The Penguin Book of French Sho

THE
PENGUIN BOOK
of
FRENCH
SHORT
STORIES

VOLUME 2

PATRICK McGUINNESS

ALLEN LANE
an imprint of
PENGUIN BOOKS

ALLEN LANE

UK | USA | Canada | Ireland | Australia
India | New Zealand | South Africa

Allen Lane is part of the Penguin Random House group of companies
whose addresses can be found at global.penguinrandomhouse.com

First published 2022
001

Introduction copyright © Patrick McGuinness, 2022
Text copyright information can be found in 'Acknowledgements' on page 335

The moral right of the authors and translators has been asserted

Set in 11.25/14.75 pt Adobe Caslon Pro
Typeset by Jouve (UK), Milton Keynes
Printed and bound in Great Britain by Clays Ltd, Elcograf S.p.A.

The authorized representative in the EEA is Penguin Random House Ireland,
Morrison Chambers, 32 Nassau Street, Dublin D02 YH68

A CIP catalogue record for this book is available from the British Library

ISBN: 978–0–241–46205–8

Contents

Contents

extreme example, but he shows us that the best short stories use their length as a resource, rather than just inhabiting it as a limit: they combine the immediacy of theatre, the compression of a poem and the latitude of a novel.

A further advantage of the short story is uninterruptedness, the way it can be read (or heard) in one sitting. Although some people can sit for longer than others, we all know what we mean by 'a sitting': an arrangement between the mind and the body, between the limits of our attention span and the moment pins and needles set in. The playwright August Strindberg claimed that the one-act play was the most effective kind of drama because it lacked intervals, and because, as he put it, the audience was 'prisoner' for the duration. Something similar can be said of the short story: that it shares with the one-act play the pressure of an imminent ending as it bears down upon the *nowness* of reading or listening.

Fénéon's three-line novellas appeared in the daily newspaper *Le Matin* between 1903 and 1937 and remind us that everyday life is a mine of scenarios as full of drama, mystery, absurdity and plot twists as the most *outré* fiction. They also remind us that the literary short story – a piece of artistically-designed and mostly (but not exclusively) fictional prose – is just one strand of narrative in a world saturated with stories. It is no coincidence that the high point of the modern short story – the nineteenth and early twentieth centuries – is also a high point in print media, in news and reportage, and in an experience of speed and connectivity that, despite changes in technology, remains remarkably consistent with today's. Newspapers and magazines were hospitable to the short story and the first readers of many of the stories in this anthology encountered them in a patchwork of different kinds of narrative: news stories, court reports, 'true crime', gossip columns, journalistic scoops, political commentary and philosophical tales. They will also have picked them out from the mixed page: advertisements, recipes (which are also stories), polemics, letters, puzzles, notices and personal ads. The short story is a pragmatic, nimble genre, responsive and topical, reaching the parts of a culture other genres cannot, and reaching them fast. Where the novel stretches across our days and accompanies us through them, the short story thrives in the busy ecosystem of everyday narratives and everyday reading habits. Several of the stories in this anthology reflect that: there are stories in the form of news items, political or philosophical parables, topical polemics, dialogues and monologues, letters, psychological case studies, dream-notation and even a multiple-choice questionnaire. There are fine-tuned classics of the 'well-made' tale and works that seem to conform to no genre, or sit proudly and unfazed between genres.

Volume One begins with a bawdy, innuendo-laden tale from Philippe de Laon's *One Hundred New Tales*, written between 1464 and 1467. The final story in Volume Two dates from the early 2000s, written by Virginie Despentes, one of the most thrilling and taboo-breaking contemporary French writers.

Laon's *One Hundred New Tales* have been described both as 'the first French literary work in prose' and as 'a museum of obscenities'. Although only the first of these judgments was a compelling argument for their inclusion, the second reminds us that the short story is not some remote high-cultural object to be entombed in a university syllabus, but a diversion and an entertainment. Both *One Hundred New Tales* and Marguerite de Navarre's *The Heptameron*, from which the story 'The Substitute' is taken, are inspired (like Chaucer's *The Canterbury Tales*) by Boccaccio's *The Decameron*. They follow their model in setting stories told by diverse voices into an overarching frame narrative. In *The Decameron*, travellers who have been thrown together by circumstances tell stories as they escape the Black Death. In *The Canterbury Tales*, they are travelling on a pilgrimage. In *The Heptameron*, they are in an abbey, waiting for the bridge that will bear them to safety to be completed. What these early examples of storytelling have in common is sophistication and playfulness, tricky narrators and slippery perspectives. From the very start, the short story is testing its limits, pushing the boundaries, defying expectations.

These classic tales also show us that once we are together, around a table or in a room, and once we have assured ourselves of food and shelter, we want stories. The earliest storytellers show us that stories are our first non-physical need, and what medieval and Renaissance audiences have in common with today's readers and listeners is the understanding that we are narrative creatures: that whatever our ends and goals, however full our agendas and busy our days, there will always be time for stories.

The advantage of beginning the anthology with *The Heptameron* is that it opens up the field to include more than just the classics from the Golden Age of the short story. To have started with Voltaire or Diderot, and moved smoothly to Colette and Marcel Aymé via Maupassant and Balzac, would have been to impose an artificial beginning on a thrillingly messy and hybrid tradition. Diverging from the familiar path, this anthology contains hitherto untranslated sixteenth-century stories by Jean-Pierre Camus and François de Rosset. These garish, sensational narratives, nicknamed 'histoires sanglantes' or 'bloody tales', are the ancestors of today's 'true crime' genre.

As we move through the centuries, we encounter works, many of them little-known in English, that might be considered to stretch the definition of a story. But the short story has never been a pure, clear-cut genre, and I have been fascinated by the way in which classic stories share so much of their narrative DNA with other forms of writing: the prose poem, for instance, with Baudelaire, Mallarmé and Charles Cros, who are included here; or with strange dream-narratives such as Xavier Forneret's 'A Dream'. In Forneret's short tale, the nineteenth century's fascination with the unconscious, and with the sleeping mind's bizarre connectivity, is distilled into a single, surreal text. As Forneret claimed: 'Since I write while I'm dreaming, you can read me while you're sleeping.' No wonder the surrealists claimed him as a trailblazing predecessor. Closer to the twenty-first century, Simone de Beauvoir's 'Monologue' or Béatrix Beck's 'The Adam Affair', a dialogue between God and a particularly obtuse Adam, give the short story the dynamism of drama.

The question is not 'what is a short story?' but 'what can a short story *be*?'. French thought has a reputation for classifying and defining, and French literary history is the home of '–isms': Naturalism, Symbolism, Surrealism, Existentialism, to name just a few movements that enjoyed worldwide influence. This fondness for categorizing has the unexpected and paradoxical effect of giving writers more categories to blur. When Diderot titled his story 'This Is Not a Story' and included 'a character whose role is more or less that of the reader', he was breaking down the fourth wall. When, 200 years later, Raymond Queneau wrote 'A Tale for Your Shaping' as a questionnaire in which the reader chooses outcomes, he was playing with the complex interrelationship between formal structure and readerly expectation in a similar spirit. That playfulness can be seen in the work of OuLiPo, or 'Ouvroir de littérature potentielle' (Workshop of Potential Literature), a group of writers that included Queneau, Italo Calvino and Georges Perec, who exploited the inventive licence granted by writing to particular rules and constraints. It can also be seen in the more ludic strains of French literary theory, in the work of Roland Barthes and in that other dominant '–ism', Structuralism: an understanding that the rules themselves are the best route to subverting the rules.

It would not be too much to say that the fondness for categorizing is exactly what makes the French literary tradition so varied and experimental.

With Voltaire, Diderot and Sade, the short story is both a self-aware genre, sophisticated and amusing, and a place to think – an opportunity for reflection, to test political and social ideas. In Voltaire's 'Micromégas', an early science-fiction story that is also a philosophical parable, an extra-terrestrial character is used to make us see ourselves from the outside. Funny, absurd, by turns intellectually playful and serious, Voltaire gives humanity – or at any rate French humanity – the sort of cultural out-of-body experience that enables it to scrutinize itself. Seriousness and play are not incompatible, and the French short story from the eighteenth to the twenty-first centuries has often directly or obliquely engaged in philosophical and social concerns.

Of the many continuities in this anthology, the reader will notice how the French short story is imbricated in its culture, in the febrile politics of its time. It has addressed injustice and discrimination, and often intervened publicly in the big debates. From Voltaire testing the tolerance of the French state and official religion to Victor Hugo's 'Claude Gueux', about the barbarism of the death penalty, writers have used the short story not just for its brevity but for the ways in which it circulates. More widely and quickly disseminated than novels and more easily digested than political tracts, it blends the efficacy of polemic with the attractions of entertainment.

Another continuity the reader will notice is the relationship between the ordinary and extraordinary, and the French short story's attraction to the 'fantastic'. Traditionally understood as a nineteenth-century speciality, its roots lie earlier and its offshoots extend into the twentieth and twenty-first centuries. This anthology contains classics such as Gautier's 'The Mummy's Foot' and Mérimée's 'The Venus of Ille', along with lesser-known masterpieces such as Villiers de l'Isle-Adam's moving story 'Véra', in which, through a sustained refusal to believe in his wife's death, a widower succeeds in returning her to life (or does he … ?). The *'fantastique'* is one of the dominant genres and thrives on bringing the everyday and the extraordinary into explosive contact. In Marcel Aymé's 'The Man who Walked Through Walls' and Jacques Sternberg's 'The Execution', fantastical events are told in such matter-of-fact, deadpan prose that the flatness of the narration accentuates rather than dulls the narrative. Meanwhile, writers such as Renée Vivien and Claude Cahun are the heirs of Perrault and his fairy tales, and Jules Verne's science fiction is in the lineage of Voltaire's space travel. While all this speaks to a desire for escapism and supernatural thrill, it reflects something more serious in all of us: the feeling that there is more to life than just the here and now. We may think of the 'fantastic' and related genres – science fiction, horror, gothic – as expressions of our need for an '*au-delà*', a 'beyond', in a utilitarian and post-religious age.

The short story is also a place where authors experiment with themes and styles that are at an angle to the work for which they are best known. Thus Apollinaire, the great modern poet of *Calligrammes* and *Alcools*, appears here with a short story about a man with the gift of blending in with his sur-roundings. Émile Zola, the Naturalist author of the twenty-novel Rougon Macquart cycle, features with a sharp and prescient story about advertising and the media. His fellow one-time Naturalist, Joris-Karl Huysmans, the decadent-turned-catholic author of *Against Nature*, is represented by the bleakly comic tale of Mr Bougran, a sacked bureaucrat who cannot bear to retire. A taste of the *fin de siècle* and decadent period is offered in a range of stories, from the erotic and depraved tales of Rachilde and Jean Lorrain to Marcel Schwob's harrowing war story, 'The *Sans Gueules*'.

Some of the major twentieth century writers I would have wished to include – notably Jean-Paul Sartre, Albert Camus, Georges Simenon and Jean Giono – were unavailable for reasons of copyright, but I have also sought to expand the range of authors traditionally available to the English-speaking audience. As well as the canonical and the classic (Colette, Marguerite Duras, Marguerite Yourcenar, Georges Perec, Françoise Sagan), I have included authors who are less familiar to readers in the anglosphere. These include Emmanuel Bove, Béatrix Beck, Charles-Albert Cingria, Jacqueline Harpman, Madeleine Bourdouxhe and Thomas Owen, as well as contemporary writers such as Gilles Ortlieb, Ananda Devi and Christian Garcin. In the works of Birago Diop, Boualem Sansal, Leïla Sebbar and Assia Djebar, among others, the short story brings its unique focus to bear on the legacies of colonialism and the cultural, linguistic and religious fault lines of contemporary France and its former colonies. Many authors are translated here for the first time; their work enriches not just the French literary tradition, but the range of French writing available in English.

I think of every story not just as a standalone fiction, but as part of a whole, a busy, imbricated set of contexts. In theatrical terms, I like to imagine the 'noises off' behind and to the side of them. They may be free-standing works of art but they are not sealed off from the worlds that produced them. They are also little keys to their cultures, their times and places: from Renaissance France to the multicultural global *francophonie* of the twentieth and twenty-first centuries.

My aim in this selection has been to entertain, to provide variety and to reveal the unexpected continuities between different periods and different literary traditions. I have aimed for variety among the stories and diversity among the authors. The pluralism of my definition of the short story is matched by the pluralism of my definition of French, and I include many writers from the francophone world. I have chosen writers substantially published in France, or resident there, or writers who are part of the literary culture in terms of their publishing houses, their eligibility for prizes, or their media presence. Here, too, I have been permissive: though they have all written French short stories, none of the authors in these pages has been required to show their passport or provide proof of residence.

Acknowledgments

Preparing an anthology like this, an editor runs up a marathon of debts. My first *tranche* of thanks goes to Simon Winder, who commissioned it and tracked its progress attentively and with encouragement. I am also grateful to Eva Hodgkin for her advice and for her careful and nuanced reading of both French originals and English translations. Claire Péligry was a tremendous copy editor and Anna Wilson at Penguin turned complicated manuscripts into clear and elegant pages.

I have benefited from the advice of several friends and colleagues at Oxford and elsewhere: Clément Dessy, Catherine Emerson, Andrew Kahn, Will McMorran, Stephen Romer, Catriona Seth, Helen Swift, Kate Tunstall, Caroline Warman and Jenny Yee. At St Anne's College, I am especially grateful to my fellow modern languages tutors, Geraldine Hazbun and Simon Park, and to my students, whose curiosity has kept me abreast of French literature over almost three decades of teaching. My greatest thanks go to the translators who have contributed to these volumes: translation is how cultures speak to each other and we continue to be indebted to those who practice it.

COLETTE

Green Sealing Wax

Around fifteen, I was at the height of a mania for 'desk furniture'. In this I was only imitating my father, whose mania for it lasted in full force all his life. At the age when every kind of vice gets its claws into adolescence, like the hundred little hooks of a burr sticking into one's hair, a girl of fifteen runs plenty of risks. My glorious freedom exposed me to all of them and I believed it to be unbounded, unaware that Sido's maternal instinct, which disdained any form of spying, worked by flashes of intuition and leaped telepathically to the danger point.

When I had just turned fifteen, Sido gave me a dazzling proof of her second sight. She guessed that a man above suspicion had designs on my little pointed face, the plaits that whipped against my calves, and my well-made body. Having entrusted me to this man's family during the holidays, she received a warning as clear and shattering as the gift of sudden faith and she cursed herself for having sent me away to strangers. Promptly she put on her little bonnet that tied under the chin, got into the clanking, jolting train – they were beginning to send antique coaches along a brand-new line – and found me in a garden, playing with two other little girls, under the eyes of a taciturn man, leaning on his elbow like the meditative Demon on the ledge of Notre-Dame.

Such a spectacle of peaceful family life could not deceive Sido. She noticed, moreover, that I looked prettier than I did at home. That is how girls blossom in the warmth of a man's desire, whether they are fifteen or thirty. There was no question of scolding me and Sido took me away with her without the irreproachably respectable man's having dared to ask the reason for her arrival or for our departure. In the train, she fell asleep before my eyes, worn out like someone who had won a battle. I remember that

I

lunchtime went by and I complained of being hungry. Instead of flushing, looking at her watch, promising me my favourite delicacies – wholemeal bread, cream cheese and pink onions – all she did was to shrug her shoulders. Little did she care about my hunger pangs, she had saved the most precious thing of all.

I had done nothing wrong, nor had I abetted this man, except by my torpor. But torpor is a far graver peril for a girl of fifteen than all the usual excited giggling and blushing and clumsy attempts at flirtation. Only a few men can induce that torpor from which girls awake to find themselves lost. That, so to speak, surgical intervention of Sido's cleared up all the confusion inside me and I had one of those relapses into childishness in which adolescence revels when it is simultaneously ashamed of itself and intoxicated by its own ego.

My father, a born writer, left few pages behind him. At the actual moment of writing, he dissipated his desire in material arrangements, setting out all the objects a writer needs and a number of superfluous ones as well. Because of him, I am not proof against this mania myself. As a result of having admired and coveted the perfect equipment of a writer's worktable, I am still exacting about the tools on my desk. Since adolescence does nothing by halves, I stole from my father's work table, first a little mahogany set square that smelled like a cigar box, then a white metal ruler. Not to mention the scolding, I received full in my face the glare of a small, blazing grey eye, the eye of a rival, so fierce that I did not risk it a third time. I confined myself to prowling, hungrily, with my mind full of evil thoughts, around all these treasures of stationery. A pad of virgin blotting paper; an ebony ruler; one, two, four, six pencils, sharpened with a penknife and all of different colours; pens with medium nibs and fine nibs, pens with enormously broad nibs, drawing pens no thicker than a blackbird's quill; sealing wax, red, green, and violet; a hand blotter; a bottle of liquid glue, not to mention slabs of transparent amber-coloured stuff known as 'mouth glue'; the minute remains of a spahi's cloak reduced to the dimensions of a pen wiper with scalloped edges; a big ink pot flanked by a small ink pot, both in bronze; and a lacquer bowl filled with a golden powder to dry the wet page; another bowl containing sealing wafers of all colours (I used to eat the white ones); to right and left of the table, reams of paper, cream-laid, ruled, watermarked; and, of course, that little stamping machine that bit into the white sheet, and, with one snap of its jaws, adorned it with an embossed name: *J.–J. Colette*. There was also a glass of water for washing paintbrushes, a box of watercolours, an address book, the bottles of red, black and violet ink, the mahogany set square, a pocket case of mathematical instruments, the tobacco jar, a pipe, the spirit lamp for melting the sealing wax.

A property owner tries to extend his domain; my father therefore tried to acclimatize adventitious subjects on his vast table. At one time there appeared on it a machine that could cut through a pile of a hundred sheets, and some frames filled with a white jelly on which you laid a written page face downward and then, from this looking-glass original, pulled off blurred, sticky, anaemic copies. But my father soon wearied of such gadgets and the huge table returned to its serenity, to its classical style that was never disturbed by inspiration with its disorderly litter of crossed-out pages, cigarette butts, and 'roughs' screwed up into paper balls. I have forgotten, heaven forgive me, the paper-knife section, three or four boxwood ones, one of imitation silver, and the last of yellowed ivory, cracked from end to end.

From the age of ten I had never stopped coveting those material goods, invented for the glory and convenience of a mental power, which come under the general heading of 'desk furniture'. Children only delight in things they can hide. For a long time I secured possession of one wing, the left one, of the great four-doored double bookcase (it was eventually sold by order of the court). The doors of the upper part were glass-fronted, those of the lower, solid and made of beautiful figured mahogany. When you opened the lower left-hand door at a right angle, the flap touched the side of the chest of drawers, and as the bookcase took up nearly the whole of one panelled wall, I would immure myself in a quadrangular nook formed by the side of the chest of drawers, the wall, the left section of the bookcase and its wide-open door. Sitting on a little footstool, I could gaze at the three mahogany shelves in front of me, on which were displayed the objects of my worship, ranging from cream-laid paper to a little cup of the golden powder. 'She's a chip off the old block,' Sido would say teasingly to my father. It was ironical that, equipped with every conceivable tool for writing, my father rarely committed himself to putting pen to paper, whereas Sido – sitting at any old table, pushing aside an invading cat, a basket of plums, a pile of linen, or else just putting a dictionary on her lap by way of a desk – Sido really did write. A hundred enchanting letters prove that she did. To continue a letter or finish it off, she would tear a page out of her household account book or write on the back of a bill.

She therefore despised our useless altars. But she did not discourage me from lavishing care on my desk and adorning it to amuse myself. She even showed anxiety when I explained that my little house was becoming too small for me . . . 'Too small. Yes, much too small,' said the grey eyes. 'Fifteen . . . Where is Pussy Darling going, bursting out of her nook like a hermit crab driven out of its borrowed shell by its own growth? Already, I've snatched her from the clutches of that man. Already, I've had to forbid her to go dancing on the "Ring" on Low Sunday. Already, she's escaping and I shan't be able to follow her. Already, she wants a long dress, and if I give her one, the blindest will notice that she's a young girl. And if I refuse, everyone will look below the too-short skirt and stare at her woman's legs. Fifteen . . . How can I stop her from being fifteen, then sixteen, then seventeen years old?'

Sometimes, during that period, she would come and lean over the mahogany half door that isolated me from the world. 'What are you doing?' She could see perfectly well what I was doing but she could not understand it. I refused her the answer given her so generously by everything else she observed, the bee, the caterpillar, the hydrangea, the ice plant. But at least she could see I was there, sheltered from danger. She indulged my mania. The lovely pieces of shiny coloured wrapping paper were given me to bind my books and I made the gold string into bookmarkers. I had the first penholder sheathed in a glazed turquoise-coloured substance, with a moiré pattern on it, that appeared in Reumont's, the stationers.

One day my mother brought me a little stick of sealing wax and I recognized the stub of green wax, the prize jewel of my father's desk. No doubt I considered the gift too overwhelming, for I gave no sign of ecstatic joy. I clutched the sealing wax in my hand, and as it grew warm, it gave out a slightly Oriental fragrance of incense.

'It's very old sealing wax,' Sido told me, 'and as you can see, it's powdered with gold. Your father already had it when we were married; he'd been given it by his mother and his mother assured him that it was a stick of wax that had been used by Napoleon I. But you've got to remember that my mother-in-law lied every time she opened her mouth, so . . .'

'Is he giving it to me or have you taken it?'

Sido became impatient; she always turned irritable when she thought she was going to be forced to lie and was trying to avoid lying.

'When *will* you stop twisting a lock of hair around the end of your nose?' she cried. 'You're doing your best to have a red nose with a blob at the tip like a cherry! That sealing wax? Let's say your father's lending it to you and leave it at that. Of course, if you don't want . . .'

My wild clutch of possession made Sido laugh again, and she said, with pretended lightness: 'If he wanted it, he'd ask you to give it back, of course!'

But he did not ask me to give it back. For a few months, gold-flecked green sealing wax perfumed my narrow empire bounded by four mahogany walls; then my pleasure gradually diminished, as do all pleasures to which no one disputes our right. Besides, my devotion to stationery temporarily waned in favour of a craze to be glamorous. I asserted my right to wear a 'bustle', that is to say, I enlarged my small, round behind with a horsehair cushion, which, of course, made my skirts much shorter at the back than in front. In our village, the frenzy of adolescence turned girls between thirteen and fifteen into madwomen who stole horsehair, cotton and wool, stuffed rags in a bag, and tied on the hideous contraption known as a 'false bottom' on dark staircases, out of their mothers' sight. I also longed for a thick, frizzy fringe, leather belts so tight I could hardly breathe, high boned collars, violet scent on my handkerchief . . .

From that phase, I relapsed once more into childhood, for a feminine creature has to make several attempts before it finally hatches out. I revelled in being a Plain Jane, with my hair in pigtails and straight wisps straggling over my cheeks. I gladly renounced all my finery in favour of my old school pinafores with their pockets stuffed with nuts and string and chocolate. Paths edged with brambles, clumps of bulrushes, liquorice 'shoelaces', cats – in short, everything I still love to this day – became dear to me again. There are no words to hymn such times in one's life, no clear memories to illuminate them; looking back on them, I can only compare them to the depths of blissful sleep. The smell of haymaking sometimes brings them back to me, perhaps because, suddenly tired, as growing creatures are, I would drop for an hour into a dreamless sleep among the new-mown hay.

It was at this point there occurred the episode known for long afterwards as 'the Hervouët will affair'. Old Monsieur Hervouët died and no will could be found. The provinces have always been rich in fantastic figures. Somewhere, under old tiled roofs, yellow with lichen, in icy drawing rooms and dining rooms dedicated to eternal shade, on waxed floors strewn with death traps of knitted rugs, in kitchen-garden paths between the hard-headed cabbages and the curly parsley, queer characters are always to be found. A little town or a village prides itself on possessing a mystery. My own village acknowledged placidly, even respectfully, the rights of young Gatreau to rave unmolested. This admirable example of a romantic madman, a wooden cigar between his lips, was always wildly tossing his streaming black curls and staring fixedly at young girls with his long, Arab eyes. A voluntary recluse used to nod good morning through a windowpane and passers would say of her admiringly: 'That makes twenty-two years since Madame Sibile left her room! My mother used to see her there, just as you see her now. And, you know, there's nothing the matter with her. In one way, it's a fine life!'

But Sido used to hurry her quick step and pull me along when we passed level with the aquarium that housed the lady who had not gone out for twenty-two years. Behind her clear glass pane the prisoner would be smiling. She always wore a linen cap; sometimes her little yellow hand held a cup. A sure instinct for what is horrible and prohibited made Sido turn away from that ground-floor window and that bobbing head. But the sadism of childhood made me ask her endless questions.

'How old do you think she is, Madame Sibile? At night does she sleep by the window in her armchair? Do they undress her? Do they wash her? And how does she go to the lavatory?'

Sido would start as if she had been stung.

'Be quiet. I forbid you to think about those things.'

Monsieur Hervouët had never passed for one of those eccentrics to whom a market town extends its slightly derisive protection. For sixty years he had been well-off and ill dressed, first a 'big catch' to marry, then a big catch married. Left a widower, he had remarried. His second wife was a former postmistress, thin and full of fire.

When she struck her breastbone, exclaiming, '*That's* where I can feel it burning!' her Spanish eyes seemed to make the person she was talking to responsible for this unquenchable ardour. 'I am not easily frightened,' my father used to say; 'but heaven preserve me from being left alone with Mademoiselle Matheix!'

After his second marriage, Monsieur Hervouët no longer appeared in public. As he never left his home, no one knew exactly when he developed the gastric trouble that was to carry him off. He was a man dressed, in all weathers, in black, including a cap with earflaps. Smothered in fleecy white hair and a beard like cotton wool, he looked like an apple tree attacked by woolly aphis. High walls and a gateway that was nearly always closed protected his second season of conjugal bliss. In summer a single rosebush clothed three sides of his one-storeyed house and the thick fringe of wisteria on the crest of the wall provided food for the first bees. But we had never heard anyone say that Monsieur Hervouët was fond of flowers, and if we now and then caught sight of his black figure pacing to and fro under the pendants of the wisteria and the showering roses, he struck us as being neither responsible for nor interested in all this wealth of blossom.

When Mademoiselle Matheix became Madame Hervouët, the ex-postmistress lost none of her resemblance to a black-and-yellow wasp. With her sallow skin, her squeezed-in waist, her fine, inscrutable eyes and her mass of dark hair, touched with white and restrained in a knot on the nape of her neck, she showed no surprise at being promoted to middle-class luxury. She appeared to be fond of gardening. Sido, the impartial, thought it only fair to show some interest in her; she lent her books, and in exchange accepted cuttings and also roots of tree violets whose flowers were almost black and whose stem grew naked out of the ground like the trunk of a tiny palm tree. To me, Madame Hervouët-Matheix was an anything but sympathetic figure. I was vaguely scandalized that, when making some assertions of irreproachable banality, she did so in a tone of passionate and plaintive supplication.

'What do you expect?' said my mother. 'She's an old maid.'

'But, Mamma, she's married!'

'Do you really imagine,' retorted Sido acidly, 'people stop being old maids for a little thing like that?'

One day, my father, returning from the daily 'round of the town', by which this man who had lost one leg kept himself fit, said to my mother: 'A piece of news! The Hervouët relatives are attacking the widow.'

'*No!*'

'And going all out for her, too! People are saying the grounds of the accusation are extremely serious.'

'A new Lafarge case?'

'You're demanding a lot,' said my father.

I thrust my sharp little mug between my two parents.

'What's that, the Lafarge case?'

'A horrible business between husband and wife. There's never been a period without one. A famous poisoning case.'

'Ah!' I exclaimed excitedly. 'What a piece of luck!'

Sido gave me a look that utterly renounced me.

'There you are,' she muttered. 'That's what they're all like at that age . . . A girl ought never to be fifteen.'

'Sido, are you listening to me or not?' broke in my father. 'The relatives, put up to it by a niece of Hervouët's, are claiming that Hervouët didn't die intestate and that his wife has destroyed the will.'

'In that case,' observed Sido, 'you could bring an action against all widowers and all widows of intestates.'

'No,' retorted my father, 'men who have children don't need to make a will. The flames of Hervouët's lady can only have scorched Hervouët from the waist up since . . .'

'Colette,' my mother said to him severely, indicating me with a look.

'Well,' my father went on. 'So there she is in a nice pickle. Hervouët's niece says she saw the will, yes, saw it with her very own eyes. She can even describe it. A big envelope, five seals of green wax with gold flecks in it . . .'

'Fancy that!' I said innocently.

'. . . and on the front of it, the instructions: "To be opened after my death in the presence of my solicitor, Monsieur Hourblin or his successor."'

'And suppose the niece is lying?' I ventured to ask.

'And suppose Hervouët changed his mind and destroyed his will?' suggested Sido. 'He was perfectly free to do so, I presume?'

'There you go, the two of you! Already siding with the bull against the bullfighter!' cried my father.

'Exactly,' said my mother. 'Bullfighters are usually men with fat buttocks and that's enough to put me against them!'

'Let's get back to the point,' said my father. 'Hervouët's niece has a husband, a decidedly sinister gentleman by the name of Pellepuits.'

I soon got tired of listening. On the evidence of such words as 'The relatives are attacking the widow!' I had hoped for bloodshed and foul play and all I heard was bits of gibberish such as 'disposable portion of estate', 'holograph will', 'charge against X'.

All the same, my curiosity was reawakened when Monsieur Hervouët's widow paid us a call. Her little mantle of imitation Chantilly lace worn over hock-bottle shoulders, her black mittens from which protruded unusually thick, almost opaque nails, the luxuriance of her black-and-white hair, a big black taffeta pocket suspended from her belt that dangled over the skirt of her mourning, her 'houri eyes', as she called them; all these details, which I seemed to be seeing for the first time, took on a new, sinister significance.

Sido received the widow graciously, took her into the garden, and offered her a thimbleful of Frontignan and a wedge of homemade cake. The June afternoon buzzed over the garden, russet caterpillars dropped about us from the walnut tree, not a cloud floated in the sky. My mother's pretty voice and Madame Hervouët's imploring one exchanged tranquil remarks; as usual, they talked about nothing but salpiglossis, gladiolus, and the misdemeanours of servants. Then the visitor rose to go and my mother escorted her. 'If you don't mind,' said Madame Hervouët, 'I'll come over in a day or two and borrow some books; I'm so lonely.'

'Would you like to take them now?' suggested Sido.

'No, no, there's no hurry. Besides, I've noted down the titles of some adventure stories. Goodbye for the time being, and thank you.'

As she said this, Madame Hervouët, instead of taking the path that led to the house, took the one that circled the lawn and walked twice around the plot of grass.

'Good gracious, whatever am I doing? Do forgive me.'

She allowed herself a modest laugh and eventually reached the hall, where she groped too high and to the left of the two sides of the folding door for a latch she had twenty times found on the right. My mother opened the front door for her and, out of politeness, stood for a moment at the top of the steps. We watched Madame Hervouët go off, keeping at first very close to the house, then crossing the road very hurriedly, picking up her skirts as if she were fording a river.

My mother shut the door again and saw that I had followed her.

'She is lost,' she said.

'Who? Madame Hervouët? Why do you say that? How d'you mean, lost?'

Sido shrugged her shoulders.

'I've no idea. It's just my impression. Keep that to yourself.'

I kept silence faithfully. This was all the easier, as continuing my series of metamorphoses like a grub, I had entered a new phase – the 'enlightened bibliophile' – and I forgot Madame Hervouët in a grand turnout of my stationery shop. A few days later, I was installing Jules Verne between *Les Fleurs animées* and a relief atlas when Madame Hervouët appeared on the scene without the bell having warned me. For we left the front door open nearly all day so that our dog Domino could go in and out.

'How nice of a big girl like you to tidy up the bookshelves,' exclaimed the visitor. 'What books are you going to lend me today?'

When Madame Hervouët raised her voice, I clenched my teeth and screwed up my eyes very small.

'Jules Verne,' she read, in a plaintive voice. 'You can't read him twice. Once you know the secret, it's finished.'

'There's Balzac up there, on the big shelves,' I said, pointing to them.

'He's very heavy going,' said Madame Hervouët.

Balzac, heavy going? Balzac, my cradle, my enchanted forest, my voyage of discovery? Amazed, I looked up at the tall dark woman, a head taller than myself. She was toying with a cut rose and staring into space. Her features expressed nothing which could be remotely connected with opinions on literature. She became aware I was gazing at her and pretended to be interested in my writer's equipment.

'It's charming. What a splendid collection!'

Her mouth had grown older in the last week. She remained stooping over my relics, handling this one and that. Then she straightened herself up with a start.

'But isn't your dear mother anywhere about? I'd like to see her.'

Only too glad to move, to get away from this 'lost' lady, I rushed wildly out into the garden, calling 'Mamma!' as if I were shouting 'Fire!'

'She took a few books away with her,' Sido told me when we were alone. 'But I could positively swear she didn't even glance at their titles.'

The rest of the 'Hervouët affair' is linked, in my memory, with a vague general commotion, a kind of romantic blur. My clearest recollection of it comes to me through Sido, thanks to the extraordinary 'presence' I still have of the sound of her voice. Her stories, her conversations with my father, the intolerant way she had of arguing and refuting, those are the things that riveted a sordid provincial drama in my mind.

One day, shortly after Madame Hervouët's last visit, the entire district was exclaiming 'The will's been found!' and describing the big envelope with five seals that the widow had just deposited in Monsieur Hourblin's study. At once uneasy and triumphant, the Pellepuits-Hervouët couple and another lot, the Hervouët-Guillamats, appeared, along with the widow, at the lawyer's office. There, Madame Hervouët, all by herself, faced up to the solid, pitiless group, to what Sido called those 'gaping, legacy-hunting sharks'. 'It seems,' my mother said, telling the story, 'that she smelled of brandy.' At this point, my mother's voice is superseded by the hunchback's voice of Julia Vincent, a woman who went out ironing by the day and came to us once a week. For I don't know how many consecutive Fridays, I pressed Julia till I wrung out of her all she knew. The precise sound of that nasal voice, squeezed between the throat, the hump and the hollow, deformed chest, was a delight to me.

'The man as was most afeared was the lawyer. To begin with, he's not a tall man, not half so tall as that woman. She, all dressed in black she was, and her veil falling down in front right to her feet. Then the lawyer picked up the envelope, big as that it was' (Julia unfolded one of my father's vast handkerchiefs) 'and he passed it just as it was to the nephews so they could recognize the seals.'

'But you weren't there, Julia, were you?'

'No, it was Monsieur Hourblin's junior clerk who was watching through the keyhole. One of the nephews said a word or two. Then Madame Hervouët stared at him like a duchess. The lawyer coughed, ahem, ahem, he broke the seals, and he read it out.'

In my recollection, it is sometimes Sido talking, sometimes some scandalmonger eager to gossip about the Hervouët affair. Sometimes it seems too that some illustrator, such as Bertall or Tony Johannot, has actually etched a picture for me of the tall, thin woman who never withdrew her Spanish eyes from the group of heirs-at-law and kept licking her lip to taste the *marc* brandy she had gulped down to give herself courage.

So Monsieur Hourblin read out the will. But after the first lines, the document began to shake in his hands and he broke off, with an apology, to wipe his glasses. He resumed his reading and went right through to the end. Although the testator declared himself to be 'sound in body and mind', the will was nothing but a tissue of absurdities, among others, the acknowledgement of a debt of two million francs contracted to Louise-Léonie-Alberte Matheix, beloved spouse of Clovis-Edme Hervouët.

The reading finished in silence and not one voice was raised from the block of silent heirs.

'It seems,' said Sido, 'that, after the reading, the silence was such you could hear the wasps buzzing in the vine arbour outside the window.' The Pellepuits and the various Guillamats did nothing but stare at Madame Hervouët, without stirring a finger. Why aren't cupidity and avarice possessed of second sight? It was a female Guillamat, less stupid than the others, who said afterwards that, before anyone had spoken, Madame Hervouët began to make peculiar movements with her neck, like a hen that's swallowed a hairy caterpillar.

The story of the last scene of that meeting spread like wildfire through the streets, through people's homes, through the cafés, through the fairgrounds. Monsieur Hourblin had been the first to speak above the vibrating hum of the wasps.

'On my soul and conscience, I find myself obliged to declare that the handwriting of the will does not correspond ...'

A loud yelping interrupted him. Before him, before the heirs, there was no longer any Widow Hervouët but a sombre Fury whirling around and stamping her feet, a kind of black dervish, lacerating herself, muttering and shrieking. To her admissions of forgery, the crazy woman added others, so rich in the names of vegetable poisons, such as buckthorn and hemlock, that the lawyer, in consternation, exclaimed naively: 'Stop, my poor good lady, you're telling us far more than anyone has asked you to!'

A lunatic asylum engulfed the madwoman, and if the Hervouët affair persisted in some memories, at least, there was no 'Hervouët case' at the assizes.

'Why, Mamma?' I asked.

"Mad people aren't tried. Or else they'd have to have judges who were mad too. That wouldn't be a bad idea, when you come to think of it . . .'

To pursue her train of thought better, she dropped the task with which her hands were busy; graceful hands that she took no care of. Perhaps, that particular day, she was shelling haricot beans. Or else, with her little finger stuck in the air, she was coating my father's crutch with black varnish . . .

'Yes, judges who would be able to assess the element of calculation in madness, who could sift out the hidden grain of lucidity, of deliberate fraud.'

Translated by Antonia White

RENÉE VIVIEN

Woman of the Wolf

Narrated by Monsieur Pierre Lenoir, 69, Rue des Dames, Paris

I do not know why I undertook to court that woman. She was neither beautiful, nor pretty, nor even agreeable. As for myself (and I say this without conceit, dear ladies), there are those who have not been indifferent to me. It is not that I am extraordinarily endowed by nature, physically or mentally, but simply – may I confess it? – that I have been spoiled when it comes to the fairer sex. Oh, do not be alarmed: I am not going to inflict upon you a vain recital of my conquests. I am a modest man. In any case, this story is not about me. It is about a particular woman, or rather, a particular young lady, an Englishwoman, whose strange face enchanted me for an hour or so.

She was a peculiar specimen. When I approached her for the first time, a great beast was sleeping in the trailing folds of her skirt. I had on my lips the amiably banal remarks that break the ice between strangers. Words mean nothing in such cases; the art of pronouncing them is everything . . . But the great beast, lifting its muzzle, growled ominously just as I reached the interesting stranger.

I drew back a step, despite myself. 'You have quite a vicious dog there, mademoiselle,' I observed.

'It is a she-wolf,' she replied, somewhat sharply. 'And since she sometimes turns on people, violently and inexplicably, I think you would do well to step back a bit.' With one stern word, she silenced the wolf: 'Helga!'

I left, somewhat humiliated. It was a stupid business, you must admit. Fear is foreign to me, but I hate ridicule. The incident bothered me all the more since I thought I had seen a glimmer of liking in the young lady's eye. I certainly pleased her somewhat. She must have been as vexed as I at this regrettable setback. What a pity! A conversation that had been so promising at the outset . . .

I do not know why the frightful animal later ceased its display of hostility. I was able to approach its mistress without fear. I had never seen such a strange face. Her pale grey complexion glowed white under heavy blonde hair, which was both fiery and colourless, like burning ashes. Her emaciated body had the fine and fragile delicacy of a lovely skeleton. (We are all a little artistic in Paris, you see.) This woman radiated an impression of tough and solitary pride, of flight and of fierce recoil. Her yellow eyes resembled those of her she-wolf. They both wore an expression of sly hostility. Her footsteps were so silent that they became disturbing. No one had ever walked so quietly. She was dressed in a thick material which looked like fur. She was neither beautiful, nor pretty, nor charming. But she was the only woman on board the ship.

So, I courted her. I played by rules based on my already extensive experience. She had the intelligence not to let me see the deep pleasure my advances afforded her. Even her yellow eyes maintained their usual mistrustful expression. A remarkable example of feminine wiles! This only made me more violently attracted to her. Drawn-out resistance sometimes leads to a pleasant surprise, rendering the victory all the more brilliant . . . You would not contradict me on this point, would you, gentlemen? We all share the same sentiments to some degree. There is such complete fraternity of spirit between us that conversation is almost impossible. That is why I often flee the monotonous company of men – they are too identical to myself.

Admittedly, the Woman of the Wolf attracted me. And furthermore – dare I confess it? – the enforced chastity of that floating jail made my feelings yet more turbulent. She was a woman . . . and my courting of her, respectful until then, became each day more insistent. I built up blazing metaphors. I elegantly elaborated eloquent expressions.

Look at the extent of the woman's deceitfulness! In listening to me, she adopted an air of moonstruck distraction. One would have sworn she was interested only in the foaming wake which looked like steaming snow. (Women are by no means indifferent to flowery similes.) But I, who had long studied the feelings behind the feminine face, understood that her heavy, lowered eyelids concealed vacillating glimmers of love.

One day I was particularly bold, combining flattering gestures with delicate words, when she turned to me with the spring of a she-wolf.

'Go away,' she commanded, with almost savage decisiveness. Her teeth, like those of a wild beast, glittered strangely behind lips drawn back in menace.

I smiled, without any anxiety. You must have patience with women, must you not? And you must not believe a single word they say. When they order you to depart, you must remain. Really, gentlemen, I am rather ashamed to give you the same old mediocre banalities.

The lady considered me with her large, yellow eyes. 'You have not worked me out. You are foolishly running up against my insurmountable contempt. I know neither how to hate nor love. I have not yet met a human worthy of my hatred. Hatred, which is more patient and more tenacious than love, deserves a great adversary.'

She caressed Helga's heavy head. The wolf looked back at her with the deep eyes of a woman. 'And love? I know as little about that as you know about concealing your inherent masculine conceit, a technique which is elementary among us Anglo-Saxons. If I were a man, I would have perhaps loved a woman, for women possess the qualities I value: loyalty in passion and selflessness in affection. In general, women are simple and sincere. They give of themselves without restriction and without counting the cost. Their patience is as inexhaustible as their kindness. They are able to forgive. They are able to wait. They possess a superior kind of chastity: constancy.'

I do not lack finesse and I can take a hint. I smiled meaningfully in response to her outburst of enthusiasm. She gave me a distracted look, taking me in.

'Oh, you are strangely mistaken. I have observed women in passing who are generous in spirit and in heart. But I have never become attached to them. Their very gentleness sets them at a distance from me. My spirit is not sufficiently noble, and so I lose patience in the face of their excessive candour and devotion.'

She was beginning to bore me with her pretentious discourse. A prude and a bluestocking, and a brat too! . . . But she was the only woman on board. And she was only putting on airs of superiority to make her imminent capitulation the more precious.

'I have affection for Helga alone. And Helga knows it. As for you, you are probably a nice enough little man, but you cannot imagine how much I despise you.'

By hurting my pride, she was trying to make me want her even more. She was succeeding, too, the little hussy! I was red with anger and lust.

'Men who hover around women, any women, are like dogs sniffing after bitches.' She gave me one of her long yellow looks. 'I have for so long breathed the forest air, air that quivers with snow; I have spent so much time amid vast, barren whiteness, that my soul is not unlike the souls of fleeting she-wolves.'

The woman had finally frightened me. She perceived it and changed her tone. 'I love clarity and freshness,' she continued, with a little laugh. 'Thus, the crudeness of men is as off-putting as the stench of garlic, and their dirtiness as repulsive as the waft of a drain. Men,' she insisted, 'are only really at home in brothels. They love only courtesans. For in them they discover their own rapacity, their sentimental unintelligence, their stupid cruelty. They live for self-interest and debauchery alone. Morally, they sicken me; physically, I find them repugnant ... I have seen men kissing women on the lips while obscenely fondling them. A gorilla's performance would not have been more repellent.'

She ceased for a minute. 'Even the severest legislator only escapes by a miracle the deplorable consequences of the carnal promiscuity of his youth. I do not understand how even the least sensitive woman could endure your filthy embraces without retching. Indeed, my virgin's contempt is equal in disgust to the courtesan's nausea!'

Really, I thought, *she is overdoing it, though she understands her part very well. She is overdoing it.*

(If we were among ourselves, gentlemen, I would tell you that I have not always despised public houses, and have even picked up a few pitiful whores on the street. Parisian women were nonetheless more accommodating than that hypocrite. I am by no means smug, but one must be aware of one's own worth.)

Deeming that the conversation had gone on long enough, I took dignified leave of the Woman of the Wolf. Helga slyly followed me with her long yellow gaze.

Towering clouds loomed on the horizon. A streak of dull blue-green sky was winding like a moat beneath them. I felt as though I were being crushed between stone walls ... And the wind was getting up ...

I was seized with seasickness – I do beg your pardon for such an inelegant detail, dear ladies. I was horribly indisposed ... I fell asleep around midnight, feeling more pitiful than I could tell you.

Around two o'clock in the morning, I was awakened by a sinister impact, followed by an even more sinister grinding sound. The darkness emitted an inexpressible terror. I realized that the ship had struck a reef. For the first time in my life, I neglected my clothes. I appeared on deck in extremely skimpy attire.

A confused crowd of half-naked men were already swarming about up there. They were hurriedly launching the lifeboats. Looking at those hairy arms and shaggy chests, I could not help remembering, not without a smile, something the Woman of the Wolf had said: *'A gorilla's performance would not have been more repellent ...'* I do not know why that unimportant memory came back to mock me in the midst of the common danger.

The waves looked like monstrous volcanoes wreathed in white smoke. Or, rather, they looked like nothing at all. They were themselves – magnificent, terrible, mortal ... The wind was blowing across their enormous wrath and so increasing their frenzy. The salt bit at my eyes. I shivered in the spray as though in a cold drizzle, and the crashing of the waves obliterated all my thoughts.

The Woman of the Wolf was calmer than ever. And I was faint with terror. I could see death looming before me. I could almost touch it. I distractedly put my fingers to my forehead, where I could feel the bones of my skull bulging frightfully. The skeleton within me terrified me. Idiotically, I started to cry ...

My flesh would be black and blue, more swollen than a bulging wineskin. The sharks would snap at my dismembered limbs. And, when I sank beneath the waves, the crabs would climb sideways along my rotten corpse and gluttonously eat their fill.

The wind was blowing over the waters ...

I relived my past. I repented my idiotic life, my spoiled life, my lost life. I tried to remember one act of kindness I may have performed, either absent-mindedly or inadvertently. Had I ever been good for anything, useful to anyone? And the dark side of my conscience cried out, as horri-fying as a mute who has miraculously recovered his speech: 'No!'

The wind was blowing over the waters . . .

I vaguely remembered the sacred words which encourage repentance and which promise salvation to the contrite sinner even at the hour of death. I strove to retrieve from my memory, drier now than an empty goblet, a few words of prayer . . . And lustful thoughts came to torment me, like little red devils. I again saw the soiled beds of chance companions. I heard their stupidly obscene cries once more. I re-experienced loveless embraces. I was overwhelmed with the horror of Pleasure . . .

Faced with the terror of the Mysterious Immensity, all that survived in me was the rutting instinct, as powerful for some as the instinct of self-preservation. It was Life, crude, ugly Life, screaming its ferocious protest against Annihilation.

The wind was blowing over the waters . . .

One has peculiar ideas at times like that, all the same . . . There I was – a very decent fellow, admired by all, except for a few who were jealous of me, even loved by some – so bitterly reproaching myself for an existence which was neither better nor worse than anyone else's. I must have suc-cumbed to a moment of madness. We were all a little mad, anyway . . .

The Woman of the Wolf was looking out at the white waves, completely calm . . . Oh! they were whiter than snow at twilight! And, sitting up on her haunches, Helga was howling like a dog. She howled pitifully, like a dog baying at the moon. She *understood*.

I do not know why her howls chilled me even more than the sound of the wind and the waves. She howled at death, that damned devil-wolf. I wanted to knock her senseless just to shut her up, and I looked for a plank, a spar, an iron bar, anything on the deck to beat her with . . . I found nothing.

The lifeboat was finally ready to leave. The men leapt frantically towards salvation. Only the Woman of the Wolf did not move.

'Get in, then,' I shouted at her as I took my turn.

She came slowly over to the boat, followed by Helga.

'Mademoiselle,' said the lieutenant, who was commanding us as well as he could, 'we cannot take that animal with us. There is only enough room for people.'

'In that case, I will stay,' she said, stepping back ...

The terror-stricken men rushed forward with incoherent cries. We had to let her stay behind.

I really couldn't be bothered with such a silly girl. And she had been so insolent to me! You understand that, gentlemen, don't you? You would not have acted any differently.

Finally I was saved, or just about. Dawn broke and, my God, what a dawn! There was a shiver of chilling light, a grey stupor, a swarm of people and unformed shapes in a dusky confusion of limbs ...

And we saw the blue of distant land ...

Oh, what joy and comfort to see the trusty, welcoming sun! ... Since that horrible experience I have only once travelled by sea, and that was to return here. I won't be doing it again, you can be sure of that!

I must not be too egotistical, dear ladies. In the midst of such unspeakable uncertainty, and though I had narrowly escaped Destruction, I was still brave enough to concern myself with the fate of my companions in misfortune. The second lifeboat had been swamped by too many frenzied madmen. With horror, I saw it sink ... The Woman of the Wolf had taken refuge on a broken mast, along with her obedient animal. I was quite certain that she would be saved, as long as her strength and endurance did not fail her. I hoped so, with all my heart ... But there was the cold, her slow, fragile improvised raft, which lacked sails and rudder, her fatigue, her feminine weakness!

They were not far from land when the Woman, exhausted, turned to Helga, as if to say, 'I am finished ...'

And then a most mournful and solemn thing occurred. The she-wolf, *who had understood*, hurled her howl of despair at the close yet inaccessible shore ... Then, standing up, she put her two front paws on the shoulders of her mistress, who took her in her arms. Together, they disappeared beneath the waves.

Translated by Karla Jay and Yvonne Klein

CHARLES-ALBERT CINGRIA

The Grass Snake

This story could also be called 'The High Life', because of its very particular lakeside castle setting, and I can no longer think of a grass snake without thinking of a castle or of a castle without thinking of a grass snake. This one was a *Tropinodotus Natrix*, also known as a ring-necked snake or a water snake, a very common species in these parts and pretty much everywhere, except in the south where they are green and yellow, or white or brown, or sometimes black, and in the central regions, where a prehistoric variety with an extraordinary green livery – the green of oxidized copper – still exists and provokes a mix of amazement and unjustified terror.

But let us not talk of species when really these pages concern a personality. This lady is the cherished guest of the castle. She doesn't live there, but close by under a large flat stone that nobody has ever been able to lift. She enters by means of a hole in the stone's flank that resembles the hole in a clock where the key is inserted to wind it up. If the level of the lake varies and the gentle flooding caused by the steamboat inconveniences her a little too much – this is rare, and besides, she knows the timetable – she decamps and heads into the wall, higher up in the bushes.

Is she domesticated? Not quite. It would be a shame if she lost her wild nature in the service she renders to others. Nonetheless, she is unsurprised to find herself the occasional object – on Sundays, for instance – of some well-meaning ministrations, such as a little cup of milk laid beside her stone.

People watching through opera glasses from the castle are surprised by her slowness: they would like to see her emerge and plunge her head in, as seen in illustrations from textbooks or in engravings. But no, nothing happens, which is to say that the cup remains untouched, and, from their vantage point of the castle, they get tired of waiting. It should be noted that she is not always under her stone. She roams, which is how it should be. Never very far, truth be told, and preferably in the water rather than on the ground. That's why suddenly you will see her slurp the contents of the cup with delight, alas too late for those who were just at the window, and who have now moved on.

She is much loved at the castle, though everyone is a little afraid of her, because, after all those years sleeping in the winter and waking up in spring, safe from any predators, she is 1 metre 30 centimetres long. Everyone is made aware of her: the new gardener, the gatekeeper, the electricians, the tradesmen. There's only the railway track that could slice her in half, but she knows this and doesn't venture too much in that direction. The biggest danger would be the Sunday walkers – idiots who climb over the estate walls despite the signs threatening such actions with a heavy fine. Swimmers could also pose a danger – those who think that this little scrubby beach, where a few plums drop down from over a wall, is public property. But it's rather the other way around, because she takes the initiative; in other words, she is already in the lake, and, if we suddenly hear terrified screams, it's no surprise: she is incorrigibly playful. Do you know what she does? She waits until the waves from the passing steamboat have forced a few frightened swimmers to stand up in the lake (if the water is turbulent, they won't dare to swim) and slips between their legs, with the immediate effect that they are transfixed with icy terror. They run away in contorted, liquid, postures, like the late Graeco-Roman bas-reliefs from South-East Asia you find in museums. They stumble towards the rocky limestone steps, then the bridge, and then, still in shock, cross the rail tracks to fetch their clothes. They cannot walk naked like this on the road; decency prevails.

Come to think of it, do you know what else she does? Even when the lake is calm as a mirror, and thus without the element of surprise offered by the steamboat's ripples, she sometimes launches herself, not out of anger but out of a natural and vehement love, as an eel in the Sargasso Sea launches itself at another eel, at a swimmer who is as beautiful as the snow, and who is not in the least petrified with horror at her embrace. On the contrary. What strange phenomena these are. Ah, but I must hold my tongue. It would be indiscreet to mention here individuals who might recognize themselves.

Lastly, there is the sun to describe. It's so pleasant to sit there letting the plums drop on to you while listening to the train rumbling as if it was coming to annihilate you. In the old days, baccalaureate students would choose this means of death on account of a failed exam. These days, we reserve our despair for things that really warrant it. It's cats who get sliced in two. Not from despair, but because they are so extraordinarily careless. Or because they are deaf – especially the Angoras. In their case, they can't hear the train even though it stops twice (two stations almost adjacent to each other), and the noise from its brakes makes a frightful screeching sound that echoes all over.

Oh, and on the subject of noises, that's not the only one. There's the noise the steamboat makes, or tries to make, when it wants to whistle. It's long, painfully drawn-out, soft, low, fateful, piercing, intimate. But there's only a voiceless jet of vapour, nonetheless visible to the eye. It goes without saying that the snake finds this hugely enjoyable.

Translated by Patrick McGuinness

GUILLAUME APOLLINAIRE

The Disappearance of Honoré Subrac

Despite the most thorough investigations, the police have been unable to solve the mystery of Honoré Subrac's disappearance.

He was my friend, and, as I knew the truth about his case, I took it upon myself to inform the authorities of what had happened. After listening to my story, the judge who took down my statement addressed me with such terrified politeness that I had no difficulty realizing that he thought I was a madman. I told him. He became even more polite, and then, rising, ushered me towards the door, and I saw his clerk, standing with his fists clenched, ready to jump on me if I made a scene.

I didn't push it. The case of Honoré Subrac is indeed so strange that the truth seems unbelievable. We learned from newspaper articles that Subrac had a reputation for being odd. In winter as in summer he dressed only in slippers and a long robe. He was very rich, and because his outfit puzzled me, I asked him about it one day:

'It's so I can undress more quickly when the need arises,' he answered. 'Besides, you get used to going out without much on. It's easy to do without underwear, socks and hat. I've lived like this since I was twenty-five and I've never been ill.'

Instead of allaying my curiosity, these words piqued it all the more.

'Why on earth does Honoré Subrac need to get undressed so quickly?' I wondered, and formed a great many theories on the topic.

One night, as I was returning home – it must have been one in the morning, quarter past – I heard my name whispered. It seemed to be coming from the wall I was brushing against. I stopped, unpleasantly surprised.

'Is the street clear?' said the voice. 'It's me, Honoré Subrac.'

*

'Where on earth are you?' I cried out, looking around me, unable to tell where my friend was hiding. All I could see was his famous robe in a pile on the pavement, beside his no less famous slippers.

'Here's a situation where necessity has forced Honoré Subrac to take his clothes off in the blink of an eye,' I thought, 'and now I'm about to find out the reason why ...'

I said in a loud voice: 'The street is empty, my friend, you can come out.'

Suddenly, Honoré Subrac seemed to detach himself from the wall against which I had not seen him. He was completely naked, and immediately picked up his robe and slipped it on, buttoning it up as fast as he could. He put on his slippers and accompanied me to my door.

'You were surprised!' he said. 'But you now know why I dress so strangely. And yet you haven't understood why I was able to avoid being seen by you. It's very straightforward. It's simply a case of mimicry ... Nature is a good mother. To those of her children who have no strength to defend themselves and who are surrounded by danger, she bestowed the gift of blending into their surroundings ... But you know all this. You know that butterflies look like flowers, insects resemble leaves, the chameleon can take on the colour that conceals it best, that the arctic hare turned white as the snowy landscapes where, just as fearful as our own species, it can dart around almost invisibly.

'This is how these weak creatures escape their enemies – an instinctive ingenuity that allows them to alter their appearance.

'And I, chased endlessly by an enemy of my own – I who am fearful and incapable of defending myself in combat – am like those creatures: from sheer terror, I can blend at will into my surroundings. I used this instinctive power for the first time a number of years ago. I was twenty-five and, by and large, women found me pleasant and easy on the eye. One woman, who was married, showed me such fondness that I was unable to resist. Fateful liaison! ... One night I was at my mistress's. Her husband was apparently out of town for a few days. We were naked as the gods when suddenly the door swung open and the husband appeared with a revolver in his hand. I was terrified out of my wits, and I had only one desire, coward that I was and coward that I still am: to disappear. My back up against the wall, I wished only to blend into it. Then the unexpected happened. I took on the colour of the wallpaper, and my limbs flattened themselves out in an extraordinary instinctive stretching movement. It seemed I had become one with the wall, and that no one could see me any more. And so it was. The husband was looking for me in order to kill me. He had seen me with his own eyes and it was impossible that I'd escaped. He was mad with rage, and, turning his fury on his wife, shot her six times in the head and ran away sobbing. After he left, my body instinctively returned to its normal shape and shade. I got dressed and managed to escape before anyone arrived on the scene ... I have kept this lucky power of mimicry ever since. The husband, having failed to kill me on that occasion, has devoted his life to accomplishing the task. For years he has been following me across the globe, and I thought I had escaped him by coming to live in Paris. But I caught sight of the man a few moments before you arrived. My teeth were chattering with fear. I barely had time to get undressed and disappear against the wall. He walked right past me, looking suspiciously at the robe and the slippers abandoned on the pavement. Now you see why it makes sense for me to dress so skimpily. My mimetic power would never work if I dressed like everyone else. I wouldn't be able to strip off quickly enough to escape my pursuer, and the most important thing is for me to be naked, so that my flattened clothes against the wall don't give away my defensive disappearing act.'

I congratulated Subrac on his power, of which I now had proof, and which I envied him ...

In the days that followed, I thought only of this, and found myself taking every opportunity to test my will with the aim of modifying my shape and colour. I tried to change myself into a bus, into the Eiffel Tower, into an Academician, into a lottery winner. To no avail. I couldn't do it. My will wasn't strong enough, and besides, I lacked the holy terror and the terrible danger that had awakened Honoré Subrac's instincts ...

I had not seen him for some time when, one day, he turned up in a state of anguish:

'That man – my enemy – he's tracking me everywhere! I managed to escape three times with my mimetic power, but I'm scared my friend, scared!'

I saw he had lost weight, but I held back from mentioning it.

'There's only one thing you can do to escape such a merciless enemy,'

I exclaimed. 'Leave! Go and hide in some village. Let me look after your affairs while you head straight to the nearest station.'

He shook my hand, saying, 'Come with me, please, I'm afraid!'

We walked the street in silence. Honoré Subrac kept anxiously turning around. Suddenly he let out a cry and started to flee, tearing off his robe and slippers. I saw a man behind us, running. I tried to intercept him, but he escaped me. He held a revolver which he aimed in Honoré Subrac's direction. Subrac had just reached a long barracks wall when he disappeared as if by magic.

The man with the gun stopped in amazement, roared with rage, and, as if to avenge himself on the wall which seemed to have robbed him of his victim, emptied his revolver in the place where Honoré Subrac had vanished. Then he ran off . . .

People gathered and a few policemen dispersed them. When everyone had gone, I called my friend's name. There was no reply. I felt the wall, which was still warm, and noticed that, of the six bullets, three had hit the wall at heart-height, whereas the others had chipped the plaster higher up, at just the spot where I thought I could make out, indistinctly, the contours of a face.

Translated by Patrick McGuinness

JEAN DE LA VILLE DE MIRMONT

The Upright Piano

Miss Céréda was moving house.

She had arranged it for that Saturday a long time ago, but had neglected to fix a time with the porter.

At dawn, she was ready. At noon, she had a few cold cuts for lunch, as if on a trip; that evening, her stomach refused any food. That whole day, sacrificed to the anxiety of waiting as well as the disquiet of the temporary, every step on the stairway was for her a hope and every ring of a doorbell a disappointment. It was dark by the time she saw, having lost hope, two strangers stop at her landing, holding their caps, too polite for sober folk.

Miss Céréda's belongings did not consist of those charming and intricate trinkets which would allow one to fulfil – if such a thing were possible – our domestic dream of an elegant and intimate Louis XV interior. And it all happened so quickly. Leaving nothing behind him save a few scattered wisps of straw, the removal man headed through the dark streets, tossed about behind a horse which, had it not been white, would have been perfectly acceptable for funerals for the poor.

Miss Céréda followed the procession in resignation; the nocturnal breeze swelled her beige jacket, of that breed of trusty garments which is dying out but refuses to submit, even on the emaciated bodies of elderly lady teachers of chamber music.

The two removal men, who, after all, were very sedately drunk, restored in the new home all the comfort they had destroyed in the old one. A candle, stuck on the all-too-fake marble of the fireplace and reflected in the halo of a mirror which had seen many others, illuminated their usual labour. They screwed the bed back together, unpacked the dressing table, and wedged the *commode* in its corner; then, like people who know what they are about, they spread out the chairs and hung on the wall a photographic enlargement enhanced with charcoal, an image that very much resembled some or other deceased person.

All that remained was the piano, with which the mournful horse had been entrusted below. It was an upright piano destined from the very beginning to teach mazurka tunes to Parisian shopkeepers. Some late passers-by and the clients of the bar next door looked at the horse and piano illuminated by a street lamp. 'Only a musician would move house at such an hour! Those artistic types can never just do things like everyone else.'

Seized at last by four vigorous arms, the piano, bumped against the pavement, gave out a sound in perfect harmony with that autumnal evening, and which penetrated deep into Miss Céréda's soul. But a moment after disappearing through the doors of the building, the dishevelled carriers of that respectable musical instrument reappeared with their burden to explain, not without some verbiage, that given the lack of width in the turns of the staircase, it would be impossible for them to get the job done by the usual methods.

Nonetheless, the rain, which the morning newspapers had announced on their fourth page, along with the saint's day to celebrate, abruptly made up its mind. It made sense therefore to come to a decision as quickly as possible. Everyone shared their opinion and gave their advice. Only Miss Céréda was not heard. It was left, finally, up to the concierge, whose competence was generally acknowledged in the local area. He did not hesitate in recommending the audacious system of a hoist, block and tackle. He gestured at the mansard window on the fifth floor, lost in the shadows.

They agreed on Monday as the day for the operation. The upright piano was given shelter in the lodge, and, towards midnight, Miss Céréda was finally able to take possession of her abode, where the candle went out, after one last spasm, as soon as the door was closed.

On the Monday morning, the two removal men, accompanied by a carpenter, a locksmith and the concierge, turned up bright and early. They were carrying pullies, cables and beams. The old lady let them in, a half-open trunk beside her, just as she was tucking the last strands of grey under her bonnet.

The preparations lasted until noon . . . One would have said that Miss

Céréda, once she had the frame of the casement removed and the cast iron balcony detached, was trying to revive and install a ballistic contraption from the wars of antiquity. The piano left the ground and rose with ease, to the rhythm of the 'heave-hos' chanted by the concierge. Its great swinging shadow piqued the curiosity of the fashion boutique, *Au caprice des dames*, on the entresol floor; it caused some surprise to the young maid on the first floor, who, born far from the tumult of the metropolises, still had the readily enthralled face of her childhood; it disturbed the work of the midwife on the second floor and dizzied all the lodgers on the upper floors. But once at the right height, the piano, however they went about it, whether head on, sideways, at a three-quarters angle, vertically, diagonally or horizontally, could not penetrate by the expected orifice and had to descend again with infinite care.

Thereafter, and for a long time, Miss Céréda's 'home' was transformed into a building site ringing with the noise of tools and the manly trill of the builders. One by one the teacher lost her last students of music theory. The day would come, however, when the masons would have enlarged the window sufficiently and it was to be hoped that the piano would take its rightful place back in front of the adjustable stool waiting for it by the fireplace.

On that day, the result was conclusive, but contrary to all predictions. A cable gave way at the most critical moment and the piano, its lid flapping and its copper candlestick holders shaking madly, plummeted straight down and broke the backs of two dappled horses of an omnibus which was making its way, as usual, along the public highway.

We shall not attempt to describe the relatives' despair ... As for Miss Céréda, she is now considered the most docile resident of a sanatorium in Loir-et-Cher. She alone is entrusted with the task of putting together the programme of modest musical festivities her companions are in the habit of offering the director's wife on her birthday.

Translated by Will McMorran

CLAUDE CAHUN

Cinderella, the Humble and Haughty Child

'She dropped one of her glass slippers, and the prince picked it up very carefully.'

– Perrault

My father got remarried, which overjoyed me. I'd always dreamed of having an evil stepmother. The heavens granted me even more, giving me two stepsisters. They were deliciously cruel. I especially liked the older one, who despised me so much it thrilled me. Seeing me always seated in the fireplace's cinders, whose heat penetrated me delectably (sometimes even burning me), with her sweet, familiar voice, didn't she call me *Cinderass*? Never was a word so sweet to my ears.

Unfortunately, they were pretty girls, suitable for marriage. They soon left us, leaving me with my parents who, devoted to one another, regarded the world with a drunken tenderness. And I too was enveloped by their splendid, universal indifference. I would do anything to avoid such a marriage ... But how would I, since I was of an amorous mind, and so submissive?

Furthermore, I felt my pleasure diminish each day, and my ecstasy wane. I understood why (for lack of anything better, I had given myself to solitary reveries and reflected a lot): such delights fade with habit. At present, I was too downcast, too humiliated, to experience the joy of daily humiliation. I had to climb back on to the bank, on to a tall bank, to dive back into the infinite sea of human voluptuousness. A princess, ah! *If I were a queen!* ... To wed, publicly, the least of my vassals, to get him to force me to abdicate, to abuse me, to prefer the whores of his village to me! *Can one make such fantasies come true?*

31

My very wise godmother, Madame Fairy, to whom I confessed my desires, came to my rescue. She knew our Prince very well (long ago, she had even attended his baptism) and revealed to me the *curious particularities* by which he could be seduced:

He had a passion for women's shoes. Touching them, kissing them, letting himself be walked on with their charming heels (pointed heels with a scarlet tint so they looked as if they were splattered with blood) – these were the simple pleasures he'd been looking for since he was a child. The ladies at court could not satisfy him. Awkward and timid, lest they wound the heir to the throne, they wear house slippers. And fearing he would lower himself to kiss their feet, they raise them, with all the signs of respect, to his mouth, which is august, but bitter, unyielding to smiles . . . What this royal lover needs is a haughty and dominating mistress, with hard heels and no pity, the one I could be – me, the one who understands!

'Godmother, you are demanding a terrible sacrifice of me! This man is the opposite of the one my heart desires.'

'I know, my dear. But it's for a purpose. *Every sacrifice has its own reward.* By playing your role, you will experience an excitement more profound than any of the all-too-common ones you've known until now. My blasé Cinderella, listen to me: the sharpest pain on earth (for you, the greatest pleasure) is to go against one's instinct, to violate it and to chasten it time and again . . .'

Convinced by my good godmother, I accepted her presents – three pairs of cinder-grey horses, a carriage, a driver and six lackeys; clothes of velour and gold; and cute *vair* slippers (he adores fur) that she entrusted to me just for him . . .

She advised me to be proud and fierce, mysterious to perfection, and to flee at the stroke of midnight – and to do so the second night, in the process losing my little left slipper (but in full light and under the eyes of the Prince who would follow me).

(My feet are small and compact, and sort of stunted – since I have the habit of binding them in a vice of stiff cloth laced firmly in the Chinese fashion. This exquisite and most effective torture fills me with utter satisfaction. . .)

I obeyed. Yesterday, I saw the Prince, who disturbed me greatly. Alas!

I guess his thoughts all too well! And I noticed many essential details . . . *He blushed at the mention of boots. He blushes*, he told me naively, *if he walks in front of a display of shoes, which seems to him to be the worst inconvenience*; but a display of flesh does not affect his modest and tolerant soul. He is astonished that games so foolish and even a bit repugnant can be pleasing.

I agree with him. And perhaps I would truly love him if he occasionally wanted to switch roles . . . I can't entertain the thought for a second, for if I were to ruin his illusions, he would send his cricket back home all too quickly! I'll have to deceive him to the grave.

The important thing is being a Princess. When I'm a Princess, with the help of my godmother, I'll be able to get the lowliest of my valets to beat me.

Then, I'll once again put on my scullery maid dress, precious rags the colour and odour of cinders, in which I'll secretly bury my crazed head every day. I'll go out at night. I'll meet passers-by (there's no lack of poor or ugly, even dishonest people). And the better I play my role for the dear Prince, the more marvellously intense the contrast of these humiliating contacts will be for me.

Translated by Gretchen Schultz and Lewis Seifert

EMMANUEL BOVE

What I Saw

I don't often write on an impulse like this. Something very serious has to have happened to me for me to decide to do so. So I shall ask, dear sir, for your indulgence. It is not an author you find before you. It is a man who is suffering and who is seeking the one word that will explain everything.

Slowly I had recovered from the great shock I'd had. Everything was going well. I felt strong again and then, suddenly, once more I began to doubt.

It would be impossible to explain why I am overwhelmed by anxiety. It returned, all-powerful, without my having any say in the matter. I was at home reading a book when, for no apparent reason, I realized I had not been mistaken. I tried not to think about it any more, but you know that the harder you attempt to forget an ordeal, the more it clings to you.

Yes, I was reading a book that was as interesting to me as any book can be. I was so deep into this novel that I forgot where I was when, all of a sudden while turning a page, during that brief moment of distraction that interrupts the story with each new page, I had the clear realization that I had not been wrong.

I had seen the thing with my own eyes and, as a result, it was true. My girlfriend could deny it all she wanted, but because I had seen it, it was true. The proof that I was wrong is all around me. My friends, to whom I made the mistake of telling this story, disagreed with me. My girlfriend's parents hinted that I had taken leave of my senses. Even my Henriette, after having heatedly defended herself, in the end simply shrugged whenever I mentioned this scene.

And so I managed, by the strength of my will, to doubt my own eyes. Gradually I forgot what I had seen. I forced myself to think I had been wrong. Life became bearable again. My girlfriend was ever more loving.

And now, in some idiotic way, I have begun thinking about this episode again. And so, all my efforts have been in vain! That painstaking and salutary process I suffered through in order to find peace was for naught!

Ridiculously, I again find myself anxious and desperate, like on the first day.

Yet I believe I was wrong, that my girlfriend is innocent, and that I was the victim of a hallucination. I want to believe this, even though my eyes will not let me. But despite all my efforts, I feel I will always have before me that ludicrous vision that pains me so.

This is why I am writing to you, so as not to be alone with my doubts. And perhaps for you to give me some advice. I must confess that I feel the need to ask you to forgive me for writing. When a man suffers as I am suffering, writing should not be a consolation. Forgive me, dear sir, for speaking to you like this. You are not used to such confessions. They seem to you some artifice meant to hold your attention, whereas in reality they are the proof of deep despair. It's true. I feel some embarrassment in writing. I know I shouldn't tell you this. One never admits that the person who is writing to us is doing so reluctantly – and with good reason. If, at the theatre, an actor were to say he did not want to play his part, that it annoyed him to do so, I admit that I, like any theatregoer, would boo him off the stage.

But this, I must say, is a different situation. I am suffering as much as a man can suffer. And I am not writing to entertain or interest you, but simply to ask you what I should do.

I will expose the facts one by one, very clearly. I will tell you everything I know about my girlfriend and will ask you, afterwards, to tell me if I was mistaken or not. I am addressing myself to you because as an outsider you will be able to be an impartial judge. It is in the interest of my parents and friends for everything to work out. They know me. They know I am impressionable. And they will believe me less than you, who do not know me.

Because you have agreed to hear me out, I must first tell you what happened. You can see from the tone of what I just wrote that I am a sincere man, that I do not lie. I therefore beg you, while I am telling you this story, not to think you need to know my girlfriend's version before you form an opinion. Only the spineless want to know the pros and cons in order not to take sides. So I am asking you to judge this story simply through what I tell you, otherwise you will cause me great pain.

I shall recount the story you are about to read as if I were not the main character. I shall have no bias. On the contrary, I shall not mention anything that casts me in a good light. I shall lay out clearly everything that does credit to my Henriette. You can see that all I long for is to be wrong.

So I will begin. Pay close attention. Do not skip over anything, because my happiness is at stake. Some other time, I will write a long letter to amuse you, a letter full of youthful imagination. And if it annoys you, do not finish it. It will not matter. But today, I beg you, pay attention. At the risk of repeating myself, let me say yet again that my happiness is in your hands.

My girlfriend is as sweet as an angel. I must tell you that, although she was pure when she gave herself to me, she did not wait until we were married to abandon herself and I am open-minded enough not to reproach her for this. It would be human enough for me to use this fact to degrade her in your eyes. Believe me, I see nothing in this proof of love that could allow what my dear Henriette did to be predicted. If she gave herself to me without our being married, it is my fault.

A thousand signs prove to me that my girlfriend adores me. She has forgiven me what many women would never have forgiven. Even though she is beautiful, she recognizes that a man's lapse is not as great as a woman's. Naturally, she did not say this to me, but I felt, deep down inside, she knew it. When in the past I did what I should not have done, she was not angry with me, but rather, with man's very nature. And this fact alone demonstrates my girlfriend's immense goodness.

There are additional signs that make her pure in my eyes. Other men do not exist for her. I believe I can discern, from certain details, from certain attitudes, that they repulse her just as they do me. She often says exactly what I would say about a man were I a woman. She could not invent these feelings if she did not have them. And this is another reason why I love her so much.

36

A few times I asked her what she would do if I lost a leg. And she always responded ardently that she would love me just as much.

Please forgive me for providing such details but, when you want to prove a woman loves you, they are necessary.

There is something else that proves her love, and that is the way she admires me. She takes all my opinions for her own. Sometimes, when I have not finished voicing my opinion on a subject, embarrassed by the difficulty I have expressing myself, she will finish my thought differently from how I would have. As soon as she realizes this, she stops herself and is even ready to contradict herself until we agree. Is this not the mark of great love, to show such self-abnegation? Do you believe that if my adored Henriette did not love me she would follow my line of thinking in this way, step by step? No, of course not.

That's not all. So many things at every moment of the day and night demonstrate her love. When we are lying next to each other, I am always the first to turn away. Candy, cake, fruit – she always goes without in order to offer them to me and, if I don't take them, because I know how fond she is of them, she insists with so much love that I would be hurting her if I continued to refuse them. Nothing exists for her. She sees all of life through me. And when she arrives late for one of our dates, do not think it is because she is trying to be coy. She wants to imitate other women. She forces herself to be late because she is a woman and sometimes she is afraid she will lose me if she is not enough of one.

No, my Henriette, you did not do that, and yet . . .

One day she asked me if I ever had the feeling when I was away from her that I had not been as kind to her as I could have been. Without thinking, I said no. How can you detect in a question asked in an ordinary voice everything that someone expects from your answer? She became a bit sad. She did not say anything right then, but later in the evening she told me I was not kind, that I did not love her as much as she loved me. And she added that whenever she was away from me, she had the impression she had not pleased me enough.

Often she reminds me of things I said that I had forgotten and that she had thought about for a long time without my suspecting. Her sweet little brain works tirelessly to make me happy.

With her, as with little children, I never mention death. But I have the feeling if I asked her to die with me, she would. She led me to understand as much without pronouncing the word 'death', out of modesty.

Now that you are familiar with my girlfriend from what I have said about her, I ask you to believe the portrait I have painted of her. Everyone will only have good things to tell you about her. Love has not deformed my judgement. This is how she is. And although it may be difficult to believe the portrait that one person paints of another, it is less difficult than believing in true love.

You know her well now, or at least you know how much she loves me, and that is what is important. So I am going to tell you what happened.

This is what happened. Two months ago, I was not feeling well. It was a Friday. The day was a cold one, but the sun was shining in the blue sky. We'd had lunch at home. We were just finishing up when Henriette came over to me and kissed me.

'Darling, will you let me take a little walk?'

'Of course.'

'I'd like to buy a few things.'

'Shall I come along?'

'Why not, my darling?'

Then she changed the subject, busied herself with this and that and, picking up one of my books, sat down in an armchair. Jokingly, I said to her:

'You're going to know that one by heart!'

Indeed, she only reads the books I have written, and since there aren't many, she reads them over and over.

'That's what I want, my love. I am jealous of your thoughts.'

I did not really understand what she meant, but I felt she was trying to make me understand that my work represented a rival to her.

I know that, even though she loved me very much, what she said was not completely sincere. She said it because women are supposed to be jealous of their husbands' work. But I am indulgent. What is the use of taking offence at that? One shouldn't ask too much of a woman. And then again, this lack of sincerity is also a kind of love.

She sat back down and continued reading. Although she admired my writing, she closed the book before the end of a chapter, stood up, and said to me:

'You are really amazing! You notice everything. Well, I'm going out, darling.'

'Don't you want me to come with you?'

'Yes, of course. But wait, there is still something at the end of your book that I want to reread. You know, the story about the unfaithful wife. It's amazing. Don't tell me you haven't been acquainted with a woman like her.'

'You're mad, darling! You know how trustworthy I am.'

'Still, there's something of you in this story. You are a bit like the husband.'

So she reread the story of the unfaithful wife. Then, getting up, she went to dress without saying anything. She came back a few minutes later.

'Goodbye, darling. I'll be back around six o'clock. Be good and work well.'

'You don't want me to come along?'

'How foolish you are! You are feeling poorly. You told me yourself you have a headache. It's cold outside. You have a slight fever. Give me your hand. See, your hand is burning!'

'Yes, but if I dress warmly?'

'I don't think it would be wise. A man like you must be well cared for.'

'You know I don't like to stay home alone, darling.'

'But I'll be back before six!'

And she left. It is obvious she did not want me to accompany her. But I pay this no mind. I understand that a woman can feel the need to be alone from time to time. It could even be that she truly did not want me to go out because I was feeling poorly. Perhaps she was thinking about my health, perhaps not. She wanted to be alone for no reason; she wanted to be alone for a variety of reasons. I know that just because one is hiding something, it does not mean that one is guilty. She could easily have been hiding the fact that she was going to see someone, meeting a girlfriend, without necessarily being unfaithful to me.

And so, I soon stopped thinking about her. Have you noticed that it takes several hours of absence before you think about the woman you love when she has gone out freely, happily, with her errands to run?

I sat down at my desk with the intention of writing. Do not think some vague suspicion was keeping me from working. I assure you I was not thinking about her. If I was incapable of doing anything at all it was more because I felt lazy than because I was worried.

To my great sadness it was then that, bored with my indolence, I decided to go out.

I shall always remember that radiant winter afternoon. No wind. A blue sky that grows dark before the evening papers come out. A pure sky where the sun seems to be an intruder. A white dust that surprises you because the previous day it was raining.

I was strolling calmly. It was pleasant to feel that my fever gave me permission not to hurry. Like a convalescent, I walked down a boulevard, taking interest in small things. Whenever our life is peaceful, whenever everything smiles on us, how agreeable it is to take interest in small things! You stop, you look. No one pays attention to you. These small things don't really interest us. It's our soul that is content with simple things, our soul that wants to find its youth again because it is happy contemplating small things, for no reason, simply not to think.

Such joy in being alive! And to imagine that we struggle to push away everything that could prevent us from moving along like this, gently, slowly, towards some intangible goal, almost unconsciously, happy to listen to the sounds, smell the aromas, see the light, touch a few objects.

A clock chimed. I did not count the chimes, but I sensed from the duration of the ringing that it was four o'clock.

And at that moment, dear sir, something horrible occurred. Have the kindness to read what follows attentively. I must tell you yet again that my happiness is in your hands. You know what a great responsibility it is for someone's happiness to depend on you. Think of a person in your life who made you suffer. Think that, in his shoes, you would not have acted as he did. I am not asking you to do for a stranger what you would have done for a loved one. I'm simply asking you to attempt to understand and advise me.

I looked at a storefront. I looked at it distractedly, like people do when they have no one with whom to share what they notice. Then I turned around. Now you will find out what happened.

For merely a second, I saw a taxi pass close to me and, in the taxi, my girlfriend was kissing a man.

You've grasped what I just said. I saw a taxi and, in this taxi, my girlfriend was kissing a man. She was blocking my view of him, but not entirely; I could see that he was hatless.

I swear on everything that is most sacred in the world that I saw my girlfriend kissing a man in a taxi. I swear. I saw them. He was letting himself be kissed. It was she who was leaning towards him. The taxi passed a few feet in front of me. I saw them. I'm sure of it, absolutely sure. Why would I say that if I had not seen them? I even remember today, two months later, all the details with extraordinary precision. She was to the left of this man. And her left knee was higher than the right and hid the man's legs. I did not have the time to see her hands. I don't know where they were. But, on reflection, I really have the impression that her right hand was behind her companion's back, while her left hand must have been holding him around the neck. There is no possible doubt. She was kissing a man. I saw the bright colour of the hat she had put on before going out. I saw her, my girlfriend, in this taxi and I also saw a bit of the man she was kissing. Yes, it was her. But, then, I just don't understand. If she doesn't love me, why doesn't she leave me? It was her. I saw her. I was not thinking about her when I saw her. Otherwise it would be easy to imagine that, since I was thinking of her so vividly, I gave her features to the first woman I saw.

And now, since I have offered you all my certainty, let me tell you again that it is true: I saw her in this taxi; it was her.

I went back home, completely demoralized. Before my eyes I continually saw the inside of this taxi that in my mind – a bit dark, lit from the front, with its cushions – resembled a small bedroom. I even imagined flowers in this taxi, flowers I had not seen. It is impossible to describe what I was feeling. I would have to choose among a thousand fleeting thoughts. I need to present you, dear sir, with a few of these inconsistent thoughts that, in my head, followed one another with dizzying speed. And if I could manage to sort some of them out, to see them separately from the others, it would seem, by their insignificance, that my pain was not as great as I claim. So I shall not describe my pain. Can one really portray suffering with words? In this account, I don't think so. I am too removed from what happened. Any perfect description of pain presupposes an effort I can no longer make. I can only write as I am writing, just clearly enough for you to understand me.

I went home and lay down on a bed. Remaining motionless seemed odious to me, but by forcing myself to lie down, I wanted to prove I was still in control of myself.

Until my girlfriend returned, I never ceased thinking about her. No, I had not been mistaken. If I'd had even the slightest doubt, I would have done everything I could to fuel it until it became a certainty. But there was not even the shadow of a doubt. It is dreadful to find yourself confronting reality in this way. No matter what line of reasoning you come up with to forget it, it reappears quickly, more real than ever.

I spent two interminable hours like this, thinking, all the while waiting for the one I love.

Suddenly the door opened. She was there.

'I've been looking for you everywhere, darling. Why are you here? Do you feel ill? You should have undressed and gone under the blankets.'

I did not answer. I was torn between the desire to tell her everything I had seen, immediately, and the desire to remain silent in order to hold on to a reason to be sad, in order to take an incomprehensible pleasure in hearing my girlfriend lie. I hid my confusion behind an imaginary headache.

'Get under the blankets, my love. If I had known you were so sick, I would not have gone out. I would have taken care of you. Lie down now. I'll make you something warm. And I'll sit next to you and read you the papers. I have never seen you so ill. What's wrong? Do you want me to go get a doctor?'

'He wouldn't be able to cure me.'

My voice was filled with sadness as I pronounced this sentence. In my mind, it had a different meaning than the one my girlfriend heard and, like all such sentences, it required a disabused tone. I like those sentences, and you will see what I did with them.

'Go lie down now.'

'What's the point?'

'Come now, don't be so discouraged. The minute you are a tiny bit ill you think you're going to die.'

'I wish it were true.'

My girlfriend, despite all my efforts, did not notice that my pain was entirely emotional. I would have wanted her to see it for herself so I could deny it feebly, and in the end explain to her why, so that she could reassure me. But she did not notice.

She undressed me by force, as badly as I would have undressed her.

'Now lie down. Close your eyes, my darling. I'll bring you something warm.'

I obeyed. I felt I would not be able to keep what I had seen to myself. In spite of how sure I was of my girlfriend's unfaithfulness, I still wanted to believe that a word from her would dispel my certainty.

'Henriette, what did you do this afternoon?'

'Errands of no interest to you, my little lamb. I brought you the papers. You see, I thought of you.'

'But what kind of errands?'

'How jealous you are, Jean.'

'I'm not jealous, my darling. I'm interested in everything you do.'

'Well, in that case: I went to the milliner's. Then to Anne's. We went for a walk together. Then she felt ill. We went into a café. And you know, when I was at the milliner's, there was some old man who waited for me for at least an hour at the door. If you had seen him! He was looking at hats, but how he looked at me! In the café, it was the same thing. Two young men wanted to sit down at our table. You can imagine how Anne, who wasn't feeling well, sent them packing!'

'And if she had been feeling well?'

'Oh! You are mad! You see everything in a distorted way. You know I would never talk to a man I didn't know.'

'And you didn't go down Rue Saint-Lazare?'

As I said these words, I stared at my girlfriend, as much as one can when one is lying down. She answered me without hesitating at all:

'No, why?'

'Because I saw you.'

'You saw me?'

'Yes.'

'So you went out? That was not wise, sick as you are. You should have told me you wanted to go out. We would have gone out together.'

'I saw you.'

'You're mistaken. What would I have been doing on Rue Saint-Lazare? I was not even in that neighbourhood. You dreamed it, and it doesn't surprise me, my adorable little lamb.'

'I saw you in a taxi.'

'Well, that takes the cake! In a taxi, now! I swear I wasn't. If I had taken a taxi, I wouldn't hide it. And why would I have taken a taxi?'

'To kiss a man.'

My girlfriend, who was stirring a cup of tea, stopped. She looked at me with large, surprised eyes in which there was that hint of calm that precedes indignation.

'To kiss a man?'

'Yes.'

'My poor Jean, what is the matter with you? You are going mad, mad, mad. How can you think such a thing of me? Me, kiss another man? So you take me for a streetwalker? You are mad, completely mad.'

'I saw you.'

'Listen, Jean. You don't know what you're saying. You have a fever. You are so jealous that you're losing your mind.'

'I saw you. Do you understand what that means? I saw you, you who are in front of me. I saw you kissing a man.'

'You're lying. I swear on my life that I didn't take a taxi, and that I have never kissed a man besides you.'

'But I saw you.'

'That's impossible. What would keep me here if not love? We are not married. If I loved someone else, I would not be able to put on such a loathsome act, I would be incapable of concealing it. You know how frank I am. If I loved someone else, I would tell you. Even if it would make you suffer, I would tell you. You could not have seen me. It's impossible. I belong to you alone.'

'I saw you.'

'Perhaps you saw someone who looks like me.'

I had been waiting for these words for several minutes and yet I did not know how to answer them immediately. I was afraid of them. I knew that they alone were capable of making me doubt my eyes without providing proof of my girlfriend's innocence.

You, dear sir, will perhaps think what my friends thought, that I fell victim to a resemblance. When one is trying to console someone, one always manages to make statements that one would not believe oneself. To claim I fell victim to a resemblance is such a statement.

Let me tell you, sir, that I recognized my girlfriend, not just her clothing, but her neck, the colour of her hair.

'You are the one I saw in the taxi.'

'It was not me. I told you exactly what I did and when. You can ask Anne if I spent the afternoon with her. You can come with me to the milliner's, and to the café where we went when she felt ill. You can ask the waiter, if it's the same one, what we had to drink. I cannot do any more, my Jean, to prove to you that I am faithful.'

I listened to these words without believing them. I know I would have got lost trying to figure out my girlfriend's schedule. Yes, I could have seen a waiter who would have told me 'It seems to me that I waited on those two women,' or who would not have remembered. My girlfriend would have shown me the table where she sat. But what would that have proved? The fact remained that I had seen her, in this taxi, kissing a man.

Or if she had said to me, 'Yes, I took a taxi with Anne and I kissed her,' I would have believed that. I did not have enough time to see the person who was with my girlfriend and to be sure it was a man. But the fact that she denied so obstinately that she had taken a taxi proves to me she was unfaithful.

'I saw you.'

'Listen to me, Jean. I swear to you on our love, on your life, on my parents' life, that I did not take a taxi, that I was not unfaithful to you, that I love you more than anything in the world, more than my family, and I am ready to do anything you tell me, I am your slave and your wife. I swear to you, my love, that if you were to die tomorrow, I could not survive. You are my sole joy in this world. I only live for you and through you. Look me in the eyes. You see, I don't lower my lids. Do you believe if I had done what you say I would not die of shame beneath your gaze?'

Dear sir, I wound up believing my girlfriend. I wound up believing her but, in spite of everything, some doubt has remained in me. It is this doubt I am asking you to drive out. I repeated word for word what the woman whom I still love said. I also told you that, while I wound up believing my girlfriend, I am still sure I saw her in the taxi. It seems that nothing can shake this certainty. And yet, Henriette loves me so, she is so honest! Let me tell you as well that, if you had been in my shoes, you certainly would have recognized my girlfriend. You would have recognized her as I did. So it is useless to tell me that perhaps I did not see clearly.

Before you can reach your decision, you probably think you will need to know my girlfriend better. It is not worth the trouble. You know her. She is unable to do anything behind my back. She loves me. You were able to see that. Do not think I am blinded by love. She is exactly as I have presented her to you. And as sure as I am of having seen her kiss someone else, I am just as sure of her total love.

I am waiting, dear sir, for a letter from you that will allow me to know the truth. If you are not sensitive to my pain, perhaps you will respond with indifference. Know that I shall read your words with the same attention, for I am hoping nonetheless to find in what you say the word that will bring me peace.

Translated by Alyson Waters

MARCEL AYMÉ

The Man Who Walked Through Walls

In Montmartre, on the third floor of 75b Rue d'Orchampt, there lived an excellent gentleman called Dutilleul, who possessed the singular gift of passing through walls without any trouble at all. He wore pince-nez and a small black goatee, and was a lowly clerk in the Ministry of Records. In winter he would take the bus to work, and in fine weather he would make the journey on foot, in his bowler hat.

Dutilleul had just entered his forty-third year when he discovered his power. One evening, a brief electricity cut caught him in the hallway of his small bachelor's apartment. He groped for a while in the darkness and, when the lights came back on, found himself outside on the third-floor landing. Since his front door was locked from the inside, the incident gave him food for thought and, despite the objections of common sense, he decided to go back inside just as he had come out, by passing through the wall. This peculiar skill, apparently unrelated to any aspiration of his, rather disturbed him. So, the next day being Saturday, he took advantage of his English-style five-day week to visit a local doctor and explain his case. The doctor was soon persuaded that Dutilleul was telling the truth and, following a full examination, located the cause of the problem in a helicoid hardening of the strangulary wall in the thyroid gland. He prescribed sustained over-exertion and a twice-yearly dose of one powdered tetravalent pirette pill, a mixture of rice flour and centaur hormones.

Having taken the first pill, Dutilleul put the medicine away in a drawer and forgot about it. As for the intensive over-exertion, as a civil servant his rate of work was governed by practices that permitted no excess, nor did his leisure time, divided between reading the newspapers and tending his stamp collection, involve him in any excessive expenditure of energy either. A year later, therefore, his ability to walk through walls remained intact, but he never used it, apart from inadvertently, being uninterested in adventure and resistant towards the seductions of his imagination. He never even thought of entering his home by any route other than the front door and then only after having opened it by means of key and lock. Perhaps he would have grown old in the comfort of his habits, never tempted to put his gift to the test, had an extraordinary event not suddenly turned his life upside down. Being called to other duties, his deputy chief clerk Monsieur Mouron was replaced by a certain Monsieur Lécuyer, a man of abrupt speech who wore a nail-brush moustache. From his first day, the new deputy chief clerk looked unfavourably on Dutilleul's wearing of pince-nez with a chain and a black goatee, and made a show of treating him like an irritating, shabby old thing. But the worst of it was that he intended to introduce reforms of considerable scope into his department – just the thing to disturb his subordinate's peace. For twenty years now, Dutilleul had commenced his official letters with the following formula: 'With reference to your esteemed communication of the nth of this month and, for the record, to all previous exchange of letters, I have the honour to inform you that . . .' A formula for which Monsieur Lécuyer intended to substitute another, much more American in tone: 'In reply to your letter of n, I inform you that . . .' Dutilleul could not get used to these new epistolary fashions. In spite of himself, he would go back to his traditional ways, with a machine-like obstinacy that earned him the deputy clerk's growing hostility. The atmosphere inside the Ministry of Records became almost oppressive. In the morning he would come in to work full of apprehension, and in bed in the evenings, it often happened that he stayed awake thinking for a whole fifteen minutes before falling asleep.

Disgusted by this backward thinking that was threatening the success of his reforms, Monsieur Lécuyer had banished Dutilleul to a badly lit cubbyhole that led off his own office. It was reached by a low and narrow door in the corridor and still displayed in capital letters the inscription: BROOM CUPBOARD. Dutilleul resigned himself to accepting this unprecedented humiliation, but at home, reading a news item on some bloodthirsty crime, he found himself picturing Monsieur Lécuyer as the victim.

One day, the deputy clerk burst into Dutilleul's cubbyhole brandishing a letter and began to bellow:

'Rewrite this tripe! Rewrite this piece of unspeakable dross that brings shame on my department!'

Dutilleul tried to protest, but Monsieur Lécuyer raged on, calling him a procedure-addicted cockroach and, before storming out, crumpled the letter in his hand and threw it in Dutilleul's face. Dutilleul was modest but proud. Sitting alone in his cubbyhole, he grew rather hot under the collar and suddenly felt a flash of inspiration. Leaving his seat, he stepped into the wall that divided his office from that of the deputy clerk – but stepped carefully, in such a way that only his head emerged on the other side. Sitting at his desk, his hand still shaking, Monsieur Lécuyer was shifting a comma in an underling's draft that had been submitted for his approbation, when he heard a cough inside his office. Looking up, with an unspeakable fright, he found Dutilleul's head mounted on the wall like a hunting trophy. But the head was still alive. Through its pince-nez, the head flashed a look of hatred at him. Even better, the head began to speak.

'Sir,' it said, 'you are a ruffian, a boor and a scoundrel.'

Gaping in horror, Monsieur Lécuyer was unable to tear his eyes from this apparition. At last, hefting himself out of his armchair, he leapt into the corridor and ran round to the cubbyhole. Dutilleul, pen in hand, was sitting in his usual place, in a peaceful, hard-working attitude. The deputy clerk gave him a long stare and then, after stammering a few words, went back to his office. Hardly had he sat down when the head reappeared on the wall.

'Sir, you are a ruffian, a boor and a scoundrel.'

In the course of that day alone, the frightful head appeared on the wall twenty-three times and kept up the same frequency in the days that followed. Dutilleul, who had acquired a degree of skill in this game, was no longer satisfied with simply insulting the deputy clerk. He uttered obscure threats, exclaiming for example in a sepulchral voice, punctuated by truly demonic laughter:

'Werewolf! Werewolf! Hair of a beast!' (laughter). 'A horror is lurking the owls have unleashed!' (laughter).

On hearing which, the poor deputy clerk grew even paler and even more choked, and his hair stood up quite straight on his head while down his back dribbled horrid cold sweat. On the first day, he lost a pound in weight. In the following week, apart from melting away almost visibly, he began to eat his soup with a fork and to give passing policemen full military salutes. At the beginning of the second week, an ambulance came to collect him at home and took him to a mental asylum.

Delivered from Monsieur Lécuyer's tyranny, Dutilleul was free to return to his cherished formalities: 'With reference to your esteemed communication of the nth of this month . . .' And yet, he was not satisfied. There was a craving inside him, a new, imperious urge – it was nothing less than the urge to walk through walls. Of course, this was easily satisfied, for example at home, and there indeed he went ahead. But a man in possession of brilliant gifts cannot long be content to exercise them in pursuit of mediocre goals. Besides, walking through walls cannot constitute an end in itself. It is the beginning of an adventure, which calls for a sequel, for elaboration and, in the end, for some reward. Dutilleul quite understood this. He felt within him a need for expansion, a growing desire to fulfil and surpass himself, and a stab of longing, which was something like the call of what lay through the wall. Unfortunately, he lacked an objective. He looked for inspiration in the newspaper, particularly in the politics and sports sections, since he felt these were honourable activities, but finally realizing that they offered no outlets for people who walk through walls, he made do with the most promising of the 'in brief' news items.

The first break-in that Dutilleul carried out was at a large credit institution on the right bank of the river. After walking through a dozen walls and partitions, he forced a number of safes, filled his pockets with banknotes and, before leaving, autographed the scene of his theft in red chalk with the pseudonym The Werewolf, with a very elegant flourish that was reproduced the next day in all the newspapers. By the end of the week, The Werewolf's name had become spectacularly famous. Public sympathy was unreservedly on the side of this superior burglar who was so cleverly mocking the police. He distinguished himself each succeeding night with the accomplishment of a new exploit, whether at the expense of a bank or a jeweller or some wealthy individual. There was not one among the dreamy type of Parisienne or country miss who did not passionately wish they belonged body and soul to the terrible Werewolf. After the theft of the famous Burdigala diamond and the burglary at the state pawnbroker's, which took place in the same week, the fervour of the masses reached the point of delirium. The Minister for the Interior was forced to resign, bringing the Minister for Records down with him. In spite of this, Dutilleul became one of the richest men in Paris, always came to work on time and was talked of as a strong candidate for the *palmes académiques*, for his contribution to French culture. In the mornings at the Ministry of Records, he enjoyed listening to colleagues discussing his exploits of the night before. 'This Werewolf,' they said, 'is amazing, a superman, a genius.' Hearing such praise, Dutilleul blushed pink with embarrassment and, behind his pince-nez and chain, his eyes shone with warmth and gratitude.

One day, this sympathetic atmosphere won him over so completely that he felt he could not keep his secret for much longer. With some residual shyness, he considered his colleagues, gathered around a newspaper that announced his theft at the Bank of France, and declared in modest tones: 'You know, I am The Werewolf.' Hearty laughter greeted Dutilleul's confession and won him the mocking nickname 'Werewolf'. That evening, as they were leaving the Ministry, his colleagues made him the butt of endless jokes, and his life seemed less sweet.

A few days later, The Werewolf was caught by a night patrol in a jeweller's shop on the Rue de la Paix. He had added his signature to the counter and had begun to sing a drinking song while smashing various display cases with the help of a solid gold chalice. It would have been easy for him to sink into a wall and so escape the night patrol, but all the evidence suggests that he wanted to be arrested – probably solely in order to disconcert his colleagues, whose incredulity had mortified him. Indeed they were very surprised when the next day's papers ran a photograph of Dutilleul on their front pages. They bitterly regretted having misjudged their brilliant comrade and paid homage to him by all growing small goatees. Carried away by remorse and admiration, some were even tempted to try their hand at their friends' and acquaintances' wallets and heirloom watches.

It will doubtless be supposed that letting oneself get caught by the police simply in order to surprise a few colleagues shows a great deal of frivolity, unworthy of an exceptional man, but the obvious motivations count for very little with this kind of resolution. In giving up his liberty, Dutilleul believed he was giving in to an arrogant desire for revenge, while in truth he was simply slipping down the slope of his destiny. For a man who walks through walls, there can be no dazzling career if he hasn't at least once seen the inside of a prison.

When Dutilleul entered the premises of La Santé Prison, he felt that fate was spoiling him. The thickness of the walls was a veritable feast. Only a day after his incarceration, the astonished guards found that the prisoner had hammered a nail into his cell wall on which now hung a gold watch belonging to the warden. He either could not or would not reveal how this item had come into his possession. The watch was returned to its owner and, the following day, found once more at The Werewolf's bedside, along with the first volume of *The Three Musketeers* borrowed from the warden's personal library. The staff at La Santé grew very tense. Furthermore, the guards were complaining of kicks in their backsides of inexplicable provenance. It seemed that the walls no longer had ears but feet. The Werewolf's detention had lasted a week when, on entering his office one morning, the warden found the following letter on his desk:

Dear Warden,

With reference to our interview of the seventeenth of this month and, for the record, to your general instructions dating from fifteenth of May of the previous year, I have the honour to inform you that I have just finished reading the second volume of The Three Musketeers *and that I intend to escape tonight between eleven twenty-five and eleven thirty-five.*

I remain, dear Warden, yours respectfully,
The Werewolf.

In spite of the close surveillance to which he was subjected that night, Dutilleul escaped at half past eleven. Broadcast to the public the following morning, the news stirred deep admiration up and down the country. Nevertheless, after this latest feat, which had brought his popularity to even greater heights, Dutilleul hardly seemed concerned about secrecy and moved around Montmartre without any precautions. Three days after his escape, a little before noon, he was arrested on Rue Caulaincourt at the Café du Rêve, where he was enjoying a glass of white wine with lemon among friends.

Marched back to La Santé and triple-locked into a murky cell, The Werewolf escaped that very evening and went to sleep in the warden's own apartment, in the guest bedroom. The next morning at about nine o'clock, he called the maid for his breakfast and allowed himself to be plucked from his bed, without resisting, by belatedly alerted guards. Outraged, the warden set a guard at the door of Dutilleul's cell and put him on dry bread. Around noon, the prisoner went to lunch in a nearby restaurant and then, after his coffee, called the warden.

'Hello! Warden sir, I'm a little embarrassed but a moment ago, as I was leaving, I forgot to take your wallet with me, so here I am stuck for cash in this restaurant. Would you be so good as to send someone to pay the bill?'

The warden rushed over himself, so furious that he overflowed with threats and oaths. Personally offended, Dutilleul escaped the next night, this time never to return. He took the precaution of shaving off his black goatee and replacing his lorgnette and chain with tortoiseshell spectacles. A sports cap and a loud checked suit with plus fours completed his transformation. He set himself up in a small apartment on Avenue Junot to which, since his first arrest, he had sent a selection of furnishings and his most prized objects. He was getting tired of the fuss over his fame and, since his stay in La Santé, he had become rather blasé about the pleasure of walking through walls. The thickest, the proudest of them now seemed to him mere Japanese screens, and he dreamed of plunging into the heart of some immense pyramid. While planning a journey to Egypt, he continued to live a very peaceful life, dividing his time between his stamp collection, the cinema and long strolls around Montmartre. His metamorphosis was so complete that, beardless and bespectacled, he could walk right past his best friends without being recognized by any of them. Only the painter Gen Paul, who picked up the least physiological change in the old denizens of the neighbourhood, at last managed to discover Dutilleul's true identity. One morning, finding himself face to face with Dutilleul at the corner of the Rue de l'Abreuvoir, he could not stop himself from saying, in his rough way:

'Well stone me, I see you've decked y'self out in fine new whistles to put the todd off the scent.' (Which in common parlance means more or less: 'I see you've disguised yourself as a gentleman in order to confuse the detectives.')

'Ah!' murmured Dutilleul. 'You've recognized me!'

This troubled him and he decided to hasten his departure for Egypt. It was the afternoon of that very same day that he fell in love with a blonde beauty whom he bumped into twice in fifteen minutes on the Rue Lepic. Straightaway he forgot his stamp collection and Egypt and the Pyramids. For her part, the blonde had looked at him with genuine interest. Nothing speaks more eloquently to the imagination of today's young woman than plus fours and a pair of tortoiseshell spectacles. She will scent her big break, and dream of cocktails and nights in California. Unfortunately, Dutilleul was informed by Gen Paul, the beauty was married to a man both brutal and jealous. This suspicious husband, who happened to have a wild and disreputable lifestyle, regularly deserted his wife between ten at night and four in the morning, double-locked in her room, with all her shutters also padlocked. During the day he kept her under close supervision, sometimes even following her through the streets of Montmartre.

'Always on the lookout, him. S'just a great bob who can't stand the thought of other Bengals fishing in his pond.'

But Gen Paul's warning only fired up Dutilleul even more. Bumping into the young lady on Rue Tholozé the next day, he dared to follow her into a creamery and, while she was waiting to be served, he said that he loved her most respectfully, that he knew about everything – the dreadful husband, the locked door and the shutters, but that he would see her that very evening in her bedroom. The blonde blushed, her milk jug trembled in her hand and, her eyes moist with yearning, she sighed softly: 'Alas! Monsieur, it is impossible.'

On the evening of this glorious day, by around ten o'clock, Dutilleul was keeping watch in Rue Norvins, observing a robust outer wall behind which stood a small house, the only signs of which were the weathervane and a chimney. A door in the wall opened and a man emerged who, after carefully locking the door behind him, walked off down the hill towards Avenue Junot. Dutilleul watched him vanish from view, far away at a bend in the road below, then counted to ten. Then he leapt forward, strode through the wall like an athlete and, after dashing through every obstacle, finally penetrated the bedroom belonging to the beautiful recluse. She welcomed him rapturously and they made love until late into the night.

The following morning, Dutilleul was annoyed to wake up with a nasty headache. It did not bother him badly and he wasn't going to let such a minor thing keep him from his next rendezvous. Still, when he happened to find a few pills scattered at the back of a drawer, he gulped down one that morning and one in the afternoon. By evening, his headache was bearable and in his elation he managed to forget it completely. The young woman was waiting for him with an impatience fanned by memories of the night before, and that night they made love until three o'clock in the morning.

When he was leaving, while walking through the partitions and walls of the house, Dutilleul had the unfamiliar feeling that they were rubbing on his hips and at his shoulders. Nevertheless, he thought it best not to pay much attention to this. Besides, it was only on entering the outer wall that he really met with considerable resistance. It felt as though he were moving through a substance that, while still fluid, was growing sticky and, at every effort he made, taking on greater density. Having managed to push himself right into the wall, he realized that he was no longer moving forward and, horrified, remembered the two pills he had taken during the day. Those pills, which he had thought were aspirin, in fact contained the powder of tetravalent pirette that the doctor had prescribed him the year before. The medication's effects combined with that of intensive over-exertion were now, suddenly, being realized.

Dutilleul was as if transfixed within the wall. He is still there today, incorporated into the stonework. Night-time revellers walking down Rue Norvins at an hour when the buzz of Paris dies down can hear a muffled voice that seems to reach them from beyond the tomb and which they take for the moans of the wind as it blows through the crossroads of Montmartre. It is Werewolf Dutilleul, lamenting the end of his glorious career and the sorrows of a love cut short. On some winter nights, the painter Gen Paul may happen to take down his guitar and venture out into the sonorous solitude of Rue Norvins to console the poor prisoner with a song, and the notes of his guitar, rising from his swollen fingers, pierce to the heart of the wall like drops of moonlight.

Translated by Sophie Lewis

RAYMOND QUENEAU

A Tale for Your Shaping

1 – Would you like to know the story of the three lively little peas?

if yes, go on to 4
if no, go on to 2

2 – Would you prefer the story of the three tall thin beanpoles?

if yes, go on to 16
if no, go on to 3

3 – Would you prefer the story of the three middle-sized middling bushes?

if yes, go on to 17
if no, go on to 21

4 – Once upon a time there were three little peas dressed all in green who slept comfily in their pod. They had plump round faces and when they were breathing through the cavities of their nostrils you could hear their soft and harmonious snoring.

if you would prefer another description, go on to 9
if this one suits you, go on to 5

5 – They were not dreaming. In fact these little beings never dream.

if you would prefer that they do dream, go on to 6
otherwise, go on to 7

6 – They were dreaming. In fact these little beings always dream and their nights exude delightful visions.

if you would like to know these visions, go on to 11
if you don't want to pursue the matter, go on to 7

7 – Their dainty feet were enveloped in warm socks and they wore black velvet gloves in bed.

if you would prefer gloves of a different colour, go on to 8
if this colour suits you, go on to 10

8 – They wore blue velvet gloves in bed.

if you would prefer gloves of a different colour, go on to 7
if this colour suits you, go on to 10

9 – Once upon a time there were three little peas who roved around on the open road. When evening approached, tired and weary, they would go to sleep very quickly.

if you would like to know what happened next, go on to 5
if not, go on to 21

10 – All three had the same dream, for in fact they loved one another dearly and, good old fellows as they were, always dreamed identically.

if you would like to know their dream, go on to 11
if not, go on to 12

11 – They dreamed that they had gone to get their soup from the soup kitchen and when they opened their canteens they discovered that it was vetch soup. Horrified, they awoke.

if you want to know why they awoke in horror, consult your
   OED at the entry 'vetch' and think it over
if you deem it pointless to investigate the question, go on to 12

12 – Opopoï! they shrieked as they opened their eyes. Opopoï! what a dream we've dreamed! An ill omen, said the first. Yes indeedy, said the second, that's true enough, it's quite got me down. Don't trouble yourselves so, said the third, the brightest of them, there's no point getting alarmed instead of understanding; in a word, I'm going to analyse it for you.

> if you would like to know the interpretation of the dream straightaway, go on to 15
> if you wish on the other hand to know the reactions of the other two, go on to 13

13 – You're putting us on, said the first. Since when have you known how to analyse dreams? Yes, since when? added the second.

> if you too would like to know since when, go on to 14
> if not, go on to 14 just the same, as you'll be none the wiser

14 – Since when? shrieked the third. How should I know! The thing is, I do it. You wait and see!

> if you too want to see, go on to 15
> if not, likewise go on to 15, as you won't see anything

15 – OK, let's see, said his brothers. Your mockery doesn't please me, replied the other, and you shan't find out a thing. Besides, in the course of this rather lively discussion, hasn't your feeling of horror faded? vanished even? So why stir up the muck of your papilionaceous unconscious? Let us rather wash ourselves in the fountain and salute this blithe morn in a state of hygiene and sainted euphoria! No sooner said than done: they slid out of their pod, let themselves roll in the sunlight and then at a jog-trot merrily attained to the theatre of their ablutions.

> if you would like to know what happened at the theatre of their ablutions, go on to 16
> if you wouldn't like to, go on to 21

16 – Three tall thin beanpoles were watching them.

if the three tall thin beanpoles displease you, go on to 17
if they suit you, go on to 18.

17 – Three middle-sized middling bushes were watching them.

if the three middle-sized middling bushes displease you, go on
    to 21
if they suit you, go on to 18

18 – Seeing that they were being ogled, the three lively little peas,
who were very bashful, made off.

if you would like to know what they did next, go on to 19
if you wouldn't like to, go on to 21

19 – They ran very hard until they got back to their pod and, closing
it behind them, went to sleep again.

if you would like to know the sequel, go on to 20
if you wouldn't like to, go to 21

20 – There isn't any sequel, the tale has ended.

21 – In this case, the tale has likewise ended.

Translated by Harry Gilonis

MARGUERITE YOURCENAR

The Man Who Loved Nereids

He stood on bare feet in the dust, heat and stale smells of the port, beneath the narrow awning of a small café where several customers had let themselves fall on the chairs in the vain hope of protecting themselves from the sun. His old rust-coloured trousers barely reached his ankles, and his pointed anklebones, the tips of his heels, his long, grazed, callused soles, his supple toes, all belonged to that race of intelligent feet, accustomed to the constant embrace of the air and the earth, hardened by the roughness of the stones, which in Mediterranean countries still allow a clothed man a little of the freedom of a man who is naked. These were agile feet, so different from the awkward, heavy ones trapped inside northern footwear . . . The faded blue of his shirt matched the tones of the sky bleached by the summer light; his shoulders and shoulder blades pierced through the tears in the cloth like lean rocks; his longish ears framed his head obliquely like the handles of a Greek vase; undoubtable traces of beauty could still be seen on his wan and vacant face, like the surfacing of an ancient broken statue in a wasteland. His eyes, like those of a sick animal, hid without distrust behind eyelashes as long as the eyelashes of mules; he held his right hand continuously stretched out, with the obstinate and insistent gesture of the archaic idols in the museums, who seem to demand from visitors the alms of their admiration; and an inarticulate braying issued from his wide-open mouth full of crooked teeth.

'Is he deaf and dumb?'

'He's certainly not deaf.'

Jean Demetriadis, the owner of the large soap factory on the island, took advantage of a momentary distraction, during which the idiot's vague glance lost itself upon the sea, to let a drachma fall on the smooth stone

slab. The light clink, half muffled by a fine coat of sand, was not lost on
the beggar, who greedily picked up the small piece of white metal and
then returned to his gazing and mournful position, much like a seagull
perched on a quay.

'He's not deaf,' Jean Demetriadis repeated, putting down in front of
him his cup half full of unctuous black lees. 'Both speech and reason were
taken from him under such extraordinary conditions that sometimes I
find myself envying him: I, a rich man, a reasonable man, who often finds
nothing but boredom and emptiness along my path. This fellow Panegyotis, as he is called, was struck dumb at the age of eighteen for having seen
the Nereids naked.'

A shy smile appeared on Panegyotis's lips, hearing his name being
mentioned. He did not seem to understand the meaning of the words
spoken by this important man in whom he vaguely recognized someone
who would protect him, but the tone, if not the words themselves, touched
him. Happy in the knowledge that he was the subject of the conversation,
and that perhaps there were more alms to be expected, he put forward his
hand imperceptibly, with the wary movement of a dog brushing his master's knee with his paw, so as not to be forgotten at dinnertime.

'He is the son of one of the wealthiest peasants in my village,' continued
Jean Demetriadis, 'and, an exception among my people, his parents are
truly rich folk. They have more land than they know what to do with, a
fine stone house, an orchard with several kinds of fruit trees, and vegetables
in the garden; an alarm clock in the kitchen, a lamp lit on the icon wall – in
a word, everything you could wish for. You could have said of Panegyotis
what can rarely be said of a young Greek: that he had his fortune made
for him. You could also say that he had the path of his future life laid out
for him, a Greek path, dusty, stony and monotonous, but here and there
along the path, crickets sing, and you can stop at the door of taverns, which
is pleasant enough. He used to help the old women beat the olives out of
the trees; he oversaw the packing of the crates of grapes and the weighing
of the bales of wool; in the discussions with the tobacco merchants, he
discreetly stood up for his father, spitting in disgust at any proposal below
the desired price; he was betrothed to the animal doctor's daughter, a good
girl who once worked in my factory. As he was very handsome, folk sad-
dled him with as many mistresses as there are women liking to be made

love to in our country; it was rumoured that he slept with the priest's wife; if the rumour was true, the priest did not hold it against him, because the priest did not care much for women in general, or for his own in particular, who, in any case, offers herself to anyone. Imagine Panegyotis's humble happiness: the love of beautiful women, the envy of men and sometimes their longing, a silver wristwatch, every two or three days a shirt, marvellously white, ironed by his mother, rice pilaf at midday and scented sea-green ouzo before supper. But happiness is brittle, and if men and circumstances don't destroy it, it is threatened by ghosts. Our ghosts are not like your northern spirits who come out only at night and live during the day in graveyards. Ours forgo the white sheets, and their skeletons are covered with flesh. But perhaps they are more dangerous than the spirits of the dead who at least have been baptized, have tasted life, have known what it is to suffer. These Nereids of our countryside are as innocent and as wicked as Nature, which at times protects and at times destroys us. The ancient gods and goddesses are certainly dead, and the museums hold nothing but their marble corpses. Our nymphs are more like your fairies than like the image Praxiteles has led you to conceive. But our people believe in their powers; they exist as the earth exists, as the water and the dangerous sun. Summer light becomes flesh in them, and because of this the sight of them provokes vertigo and stupor. They come out only at the tragic hour of midday; they seem immersed in the mystery of high noon. If the peasants bar the doors of their houses before lying down for their afternoon nap, it is not against the sun, it is against them; these truly fatal fairies are beautiful, naked, refreshing and nefarious as water in which one drinks the germs of fever; those who have seen them languish sweetly with apathy and desire; those who have had the temerity to approach them are struck dumb for life, because the secrets of their love must never be revealed to common mortals. Now, one July morning, two of the sheep in Panegyotis's father's herd began to turn in circles. The epidemic spread quickly to the best animals, and the front yard of beaten earth soon became a bedlam of demented beasts. Panegyotis left all on his own, in the midday heat, under the midday sun, in search of the animal doctor, who lives on the far side of Mount Saint Elias, in a little village hidden along the seashore. At sunset, he had not returned. The concern of Panegyotis's father passed from his sheep to his son; the surrounding fields and the valleys were searched in vain; all night long, the women of the family prayed in the village chapel, which is simply a barn lit by two dozen candles, and where it seems as if at any minute Mary will come in to give birth to Jesus. On the following evening, after work, when the men usually sit in the village square in front of a tiny cup of coffee, a glass of water or a spoonful of jam, a transfigured Panegyotis made his appearance, as changed as if he had walked through the Valley of Death. His eyes sparkled, but it seemed as if the whites and the pupils had devoured the irises; two months of malaria would not have given his skin a yellower hue; a slightly disgusting smile deformed his lips, from which no words poured forth.

'However, he had not yet become totally dumb. Broken syllables escaped from his mouth like the final gurgling of a dying fountain: "The Nereids . . . Ladies . . . Nereids . . . Beautiful . . . Naked . . . Astounding . . . Blond . . . The hair, all blond . . ."

'These were the only words they managed to get out of him. Many times, during the following days, he could be heard gently repeating to himself: "Blond hair . . . Blond . . .' as if he were stroking silk. That was all. His eyes stopped shining, but his sight, which had acquired a fixed and vacant look, now possesses singular properties: he can stare at the sun without blinking; perhaps he finds pleasure in looking upon this dazzling blond object. I was in the village during the first few weeks of his delirium: no fever, no symptoms of sunstroke or madness. In order to have him exorcized, his parents took him to a celebrated monastery not far from here: he allowed himself to be handled with the meekness of a sick lamb; but neither the ceremonies of the Church nor the fumigations of incense nor the magic rites performed by the old wives in the village managed to expel from his blood the mad sun-coloured nymphs. The first days of his newly acquired state passed in incessant comings and goings: tirelessly, he returned to the spot where the apparition had taken place. A spring flows there, a spring where fishermen sometimes come to get fresh water, a hollow valley, a field of fig trees from which a path descends towards the sea. The people of the village thought they had discovered light traces of female feet on the thin grass and places crushed by the weight of bodies. You can well imagine the scene: the patches of sunlight in the shadow of the fig trees, which is not really a shadow but a greener, softer shade of light; the young man warned by the female laughter and cries, like a hunter by the sound of beating wings; the divine young women lifting their white arms on which blond hairs caught the sun; the shadow of a leaf moving over a naked belly; a clear breast whose tip is pink and not violet; Panegyotis's kisses devouring those heads of blond hair, giving him the impression of filling his mouth with honey; his desire losing itself between those blond legs. Just as there is no love without a dazzling of the heart, there is no true voluptuousness without the startling wonder of beauty. Everything else is, at the most, a mechanical function, like hunger or thirst. To the reckless young man the Nereids opened the gates of a feminine world as different from that of the island's girls as these are different from the ewes in the herd; they made him drunk on the unknown, they made him taste the exhaustion of a miracle, they made him gaze on the evil sparks of happiness. Some people say that he never stopped meeting them, in the hot hours when these lovely midday she-devils roam the countryside in search of love. He seems to have forgotten even the face of his betrothed, from whom he turns away as if she were a disgusting ape; he spits on the path of the priest's wife, who was in tears for a good two months before consoling herself. The Nymphs stripped him of his senses in order to better entangle him in their games, like a sort of innocent faun. He no longer works; he no longer cares about the passing of months or days; he has become a beggar, and simply eats when he is hungry. He wanders about the island, avoiding as far as possible the major roads; he crosses fields and pine forests between bare hills; and some say that a jasmine blossom placed on a drystone wall, a white pebble at the foot of a cypress, are messages which tell him the time and place of his next meeting with the fairies. The peasants say that he will not grow old: like all those on whom an evil spell has been cast, he will whither without our ever knowing whether he is eighteen or forty years old. But his knees tremble and shake, his soul has left him never to return, and words will not come to his lips ever again. Homer knew that those who sleep with the golden goddesses have their intelligence and their strength drained from them. And yet I envy Panegyotis. He has left the world of facts to enter that of illusions, and sometimes I think that an illusion is perhaps the shape that the innermost secret realities take in the mind's eye of common folk.'

'But look here, Jean,' his wife said irritably. 'You don't really believe that Panegyotis actually saw the Nereids?'

Jean Demetriadis did not answer, too busy half lifting himself out of his chair to return the haughty greeting of three passing foreigners. Three young American girls in their comfortable white linen clothes were walking listlessly across the sun-drenched quay, followed by an old porter bent over with the weight of provisions bought at the market; they held hands, like three girls on their way home from school. One of them walked bareheaded, myrtle sprigs stuck in her red hair, but the second one wore an immense Mexican straw hat, and the third a peasant woman's cotton scarf; dark sunglasses protected her eyes like a mask. The three girls had settled on the island and had bought a house far from the main roads: at night they fished with a trident in their very own boat, and in autumn they hunted for quail; they socialized with no one and looked after themselves, fearful of letting a housekeeper enter their tightly knit everyday life; they isolated themselves to avoid gossip, preferring perhaps the slander. In vain I tried to intercept the look Panegyotis cast upon these three goddesses, but his distracted eyes remained empty and lifeless: obviously, he failed to recognize his Nereids dressed up as women. Suddenly he bent over, with animal grace, to pick up yet another drachma that had fallen out of one of our pockets, and I saw, caught in the rough grain of his pea jacket, which he carried hanging over one shoulder, clipped on to his suspenders, the only thing that could lend an imponderable proof to my conviction: the silky, slender, the lost thread of a single blond hair.

Translated by Alberto Manguel

IRÈNE NEMIROVSKY

Sunday

In Rue Las Cases it was as quiet as during the height of summer, and every open window was screened by a yellow blind. The fine weather had returned: it was the first Sunday of spring, a warm and restless day that took people out of their houses and out of the city. The sky glowed with a gentle radiance. The birds in Place Sainte-Clotilde chirped lazily, while the raucous screeching of cars leaving for the country echoed in the peaceful streets. The only cloud in the sky was a delicately curled white shell that floated upwards for a moment, then melted into the ether. People raised their heads with surprise and anticipation; they sniffed the air and smiled.

Agnès half closed the shutters: the sun was hot and the roses would open too quickly and die. Nanette ran in and stood hopping from one foot to the other.

'May I go out, Mother? It's such nice weather.'

Mass was almost over. The children were already coming down the street in their bright sleeveless dresses, holding their prayer books in their white-gloved hands and clustering round a little girl who had just taken her first communion. Her round cheeks were pink and shining under her veil. A procession of bare legs, all pink and gold, as downy as the skin of a peach, sparkled in the sunshine. The bells were still ringing, slowly and sadly as if to say: 'Off you go, good people, we are sorry not to be able to keep you any longer. We have sheltered you for as long as we could, but now we have to give you back to the world and to your everyday life. Time to go. Mass is over.'

The bells fell silent. The smell of hot bread filled the street, wafting up from the open bakery; you could see the freshly washed floor gleaming, and the narrow mirrors on the walls glinting faintly in the shadows. Then everyone had gone home.

Agnès said: 'Nanette, go and see if Papa is ready, and tell Nadine that lunch is on the table.'

Guillaume came in, radiating the scent of lavender water and good cigars which always made her feel slightly nauseated. He seemed even more high-spirited, healthy and plump than usual.

As soon as they had sat down, he announced: 'I'll be going out after lunch. When you've been suffocating in Paris all week, it's the least . . . Are you really not tempted?'

'I don't want to leave the little one.'

Nanette was sitting opposite him and Guillaume smiled at her and tweaked her hair. The previous night she had had a temperature, but so slight that her fresh complexion showed no sign of pallor.

'She's not really ill. She has a good appetite.'

'Oh, I'm not worried, thank God,' said Agnès. 'I'll let her go out until four o'clock. Where are you going?'

Guillaume's face visibly clouded over. 'I . . . oh, I don't know yet . . . You always want to organize things in advance . . . Somewhere around Fontainebleau or Chartres, I'll see, wherever I end up. So? Will you come with me?'

'I'd love to see the look on his face if I agreed,' thought Agnès. The set smile on her lips annoyed her husband. But she answered, as she always did: 'I've got things to do at home.'

She thought, 'Who is it this time?'

Guillaume's mistresses: her jealousy, her anxiety, the sleepless nights, were now in the long distant past. He was tall and overweight, going bald, his whole body solidly balanced, his head firmly planted on a thick, strong neck. He was forty-five, the age at which men are at their most powerful, dominant and self-confident, the blood coursing thickly through their veins. When he laughed he thrust his jaw forward, to reveal a row of nearly perfect white teeth.

'Which one of them told him, "You look like a wolf or a wild animal when you smile"?' wondered Agnès. 'He must have been incredibly flattered. He never used to laugh like that.'

She remembered how he used to weep in her arms every time a love affair ended, gulping as if he was trying to inhale his tears. Poor Guillaume . . .

'Well, I ...' said Nadine.

She started each sentence like that. It was impossible to detect a single word or a single idea in anything she thought or said that did not relate to herself, her clothes, her friends, the ladders in her stockings, her pocket money, her own pleasure. She was ... triumphant. Her skin had the pale, velvety brightness of jasmine and of camellias, and you could see the blood beating just beneath the surface: it rose girlishly in her cheeks, swelling her lips so that it looked as though a pink, heady wine was about to gush from them. Her green eyes sparkled.

'She's twenty,' thought Agnès, trying, as so often, to keep her eyes closed and not to be wounded by her daughter's almost overwhelming beauty, the peals of laughter, the egoism, the fervour, the diamond-like hardness. 'She's twenty years old, it's not her fault ... Life will tame her, soften her, make her grow up.'

'Mother, may I take your red scarf? I won't lose it. And, Mother, may I come back late?'

'And where are you going?'

'Mother, you know perfectly well! To Chantal Aumont's house in Saint-Cloud. Arlette is coming to fetch me. May I come home late? After eight o'clock, anyway? You won't be angry? Then I won't have to go through Saint-Cloud at seven o'clock on a Sunday evening.'

'She's quite right,' said Guillaume.

Lunch was nearly over. Mariette was serving the meal quickly. Sunday ... As soon as the washing-up was done, she too would be going out.

They ate orange-flavoured crêpes; Agnès had helped Mariette make the batter.

'Delicious,' said Guillaume appreciatively.

The clattering of dishes could be heard through the open windows: it was only a faint sound from the dark ground-floor flat where two spinsters lived in the gloom, but was louder and livelier in the house across the way where there was a table laid for twelve with the place settings gleaming on the neat folds of the damask tablecloth, and a basket of white roses for a first communion decorating the centre.

'I'm going to get ready, Mother. I don't want any coffee.'

Guillaume swallowed his quickly and silently. Mariette began to clear the table.

'What a hurry they're in,' thought Agnès, as her thin, skilful hands deftly folded Nanette's napkin. 'Only I . . .'

She was the only one for whom this wonderful Sunday held no attraction.

'I never imagined she'd become so stay-at-home and dull,' thought Guillaume as he looked at her. He took a deep inward breath and, proudly conscious of the sense of vigour that surged through his body, felt his chest expand with the fine weather. 'I'm in rather good shape, holding up surprisingly well,' he thought, as his mind turned to all the reasons (the political crisis, money worries, the taxes he owed, Germaine – who cramped his style, devil take her) why he could justifiably feel as miserable and depressed as anyone else. But on the contrary! 'I've always been the same. A ray of sunshine, the prospect of a Sunday away from Paris, a nice bottle of wine, freedom, a pretty woman at my side – and I'm twenty again! I'm alive,' he congratulated himself, looking at his wife with veiled hostility; her cold beauty and the tense, mocking line of her lips irritated him. He said aloud: 'Of course, I'll telephone you if I spend the night in Chartres. In any case, I'll be back tomorrow morning, and I'll drop in at home before I go to the office.'

Agnès thought, with a strange, weary detachment, 'One day, after a lavish lunch, just as he's kissing the woman he's with, the car he's driving will crash into a tree. I'll get a phone call from Senlis or Auxerre.' Will you suffer? she demanded curiously of the mute, invisible image of herself waiting in the shadows. But the image, silent and indifferent, did not reply, and the powerful silhouette of Guillaume came between it and her.

'See you soon, darling.'

'See you soon, dear.'

Then Guillaume was gone.

'Shall I lay tea in the drawing room, madame?' asked Mariette.

'No, I'll do it. You may go as soon as you've tidied the kitchen.'

'Thank you, madame,' said the girl, blushing fiercely as if she was near a blazing fire. 'Thank you, madame,' she repeated, with a dreamy expression that made Agnès shrug sardonically.

Agnès stroked Nanette's smooth, black hair, as the little girl first hid in the folds of her dress and then poked her head out giggling.

'We'll be perfectly happy, just the two of us, sweetheart.'

Meanwhile, in her room, Nadine was quickly changing her clothes, powdering her neck, her bare arms, and the curve of her breast where, unseen in the car, Rémi had placed his dry, passionate lips, caressing her with quick, burning kisses. Half past two ... Arlette had still not arrived. 'With Arlette here, Mother won't suspect anything.' The rendezvous was at three. 'To think that Mother doesn't notice anything. And she was young once ...' she thought, trying in vain to imagine her mother's youth, her engagement and her early married life.

'She must always have been like this. Everything calm, orderly, wearing those white lawn collars ... "Guillaume, don't spoil my roses." Whereas, I ...'

She shivered, gently biting her lips as she looked at herself in the mirror. Nothing gave her more pleasure than her body, her eyes, her face, and the shape of her young, white neck as straight as a column. 'It's wonderful to be twenty,' she thought fervently. 'Do all young women feel like me, do they relish their happiness, their energy, the fire in their blood? Do they feel these things as fiercely and deeply as I do? For a woman, being twenty in 1934 is ... is incredible,' she told herself. She summoned up disjointed memories of nights on a campsite, coming back at dawn in Rémi's car (and there were her parents thinking she was on an innocent trip with her friends on the Île Saint-Louis, watching the sun rise over the Seine), skiing, swimming, the pure air and cold water on her body, Rémi digging his nails into her neck, gently pulling back her short hair ... 'And my parents are blind to it all! I suppose in their day ... I can imagine my mother at my age, at her first ball, her eyes modestly lowered. Rémi ... I'm in love,' she told her reflection, smiling into the mirror. 'But I must be careful of him – he's so good-looking and so sure of himself, he's been spoilt by women, by flattery. He must like making people suffer.

'But then, we'll see who'll be the strongest,' she muttered, as she nervously clenched her fists, feeling her love pounding in her heart, making her long to take part in this game of cruelty and passion.

She laughed out loud. And her laugh rang out so clearly and arrogantly in the silence that she stopped to listen, as if enchanted by the beauty of a rare and perfect musical instrument.

'There are times when I think I'm in love with myself more than anything else,' she thought, as she put on her green necklace, every bead of which gleamed and reflected the sun. Her smooth, firm skin had the brilliant glow of young animals, flowers, or blossom in May, a glossiness that is fleeting but completely perfect. 'I shall never be as beautiful again.'

She sprayed perfume on her face and shoulders, deliberately wasting it; today anything sparkling and extravagant suited her! 'I'd love a bright red dress and gypsy jewellery.' She thought of her mother's tender, weary voice: 'Moderation in all things, Nadine!'

'The old!' she thought contemptuously.

In the street Arlette's car had stopped outside the house. Nadine grabbed her bag and, cramming her beret on her head as she ran, shouted 'Goodbye, Mother' and disappeared.

'I want you to have a little rest on the sofa, Nanette. You slept so badly last night. I'll sit next to you and do some work,' said Agnès. 'Then you may go out with mademoiselle.'

Nanette rolled her pink smock in her fingers for a while, rubbed her face against the cushions as she turned over and over, yawned, and went to sleep. She was five and, like Agnès, had the pale, fresh complexion of someone fair-haired, yet had black hair and dark eyes.

Agnès sat down quietly next to her. The house was sleeping silently. Outside, the smell of coffee hung in the air. The room was flooded with a soft, warm, yellow light. Agnès heard Mariette carefully close the kitchen door and walk through the flat; she listened to her footsteps fading away down the back stairs. She sighed: a strange, melancholy happiness and a delicious feeling of peace overcame her. Silence fell over the empty rooms and she knew that nobody would disturb her until evening; not a single footstep, nor any unknown voice would find its way into the house, her refuge . . . The street was empty and quiet. There was only an invisible woman playing the piano, hidden behind her closed shutters. Then all was quiet. At that very moment Mariette, clutching her Sunday imitation pigskin bag in her large, bare hands, was hurrying to the station where her lover was waiting for her, and Guillaume, in the woods at Compiègne, was saying to the fat, blonde woman sitting next to him: 'It's easy to blame me, I'm not really a bad husband, but my wife . . .' Nadine was in Arlette's little green car, driving past the gates of the Luxembourg Gardens. The chestnut trees were in flower. Children ran about in little sleeveless knitted tops. Arlette was thinking bitterly that nobody was waiting for her; nobody loved her. Her friends put up with her because of her precious green car and, behind their horn-rimmed glasses, her round eyes made mothers trust her. Lucky Nadine!

A sharp wind was blowing; the water from the fountains splashed sideways, covering passers-by with spray. The saplings in Place Sainte-Clotilde swayed gently.

'It's so peaceful,' thought Agnès.

She smiled; neither her husband nor her elder daughter had ever seen this rare, slow, confident smile on her lips.

She got up and quietly went to change the water for the roses; carefully she cut their stems; they were gradually coming into flower although their petals seemed to be opening reluctantly, fearfully, as if with some kind of divine modesty.

'How lovely it is here,' she thought.

Her house was a refuge, a warm enclosed shell sealed against the noise outside. When, in the wintry dusk, she walked along the Rue Las Cases, an island of shadows, and saw the stone sculpture of the smiling woman above the door, that sweet, familiar face decorated with narrow, carved ribbons, she felt oddly relaxed and peaceful, floating in waves of happiness and calm. Her house ... how she loved the delicious silence, the slight, furtive creaking of the furniture, the delicate inlaid tables shining palely in the gloom. She sat down; although she normally held herself so erect, now she curled up in an armchair.

'Guillaume says I like objects more than human beings ... That may be true.'

Objects enfolded her in a gentle, wordless spell. The copper and tortoiseshell clock ticked slowly and peacefully in the silence.

The familiar musical clinking of a silver cup gleaming in the shadows responded to her every movement, her every sigh, as if it were her friend.

Where do we find happiness? 'We pursue it, search for it, kill ourselves trying to find it, and all the time it's just here,' she said to herself. 'It comes just when we've stopped expecting anything, stopped hoping, stopped being afraid. Of course there is the children's health ...' and she bent automatically to kiss Nanette's forehead. 'Fresh as a flower, thank God. It would be such a relief not to hope for anything any more. How I've changed,' she thought, remembering the past, her insane love for Guil-laume, that little hidden square in Passy where she used to wait for him on spring evenings. She thought of his family, her hateful mother-in-law, the noise his sisters made in their miserable, gloomy drawing room. 'Ah, I can never have enough silence!' She smiled, whispering as if the Agnès of an earlier time were sitting next to her, listening incredulously, her dark plaits framing her pale young face:

'Yes, aren't you surprised? I've changed, haven't I?'

She shook her head. In her memory every day in the past was rainy and sad, every effort was in vain, and every word that was uttered was either cruel or full of lies.

Ah, how can one regret being in love? But, luckily, Nadine is not like me. Today's young girls are so cold, so unemotional. Nadine is a child, but even later on she'll never love or suffer as I did. So much the better, thank God, so much the better. And by the look of things Nanette will be like her sister.'

She smiled: it was strange to think that these smooth, chubby, pink cheeks and unformed features would turn into a woman's face. She put out a hand to stroke the fine black hair. 'These are the only moments when my soul is at peace,' she thought, remembering a childhood friend who used to say, 'My soul is at peace,' as she half-closed her eyes and lit a cig-arette. But Agnès did not smoke. And it was not that she liked to dream, more that she preferred to sit and occupy herself with some humdrum but specific task: she would sew or knit, stifle her thoughts, and force herself to stay calm and silent as she tidied books away or, one at a time, carefully washed and dried the Bohemian glassware, the tall, thin antique glasses with gold rims that they used for champagne. 'Yes, at twenty happiness seemed different to me, rather terrible and overwhelming; yet one's desires become easier to achieve once they have largely run their course,' she thought, as she picked up her sewing basket, with its piece of needlework, some silk thread, her thimble and her little gold scissors. 'What more does a woman need who is not in love with love?'

'Let me out here, Arlette, will you?' Nadine asked. It was three o'clock. 'I'll walk for a bit,' she said to herself, 'I don't want to get there first.'

Arlette did as she asked. Nadine jumped out of the car.

'Thank you, *chérie*.'

Arlette drove off. Nadine walked up the Rue de l'Odéon, forcing herself to slow down and suppress the excitement spreading through her body. 'I like being out in the street,' she thought, happily looking round at everything. 'I'm stifled at home. They can't understand that I'm young, I'm twenty years old, I can't stop myself singing, dancing, laughing, shouting. It's because I'm full of joy.' The breeze, fanning her legs through the thin material of her dress, was delicious. She felt light, ethereal, floating: and just then it seemed to her that nothing could tether her to the ground. 'There are times when I could easily fly away,' she thought, buoyed up with hope. The world was so beautiful, so kind! The glare of the midday sun had softened and was turning into a pale, gentle glow; on every street corner women were holding out bunches of daffodils, offering them for sale to passers-by. Families were happily sitting outside the cafés, drinking fruit juice as they clustered round a little girl fresh from communion, her cheeks flushed, her eyes shining. Soldiers strolled slowly along, blocking the pavement, walking beside women dressed in black with large, red, bare hands. 'Nice,' said a boy walking past, blowing a kiss to Nadine as he eyed her. She laughed.

Sometimes love itself, even the image of Rémi, disappeared. There remained simply a feeling of exultation, and a feverish, piercing happiness, both of which were almost agonizingly unbearable.

'Love? Does Rémi love me?' she asked herself suddenly, as she reached the little bistro where he was due to meet her. 'What do I feel? We're mostly just friends, but what good is that? Friendship and trust are all right for old people. Even tenderness is not for us. Love, well that's something else.' She remembered the sharp pain that tender words and kisses sometimes seemed to conceal. She went inside.

The café was empty. The sun was shining. A clock on the wall ticked. The small inside room where she sat down smelt of wine and the dank air from the cellar.

He was not there. She felt her heart tighten slowly in her chest. 'I know it's quarter past three, but surely he would have waited for me?'

She ordered a drink.

Each time the door opened, each time a man's shadow appeared, her heart beat faster and she was filled with happiness; each time it was a stranger who came in, gave her a distracted look and went to sit down in the shadows. She clasped and unclasped her hands nervously under the table.

'But where can he be? Why doesn't he come?'

Then she lowered her head and continued to wait.

Inexorably, the clock struck every quarter of an hour. Staring at its hands, she waited without moving a muscle, as if complete silence, complete stillness, would somehow slow the passing of time. Three thirty. Three forty-five. That was nothing, one side or the other of the half hour made little difference, even when it was three forty, but if you said 'twenty to four, quarter to four', then you were lost, everything was ruined, gone for ever. He wasn't coming, he was laughing at her! Who was he with at that very moment? To whom was he saying: 'That Nadine Padouan? I've really taken her for a ride!' She felt sharp, bitter little tears prick her eyes. No, no, not that! Four o'clock. Her lips were trembling. She opened her bag and blew on her powder puff, the powder enveloping her in a stifling, perfumed cloud; as she looked in the little mirror she noticed that her face was quivering and distorted as if under water. 'No, I'm not going to cry,' she thought, savagely clenching her teeth together. With shaking hands she took out her lipstick and outlined her lips, then powdered the satin-smooth, bluish hollow under her eyes where, one day, the first wrinkle would appear. 'Why has he done this? Did he just want a kiss one evening, is that all?' For a moment she felt despairing and worthless. All the painful memories that are part of even a happy and secure childhood flooded into her mind: the undeserved slap her father had given her when she was twelve; the unfair teacher; those little English girls who, so long in the past, so long ago, had laughed at her and said, 'We won't play with you. We don't play with kids.'

'It hurts. I never knew it could hurt so much.'

She gave up watching the clock but stayed where she was, quite still. Where could she go? She felt safe here and comfortable. How many other women had waited like her, swallowing their tears like her, unthinkingly stroking the old imitation-leather banquette, warm and soft as an animal's coat? Then, all at once, she felt proud and strong again. What did any of it matter? 'I'm in agony, I'm unhappy.' Oh, what fine new words these were: love, unhappiness, desire. She rolled them silently on her lips.

'I want him to love me. I'm young and beautiful. He will love me, and if he doesn't, others will,' she muttered as she nervously clenched her hands, her nails as shining and sharp as claws.

Five o'clock . . . The dim little room suddenly shone like a furnace. The sun had moved round. It lit up the golden liqueur in her glass and the telephone booth opposite her.

'A phone call?' she thought feverishly. 'Maybe he's ill?'

'Oh, come on,' she said, with a furious shrug. She had spoken out loud; she shivered. 'What's the matter with me?' She imagined him lying bleeding, dead in the road; he drives like a madman . . .

'Supposing I telephoned? No!' she murmured, acknowledging for the first time how weak and downcast she felt.

At the same time, deep down, a mysterious voice seemed to be whispering: 'Look. Listen. Remember. You'll never forget today. You'll grow old. But at the instant of your death you'll see that door opening, banging in the sunshine. You'll hear the clock chiming the quarters and the noise in the street.'

She stood up and went into the telephone booth, which smelt of dust and chalk; the walls were covered with scribbles. She looked for a long time at a drawing of a woman in the corner. At last she dialled Jasmin 10-32.

'Hello,' said a woman's voice, a voice she did not recognize.

'Is that Monsieur Rémi Alquier's apartment?' she asked, and she was struck by the sound of her words: her voice shook.

'Yes, who is it?'

Nadine said nothing; she could clearly hear a soft, lazy laugh and a voice calling out:

'Rémi, there's a young girl asking for you . . . What? Monsieur Alquier isn't in, mademoiselle.'

Slowly, Nadine hung up and went outside. It was six o'clock and the brightness of the May sunshine had faded; a sad, pale dusk had taken over. The smell of plants and freshly watered flowers rose from the Luxembourg Gardens. Nadine walked aimlessly down one street, then down another. She whistled quietly as she walked. The first lights were coming on in the houses, and although the streets were not yet dark, the first gas lamps were being lit: their flickering light shone through her tears.

*

In Rue Las Cases Agnès had put Nanette to bed; half-asleep, she was still talking quietly to herself, shyly confiding in her toys and the shadows in the room. As soon as she heard Agnès, however, she cautiously stopped.

'Already,' Agnès thought.

She went into the drawing room. She walked across it without turning on the lights, and leaned by the window. It was getting dark. She sighed. The spring day concealed a latent bitterness which seemed to emerge as evening came, just as sweet-smelling peaches can leave a sour taste in the mouth. Where was Guillaume? 'He probably won't come back tonight. So much the better,' she said to herself, as she thought of her cool, empty bed. She touched the cold window. How many times had she waited like this for Guillaume? Evening after evening, listening to the clock ticking in the silence and the creaking of the lift as it slowly went up, up, past her door, and then back down. Evening after evening, at first in despair, then with resignation, then with a heavy and deadly indifference. And now? Sadly, she shrugged her shoulders.

The street was empty and a bluish mist seemed to float over everything, as if a fine shower of ash had begun to fall gently from the overcast sky. The golden star of a street lamp lit up the shadows, and the towers of Sainte-Clotilde looked as if they were retreating and melting into the distance. A little car full of flowers, returning from the country, went past; there was just enough light to see bunches of daffodils tied on to the headlights. Concierges sat outside on their wicker chairs, hands folded loosely in their laps, not talking. Shutters were being closed at every window and only the faint pink light of a lamp could be glimpsed through the slats.

'In the old days,' remembered Agnès, 'when I was Nadine's age, I was already spending long hours waiting in vain for Guillaume.' She shut her eyes, trying to see him as he was then, or at least how he had seemed to her then. Had he been so handsome? So charming? My God, he had certainly been thinner than he was now, his face leaner and more expressive, with a beautiful mouth. His kisses . . . she let out a sad, bitter little laugh.

'How I loved him . . . the idiot I was . . . stupid idiot . . . He didn't say anything loving to me. He just used to kiss me, kiss me until my heart melted with sweetness and pain. For eighteen months he never once said

"I love you", or "I want to marry you" . . . I always had to be there, at his feet. "At my disposal," he would say. And, fool that I was, I found pleasure in it. I was at that age when even defeat is intoxicating. And I would think: "He will love me. I will be his wife. If I give him enough devotion and love, he will love me.'"

All of a sudden she had an extraordinarily precise vision of a spring evening long ago. But not a fine, mild one like this evening; it was one of those rainy, cold Parisian springs when heavy, icy showers start at dawn, streaming through the leafy trees. The chestnut trees in blossom, the long day and the warm air seem like a cruel joke. She was sitting on a bench in an empty square, waiting for him; the soaking box hedges gave off a bitter smell; the raindrops falling on the pond slowly sadly marked the minutes drifting inexorably by. Cold tears ran down her cheeks. He wasn't coming. A woman had sat down next to her, looked at her without speaking, hunching her back against the rain and tightly pinching her lips together, as if thinking, 'Here's another one.'

She bowed her head a little, resting it on her arms as she used to do in the old days. A deep sadness overcame her.

'What is the matter with me? I am happy, really; I feel very calm and peaceful. What's the good of remembering things? For heaven's sake, it will only make me resentful, and so pointlessly angry!'

And a picture came into her mind of her sitting in a taxi driving along the dark, wet avenues of the Bois de Boulogne; it was as if she could once again taste and smell the pure, cold air coming in through the open window, as Guillaume gently and cruelly felt her naked breast, as if he were squeezing the juice from a fruit. All those quarrels, reconciliations, bitter tears, lies, bad behaviour, and then that rush of sweet happiness when he touched her hand, laughing, as he said: 'Are you angry? I like making you suffer a bit.'

'That's all gone, it will never happen again,' she said aloud despairingly. And all at once, she was aware of tears pouring down her face. 'I want to suffer again.

'To suffer, to despair, to long for someone! I have no one in the world left to wait for! I'm old. I hate this house,' she thought feverishly, 'and this peace and calm! But what about the children? Oh yes, the illusion of motherhood is the strongest and yet the most futile. Of course I love them, they're all I have in the world. But that's not enough. I want to rediscover those lost years, the suffering of the past. But at my age love would be unpleasant. I'd like to be twenty! Lucky Nadine! She's in Saint-Cloud, probably playing golf! She doesn't have to worry about love! Lucky Nadine!'

She started. She had not heard the door open, nor Nadine's footsteps on the carpet. Wiping her eyes, she said abruptly: 'Don't put the light on.'

Without replying, Nadine came to sit next to her. It was dark now. They did not look at each other.

After a while Agnès asked:

'Did you have a nice time, sweetheart?'

'Yes, thank you, Mother,' said Nadine.

'What time is it?'

'Almost seven, I think.'

'You've come back earlier than you thought,' Agnès said absent-mindedly.

Nadine did not answer, wordlessly tinkling the thin gold bracelets on her bare arms.

'How quiet she is,' Agnès thought, slightly surprised. She said aloud: 'What is it, sweetheart? Are you tired?'

'A bit.'

'You must go to bed early. Now go and wash, we're going to eat in five minutes. Don't make a noise in the hall, Nanette is asleep.'

As she spoke the telephone started ringing. Nadine suddenly looked up. Mariette appeared:

'It's for Miss Nadine.'

Nadine left the room, her heart pounding, conscious of her mother's eyes on her. She silently closed the door of the little office where the telephone was kept.

'Nadine? . . . It's me, Rémi . . . Oh, we are angry, are we? Look, forgive me . . . Don't be horrid . . . Well, I'm saying sorry! There, there,' he said, as if coaxing a restive animal. 'Be kind to me, my sweet . . . What could I do? She was an old flame, I was being charitable. Ah, Nadine, you can't think the sweet nothings you give me are enough? Do you? Well, do you?' he repeated, as she heard the sweet, voluptuous sound of his laugh through his tightly closed lips. 'You must forgive me. It's true I don't dislike kissing you when you're cross, when your green eyes are blazing. I can see them now. They're smouldering, aren't they? How about tomorrow? Do you want to meet tomorrow at the same time? What? I swear I won't stand you up . . . What? You're not free? What a joke! Tomorrow? Same place, same time. I've said, I swear . . . Tomorrow?' he said again.

Nadine said:

'Tomorrow.'

He laughed:

'There's a good girl,' he said in English. 'Good little girlie. Bye-bye.'

Nadine ran into the drawing room. Her mother had not moved.

'What are you doing, Mother?' she cried, and her voice, her burst of laughter, made Agnès feel bitter and troubled, almost envious. 'It's dark in here!'

She put all the lights on. Her eyes, still wet with tears, were sparkling; a dark flush had spread over her cheeks. Humming to herself, she went up to the mirror and tidied her hair, smiling at her face, which was now alight with happiness, and at her quivering, parted lips.

'Well, you're happy, all of a sudden,' Agnès said. She tried to laugh, but only a sad, grating little sound escaped her. She thought: 'I've been blind! The girl's in love! Ah, she has too much freedom, I'm too weak, that's what worries me.' But she recognized the bitterness, the suffering in her heart. She greeted it like an old friend: 'My God, I'm jealous!'

'Who was that on the telephone? You know perfectly well that your father doesn't like telephone calls from people we don't know, or these mysterious meetings.'

'I don't understand what you mean, Mother,' Nadine said, as she looked at her mother with bright, innocent eyes that made it impossible to read the secret thoughts within them: mother, the eternal enemy, pathetic in her old age, understanding nothing, seeing nothing, withdrawing into her shell, her only aim to stop youth from being alive! 'I really don't understand. It was only that the tennis match which should have happened on Saturday has been postponed until tomorrow. That's all.'

'That's all, is it!' Agnès said, and she was struck by how dry and harsh her own voice sounded.

She looked at Nadine. 'I'm mad. It must have been my remembering the past. She's still only a child.' For a moment she had a vision of a young girl with long black hair sitting in a desolate square in the mist and rain; she looked at her sadly and then banished her for ever from her mind.

Gently she touched Nadine's arm.

'Come along,' she said.

Nadine stifled a sardonic laugh. 'Will I be as . . . gullible, when I'm her age? And as placid? Lucky mother,' she thought with gentle scorn. 'It must be wonderful to be so naive and to have such an untroubled heart.'

Translated by Bridget Patterson

BIRAGO DIOP

Sarzan

Ruins lay piled up indistinguishable from ant-heaps, and only an ostrich eggshell stuck on the point of a stake, cracked and yellowed from exposure to the weather, still indicated the site of the *mirab,* the mosque built by El Hadj Omar's warriors. The Toucouleur conqueror had cut off the long hair and shaven the heads of the fathers of those who are now the elders of the village. He had cut off the heads of all those who would not submit to the law of the Koran. The elders of the village now wear their hair long once more. The sacred wood that the fanatical *talibes** burnt down long ago has grown again and once more shelters the ritual vessels, blanched with millet porridge, or stained brown with the clotted blood of the sacrificial dogs and chickens.

Like branches felled by a chance blow from the flail, like ripe fruit falling from sap-filled boughs, whole families had left Dougouba. The young men left to seek work at Segou, at Bamako, at Kayes, at Dakar; others went off to plough the groundnut fields of Senegal, only to return when the harvest was done and there was an end of the trading. All knew that the roots of their life were in Dougouba, which had now wiped out all trace of the Islamic hordes and resumed the teachings of its ancestors.

One child of Dougouba had gone further afield and stayed longer away than the others: he was Thiémokho Kéita.

From Dougouba he had gone to the district headquarters, from there to Kati, from Kati to Dakar, from Dakar to Casablanca, from Casablanca to Frejus, and thence to Damascus. Having left the Sudan as a private

---

* *Talibes*: devout disciples of a 'Marabout' or Moslem dignitary, who exercises a great influence over the community.

Thiémokho Kéita had trained in Senegal, fought in Morocco, mounted guard in France and patrolled in Lebanon. With the rank of sergeant he travelled back with me to Dougouba.

During my rounds in this district, which is in the heart of Senegal, I had found Kéita in the Administrator's office; he had just been demobilized and wanted to enlist in the corps of local guards or of interpreters. 'No,' the District Administrator had said to him. 'You will be of greater service to the administration by going back to your village. You have travelled much and seen many things, you must teach the others something of how the white people live. You must "civilize" them a bit. Look,' he went on, turning to me, 'as you are going that way, take Kéita with you; you will save him some time and spare him a tiring journey. It's twenty years since he left his hole.' And so we set off.

In the van, in which he and I shared the front seat with the driver, while the relief driver, the local guard, cooks and male nurses were piled in the back with the field kitchen, the camp bed and the crates of vaccine and serum, Sergeant Kéita told me of his life as a soldier, both in the ranks and later when he got his stripes; he told me about the Riff war, from the point of view of a black rifleman; he told me about Marseilles, Toulon, Frejus, Beyrout. He did not seem to see the corrugated road, made with cut branches covered with a layer of clay, which stretched out in front of us in the torrid heat, and which in the extreme drought turned to a fine greasy dust, plastering our faces like a yellow mask, grating between our teeth, hiding in our wake the dog-faced baboons and the frightened leaping buck. He seemed to see, in the chalky panting mist, the minarets of Fez, the teeming crowds of Marseilles, the tall dwellings of France, the impossible blue of the sea.

By midday we had reached the village of Madougou; the marked road finished here, so we took ponies and bearers so as to reach Dougouba by nightfall.

'When you come back this way again,' Kéita said, 'you will be able to get as far as Dougouba by car, for from tomorrow I am going to get them to work on the road.'

The muffled beating of a tom-tom announced the approach to the village; then the grey mass of the huts could be seen, topped by the darker grey of three palm trees against the light grey of the sky. The tom-toms thrummed on three notes now, accompanying the shrill voice of a flute. The tops of the palm trees were licked by gleams of light. We had reached Dougouba. I dismounted first and asked for the village chief, saying:

'*Dougou-tigui* (village chief), here is your son, Sergeant Kéita.'

Thiémokho Kéita leapt from his horse. As if the noise of his shoes on the ground had been a signal, the tom-toms ceased and the flutes were silent. The old chief took Kéita's two hands, while other old men touched his arms, his shoulders and his medals. Old women gathered and knelt down to touch his puttees; and on the grey faces tears shone among the wrinkles, criss-crossed by scars, and all said:

'Kéita! Kéita! Kéita!'

'Those people,' quavered the old chief at last, 'those people who led your steps back to your village this day, are kind and good.'

It was in fact a day that was different from other days in Dougouba. It was the day of *Kotéba*, the day of Testing.

The tom-tom had resumed its thrumming, pierced by the shrill note of the flute. The women, children and grown men formed a circle within which the young men, naked to the waist, moved round to the rhythm of the tom-tom, holding long stripped wands of the balazon tree. In the centre of the moving circle crouched the flute player, with elbows and knees on the ground, keeping up the same three notes. A youth had just taken up his position, standing over him with his legs apart, his arms outstretched, like a cross, and as each of the others passed him their whips swished down; the blows fell across his shoulders leaving a weal as thick as a thumb, sometimes breaking the skin. The shrill voice of the flute was raised a tone, the tom-toms became more muffled, the whips swished, the blood flowed. On the black-brown skin was reflected the gleam of the burning branches and the dried millet-stalks, whose flames mounted to the tops of the palm trees, groaning faintly in the light breeze.

Kotéba! The test of endurance, the test of insensibility to pain. The child who cries when he hurts himself is still only a child; the child who weeps when others hurt him will never make a man.

Kotéba! Offer your back, receive the blow, turn around and give it back.
Kotéba!

'They still behave like savages!'

I turned round; it was Sergeant Kéita who had just joined me at the tom-tom.

Behaviour of savages? This test which made them, among other things, tough men, hardened men! Which had enabled the elders of these young men to march for days on end with enormous loads on their heads; which had enabled Thiémokho Kéita and those like him, to fight valiantly in that far country, under the grey skies where the sun itself is often sick, to labour with knapsack on back, to endure cold, thirst and hunger.

Behaviour of savages? Perhaps so. But I thought that elsewhere in our land we had given up the first initiation, except for young conscripts; the 'men's hut' no longer existed, in which the body, the mind and the character were tempered; where the *passines* (riddles with double meanings) were implanted in the mind by means of blows on the back or the fingers and the *kassaks* (the memory-training songs) whose words come back to us from dark nights, were burnt into our brains by means of red-hot coals that scorched the palms of our hands. I thought that perhaps we might have gained nothing by so doing, and that maybe we had gone too far in the wrong direction.

The tom-tom was still thrumming in time with the shrill voice of the flute. The fires died down and sprang up again. I went back to the hut that had been prepared for me. Mingled with the thick smell of the *banco** there floated a more subtle smell, that of the dead. There were three of them, indicated by horns fixed to the wall at the height of a man. For in Dougouba the cemetery had also disappeared and the dead continued to live with the living: they were buried in the huts.

The sun was already hot, but Dougouba was still asleep, drunk with fatigue and *dolo*,† when I started on my way back.

'Goodbye,' said Kéita, 'when you come back this way again the road will be made. That's a promise.'

Work in other sectors and other districts prevented me from returning to Dougouba for a year.

*

---

* *Banco*: clay kneaded with chopped rotten straw which becomes waterproof when dry.
† *Dolo*: millet beer.

It was the end of the afternoon of a sultry day, the air was like a thick mass through which we cut our way with difficulty.

Sergeant Kéita had kept his word; the road went as far as Dougouba. At the noise of the car, as in all villages, a swarm of naked children, their bodies grey-white with dust, appeared at the side of the road, followed by russet-coloured dogs, with docked ears and protruding ribs. In the midst of the children stood a man who gesticulated and waved a cow's tail attached to his right wrist. When the car stopped I saw that it was Sergeant Thiémokho Kéita, surrounded by children and dogs. Under his now faded army jacket, which had lost its buttons and stripes, he wore a *boubou** and breeches made of strips of yellowish-brown cotton, as did the other elders of the village. The breeches reached his knees and were held in place by string. He still had his puttees, which were in rags. He was barefoot and wore his peaked army cap.

I held out my hand and said: 'Kéita!'

The children scattered, like a swarm of millet-eating sparrows, chirping, '*Ayi! Ayi!* (No! No!)'

Théimokho Kéita did not take my hand. He looked at me, but without seeming to see me. His gaze was so distant that I could not help turning round to see what his eyes were staring at, through mine. Suddenly waving his cow's tail, he began to shout in a hoarse voice:

> *Listen more often*
> *To things than to creatures,*
> *The voice of the fire can be heard,*
> *Listen to the voice of the water.*
> *Listen to the wind,*
> *To the sobbing of the bushes:*
> *'Tis the breath of the ancestors.*

'He's completely *fato* (mad),' said my driver, whom I bade be silent. Sergeant Kéita still shouted:

---

* *Boubou*: a full cotton garment; draping the whole figure, worn by men and women in West Africa.

Sarzan

Those who have died have not departed
They are in the shadow that lightens
They are in the shadow that deepens,
The dead are not beneath the ground
They are in the tree that quivers,
They are in the moaning forest,
They are in the flowing water,
They are in the sleeping water,
They are in the dwelling, they are in the crowd
The dead are not dead.

      Listen more often
      To things than to creatures,
      Listen to the voice of the water.
      Listen to the wind
      To the sobbing of the bushes:
      'Tis the breath of the ancestors.
      The breath of the dead ancestors
      Who have not departed,
      Who are not beneath the ground,
      Who are not dead.

Those who have died have never departed,
They are in the breasts of a woman,
They are in the wailing infant
And in the freshly blazing firebrand.
The dead are not beneath the ground,
They are in the dying embers,
They are in the echoing rock-face,
They are in the weeping grasses,
They are in the forest, they are in the dwelling,
The dead are not dead.

      Listen more often
      To things than to creatures,
      The voice of fire can be heard,
      Listen to the voice of the water.
      Listen to the wind

> *To the sobbing of the bushes:*
> *'Tis the breath of the ancestors.*
> *It repeats each day the pact,*
> *The great pact which binds,*
> *Which binds our fate to the law;*
> *To the acts of the strongest breaths*
> *The fate of our dead who are not dead;*
> *The heavy pact that links us to life,*
> *The heavy law that binds us to the acts*
> *Of the breaths that die.*
> *On the banks and in the river-bed,*
> *Breaths that move*
> *In the rock that groans, in the grass that weeps.*
> *Breaths which dwell*
> *In the shadow that lightens, in the shadow grown longer*
> *In the tree that groans, in the wood that moans,*
> *In the water that runs and the water that sleeps,*
> *Breaths that are stronger,*
> *Breaths which have taken*
> *The breath of the dead who are not dead,*
> *Of the dead who have not departed,*
> *Of the dead who are not underground.*
> > *Listen more often*
> > *To things than to creatures . . .*

The children returned to surround the old village chief and his headmen. After the customary greetings I asked them what had happened to Sergeant Kéita.

'*Ayi*! *Ayi*!' said the old man. '*Ayi*! *Ayi*!' squeaked the children.

'No, not Kéita!' said the old father. 'Sarzan! just Sarzan! (Sergeant). One must not anger those who have departed. Sarzan is no longer a Kéita. The dead and the spirits have avenged themselves for his insults.'

It had begun the very next day after his arrival, the very day of my departure from Dougouba.

Sergeant Thiémokho Kéita had tried to prevent his father from sacrificing a white chicken to the shades of his ancestors, to thank them for having brought him back safe and sound. He had declared that if he had returned it was simply because he had to return, and the ancestors had had nothing to do with it. 'Leave the dead in peace,' he had said; 'they can do nothing more for the living.' The old village chief had insisted and the chicken had been sacrificed.

At the ploughing season Thiémokho had thought it useless and even stupid to kill black chickens and to sprinkle their blood in one corner of the fields. 'Work is all one needs,' he had said, 'and the rain will fall if it is to fall. The millet, maize, groundnuts, sweet-potatoes and beans will grow by themselves and will grow all the better if you use the ploughs that the district commandant has sent.' He cut down and burnt the branches of the *Dassiri*, the sacred tree that protected the village and the ploughlands, and at whose foot dogs had been sacrificed.

On the day when young boys were circumcised and the little girls excised Sergeant Kéita had leapt upon the *Gangourang* (the master of the children) as he danced and sang. He had snatched away the bundle of porcupine quills and the net that veiled his body. From Mama Djomba, the master of the girls, he had torn off the cone of yellow stuff that he wore, surmounted by a tuft of magic charms and ribbons. Sergeant Kéita had declared that this was the 'behaviour of savages' – and yet he had seen the Carnaval at Nice with its hilarious or terrifying masks. Of course it is true that the White men wore their masks simply to amuse people and not to teach their children the rudiments of the wisdom of the ancestors.

Sergeant Kéita had taken down the little bag hanging in his hut, which contained the *Nyana-boli*, the Spirit of old Kéita's family, and had thrown it out into the courtyard, where the hungry dogs were about to snatch it from the little children just as the old chief arrived.

One morning he had gone into the sacred wood and had broken the vessels containing millet porridge and sour milk. He had overturned the statuettes and the forked stakes to which hens' feathers were stuck with clotted blood. 'The behaviour of savages,' he had decreed. Yet Sergeant Kéita had been into churches, he had seen statuettes of the Holy Virgin, with candles burning before them. It is true that those statuettes were covered with gilding and bright colours, blues, reds and yellows, and were certainly more beautiful than the blackened dwarfs with long arms and short, bandy legs, carved out of mahogany or ebony, which peopled the sacred wood.

The District Administrator had said, 'You must "civilize" them a bit,' and Sergeant Thiémokho Kéita was going to 'civilize' his people. They must break with tradition, kill the beliefs on which the life of the village had always rested and which were the basis of family life and people's actions. Superstition had to be rooted out. The behaviour of savages, such was the harsh treatment inflicted on the young circumcised boys in order to open their minds and train their characters, and teach them that nowhere, at any time of their lives, could they, must they be alone. The behaviour of savages, the *Kotéba*, which forges true men, on whom pain can have no hold . . . The behaviour of savages, the sacrifices, blood offered to the ancestors and to the earth . . . The behaviour of savages, the millet porridge and the curdled milk offered to the wandering spirits and the protecting genii . . .

That is what Sergeant Kéita had said in the shade of the palaver-tree to the young men and the elders of the village.

It was at the approach of twilight that Sergeant Thiémokho Kéita lost his wits. Leaning against the palaver-tree he talked and talked – against the witch-doctor who had sacrificed dogs that very morning, against the elders who did not want to listen to him, against the young men who still listened to the elders. He was still talking when he felt something like a sting on his left shoulder and he turned around. When he looked at his audience again his eyes had a peculiar look in them. A white froth appeared at the corners of his lips. He spoke and the words that his mouth uttered were no longer the same. The ghosts had taken his wits and now they were crying out their fears.

'*Black night! Black night!*'
he cried at nightfall, and women and children trembled in the huts.

'*Black night! Black night!*'
he shouted at daybreak.

'*Black night! Black night!*'
he screamed at high noon. Night and day he talked and shouted and sang with the voices of the spirits and the genii and the ancestors . . .

. . . It was not till dawn that I was able to doze off in the hut where the dead dwelt, and the whole night through I heard Sergeant Kéita coming and going, screaming, singing, weeping,

In the dim and darkened wood
Tu-whit, tu-whoo hoot the hunting horns
To the frenzied beat of the tom-toms damned
Black night! Black night!
The milk has soured
In the hanging gourds
The porridge grown hard
In the pots
And in the huts
Fear goes by, and again goes by,
Black night! Black night!
The torches are lit
And cast on the air
Their bodiless beam
Without flash, without gleam;
The torches smoke,
Black night! Black night!
The spirits roam,
Surprised, they moan
Murmuring long-forgotten words,
Shuddering, trembling words they groan,
Black night! Black night!
From the cold bodies of the birds
From the still-warm, moving corpse
No drop has flowed
Of blood that is black, of blood that is red,
Black night! Black night!
Tu-whit, tu-whoo hoot the hunting horns
To the frenzied beat of the tom-toms damned.
Fearfully the orphan stream
Weeps as it calls to appear again
The folk who have vanished from its shores
To wander without aim, to wander in vain,

Black night! Black night!
And in the savannah that has no soul
Deserted by the ancients' ghosts
Tu-whit, tu-whoo hoot the hunting horns
To the frenzied beat of the tom-toms damned,
Black night! Black night!
The troubled trees
Whose sap congeals
In the trunks and in the leaves
Can no longer pray
To the elders of days gone by,
Black night! Black night!
In the hut where fear goes by
In the air where the torch goes out
On the river bereft of kin
In the forest soul-less weary
Under the troubled pallid trees
In the dim and darkened woods
Tu-whit, tu-whoo hoot the hunting horns
To the frenzied beat of the tom-toms damned,
Black night! Black night!

No one dared to call him by his own name any more, for the spirits and the ancestors had made another man of him. Thiémokho Kéita had departed as far as the village was concerned, and there only remained Sarzan, Sarzan-the-Madman.

Translated by Dorothy S. Blair

MADELEINE BOURDOUXHE

A Nail, a Rose

Walking through the streets, Irene could see no light. She passed other people on the pavements and in the streets, but couldn't see them either. All she could see was the image of Danny, picking up his glass in both hands and twisting it so that the beer swirled around in the bottom. He wasn't saying anything. Irene was talking and going slowly mad.

'There is something,' she had said, 'there is something you're not telling me . . . it might be something that you think is true but isn't at all . . . Tell me,' she said. 'Explain to me, speak, just speak to me . . .'

He hadn't answered; but then they weren't in the habit of explaining things to each other. That was how it was between them, they had no need of words. Then she'd said to herself that all she had to do was to walk out, all she had to do was to leave behind her, just as it was, this thing that she would never understand.

She could no longer remember whether she had said goodbye. She thought she hadn't; she thought she had just got up, walked across the room and opened the door. He didn't move or follow her. They were in the café where they often used to meet – the sign outside had the name of a flower on it, something like lily of the valley, or wallflower. It wasn't that she'd forgotten, but she always tried not to think of it. She walked into the street, but he didn't come after her, he didn't shout: 'Irene!'

She was walking in the dark roads. It hadn't happened that day, nor even the day before: it was a long time ago now. But ever since, whenever she walked through the streets, she always saw the same image, of Danny picking up his glass in both hands, swirling the beer at the bottom of it and saying nothing, whilst she talked and went slowly mad.

She was tired and the road was steep, so she waited at a tram stop. Sitting in the carriage, she closed her eyes, but images continued to assault her: his face, his hair, the hands she loved so much. Tears began to rise up through her body. She didn't like crying in the tram; it was much better to talk to yourself instead. Whatever it was, she would never understand it now . . .

Danny and Irene: that she did understand, she understood it perfectly, and she thought it meant she could understand the rest of the world as well: Danny and Irene, and the whole world. But she would never now understand the line that ran between them, like an arrow with a sharp point at either end. And the whole world was now this line.

Whenever they had met again after a parting, they had come together like two hands joining. They were like two hands of one being, finger against finger of the same length, palm against palm. And two hands of the same being are clasped together because of the same joy or the same agony. He didn't say, 'I love you,' and nor did she. Plenty of people say 'I love you,' but what existed between them wasn't the same as what exists between those people. Instead of saying 'I love you,' he said 'Irene'. And she said 'Danny'.

Sometimes they were at the heart of love, like a bee in a closed flower. But only sometimes, because that wasn't the sole aim of their encounters. Two hands can join together in joy, in torment, in emotion, in prayer, or in revolt; but their love-making was a whole in which they touched on hope and despair. Because their love-making was savage and it was pure. They made love in heather, in orchards, in fields of cut corn; in bedrooms, too, and in other people's beds: that was their right.

When they made love the only words they spoke were 'Danny' and 'Irene'. Danny never gave her lilies of the valley, nor perfume, scarves or rings; his presents would be an ear of corn, a nail or a leaf. He sometimes gave her fruit; but not the sort of fruit that changes and turns putrid – the fruit that he gave her had hard, dry outlines and a fixed shape, like kernels.

She had got off the tram and was walking again, towards her house, in the slippery, deserted streets of the outskirts. A recent fall of snow, now half melted, had been hardened by frost, and there were sheets of ice all over the place: she had to walk slowly. She could hear footsteps behind her, but they were some way away, and she paid no attention to them. A leaf, a nail, a kernel. How she had loved his hands, and his fair hair . . . in heather, in orchards, in fields of cut corn . . .

By now night had fallen, and the verges and the waste ground seemed to be etched in black and white: the only branches she could see were those on which snow was still lying. She was living through a present without a future, she was carrying inside her a love with no tomorrow. The world was empty, and she was walking along a road of hardened mud and snow.

It was a black night. In this year 1944 the darkness was total, the few houses that she passed black and dead. The road was deserted apart from those footsteps behind her; they were getting closer but still she paid them no attention. In heather, in orchards, in fields of cut corn . . . Now the man's footsteps were right behind her, he was close up to her, almost at her back, and he was hitting her on the head. Irene felt the blow while still lost in the memory of love. She turned round and saw a man wearing a cap, with a hammer in his raised hand.

'Take everything I have,' she said, 'just don't hit me any more.'

Her voice was choked. Could he hear what she was saying? She held out her handbag and case, but he didn't take them. His right hand was still raised, and with his left he grabbed the belt of her coat and held her close to him. She looked him full in the face – hoping to dissipate the feeling of vertigo brought on by his blows, and to banish the flame of pain that was dancing before her eyes. In the darkness she couldn't see the man's face clearly, but she felt that she could smell his body: she was soaking in his body smell.

'You're out of luck,' she said, 'you've wasted your time, attacking a woman with no furs or jewels . . . also, you're a lousy assailant – you're a fool, because if I'd started to cry out when you struck me so feebly, people would have come out of these black houses and run after you. There you are, have a look in there, take what interests you and leave me the rest.'

Still holding the hammer in his right hand, he let go of her coat and with his free hand took possession of the handbag and case.

'Oh no,' she said, 'you're not going off with the whole lot. What I said was that you could have a look at it all and that we'd divide it up. I didn't say you could take everything.'

'What are you going on about?'

'Don't shout so loud, someone might hear us.'

'That's true . . .'

'Let's sit down over there, on that bank. Have you got an electric torch?'

'Yes.'

'Put that hammer in your pocket, I don't like looking at it.'

'Are you frightened?'

'No, but I've been hurt. You hurt me.'

'Do you still feel bad?'

'I don't know . . . I don't care.'

'I'm going to tell you everything. Because you were moving, the hammer slipped, that's why I didn't hit you properly. What I really meant to do was to hit you bang on, on the top of the head.'

'Ping! with your metal hammer. That's a likely story!'

'Are you still afraid of my hammer?'

'No. Let's have a look at it.'

'Here.'

'It's really heavy . . . I had a narrow escape.'

'But tell me, what on earth were you up to, all alone in the dark?'

'I was just walking, walking and thinking.'

'What were you thinking about?'

'About my love life.'

'Do you mind if I look at you with the torch? . . . Yes, you're a lovely girl.'

'Present without future, a love with no tomorrow, an empty world. We can touch neither perfection nor eternity.'

'What?'

'Nothing, I was talking to myself. So, are we going to divide up my fortune?'

'If you like. Let's have a look. A packet of cigarettes . . .'

'That's for you.'

'Thanks. A lipstick . . . You can keep that.'

'Money – you take it,' she said. 'There must be about a hundred francs there. And there's another fifty francs in an envelope; here you are.'

'Thanks. A nail . . .'

'Yes, a nail.'

'A nail from a horse's hoof?'

'Yes, from a horse's hoof.'

'It's quite new, it's never been used.'

'No, it's never been used.'

'It's for you,' he said.

'Yes, it's for me.'

'Here you are.'

'Thanks,' she said. 'Listen, you own the cigarettes now – what would you say if we had a smoke?'

'Sure.'

All around them, the earth was black and white. A beautiful winter night smell rose up from the black and white earth. A vast night meadow, the colour of the earth, flowed out before and beneath her, stretched to infinity, because the mass of the darkened town beyond it, sunk in the apathy of a town under Occupation, could not be clearly distinguished. From the heart of the town she expected there to rise the alarm of the sirens, she expected an anguish to be born that would rise up in sea swells from the darkened town and unfurl over the fields, the countryside, the world. And she expected there to rise up at the same time a wave of mould that would swell and spread all over the world, and into her heart. The world is empty, and so is the sky, we can touch neither perfection nor eternity. But how beautiful the earth is, black with mud, white with frost. How beautiful it is, under its winter night smell that rises from the earth, the trees, the air.

'Well then,' she said, 'shall we divide up my food coupons?'

'Yes,' he said. 'I'd be interested in those all right. Hey, you've got milk coupons – you have a kid?'

'Yes.'

'You're married?'

'Nothing to do with you.'

'But the kid . . . ?'

'Given to me by the man I love. Will that do?'

'You've been lucky, then. Not everyone gets to have a kid by the man they love.'

'No, not everyone.'

'Kiss me.'

'If you like.'

'No, not like that. Kiss me properly.'

'If you like.'

'Come on, let me hold you close, in my arms.'

'No.'

'I only want to hold you close, in my arms. I won't do anything you don't want me to. I promise.'

'What would be the point? Why do you want to hold me close?'

'Because I didn't kill you.'

She got up and he held her against him for a moment, pressing his hands against her back. She could smell and feel his body, long and straight and smooth apart from two bumps in the middle – one inert (the head of the hammer which he had slipped into his pocket), the other very much alive. 'I'm going to faint,' she said. 'I'm surely going to faint . . . Please, let me get my breath. I'm not feeling too good.'

'What's the matter? Is your head hurting?'

'Yes, but it's not that. My heart's racing.'

'Did I hold you too tight? Have I done something to annoy you?'

'What an idea! Listen, try and take it in: you're walking along the street, you're seeing all sorts of things inside your head as you walk along, and someone comes up on you from behind and hits you on the head, suddenly, just like that. Wham! A shot in the back, from behind – it's revolting.'

She ran her hand over her face, her forehead, her whole head.

'Oh no,' she said. 'Let's have your torch.'

She held out her hand in the narrow beam of light. It was covered with blood.

He inspected her thoroughly with his torch: there was blood all over her hair and it was running on to her shoulders and coat.

'I didn't realize,' she said. 'Why didn't I feel it trickling down my neck?'

'Because your hair acted like a gutter.'

'You've done a great job, haven't you? You really are a swine.'

'Yes,' he said.

He got out his handkerchief and tried to clean her hair, to staunch the wound. She was standing up, her heart racing. A man was wiping blood from her hair – and although he was doing it gently, she was in pain. He was holding the torch on a level with their faces, and she could see his pale greyish skin and the lock of brown hair that fell on to his forehead. He'd pushed his cap back and his face looked young and very thin. It was the face of an archangel or a fool: that look could belong to either one or the other. Beyond the slope, the night fields stretched out, rejoined the horizon, rose up and reappeared in a dome above them, black from top to bottom. The earth was less black than the sky, with patches of ice criss-crossing it. The sky was empty; and she was in pain. At the corner of the road there rose up, like a miracle, a tree covered with hoar frost.

'I ought to be getting back,' she said.

'I'll come with you for a bit,' he said. 'The roads aren't safe.'

He was still cleaning her up.

'All this blood,' he said. 'What are you going to tell them at home?'

'I'll say I slipped on some ice. I'll say I fell backwards, and that my head hit the pavement hard.'

'You came up with that one quickly – you're a pretty good liar, aren't you?'

'About my things, is there anything else that interests you?'

'No. Here, take your cigarettes.'

'No, you keep them.'

'I insist, take them back.'

'Aren't we polite to each other . . .'

'Tell me, where do you live?'

'Very near here. I'll be fine on my own now.'

'Who do you live with?'

'With my brother, my father, my father's four brothers and their six sons. If my brother saw you, he'd take hold of you and turn your body into a knot in one second flat. Have you seen that Charlie Chaplin film where the policeman bends street lamps? He's a bit like him, my brother.'

'Are you teasing me?'

'I'm teasing you.'

'But seriously, where do you live?'

'Very near here. You'll be able to see me going in. Just stay where you are and let me go now. Goodbye . . .'

'Goodbye. What's your name?'

'Irene. And yours?'

'Jean.'

'Cheers, Jean.'

'Cheers, Irene.'

She went in without making the slightest sound. Half-opening the door of the bedroom she could see that Dan was asleep and so was Maggy, the kid who looked after him. She gently closed the door behind her and picked up a hand mirror. Standing in front of the looking-glass above the fireplace and holding the mirror behind her head, she tried to take stock. The lights were blacked out, which made it hard to see, so she struck a match and held it close to her head. That was no good because she had the mirror in one hand and the match in the other, and besides, she was too far from the looking-glass. Her hair was all stuck together at the roots: she really ought to wash it, and her scalp ought to have some stitches.

She called a doctor, but he lived too far away to come on foot, and didn't dare venture out by car because of the ice. Too bad – she hated having stitches anyway. She lay down on the bare floorboards, on her stomach, so as not to lean her head on the ground, and tucked her face inside her folded arms: that was the way to do it. Maggy had washed the floor, and it gave off the smell of damp wood. Inside her folded arms, she closed her eyes.

A nail from a horse's hoof . . . in bedrooms, too . . . in Lorraine, in the country I was chased from by the war. But the war is everywhere. In Lorraine there are towns covered with gold. It was in Lorraine, leaning against some flowers on a wall, that I said to you: 'If one day you no longer love me, you must tell me so.' Why did you swirl the beer in the bottom of your glass without saying anything? Why didn't you say anything when I said to you, 'Speak to me, speak to me,' whilst I was going slowly mad? In heather, in orchards, in ferns, in fields of cut corn . . . My too faithful memory has no future: it's closed to today, affirming and consuming itself at once. I live in the memory of a flower without a name. Oh my love, why did you abandon me? I live in the memory of a lost flower, I live in my devastated kingdom. And here I am inside my folded arms, hands clasped in anguish, while a vast mould spreads all over the world.

Next morning, the man came back, and stood waiting by the garden fence. Irene went down to the gate and opened it.

'I'm not coming in,' he said. 'I've just come to find out how you are.'

'I'm better. It wasn't very serious.'

'I've brought you a bottle of milk and some porridge oats.'

'Thank you,' she said, 'but you shouldn't deprive yourself. What you took from me isn't going to put you back on your feet.'

'It's OK . . . Since then, I've found what I was looking for.'

He reached out and felt her hair.

'Show me your head . . . Your hair is still all red.'

'It's not easy to wash out. Would you like a cig or two?'

'I sure would.'

He stayed by the gate while she went back into the house and came back with some cigarettes.

'Tell me, did you tell the police about me?'

'Are you daft or something?'

'Sorry. Look, here's my address.'

He held out a bit of paper.

'What could I do for you?' he asked. 'If there's anything you need doing around the house, you must drop me a line – if you've any wood that needs chopping, for instance, that sort of thing.'

'I like to chop my own wood. You mustn't take my little pleasures away from me.'

'All right. I'd like to give you a present. What would you like?'

'I don't like presents much . . .'

'Is there really nothing you want?'

'Oh, I don't know . . . It's difficult to say.'

When he had gone, Irene stayed by the gate. What a strange episode, this man who'd not been afraid to return. Neither perfection nor eternity; some good, some evil. And while she waited, the mould was rising in layers, on the world and in her heart. Because of Danny. Why is it that we don't see each other any more, why do we no longer come together, like the two hands we once were? I'll never understand. 'I'd like to give you a present – what would you like?' A present for Irene . . .

The man had gone and she could answer now, since it was not him that she was answering.

'I'd like a rose of Jericho.'

Translated by Faith Evans

MAURICE BLANCHOT

The Madness of the Day

I am not learned; I am not ignorant. I have known joys. That is saying too little: I am alive, and this life gives me the greatest pleasure. And what about death? When I die (perhaps any minute now), I will feel immense pleasure. I am not talking about the foretaste of death, which is stale and often disagreeable. Suffering dulls the senses. But this is the remarkable truth, and I am sure of it: I experience boundless pleasure in living, and I will take boundless satisfaction in dying.

I have wandered; I have gone from place to place. I have stayed in one place, lived in a single room. I have been poor, then richer, then poorer than many people. As a child I had great passions, and everything I wanted was given to me. My childhood has disappeared, my youth is behind me. It doesn't matter. I am happy about what has been, I am pleased by what is, and what is to come suits me well enough.

Is my life better than other people's lives? Perhaps. I have a roof over my head and many do not. I do not have leprosy, I am not blind, I see the world – what extraordinary happiness! I see this day, and outside it there is nothing. Who could take that away from me? And when this day fades, I will fade along with it – a thought, a certainty, that enraptures me.

I have loved people, I have lost them. I went mad when that blow struck me, because it is hell. But there was no witness to my madness, my frenzy was not evident; only my innermost being was mad. Sometimes I became enraged. People would say to me, 'Why are you so calm?' But I was scorched from head to foot; at night I would run through the streets and howl; during the day I would work calmly.

Shortly afterwards, the madness of the world broke out. I was made to stand against the wall like many others. Why? For no reason. The guns did not go off. I said to myself, God, what are you doing? At that point I stopped being insane. The world hesitated, then regained its equilibrium.

As reason returned to me, memory came with it, and I saw that even on the worst days, when I thought I was utterly and completely miserable, I was nevertheless, and nearly all the time, extremely happy. That gave me something to think about. The discovery was not a pleasant one. It seemed to me that I was losing a great deal. I asked myself, wasn't I sad, hadn't I felt my life breaking up? Yes, that had been true; but each minute, when I stayed without moving in a corner of the room, the cool of the night and the stability of the ground made me breathe and rest on gladness.

Men want to escape from death, strange beings that they are. And some of them cry out 'Die, die' because they want to escape from life. 'What a life. I'll kill myself. I'll give in.' This is lamentable and strange; it is a mistake.

Yet I have met people who have never said to life, 'Quiet!', who have never said to death, 'Go away!' Almost always women, beautiful creatures. Men are assaulted by terror, the night breaks through them, they see their plans annihilated, their work turned to dust. They who were so important, who wanted to create the world, are dumfounded; everything crumbles.

Can I describe my trials? I was not able to walk, or breathe, or eat. My breath was made of stone, my body of water, and yet I was dying of thirst. One day they thrust me into the ground; the doctors covered me with mud. What work went on at the bottom of that earth! Who says it's cold? It's a bed of fire, it's a bramble bush. When I got up I could feel nothing. My sense of touch was floating six feet away from me; if anyone entered my room, I would cry out, but the knife was serenely cutting me up. Yes, I became a skeleton. At night my thinness would rise up before me to terrify me. As it came and went it insulted me, it tired me out; oh, I was certainly very tired.

Am I an egoist? I feel drawn to only a few people, pity no one, rarely wish to please, rarely wish to be pleased, and I, who am almost unfeeling where I myself am concerned, suffer only in them, so that their slightest worry becomes an infinitely great misfortune for me, and even so, if I have to, I deliberately sacrifice them, I deprive them of every feeling of happiness (sometimes I kill them).

I came out of the muddy pit with the strength of maturity. What was I before? I was a bag of water, a lifeless extension, a motionless abyss. (Yet I knew who I was; I lived on, did not fall into nothingness.) People came to see me from far away. Children played near me. Women lay down on the ground to give me their hands. I have been young, too. But the void certainly disappointed me.

I am not timid, I've been knocked around. Someone (a man at his wits' end) took my hand and drove his knife into it. Blood everywhere. Afterward he was trembling. He held out his hand to me so that I could nail it to the table or against a door. Because he had gashed me like that, the man, a lunatic, thought he was now my friend; he pushed his wife into my arms; he followed me through the streets crying, 'I am damned, I am the plaything of an immoral delirium, I confess, I confess.' A strange sort of lunatic. Meanwhile the blood was dripping on my only suit.

I lived in cities most of the time. For a while I led a public life. I was attracted to the law, I liked crowds. Among other people I was unknown. As nobody, I was sovereign. But one day I grew tired of being the stone that beats solitary men to death. To tempt the law, I called softly to her, 'Come here; let me see you face to face.' (For a moment I wanted to take her aside.) It was a foolhardy appeal. What would I have done if she had answered?

I must admit I have read many books. When I disappear, all those volumes will change imperceptibly; the margins will become wider, the thought more cowardly. Yes, I have talked to too many people, I am struck by that now; to me, each person was an entire people. That vast other person made me much more than I would have liked. Now my life is surprisingly secure; even fatal diseases find me too tough. I'm sorry, but I must bury a few others before I bury myself.

I was beginning to sink into poverty. Slowly, it was drawing circles around me; the first seemed to leave me everything, the last would leave me only myself. One day, I found myself confined in the city; travelling was no longer more than a fantasy. I could not get through on the telephone. My clothes were wearing out. I was suffering from the cold; springtime, quick. I went to libraries. I had become friends with someone who worked in one, and he took me down to the overheated basement. In order to be useful to him I blissfully galloped along tiny gangways and brought him books which he then sent on to the gloomy spirit of reading. But that spirit hurled against me words that were not very kind; I shrank before its eyes; it saw me for what I was, an insect, a creature with mandibles who had come up from the dark regions of poverty. Who was I? It would have thrown me into great perplexity to answer that question.

Outdoors, I had a brief vision: a few steps away from me, just at the corner of the street I was about to leave, a woman with a baby carriage had stopped, I could not see her very well, she was manoeuvring the carriage to get it through the outer door. At that moment a man whom I had not seen approaching went in through that door. He had already stepped across the sill when he moved backward and came out again. While he stood next to the door, the baby carriage, passing in front of him, lifted slightly to cross the sill, and the young woman, after raising her head to look at him, also disappeared inside.

This brief scene excited me to the point of delirium. I was undoubtedly not able to explain it to myself fully and yet I was sure of it, that I had seized the moment when the day, having stumbled against a real event, would begin hurrying to its end. Here it comes, I said to myself, the end is coming; something is happening, the end is beginning. I was seized by joy.

I went to the house but did not enter. Through the opening I saw the black edge of a courtyard. I leaned against the outer wall; I was really very cold. As the cold wrapped around me from head to foot, I slowly felt my great height take on the dimensions of this boundless cold; it grew tranquilly, according to the laws of its true nature, and I lingered in the joy and perfection of this happiness, for one moment my head as high as the stone of the sky and my feet on the pavement.

All that was real; take note.

I had no enemies. No one bothered me. Sometimes a vast solitude opened in my head and the entire world disappeared inside it, but came out again intact, without a scratch, with nothing missing. I nearly lost my sight, because someone crushed glass in my eyes. That blow unnerved me, I must admit. I had the feeling I was going back into the wall, or straying into a thicket of flint. The worst thing was the sudden, shocking cruelty of the day; I could not look, but I could not help looking. To see was terrifying, and to stop seeing tore me apart from my forehead to my throat.

What was more, I heard hyena cries that exposed me to the threat of a wild animal (I think those cries were my own).

Once the glass had been removed, they slipped a thin film under my eyelids and over my eyelids they laid walls of cotton wool. I was not supposed to talk because talking pulled at the anchors of the bandage. 'You were asleep,' the doctor told me later. I was asleep! I had to hold my own against the light of seven days – a fine conflagration! Yes, seven days at once, the seven deadly lights, become the spark of a single moment, were calling me to account. Who would have imagined that? At times I said to myself, 'This is death. In spite of everything, it's really worth it, it's impressive.' But often I lay dying without saying anything. In the end, I grew convinced that I was face to face with the madness of the day. That was the truth: the light was going mad, the brightness had lost all reason; it assailed me irrationally, without control, without purpose. That discovery bit straight through my life.

I was asleep! When I woke up I had to listen to a man ask me, 'Are you going to sue?' A curious question to ask someone who has just been directly dealing with the day.

Even after I recovered, I doubted that I was well. I could not read or write. I was surrounded by a misty North. But this was what was strange: although I had not forgotten the agonizing contact with the day, I was wasting away from living behind curtains in dark glasses. I wanted to see something in full daylight; I was sated with the pleasure and comfort of the half light; I had the same desire for the daylight as for water and air. And if seeing was fire, I required the plenitude of fire, and if seeing would infect me with madness, I madly wanted that madness.

They gave me a modest position in the institution. I answered the telephone. The doctor ran a pathology laboratory (he was interested in blood), and people would come and drink some kind of drug. Stretched out on small beds, they would fall asleep. One of them used a remarkable stratagem: after drinking the prescribed drug, he took poison and fell into a coma. The doctor called it a rotten trick. He revived him and 'brought suit' against him for this fraudulent sleep. Really! It seems to me this sick man deserved better.

Even though my sight had hardly weakened at all, I walked through the streets like a crab, holding tightly on to the walls, and whenever I let go of them dizziness surrounded my steps. I often saw the same poster on these walls; it was a simple poster with rather large letters: *You want this too.* Of course I wanted it, and every time I came upon these prominent words, I wanted it.

Yet something in me quickly stopped wanting. Reading was a great weariness for me. Reading tired me no less than speaking, and the slightest true speech I uttered required some kind of strength that I did not have. I was told, 'You accept your difficulties very complacently.' This astonished me. At the age of twenty, in the same situation, no one would have noticed me. At forty, somewhat poor, I was becoming destitute. And where had this distressing appearance come from? I think I picked it up in the street. The streets did not enrich me, as by all rights they should have. Quite the contrary. As I walked along the sidewalks, plunged into the bright lights of the subways, turned down beautiful avenues where the city radiated superbly, I became extremely dull, modest and tired. Absorbing an inordinate share of the anonymous ruin, I then attracted all the more attention because this ruin was not meant for me and was making of me something rather vague and formless; for this reason it seemed affected, unashamed. What is irritating about poverty is that it is visible, and anyone who sees it thinks: You see, I'm being accused; who is attacking me? But I did not in the least wish to carry justice around on my clothes.

They said to me (sometimes it was the doctor, sometimes the nurses), 'You're an educated man, you have talents; by not using abilities which, if they were divided among ten people who lack them, would allow them to live, you are depriving them of what they don't have, and your poverty, which could be avoided, is an insult to their needs.' I asked, 'Why these lectures? Am I stealing my own place? Take it back from me.' I felt I was surrounded by unjust thoughts and spiteful reasoning. And who were they setting against me? An invisible learning that no one could prove and that I myself searched for without success. I was an educated man! But perhaps not all the time. Talented? Where were these talents that were made to speak like gowned judges sitting on benches, ready to condemn me day and night?

I liked the doctors quite well, and I did not feel belittled by their doubts. The annoying thing was that their authority loomed larger by the hour. One is not aware of it, but these men are kings. Throwing open my rooms, they would say, 'Everything here belongs to us.' They would fall upon my scraps of thought: 'This is ours.' They would challenge my story: 'Talk,' and my story would put itself at their service. In haste, I would rid myself of myself. I distributed my blood, my innermost being among them, lent them the universe, gave them the day. Right before their eyes, though they were not at all startled, I became a drop of water, a spot of ink. I reduced myself to them. The whole of me passed in full view before them, and when at last nothing was present but my perfect nothingness and there was nothing more to see, they ceased to see me too. Very irritated, they stood up and cried out, 'All right, where are you? Where are you hiding? Hiding is forbidden, it is an offence,' etc.

Behind their backs I saw the silhouette of the law. Not the law everyone knows, which is severe and hardly very agreeable; this law was different. Far from falling prey to her menace, I was the one who seemed to terrify her. According to her, my glance was a bolt of lightning and my hands were motives for perishing. What's more, the law absurdly credited me with all powers; she declared herself perpetually on her knees before me. But she did not let me ask anything and when she had recognized my right to be everywhere, it meant I had no place anywhere. When she set me above the authorities, it meant, You are not authorized to do anything. If she humbled herself, You don't respect me.

I knew that one of her aims was to make me 'see justice done'. She would say to me, 'Now you are a special case; no one can do anything to you. You can talk, nothing commits you; oaths are no longer binding to you; your acts remain without a consequence. You step all over me, and here I am, your servant for ever.' Servant? I did not want a servant at any price.

She would say to me, 'You love justice.' 'Yes, I think so.' 'Why do you let justice be offended in your person, which is so remarkable?' 'But my person is not remarkable to me.' 'If justice becomes weak in you, she will weaken in others, who will suffer because of it.' 'But this business doesn't concern her.' 'Everything concerns her.' 'But as you said, I'm a special case.' 'Special if you act – never, if you let others act.'

She was reduced to saying futile things: 'The truth is that we can never be separated again. I will follow you everywhere. I will live under your roof; we will share the same sleep.'

I had allowed myself to be locked up. Temporarily, they told me. All right, temporarily. During the outdoor hours, another resident, an old man with a white beard, jumped on my shoulders and gesticulated over my head. I said to him, 'Who are you, Tolstoy?' Because of that the doctor thought I was truly crazy. In the end I was walking everyone around on my back, a knot of tightly entwined people, a company of middle-aged men, enticed up there by a vain desire to dominate, an unfortunate child-ishness, and when I collapsed (because after all I was not a horse) most of my comrades, who had also tumbled down, beat me black and blue. Those were happy times.

The law was sharply critical of my behaviour: 'You were very different when I knew you before.' 'Very different?' 'People didn't make fun of you with impunity. To see you was worth one's life. To love you meant death. Men dug pits and buried themselves in them to get out of your sight. They would say to each other, "Has he gone by? Blessed be the earth that hides us."' 'Were they so afraid of me?' 'Fear was not enough for you, nor praise from the bottom of the heart, nor an upright life, nor humility in the dust. And above all, let no one question me. Who even dares to think of me?'

She got strangely worked up. She exalted me, but only to raise herself up in her turn. 'You are famine, discord, murder, destruction.' 'Why all that?' 'Because I am the angel of discord, murder, and the end.' 'Well,' I said to her, 'that's more than enough to get us both locked up.' The truth was that I liked her. In these surroundings, overpopulated by men, she was the only feminine element. Once she had made me touch her knee – a strange feeling. I had said as much to her: 'I am not the kind of man who is satisfied with a knee!' Her answer: 'That would be disgusting!'

This was one of her games. She would show me a part of space, between the top of the window and the ceiling. 'You are there,' she said. I looked hard at that point. 'Are you there?' I looked at it with all my might. 'Well?' I felt the scars fly off my eyes, my sight was a wound, my head a hole, a bull disembowelled. Suddenly she cried out, 'Oh, I see the day, oh God,' etc. I protested that this game was tiring me out enormously, but she was insatiably intent upon my glory.

Who threw glass in your face? That question would reappear in all the other questions. It was not posed more directly than that, but was the crossroads to which all paths led. They had pointed out to me that my answer would not reveal anything, because everything had long since been revealed. 'All the more reason not to talk.' 'Look, you're an educated man; you know that silence attracts attention. Your dumbness is betraying you in the most foolish way.' I would answer them, 'But my silence is real. If I hid it from you, you would find it again a little further on. If it betrays me, all the better for you, it helps you, and all the better for me, whom you say you are helping.' So they had to move heaven and earth to get to the bottom of it.

I had become involved in their search. We were all like masked hunters. Who was being questioned? Who was answering? One became the other. The words spoke by themselves. The silence entered them, an excellent refuge, since I was the only one who noticed it.

I had been asked: Tell us '*just* exactly' what happened. A story? I began: I am not learned; I am not ignorant. I have known joys. That is saying too little. I told them the whole story and they listened, it seems to me, with interest, at least in the beginning. But the end was a surprise to all of us. 'That was the beginning,' they said. 'Now get down to the facts.' How so? The story was over!

I had to acknowledge that I was not capable of forming a story out of these events. I had lost the sense of the story; that happens in a good many illnesses. But this explanation only made them more insistent. Then I noticed for the first time that there were two of them and that this distortion of the traditional method, even though it was explained by the fact that one of them was an eye doctor, the other a specialist in mental illness, constantly gave our conversation the character of an authoritarian interrogation, overseen and controlled by a strict set of rules. Of course neither of them was the chief of police. But because there were two of them, there were three, and this third remained firmly convinced, I am sure, that a writer, a man who speaks and who reasons with distinction, is always capable of recounting facts that he remembers.

A story? No. No stories, never again.

Translated by Lydia Davis

SIMONE DE BEAUVOIR

Monologue

– 'The monologue is her form of revenge.'

Flaubert

The silly bastards! I drew the curtains they keep the stupid coloured lanterns and the fairy lights on the Christmas trees out of the apartment but the noises come in through the walls. Engines revving brakes and now here they are starting their horns big shots is what they take themselves for behind the wheel of their dreary middle-class family cars their lousy semisports jobs their miserable little Dauphines their white convertibles. A white convertible with black seats that's terrific and the fellows whistled when I went by with slanting sunglasses on my nose and a Hermès scarf on my head and now they think they're going to impress me with their filthy old wrecks and their bawling klaxons! If they all smashed into one another right under my windows how happy I should be happy. The swine they are shattering my eardrums I've no more plugs the last two are jamming the telephone bell they are utterly repulsive yet still I'd rather have my ears shattered than hear the telephone ringing. Stop the uproar the silence: sleep. And I shan't get a wink yesterday I couldn't either I was so sick with horror because it was the day before today. I've taken so many sleeping pills they don't work any more and that doctor is a sadist he gives them to me in the form of suppositories and I can't stuff myself like a gun. I've got to get some rest I have to I must be able to cope with Tristan tomorrow: no tears no shouting. 'This is an absurd position. A ghastly mess, even from the point of view of dough! A child needs its mother.' I'm going to have another sleepless night my nerves will be completely frazzled I'll make a cock of it. Bastards! They thump

III

thump in my head I can see them I can hear them. They are stuffing themselves with cheap foie gras and burned turkey they drool over it Albert and Madame Nanard Étiennette their snooty offspring my mother: it's flying in the face of nature that my own brother my own mother should prefer my ex-husband to me. I've nothing whatever to say to them only just let them stop preventing me sleeping; you get so you are fit to be shut up you confess everything, true or false, they needn't count on that though I'm tough they won't get me down.

Celebrations with them, how they stank: it was ghastly enough quite ghastly enough on ordinary days! I always loathed Christmas Easter July 14. Papa lifted Nanard on to his shoulder so that he could see the fireworks and I stayed there on the ground squashed between them just at prick level and that randy crowd's smell of sex and Mama said 'there she is snivelling again' they stuffed an ice into my hand there was nothing I wanted to do with it I threw it away they sighed I couldn't be slapped on a July 14 evening. As for him he never touched me I was the one he liked best: 'proper little God-damn woman.' But when he kicked the bucket she didn't bother to hold in any more and she used to swipe me across the face with her rings. I never slapped Sylvie once. Nanard was the king. She used to take him into her bed in the morning and I heard them tickling one another he says it's untrue I'm disgusting of course he's not going to confess they never do confess indeed maybe he's forgotten they are very good at forgetting anything inconvenient and I say they are shits on account of I do remember: she used to wander about her brothel of a room half naked in her white silk dressing gown with its stains and cigarette holes and he clung around her legs it makes you really sick mothers with their little male jobs and I was supposed to be like them no thank you very much indeed. I wanted decent children clean children I didn't want Francis to become a fairy like Nanard. Nanard with his five kids he's a bugger for all that you can't deceive me you really must hate women to have married that cow.

It's not stopping. How many of them are there? In the streets of Paris hundreds of thousands. And it's the same in every town all over the world: three thousand million and it'll get worse and worse: famines there are not nearly enough more and more and more people: even the sky's infested with them presently they will be as thick in space as they are on the motorways and the moon you can't look at it any more without thinking that there are cunts up there spouting away. I used to like the moon it was like me; and they've mucked it up like they muck everything up they were revolting those photos – a dreary greyish dusty thing anyone at all can trample about on.

I was clean straight uncompromising. No cheating: I've had that in my bones since I was a child. I can see myself now a quaint little brat in a ragged dress Mama looked after me so badly and the kind lady simpering 'And so we love our little brother do we?' And I answered calmly 'I hate him.' The icy chill: Mama's look. It was perfectly natural that I should have been jealous all the books say so: the astonishing thing the thing I like is that I should have admitted it. No compromise no act: that proper little woman was me all right. I'm clean I'm straight I don't join in any act: that makes them mad they hate being seen through they want you to believe the stuff they hand out or at least to pretend to.

Here's some of their bloody nonsense now – rushing up the stairs laughter voices all in a tizzy. What the hell sense does that make, all working themselves up at a set date a set time just because you start using a new calendar? All my life it's made me sick, this sort of hysterical crap. I ought to tell the story of my life. Lots of women do it people print them people talk about them they strut about very pleased with themselves my book would be more interesting than all their balls: it's made me sweat but I've lived and I've lived without lies without sham how furious it would make them to see my name and picture in the shop windows and everyone would learn the real genuine truth. I'd have a whole raft of men at my feet again they're such grovelling creatures that the most dreadful slob once she's famous they make a wild rush for her. Maybe I should meet one who would know how to love me.

My father loved me. No one else. Everything comes from that. All Albert thought of was slipping off I loved him quite madly poor fool that I was. How I suffered in those days, young and as straight as they come! So of course you do silly things: maybe it was a put-up job what is there to show he didn't know Olivier? A filthy plot it knocked me completely to pieces.

Now of course that just had to happen they are dancing right over my head. My night is wrecked finished tomorrow I shall be a rag I shall have to dope myself to manage Tristan and the whole thing will end in the shit. You mustn't do it! Swine! It's all that matters to me in life sleep. Swine. They are allowed to shatter my ears and trample on me and they're making the most of it. 'The dreary bitch downstairs can't make a fuss it's New Year's Day.' Laugh away I'll find some way of getting even she'll bitch you the dreary bitch I've never let anyone walk over me ever. Albert was livid. 'No need to make a scene!' Oh yes indeed there was! He was dancing with Nina belly to belly she was sticking out her big tits she stank of scent but underneath it you got a whiff of bidet and he was jigging about with a prick on him like a bull. Scenes I've made scenes all right in my life. I've always been that proper little woman who answered 'I hate him' fearless open as a book dead straight.

They're going to break through the ceiling and come down on my head. I can see them from here it's too revolting they're rubbing together sex to sex the women the respectable women it makes them wet they're charmed with themselves because the fellow's tail is standing up. And each one of them is getting ready to give his best friend a pair of horns his dearly beloved girlfriend they'll do it that very night in the bathroom not even lying down dress hitched up on their sweating asses when you go and pee you'll tread in the mess like at Rose's the night of my scene. Maybe it's on the edge of a blue party that couple upstairs they're in their fifties at that age they need whorehouse tricks to be able to thread the needle. I'm sure Albert and his good lady have whore parties you can see from Christine's face she's ready for anything at all he wouldn't have to hold himself back with her. Poor bleeder that I was at twenty too simple-minded too shamefaced. Touching, that awkwardness: I did really deserve to be loved. Oh I've been done dirt life's given me no sort of a break.

Hell I'm dying of thirst I'm hungry but it would slay me to get up out of my armchair and go to the kitchen. You freeze to death in this hole only if I turn up the central heating the air will dry out completely there's no spit left in my mouth my nose is burning. What a bleeding mess their civilization. They can muck up the moon but can't heat a house. If they had any sense they'd invent robots that would go and fetch me fruit juice when I want some and see to the house without my having to be sweet to them and listen to all their crap.

Mariette's not coming tomorrow fine I'm sick of her old father's cancer. At least I've disciplined *her* she keeps more or less in her place. There are some that put on rubber gloves to do the washing up and play the lady that I cannot bear. I don't want them to be sluts either so you find hairs in the

salad and finger marks on the doors. Tristan is a cunt. I treat my dailies very
well. But I want them to do their jobs properly without making a fuss or
telling me the story of their lives. For that you have to train them just as
you have to train children to make worthwhile grown-ups out of them.

Tristan has not trained Francis: that bitch of a Mariette is leaving me in
the lurch. The drawing room will be a pigsty after they've been here. They'll
come with a plushy present everyone will kiss everyone else I will hand
around little cakes Francis will make the answers his father has gone over
with him he lies like a grown-up man. I should have made a decent child
of him. I shall tell Tristan a kid deprived of his mother always ends up by
going to the bad he'll turn into a hooligan or a fairy you don't want that.
My serious thoughtful voice makes me feel sick: what I should really like
to do is scream it's unnatural to take a child away from its mother! But I'm
dependent on him. 'Threaten him with divorce,' said Dédé. That made him
laugh. Men hold together so the law is so unfair and he has so much pull
that it's him that would get the decree. He would keep Francis and not
another penny and you can whistle for the rent. Nothing to be done against
this filthy blackmail – an allowance and the flat in exchange for Francis. I
am at his mercy. No money you can't stand up for yourself you're less than
nothing a zero twice over. What a numskull I didn't give a damn about
money unselfish half-wit. I didn't twist their arms a quarter enough. If I had
stayed with Florent I should have made myself a pretty little nest egg. Tristan
fell for me fell right on his face I had pity on him. And there you are! This
puffed-up little pseudo-Napoleon leaves me flat because I don't swoon go
down on my knees in admiration before him. I'll fix him. I'll tell him I'm
going to tell Francis the truth: I'm not ill I live alone because your swine of
a father ditched me he buttered me up then he tortured me he even knocked
me about. Go into hysterics in front of the boy bleed to death on their
doormat that or something else. I have weapons I'll use them he'll come
back to me I shan't go on rotting all alone in this dump with those people
on the next floor who trample me underfoot and the ones next door who
wake me every morning with their radio and no one to bring me so much
as a crust when I'm hungry. All those fat cows have a man to protect them
and kids to wait on them and me nothing: this can't go on. For a fortnight
now the plumber hasn't come a woman on her own they think they can do
anything how despicable people are when you're down they stamp on you.

I kick back I keep my end up but a woman alone is spat on. The concierge gives a dirty laugh. At ten in the morning it is *in concordance with the law* to have the radio on: if he thinks I'm impressed by his long words. I had them on the telephone four nights running they knew it was me but impossible to pin it I laughed and laughed: they've coped by having calls stopped I'll find something else. What? Drips like that sleep at night work all day go for a walk on Sunday there's nothing you can get a hold on. A man under my roof. The plumber would have come the concierge would say good day politely the neighbours would turn the volume down. Bloody hell, I want to be treated with respect I want my husband my son my home like everybody else.

A little boy of eleven it would be fun to take him to the circus to the zoo. I'd train him right away. He was easier to handle than Sylvie. She was a tough one to cope with soft and cunning like that slug Albert. Oh, I don't hold it against her poor little creep they all put her against me and she was at the age when girls loathe their mothers they call that ambivalence but it's hatred. There's another of those truths that make them mad. Étiennette dripped with fury when I told her to look at Claudie's diary. She didn't want to look, like those women who don't go to the doctor because they're afraid of having cancer so you're still the dear little mama of a dear little daughter. Sylvie was not a dear little anything I had a dose of that when I read her diary: but as for me I look things straight in the face. I didn't let it worry me all that much I knew all I had to do was wait and one day she would understand and she would say I was the one who was in the right and not them and cram it down their throats. I was patient never did I raise a hand against her. I took care of myself of course. I told her, 'You won't get me down.' Obstinate as a mule whining for hours on end days on end over a whim there wasn't the slightest reason for her to see Tristan again. A girl needs a father I ought to know if anybody does: but nobody's ever said she needs two. Albert was quite enough of a nuisance already he was taking everything the law allowed him and more I had to struggle every inch of the way he'd have corrupted her if I hadn't fought. The frocks he gave her it was immoral. I didn't want my daughter to turn into a whore like my mother. Skirts up to her knees at seventy paint all over her face! When I passed her in the street the other day I crossed over to the other sidewalk. With her strutting along like that what a fool I should have looked if she had put on the great reconciliation act. I'm sure her place is as squalid as ever with the cash she flings away at the hairdresser's she could afford herself a cleaning woman.

No more horns blowing I preferred that row to hearing them roaring and bellowing in the street: car doors slamming they shout they laugh some of them are singing they are drunk already and upstairs that racket goes on. They're making me ill there's a foul taste in my mouth and these two little pimples on my thigh they horrify me. I take care I only eat health foods but even so there are people who muck about with them hands more or less clean there's no hygiene anywhere in the world the air is polluted not only because of the cars and the factories but also these millions of filthy mouths swallowing it in and belching it out from morning till night: when I think I'm swimming in their breath I feel like rushing off into the very middle of the desert: how can you keep your body clean in such a lousy disgusting world you're contaminated through all the pores of your skin and yet I was healthy clean I can't bear them infecting me. If I had to go to bed there's not one of them that would move a finger to look after me. I could croak any minute with my poor overloaded heart no one would know anything about it that terrifies the guts out of me. They'll find a rotting corpse behind the door I'll stink I'll have shat the rats will have eaten my nose. Die alone live alone no I can't bear it. I need to have a man I want Tristan to come back lousy dunghill of a world they are shouting they are laughing and here I am withering on the shelf: forty-three it's too soon it's unfair I want to live. Big-time life that's me: the convertible the apartment the dresses everything. Florent shelled out and no horsing around – except a little in bed right's right – all he wanted to do was to go to bed with me and show me off in smart joints I was lovely my loveliest time all my girlfriends were dying with envy. It makes me sick to think of those days nobody takes me out any more I just stay here stewing in my own shit. I'm sick of it I'm sick of it sick sick sick sick sick sick sick sick sick sick sick sick sick sick sick sick sick sick sick sick sick sick sick sick sick sick sick sick sick sick sick sick sick sick sick sick sick sick sick sick sick sick sick sick sick sick sick sick sick sick sick sick sick sick sick sick sick sick sick sick sick sick sick sick sick sick sick sick sick sick sick sick sick sick sick sick sick sick.

That bastard Tristan I want him to take me out to a restaurant to a theatre I'll insist upon it I don't insist nearly enough all he does is come drooling along here either by himself or with the kid sits there with a mealy-mouthed smirk on his face and at the end of an hour he drools off again. Not so much as a sign of life even on New Year's Eve! Swine! I'm bored black I'm bored through the ground it's inhuman. If I slept that would kill the time. But there is this noise outside. And inside my head they are giving that dirty laugh and saying, 'She's all alone.' They'll laugh the other side of their faces when Tristan comes back to me. He'll come back I'll make him I certainly will. I'll go to the couturiers again I'll give cocktail parties evening parties my picture will be in *Vogue* with a neckline plunging to there I have better breasts than anyone. 'Have you seen the picture of Murielle?' They will be utterly fucked and Francis will tell them about how we go to the zoo the circus the skating rink I'll spoil him that'll make them choke on their lies their slanders. Such hatred! Clear-sighted too clear-sighted. They don't like being seen through: as for me I'm straight I don't join their act I tear masks off. They don't forgive me for that. A mother jealous of her daughter so now I've seen everything. She flung me at Albert's head to get rid of me for other reasons too no I don't want to believe it. What a dirty trick to have urged me into that marriage me so vital alive a burning flame and him stuffy middle-class cold-hearted prick like limp macaroni. I would have known the kind of man to suit Sylvie. I had her under control yes I was firm but I was always affectionate always ready to talk I wanted to be a friend to her and I would have kissed my mother's hands if she had behaved like that to me. But what a thankless heart. She's dead and so all right what of it? The dead are not saints. She wouldn't co-operate she never confided in me at all. There was someone in her life a boy or maybe a girl who can tell this gen- eration is so twisted. But there wasn't a precaution she didn't take. Not a single letter in her drawers and the last two years not a single page of diary: if she went on keeping one she hid it terribly well even after her death I didn't find anything. Blind with fury just because I was doing my duty as a mother. Me the selfish one when she ran away like that it would have been in my interest to have left her with her father. Without her I still had a chance of making a new life for myself. It was for her own good that I was having none of it. Christine with her three great lumps of children it would have suited her down to the ground to have had a big fifteen-year-old girl she could have given all the chores to poor lamb she had no notion the hysterics she put on for the benefit of the police . . . Yes the police. Was I supposed to put on kid gloves? What are the police there for? Stray cats? Albert offering me money to give up Sylvie! Always this money how grovelling men are they think everything can be bought anyhow I didn't give a damn about his money it was peanuts compared with what Tristan allows me. And even if I had been broke I'd never have sold my daughter. 'Why don't you let her go, that chick only brings you headaches,' Dédé said to me. She doesn't understand a mother's feelings she never thinks of anything but her own pleasure. But one must not always be at the receiving end one must also know how to give. I had a great deal to give Sylvie I should have made her into a fine girl: and I asked nothing from her for myself. I was completely devoted. Such ingratitude! It was perfectly natural I should ask that teacher's help. According to her diary Sylvie worshipped her and I thought she'd hold her bloody tongue the lousy half-baked intellectual. No doubt there was much more between them than I imagined I've always been so clean-minded I never see any harm these alleged brain workers are all bull dykes. Sylvie's snivelling and fuss after it and my mother who told me on the phone I had no right to intermeddle with my daughter's friendships. That was the very word she used *intermeddle*. 'Oh as far as that was concerned you never intermeddled. And don't you begin now if you please.' Straight just like that. And I hung up. My own mother it's utterly unnatural. In the end Sylvie would have realized. That was one of the things that really shattered me at the cemetery. I said to myself 'A little later she would have said I was in the right.' The ghastliness of remembering the blue sky all those flowers Albert crying in front of everyone Christ you exercise some self-control. I controlled myself yet I knew very well I'd never recover from the blow. It was me they were burying. I have been buried. They've all got together to cover me over deep. Even on this night not a sign of life. They know very well that nights when there are celebrations everybody laughing gorging stuffing one another the lonely ones the bereaved kill themselves just like that. It would suit them beautifully if I were to vanish they hide me in a hole but it doesn't work I'm a burr in their pants. I don't intend to oblige them, thank you very much indeed. I want to live I want to come to life again. Tristan will come back to me I'll be done right by I'll get out of this filthy hole. If I talked to him now I should feel better maybe I'd be able to sleep. He must be at home he's an early bedder, he saves himself up. Be calm friendly don't get his back up otherwise my night is shot to hell.

He doesn't answer. Either he's not there or he doesn't want to answer. He's jammed the bell he doesn't want to listen to what I have to say. They sit in judgement upon me find me guilty not one of them ever listens to me. I never punished Sylvie without listening to what she had to say first it was she who clammed up who wouldn't talk. Only yesterday he wouldn't let me say a quarter of what I had to say and I could hear him dozing at the other end of the line. It's disheartening. I reason I explain I prove: patiently step by step I force them to the truth I think they're following me and then I ask, 'What have I just said?' They don't know they stuff themselves with mental earplugs and if a remark happens to get through their answer is just so much balls. I start over again I pile up fresh arguments: same result. Albert is a champion at that game but Tristan is not so bad either. 'You ought to take me away with Francis for the holidays.' He doesn't answer he talks of something else. Children have to listen but they manage they forget. 'What have I said, Sylvie?' 'You said when one is messy in small things one is messy in big ones and I must tidy my room before I go out.' And then the next day she did not tidy it. When I force Tristan to listen to me and he can't find anything to reply – a boy needs his mother a mother can't do without her child it's so obvious that even the crookedest mind can't deny it – he goes to the door flies down the stairs four at a time while I shout down the well and cut myself off short in case the neighbours think I'm cracked: how cowardly it is he knows I loathe scenes particularly as I've an odd sort of a reputation in this house of course I have they behave so weirdly – unnaturally – that sometimes I do the same. Oh what the hell I used to behave so well it gave me a pain in the ass Tristan's casualness his big laugh his loud voice I should have liked to see him drop down dead when he used to horse around in public with Sylvie.

Wind! It's suddenly started to blow like fury how I should like an enormous disaster that would sweep everything away and me with it a typhoon a cyclone it would be restful to die if there were no one left to think about me: give up my body my poor little life to them no! But for everybody to plunge into nothingness that would be fine: I'm tired of fighting them even when I'm alone they harry me it's exhausting I wish it would all come to an end! Alas! I shan't have my typhoon I never have anything I want. It's only a little very ordinary wind it'll have torn off a few tiles a few chimney pots everything is mean and piddling in this world nature's as bad as men. I'm the only one that has splendid dreams and it would have been better to choke them right away everything disappoints me always.

Perhaps I ought to stuff up these sleeping things and go to bed. But I'm still too wide awake I'd only writhe about. If I had got him on the phone if we'd talked pleasantly I should have calmed down. He doesn't give a fuck. Here I am torn to pieces by heartbreaking memories I call him and he doesn't answer. Don't bawl him out don't begin by bawling him out that would muck up everything. I dread tomorrow. I shall have to be ready before four o'clock I shan't have had a wink of sleep I'll go out and buy petits fours that Francis will tread into the carpet he'll break one of my little ornaments he's not been properly brought up that child as clumsy as his father who'll drop ash all over the place and if I say anything at all Tristan will blow right up he never let me keep my house as it ought to be yet after all it's enormously important. Just now it's perfect the drawing room polished shining like the moon used to be. By seven tomorrow evening it'll be utterly filthy I'll have to spring-clean it even though I'll be all washed out. Explaining everything to him from *a* to *z* will wash me right out. He's tough. What a clot I was to drop Florent for him! Florent and I we understood one another he coughed up I lay on my back it was cleaner than those capers where you hand out tender words to one another. I'm too soft-hearted I thought it was a terrific proof of love when he offered to marry me and there was Sylvie the ungrateful little thing I wanted her to have a real home and a mother no one could say a thing against a married woman a banker's wife. For my part it gave me a pain in the ass to play the lady to be friends with crashing bores. Not so surprising that I burst out now and then. 'You're setting about it the wrong way with Tristan' Dédé used to tell me. Then later on 'I told you so!' It's true I'm headstrong I take the bit between my teeth I don't calculate. Maybe I should have learned to compromise if it hadn't been for all those disappointments. Tristan made me utterly sick I let him know it. People can't bear being told what you really think of them. They want you to believe their fine words or at least to pretend to. As for me I'm clear-sighted I'm frank I tear masks off. The dear kind lady simpering, 'So we love our little brother do we?' and my collected little voice: 'I hate him.' I'm still that proper little woman who says what she thinks and doesn't cheat. It made my guts grind to hear him holding forth and all those bloody fools on their knees before him. I came clumping along in my big boots I cut their fine words down to size for them – progress prosperity the future of mankind happiness peace aid for the underdeveloped countries peace upon earth. I'm not a racist but don't give a fuck for Algerians Jews Negroes in just the same way I don't give a fuck for Chinks Russians Yanks Frenchmen. I don't give a fuck for humanity what has it ever done for me I ask you. If they are such bleeding fools as to murder one another bomb one another plaster one another with napalm wipe one another out I'm not going to weep my eyes out. A million children have been massacred so what? Children are never anything but the seed of bastards it unclutters the planet a little they all admit it's overpopulated don't they? If I were the earth it would disgust me, all this vermin on my back, I'd shake it off. I'm quite willing to die if they all die too. I'm not going to go all soft-centred about kids that mean nothing to me. My own daughter's dead and they've stolen my son from me.

I should have won her back. I'd have made her into a worthwhile person. But it would have taken me time. Tristan did not help me the selfish bastard our quarrels bored him he used to say to me 'Leave her in peace.' You ought not to have children in a way Dédé is right they only give you one bloody headache after another. But if you do have them you ought to bring them up properly. Tristan always took Sylvie's side: now even if I had been wrong – let's say I might have been sometimes for the sake of argument – from an educational point of view it's disastrous for one parent to run out on the other. He was on her side even when I was right. Over that little Jeanne for example. It quite touches my heart to think of her again her moist adoring gaze: they can be very sweet little girls she reminded me of my own childhood badly dressed neglected slapped scolded by that concierge of a mother of hers always on the edge of tears: she thought I was lovely she stroked my furs she did little things for me and I slipped her pennies when no one was looking I gave her sweeties poor pet. She was the same age as Sylvie I should have liked them to be friends Sylvie disappointed me bitterly. She whined, 'Being with Jeanne bores me.' I told her she was a heartless thing I scolded her I punished her. Tristan stood up for her on the grounds that you can't force liking that battle lasted for ages I wanted Sylvie to learn generosity in the end it was little Jeanne who backed out.

It's quietened down a bit up there. Footsteps voices in the staircase car doors slamming there's still their bloody fool dance music but they aren't dancing any more. I know what they're at. This is the moment they make love on beds on sofas on the ground in cars the time for being sick sick sick when they bring up the turkey and the caviar it's filthy I have a feeling there's a smell of vomit I'm going to burn a joss stick. If only I could sleep I'm wide awake dawn is far away still this is a ghastly hour of the night and Sylvie died without understanding me I'll never get over it. This smell of incense is the same as at the funeral service: the candles the flowers the catafalque. My despair. Dead: it was impossible! For hours and hours I sat there by her body thinking no of course not she'll wake up I'll wake up. All that effort all those struggles scenes sacrifices – all in vain. My life's work gone up in smoke. I left nothing to chance; and chance at its cruellest reached out and hit me. Sylvie is dead. Five years already. She is dead. For ever. I can't bear it. Help it hurts it hurts too much get me out of here I can't bear the breakdown to start again no help me I can't bear it any longer don't leave me alone . . .

Who to call? Albert Bernard would hang up like a flash: he blubbered in front of everybody but tonight he's gorged and had fun and I'm the one that remembers and weeps. My mother: after all a mother is a mother I never did her any harm she was the one who mucked up my childhood she insulted me she presumed to tell me . . . I want her to take back what she said I won't go on living with those words in my ears a daughter can't bear being cursed by her mother even if she's the ultimate word in tarts.

'Was it you who called me? . . . It surprised me too but after all on a night like this it could happen you might think of my grief and say to yourself that a mother and daughter can't be on bad terms all their lives long; above all since I really can't see what you can possibly blame me for . . . Don't shout like that . . .'

She has hung up. She wants peace. She poisons my life the bitch I'll have to settle her hash. What hatred! She's always hated me: she killed two birds with one stone in marrying me to Albert. She made sure of her fun and my unhappiness. I didn't want to admit it I'm too clean too pure but it's staringly obvious. It was she who hooked him at the physical culture class and she treated herself to him slut that she was it can't have been very inviting to stuff her but what with all the men who'd been there before she must have known a whole bagful of tricks like getting astride over the guy I can just imagine it it's perfectly revolting the way respectable women make love. She was too long in the tooth to keep him she made use of me they cackled behind my back and went to work again: one day when I came back unexpectedly she was all red. How old was she when she stopped? Maybe she treats herself to gigolos she's not so poor as she says she's no doubt kept jewels that she sells off on the sly. I think that after you're fifty you ought to have the decency to give it up: I gave it up well before ever since I went into mourning. It doesn't interest me any more I'm blocked I never think of those things any more even in dreams. That old bag it makes you shudder to think of between her legs she drips with scent but underneath she smells she used to make up she titivated she didn't wash not what I call wash when she pretended to use a douche it was only to show Nanard her backside. Her son her son-in-law: it makes you feel like throwing up. They would say, 'You've got a filthy mind.' They know how to cope. If you point out that they're walking in shit they scream it's you that have dirty feet. My dear little girlfriends would have liked to have a go with my husband women they're all filthy bitches and there he was shouting at me, 'You are contemptible.' Jealousy is not contemptible real love has a beak and claws. I was not one of those women who will put up with sharing or whorehouse parties like Christine I wanted us to be a clean proper couple a decent couple. I can control myself but I'm not a complete drip I've never been afraid of making a scene. I did not allow anyone to make fun of me I can look back over my past – nothing unwholesome nothing dubious. I'm the white blackbird.

Poor white blackbird: it's the only one in the world. That's what maddens them: I'm something too far above them. They'd like to do away with me they've shut me up in a cage. Shut in locked in I'll end by dying of boredom really dying. It seems that that happens to babies even, when no one looks after them. The perfect crime that leaves no trace. Five years of this torture already. That ass Tristan who says travel you've plenty of money. Plenty to travel on the cheap like with Albert in the old days: you don't catch me doing that again. Being poor is revolting at any time but when you travel! . . . I'm not a snob I showed Tristan I wasn't impressed by deluxe palace hotels and women dripping with pearls the fancy doormen. But second-rate boarding houses and cheap restaurants, no sir. Dubious sheets filthy tablecloths sleep in other people's sweat in other people's filth eat with badly washed knives and forks you might catch lice or the pox and the smells make me sick: quite apart from the fact that I get deadly constipated because those johns where everybody goes turn me off like a tap: the brotherhood of shit only a very little for me please. Then what earthly point is there in travelling alone? We had fun Dédé and I it's terrific two pretty girls in a convertible their hair streaming in the wind: we made a terrific impression in Rome at night on the Piazza del Popolo. I've had fun with other friends too. But alone? What sort of impression do you make on beaches in casinos if you haven't got a man with you? Ruins museums I had my bellyful of them with Tristan. I'm not a hysterical enthusiast I don't swoon at the sight of broken columns or tumbledown old shacks. The people of former times my foot they're dead that's the only thing they have over the living but in their own day they were just as sickening. Picturesqueness: I don't fall for that not for one minute. Stinking filth dirty washing cabbage stalks what a pretentious fool you have to be to go into ecstasies over that! And it's the same thing everywhere all the time whether they're stuffing themselves with chips paella or pizza it's the same crew a filthy crew the rich who trample over you the poor who hate you for your money the old who dodder the young who sneer the men who show off the women who open their legs. I'd rather stay at home reading a thriller although they've become so dreary nowadays. The TV too what a clapped-out set of fools! I was made for another planet altogether I mistook the way.

Why do they have to make all that din right under my windows? They're standing there by their cars they can't make up their minds to put their stinking feet into them. What can they be going on and on about? Snotty little beasts snotty little beastesses grotesque in their miniskirts and their tights I hope they catch their deaths haven't they any mothers then? And the boys with their hair down their necks. From a distance those ones seem more or less clean. But all those louse-breeding beatniks if the chief of police had any sort of drive he'd toss them all into the brig. The youth of today! They drug they stuff one another they respect nothing. I'm going to pour a bucket of water on their heads. They might break open the door and beat me up I'm defenceless I'd better shut the window again. Rose's daughter is one of that sort it seems and Rose plays the elder sister they're always together in one another's pockets. Yet she used to hold her in so she even boxed her ears she didn't bother to bring her to reason she was impulsive arbitrary: I loathe capriciousness. Oh, Rose will pay for it all right as Dédé says she'll have Danielle on her hands pregnant … I should have made a lovely person of Sylvie. I'd have given her dresses jewels I'd have been proud of her we should have gone out together. There's no justice in the world. That's what makes me so mad – the injustice. When I think of the sort of mother I was! Tristan acknowledges it: I've forced him to acknowledge it. And then after that he tells me he's ready for anything rather than let me have Francis: they don't give a damn for logic they say absolutely anything at all and then escape at the run. He races down the stairs four at a time while I shout down the well after him. I won't be had like that. I'll force him to do me justice: cross my heart. He'll give me back my place in the home my place on earth. I'll make a splendid child of Francis they'll see what kind of a mother I am.

They are killing me the bastards. The idea of the party tomorrow destroys me. I must win. I must I must I must I must. I'll tell my fortune with the cards. No. If it went wrong I'd throw myself out of the window no I mustn't it would suit them too well. Think of something else. Cheerful things. The boy from Bordeaux. We expected nothing from one another we asked one another no questions we made one another no promises we bedded down and made love. It lasted three weeks and he left for Africa I wept wept. It's a memory that does me good. Things like that only happen once in a lifetime. What a pity! When I think back over it it seems to me that if anyone had loved me properly I should have been affection itself. Turds they bored me to death they trample everyone down right left and centre everyone can die in his hole for all they care husbands deceive their wives mothers toss off their sons not a word about it sealed lips that carefulness disgusts me and the way they don't have the courage of their convictions. 'But come really your brother is too close-fisted' it was Albert who pointed it out to me I'm too noble-minded to bother with trifles like that but it's true they had stuffed down three times as much as us and the bill was divided fifty-fifty thousands of little things like that. And afterwards he blamed me – 'You shouldn't have repeated it to him.' On the beach we went at it hammer and tongs. Étiennette cried you would have said the tears on her cheeks were melting suet. 'Now that he knows he'll turn over a new leaf,' I told her. I was simple-minded – I thought they were capable of turning over new leaves I thought you could bring them up by making them see reason. 'Come Sylvie let's think it over. You know how much that frock costs? And how many times will you ever put it on? We'll send it back.' It always had to be begun again at the beginning I wore myself out. Nanard will go on being close-fisted to the end of his days. Albert more deceitful lying secretive than ever. Tristan always just as self-satisfied just as pompous. I was knocking myself out for nothing. When I tried to teach Étiennette how to dress Nanard bawled me out – she was twenty-two and I was dressing her up as an elderly schoolteacher! She went on cramming herself into little gaudy dresses. And Rose who shouted out, 'Oh you are cruel!' I had spoken to her out of loyalty women have to stand by one another. Who has ever shown me any gratitude? I've lent them money without asking for interest not one has been grateful to me for it indeed some have whined when I asked to be paid back. Girlfriends I overwhelmed with presents accused me of showing off. And you ought to see how briskly they slipped away all those people I had done good turns to yet God knows I asked for nothing much in return. I'm not one of those people who thinks they have a right to everything. Aunt Marguerite: 'Would you lend us your apartment while you're on your cruise this summer?' Lend it hell hotels aren't built just for dogs and if they can't afford to put up in Paris they can stay in their own rotten hole. An apartment's holy I should have felt raped . . . It's like Dédé. 'You mustn't let yourself be eaten up,' she tells me. But she'd be delighted to swallow me whole. 'Have you an evening coat you can lend me? You never go out.' No I never go out but I did go out: they're my dresses my coats they remind me of masses of things I don't want a strumpet to take my place in them. And afterwards they'd smell. If I were to die Mama and Nanard would share my leavings. No no I want to live until the moths have eaten the lot or else if I have cancer I'll destroy them all. I've had enough of people making a good thing out of me – Dédé worst of all. She drank my whiskey she showed off in my convertible. Now she's playing the great-hearted friend. But she never bothered to ring me from Courchevel tonight of all nights. When her cuckold of a husband is travelling and she's bored why yes then she brings her fat backside here even when I don't want to see her at all. But it's New Year's Day I'm alone I'm eating my heart out. She's dancing she's having fun she doesn't think of me for a single minute. Nobody ever thinks of me. As if I were wiped off the face of the earth. As if I had never existed. Do I exist? Oh! I pinched myself so hard I shall have a bruise.

What silence! Not a car left not a footstep in the street not a sound in the house the silence of death. The silence of a death chamber and their eyes on me their eyes that condemn me unheard and without appeal. Oh, how strong they are! Everything they felt remorse for they clapped it on to my back the perfect scapegoat and at last they could invent an excuse for their hatred. My grief has not lessened it. Yet I should have thought the devil himself would have been sorry for me.

All my life it will be two o'clock in the afternoon one Tuesday in June. 'Mademoiselle is too fast asleep I can't get her to wake up.' My heart missed a beat I rushed in calling, 'Sylvie are you ill?' She looked as though she were asleep she was still warm. It had been all over some hours before the doctor told me. I screamed I went up and down the room like a madwoman. Sylvie Sylvie why have you done this to me? I can see her now calm relaxed and me out of my mind and the note for her father that didn't mean a thing I tore it up it was all part of the act it was only an act I was sure I am sure – a mother knows her own daughter – she had not meant to die but she had overdone the dose she was dead how appalling! It's too easy with these drugs anyone can get just like that: these teenage girls will play at suicide for a mere nothing: Sylvie went along with the fashion – she never woke up. And they all came they kissed Sylvie not one of them kissed me and my mother shouted at me 'You've killed her!' My mother my own mother. They made her be quiet but their faces their silence the weight of their silence. Yes, if I were one of those mothers who get up at seven in the morning she would have been saved I live according to another rhythm there's nothing criminal about that how could I have guessed? I was always there when she came back from school many mothers can't say as much always ready to talk to question her it was she who shut herself up in her room pretending she wanted to work. I never failed her. And my mother she who neglected me left me by myself how she dared! I couldn't manage any reply my head was spinning I no longer knew where I was. 'If I'd gone to give her a kiss that night when I came in ...' But I didn't want to wake her and during the afternoon she had seemed to me almost cheerful ... Those days, what a torment! A score of times I thought I was going to crack up. School friends teachers put flowers on the coffin without addressing a word to me: if a girl kills herself the mother is guilty: that's the way their minds worked out of hatred for their own mothers. All in at the kill. I almost let myself be got down. After the funeral I fell ill. Over and over again I said to myself, 'If I had got up at seven ... If I had gone to give her a kiss when I came in ...'

It seemed to me that everybody had heard my mother's shout I didn't dare go out any more I crept along by the wall the sun clamped me in the pillory I thought people were looking at me whispering pointing enough of that enough I'd rather die this minute than live through that time again. I lost more than twenty pounds, a skeleton, my sense of balance went I staggered. 'Psychosomatic,' said the doctor. Tristan gave me money for the nursing home. You'd never believe the questions I asked myself it might have driven me crazy. A phony suicide she had meant to hurt someone – who? I hadn't watched her closely enough I ought never to have left her for a moment I ought to have had her followed held an inquiry unmasked the guilty person a boy or a girl maybe that whore of a teacher. 'No Madame there was no one in her life.' They wouldn't yield an inch the two bitches and their eyes were murdering me: they all of them keep up the conspiracy of lies even beyond death itself. But they didn't deceive me. I know. At her age and with things as they are today it's impossible that there was no one. Perhaps she was pregnant or she'd fallen into the clutches of a lezzy or she'd got in with an immoral lot someone was blackmailing her and having her threatening to tell me everything. Oh, I must stop picturing things. You could have told me everything my Sylvie I would have got you out of that filthy mess. It must certainly have been a filthy mess for her to have written to Albert, *Papa please forgive me but I can't bear it any more.* She couldn't talk to him or to the others: they tried to get to her but they were strangers. I was the only one she could have confided in.

Without them. Without their hatred. Bastards! You nearly got me down but you didn't quite succeed. I'm not your scapegoat: your remorse – I've thrown it off. I've told you what I think of you each one has had his dose and I'm not afraid of your hatred I walk clean through it. Bastards! They are the ones who killed her. They flung mud at me they put her against me they treated her as a martyr that flattered her all girls adore playing the martyr: she took her part seriously she distrusted me she told me nothing. Poor pet. She needed my support my advice they deprived her of them they condemned her to silence she couldn't get herself out of her mess all by herself she set up this act and it killed her. Murderers! They killed Sylvie my little Sylvie my darling. I loved you. No mother on earth could have been more devoted: I never thought of anything but your own good. I open the photograph album I look at all the Sylvies. The rather drawn child's face the closed face of the adolescent. Looking deep into the eyes of my seventeen-year-old girl they murdered I say 'I was the best of mothers. You would have thanked me later on.'

Crying has comforted me and I'm beginning to feel sleepy. I mustn't go to sleep in this armchair I should wake everything would be mucked up all over again. Take my suppositories go to bed. Set the alarm clock for noon to have time to get myself ready. I must win. A man in the house my little boy I'll kiss at bedtime all this unused affection. And then it would mean rehabilitation. What? I'm going to sleep I'm relaxing. It'll be a swipe in the eye for them. Tristan is somebody they respect him. I want him to bear witness for me: they'll be forced to do me justice. I'll call him. Convince him this very night.

'Was it you who phoned me? Oh, I thought it was you. You were asleep forgive me but I'm glad to hear your voice it's so revolting tonight nobody's given the slightest sign of life yet they know that when you've had a great sorrow you can't bear celebrations all this noise these lights did you notice Paris has never been so lit up as this year they've money to waste it would be better if they were to reduce the rates I shut myself up at home so as not to see it. I can't get off to sleep I'm too sad too lonely I brood about things I must talk it over with you without any quarrelling a good friendly talk listen now what I have to say to you is really very important I shan't be able to get a wink until it's settled. You're listening to me, right? I've been thinking it over all night I had nothing else to do and I assure you this is an absurd position it can't go on like this after all we are still married what a waste these two apartments you could sell yours for at least twenty million and I'd not get in your way never fear no question of taking up married life again we're no longer in love I'd shut myself up in the room at the back don't interrupt you could have all the Fanny Hills you like I don't give a hoot but since we're still friends there's no reason why we shouldn't live under the same roof. And it's essential for Francis. Just think of him for a moment I've been doing nothing else all night and I'm tearing myself to pieces. It's bad for a child to have parents who are separated they grow sly vicious untruthful they get complexes they don't develop properly. I want Francis to develop properly. You have no right to deprive him of a real home . . . Yes yes we do have to go over all this again you always get out of it but this time I insist on your listening to me. It's too selfish indeed it's even unnatural to deprive a son of his mother a mother of her son. For no reason. I've no vices I don't drink I don't drug and you've admitted I was the most devoted of mothers. Well then? Don't interrupt. If you're thinking about your fun I tell you again I shan't prevent you from having girls. Don't tell me I'm impossible to live with that I ate you up that I wore you out. Yes I was rather difficult it's natural for me to take the bit between my teeth: but if you'd had a little patience and if you'd tried to understand me and had known how to talk to me instead of growing pig-headed things would have gone along better between us you're not a saint either so don't you think it: anyhow that's all water under the bridge: I've changed: as you know very well I've suffered I've matured I can stand things I used not to be able to stand let me speak you don't have to be afraid of scenes it'll be an easygoing coexistence and the child will be happy as he has a right to be I can't see what possible objection you can have ... Why isn't this a time for talking it over? It's a time that suits me beautifully. You can give up five minutes of sleep for me after all for my part I shan't get a wink until the matter's settled don't always be so selfish it's too dreadful to prevent people sleeping it sends them out of their minds I can't bear it. Seven years now I've been rotting here all alone like an outcast and that filthy gang laughing at me you certainly owe me my revenge let me speak you owe me a great deal you know because you gave me the madly-in-love stuff I ditched Florent and broke with my friends and now you leave me flat all your friends turn their backs on me: why did you pretend to love me? Sometimes I wonder whether it wasn't a put-up job ... Yes a put-up job – it's so unbelievable that terrific passion and now this dropping me ... You hadn't realized? Hadn't realized what? Don't you tell me again that I married you out of interest I had Florent I could have had barrowloads and get this straight the idea of being your wife didn't dazzle me at all you're not Napoleon whatever you may think don't tell me that again or I shall scream you didn't say anything but I can hear you turning the words over in your mouth don't say them it's untrue it's so untrue it makes you scream you gave me the madly-in-love jazz and I fell for it ... No don't say listen Murielle to me I know your answers by heart you've gone over and over them a hundred times no more guff it doesn't wash with me and don't you put on that exasperated look yes I said that exasperated look I can see you in the receiver. You've been even more of a cad than Albert he was young when we married you were forty-five you ought to understand the nature of your responsibilities. But still all right the past's past. I promise you I shan't reproach you. We wipe everything out we set off again on a fresh footing I can be sweet and charming you know if people aren't too beastly to me. So come on now tell me it's agreed tomorrow we'll settle the details.

'Swine! You're taking your revenge you're torturing me because I haven't drooled in admiration before you but as for me money doesn't impress me nor fine airs nor fine words. "Never not for anything on earth" we'll see all right we'll see. I shall stand up for myself. I'll talk to Francis I'll tell him what you are. And if I killed myself in front of him do you think that would be a pretty thing for him to remember? ... No it's not blackmail you silly bastard with the life I lead it wouldn't mean a thing to me to do myself in. You mustn't push people too far they reach a point when they're capable of anything indeed there are mothers who kill themselves with their children ...'

Swine! Turd! He's hung up ... He doesn't answer he won't answer. Swine. Oh! My heart's failing I'm going to die. It hurts it hurts too much they're slowly torturing me to death I can't bear it any longer I'll kill myself in his drawing room I'll slash my veins when they come back there'll be blood everywhere and I shall be dead ... Oh! I hit it too hard I've cracked my skull it's them I ought to bash. Head against the wall no no I shan't go mad they shan't let me down I'll stand up for myself I'll find weapons. What weapons swine swine I can't breathe my heart's going to give I must calm down ...

Oh God. Let it be true that you exist. Let there be a heaven and a hell I'll stroll along the walks of Paradise with my little boy and my beloved daughter and they will all be writhing in the flames of envy I'll watch them roasting and howling I'll laugh I'll laugh and the children will laugh with me. You owe me this revenge, God. I insist that you grant it me.

Translated by Patrick O'Brien

THOMAS OWEN

The Sow

The fog would not clear for some time. Quite the contrary – it was growing thicker all the time. The patches were becoming more frequent, denser, resisting the dual beams of the headlights, the sudden whiteness of a wall looming out of the night. It was becoming more and more dangerous to drive. It was as if those ethereal floating entities, springing up all over the countryside, were calling to each other, reuniting, melting little by little into a soon impenetrable mass.

Arthur Crowley had already dropped his speed. He constantly had to break sharply now before imaginary obstacles. One time he thought he saw the back of a lorry with no lights, or a tree blocking the road, or even things that made no sense round here – a dinghy, a hearse, a troupe of scouts cycling . . . He realized he could not get the better of the nauseous fatigue that was overwhelming him. He was suddenly frightened of continuing on his way. In any case, he would not get there now until the middle of the night. He dropped his speed even more and decided to stop the moment an opportunity presented itself.

Very fortunately, it did not take long. To his right, set back a little from the road, a neon sign pierced the fog. He headed in that direction, along a recently laid road, poorly surfaced, with verges of loose soil.

He arrived at the Poppy. It was a rather large cottage, of recent construction, built on the edge of an old farm, with buildings further back that formed vague and gloomy shapes in the fog.

Arthur Crowley followed the Parking sign. A black car was parked on the zigzagging concrete. He pulled in next to it. With the headlights off, the darkness instantly enveloped him. He got out and his eyes soon adjusted to the strange grey half-light. As he slammed the door, someone, pulling aside a curtain, watched from a window.

He soon reached the building by a path of neatly compacted ground brick and pushed open the door. It was a bistro like those thousands of others around the world lining main roads. A bar, shelves laden down with garishly labelled bottles, a jukebox gleaming like an electric cooker, music blaring out of it. A few tables covered with red and white gingham table-cloths. Wooden beams, rather too pale, in the ceiling.

Arthur Crowley had closed the door behind him and stood still, hesitant, inspecting this place where an atmosphere that was both rustic and Americanized held sway, to deplorable effect it seemed to him.

Sat at a table near the bar, leaning on her elbows with a cowardly air, a woman who was still young, the manageress no doubt, was chatting with a customer. She was plump, attractive, and turned to face the new arrival with laughing eyes that were puppyish but arrogant. She had dark, luxuriant hair, and was clearly a little the worse for wear. The customer opposite her was a fat ginger, a complexion the shade of brick, with a narrow-minded air and a low forehead, like a figure in a Flemish expressionist painting. In his fat mitt, he was clumsily shaking some dice, which he blew on and rolled into a wooden tray lined with green serge.

Arthur Crowley gave a nod of greeting and made for the bar, which he leaned against. The woman gave him a questioning look, without moving. He asked for a beer.

The manageress patted her partner's glowing cheek fondly for him to be patient, and got up to serve this unexpected customer.

While she was popping the cap from a bottle, Crowley asked if he could be put up for the night.

She burst into loud laughter, and, speaking to the ginger:

'He's asking if I can put him up!'

But the dimwit was lost in some inner reverie, motionless, hand on cheek, and didn't respond.

'I'm sorry,' the woman said to Arthur Crowley, 'but this isn't really a hotel.'

She spoke kindly, annoyed at her own lack of civility. She added:

'You see what I mean . . . But if you wish to stay the night, that can be arranged.'

He explained his need to stop because of the fog, and his intention to set off again fairly early the next day.

'Perfect. I'll show you to your room. Go and fetch your luggage, then. Time enough to keep that old curmudgeon waiting.'

It was all quickly taken care of and Arthur Crowley soon took possession of a very plain, cold and neat room. He pulled back the covers, as he usually did when travelling, and found the sheets to be clean, but a little damp.

The manageress watched him do so with a mischievous smile.

'Everything all right?' she asked.

'Of course. It's perfect.'

'You're not going to bed right now? You don't need me to tuck you in?'

'No. I'll go and finish my drink and have a bite. If, that is, you have something to offer me.'

'People end up finding everything they want here.'

As they were coming down the stairs, there was a great commotion downstairs and three men entered, talking loudly and giving each other friendly shoves. They greeted the manageress warmly, with more displays of friendship, tokens of affection and caresses.

The fat ginger, who knew them, became a little bolder when he saw they were not being so shy, and went to join his fat palping hands with theirs.

'Quiet, quiet!' The bitch was laughing as she calmed them down, not for the first time. 'Will you behave yourselves. We have guests!'

They piped down, each of them taking a seat at the bar, and Arthur Crowley commiserated with the merry band.

They had a few drinks. They joked around a fair bit and one of the new arrivals finally declared, after a pause:

'Now we're going to play the Sow.'

He called for the tray and the dice. The manageress shook her head, as if to say 'not in front of this guy', but the joker did not give a hoot. On the contrary, he asked Crowley:

'Will you play with us?'

'All right. But what does the game involve?'

'It's a secret.'

'Do tell.'

'The winner earns the right to go and see the Sow.'

'What's that?'

'You find out if you win.'

The stake was modest, and Arthur Crowley tempted. He played, won and was roundly applauded.

The manageress led him outside. Following her lead, he crossed a courtyard of rounded cobblestones in the direction of the farm buildings, which one could barely discern in the darkness.

He felt an electric torch being slipped into his hand.

'The battery isn't new any more,' the woman said. 'Don't waste it.'

He fiddled with the switch; a ring of light pierced the fog and danced for a moment on a building.

'It's there. I'll leave you to it.'

He would have liked to hold her back, but she had already slipped away. He heard her running in the dark, then going back into the house, its door opening for a moment to make a hole of light in the gloom.

He headed towards a sort of barn, with whitewashed walls, its entrance opening beneath a large black trellis. Inside, there was a kind of storeroom where he could see a ladder hanging on the wall, some barrels, some empty bottles, some tubs, a hosepipe and even a lady's bicycle.

At the back, a low door. The pigsty, without a doubt. He pulled back the bolt and gently pushed.

The smell of a stable hit him in the face, and the beam from his torch, cast into the gloom of this place, revealed a pale pink mass on the yellow straw which he struggled to make out at first. But he soon had to bow to the evidence. There was, before him, lying curled up in a ball, a naked woman, ageless, with a mop of blond hair, fat shoulders, and a big floppy behind. She was sound asleep and there was something poignant about her strong and regular breathing.

Arthur Crowley stayed there watching her for quite some time, stunned and sickened at the same time. He felt a sense of unease, an indefinable discomfort.

Disturbed in her sleep by the bright light, the woman stretched, grunted, looked as if she was figuring out where she was.

He turned off the torch and beat his retreat, discouraged.

Who was that old wreck? What was she doing there? To what appalling contemplations had she been doomed? How could such a thing be possible?

He returned, thoughtful and ashamed, and, as he entered, they all searched his face for signs of emotion.

'That was quick!' said the manageress.

'Was she asleep?' asked the ginger.

'Did you make her get up on her hooves?' asked another. 'There's a sharp stick behind the door. They use it for tenderizing meat. Then she raises herself up on her hands and knees.'

Arthur Crowley kept quiet, humiliated and indignant. He could not have spoken. He turned his back on them.

'In a nutshell,' said someone, 'you missed the best part of the show.'

'Another time,' said the manageress.

He went up to his room. He wanted either to cry or to vomit. He got undressed and slid into the freezing bed.

Down below, they were laughing. At him, no doubt. A little later, he heard several people crossing the courtyard, entering the barn, raising their voices, laughing and laughing . . .

He imagined what they could be doing to the Sow . . .

The spectacle of that unfortunate creature haunted him all night. His imagination, traumatized by that sight, which he was now reproaching himself for cutting short out of cowardice, filled his sleep with nightmares of harrowing sadness. The fate of that prisoner, treated like an animal, left him utterly ashamed of himself.

He pictured again that pale, fleshy mass, indecently spread out in the straw. It was as if she was dragging herself awkwardly towards him, crawling on her knees and forearms, revealing an imploring face of touching stupidity. He wanted, in his dream, to show he wanted to help, to give her a hand getting up, but his gesture led only to confusion.

The 'sow' wrapped her big pink arms around his legs, toppling him over beside her in the litter, then giving out cries of pleasure that were joined by the laughter of the drinking companions, appearing out of nowhere, jeering at her cruelly, their boorish, laughing heads squeezed into the doorway.

*

The day came at last. Arthur Crowley woke up, his nose drawn to the fine smell of fresh coffee.

A glance out the window revealed the countryside clear of all mist, a great plain of meadows scarred with wire fences, and in the distance a row of willows with a short crop of bushy leaves.

Across the courtyard, the barn he had entered, to his shame, a few hours earlier. He felt utterly nauseous at the sight of it. How were such things possible, and what monstrous conspiracy kept them from being denounced? Despite his rigorous fidelity to the principle of never meddling in other people's business, he had a strong feeling he was going to make an exception today to the line he had drawn for himself. Even if it meant upsetting his travel plans with a further delay, he had to inform the police about what was happening in this place. He in no way felt bound by any sense of solidarity with people who had very unwisely let him in on their secrets.

His suitcase packed, he went downstairs. The manageress, in a little morning négligé, greeted him nonchalantly and asked if had slept well. Did he want some bacon or ham and eggs?

'No ham! No bacon . . . !'

He couldn't have. No doubt he never could ever again.

'Scrambled egg, bread and coffee – lots of coffee!'

While she went off to the kitchen to prepare his meal, he headed out to put his case in the car. How the countryside had changed since the evening before! What spell do the fog and the night cast to make places so menacing, until daylight returns them to their former tranquillity?

Birds sang in the hedgerows by the roadside. A red lorry with a trailer slowly went by, overtaken by a small, fast car. A dog barked in the distance . . .

He crossed the courtyard of rounded cobblestones. The barn was drawing him to it, irresistibly. He gave into temptation and pushed at the door. This was indeed where he had entered a few hours earlier. The same dirt floor. The same stored tools. The ladder on the wall, the tubs, the barrels, the plastic pipe, the bottles . . .

He opened the door at the back. He recognized the smell of pine, straw and manure. There was plenty of light from a side window. His heart beat fast. He looked . . .

An enormous sow was getting to its hooves as it grunted. She turned her revolting snout towards him, looked at him with her beady little eyes, a perverse glint in her eye.

'Breakfast is served!' the manageress's voice called from outside.

He backed out of there, fascinated by this animal, the sight of which had thrown him into unspeakable confusion.

He weighed up the shocking two-faced nature of appearances, depending on whether it was dark or whether the sun was shining. He would have liked to find reasons to put his mind at ease, but he only felt half-relieved.

'Coffee!' the owner called out again.

In haste, one last time, he had another look in the pigsty to reassure himself, to never have to think about any of this ever again. The Sow was lying on her side, showing him her teated belly.

Everything was fine. There was no possible mistake. His imagination alone had created this horrid story.

And yet, and yet ... What had become of the lady's bicycle he'd seen the night before against that wall?

Translated by Will McMorran

HENRI THOMAS

The Offensive

The voice of the captain, which had sounded so loud in the company offices a short time ago, seemed thin and weak in this forest. Perhaps he really had been made hoarse by the night's march in the rain and the one-hour rest against the dripping banks of the forest path. But this was no excuse. In fact for Claude, it was yet another telling sign, this sensitivity of the captain's to bad weather. Everything was weak: the captain's voice, the ludicrous little offensive meant as help to Poland, already defeated, the arming of the troops, the fortifications left behind – and, behind these fortifications, the whole country, peasant homes, small-town cafés, and the thoughts, dreams, reason and will of the people. Even the dullest soldier should have realized that all the strength was on the other side, beyond the forests which blotted out the horizon. Instead of their taking in the situation, the attack was on, ridiculously on, in short scurries, from tree to tree.

'First section, forward!' said the captain's voice.

The first section moved off in single file beneath the trees, the sergeant who had studied for the priesthood in command; Claude saw him leave with long strides and a devout air. It would be all the same to him if he stepped on a mine.

'Second section, forward!'

This section was commanded by an Arab sergeant; Claude did not remember his name.

The captain's voice no longer trembled so much; it just seemed weaker than ever.

Claude was in the last section, the fourth. The order 'Fourth section, forward!' reached down into every nerve. 'Fourth' was no longer just an ordinal number, one in a series. 'Fourth' meant him, Claude.

He came last in the section, in charge of supplies, of which he had only the vaguest idea, and as bearer of the section's barbed-wire cutters. The section was commanded by the Corsican sergeant, Fremigacci, who moved off heavily, bent forward, like the dolt he was.

During the one-hour halt on the forest track, the lieutenant had explained that the company had a mission to rendezvous with the 21st Company of Light Infantry, engaged in fighting in the forest, from whom there had been no news.

'And another company from the 23rd, right behind us, will start out on our trail tomorrow,' said Claude, who was in the little group surrounding the lieutenant.

Nobody had noticed his words, presumably no one had heard them. Except that Sergeant Fremigacci had let out a slight grunt, which probably included the odd word, amongst incomprehensible Corsican oaths.

For some days now, Claude had hated Fremigacci. His earlier antipathy towards the Corsican sergeant had turned to hate when the company had been billeted in an evacuated Lorraine village, close at hand to the frontier. Waking one morning in the barn, Claude felt a rather sharp pain near the bottom of his right calf, just where the legging covers the boot laces. He did not look for the source, because of the bother of unrolling the legging and then rolling it up again. But he wondered about it as he made his way to the cattle trough to shave. He dragged his foot a little. Fremigacci, standing at the entrance of the barn, saw him leave. Claude did not have long to wait for the consequences. At eleven o'clock that day Fremigacci designated Claude to get the soup. The canteen was in a small hollow at least a kilometre to the rear of the village. Claude had done this fatigue two days before; he knew that his turn should not have come up again for another week. But he said nothing, having immediately understood. A protest would have got him nowhere, or would have gone too far. On his way back from the canteen, with soup rations for ten men, so difficult to carry across the fields, and with three canteens of wine on a bandolier, he felt his foot really hurting; the pain made him limp slightly. Even as he sat in the barn during the meal it made itself felt again in hot stabs every time he moved his leg.

'They've only got thirty guns over there,' said Fremigacci, when the meal was almost finished.

'And how many have we got on our side?' asked Claude.

'Didn't you hear the big guns of the Maginot line on your way over to get the soup?' said Fremigacci. 'Don't worry, you'll have the chance to hear them.'

'Don't be too sure,' said Claude.

Several quarts of wine had put Fremigacci in a good mood. He laughed: 'Nothing's ever sure with you: but just wait a while.'

They left the village at nightfall, and around midnight the company passed near the overthrown frontier post lying across the trench.

The distance between Claude and the last soldier in the section was becoming greater. It was Dauphin, a hairdresser from Lyon; he marched bent over, not turning round, with a heavy cartridge-pouch on each hip. As for the other soldiers in the section, even if they had turned round they would not have seen Claude; the trees grew close together, and bushes and high ferns rose out of the undergrowth. They left the paths, and the section followed a ravine, halfway up the slope; further on the ravine seemed to close up, and the trees, including many firs, formed a sombre barrier.

The big guns of the Maginot line could certainly be heard now. Streams of shells shot through the sky above the forest; and the whistle of each one ended in a dull explosion a long way past the dark forest barrier. After a short while Claude no longer hoped the firing would soon cease.

Shells shot across from the other direction, animating the sky even more. But there was no plane to be heard; the sky was grey and low.

Claude did not deliberately break away from the rest of the section until he heard the whistle and zip of many bullets biting into the trees. Up till then he had walked with his body almost upright; he was not carrying cartridge-pouches as Dauphin was. He doubled up, dragging his rifle butt along the ground, and, as though forced by gravity, turned towards the bottom of the ravine.

He made his way down from tree to tree, choosing the biggest ones, settled in against the roots, huddled up at the foot of the huge trunk, and rested a while there. The four sections scattered through the forest could not really have been far ahead of him; they were rather at about the same height on both sides of the ravine, to judge from their voices, which he heard faintly at times. They seemed to have come to a stop. On his left he heard the trigger catch of a machine gun being brought into action, and the gun began firing. Another gun started up on his right, and then another further to the left, and yet another. The noise of the company's four machine gunners mixed in a continual din.

They were not in front of Claude; in fact they were considerably behind him, because the gunfire whistled over him; he had the impression they were criss-crossing from one side of the ravine to the other. He went down further, and reached the bottom. A little stream flowed between enormous rocks hanging with damp mosses. Claude slid between the rocks despite the encumbrance of his rifle and kitbag. Here he could not be hit even by stray shots from any of the machine gunners; the rocks were piled up, forming hiding places whose inner walls had never been touched by rain. Claude took down the bag from his shoulders, and shoved it into a recess where he then lay down, his head on the kitbag, his rifle by his side. The machine-gun volleys were interspersed now with silences, in which Claude heard, with immense pleasure, the sound of rain falling on dead leaves and the stream murmuring nearby. Day at the bottom of the ravine was a grey twilight and Claude could no longer see the sky. Way up above, as in another world, the heavy artillery's projectiles went on with their din. Then suddenly something else, and much closer, happened: a rapid flash in the twilight obscurity, an explosion followed by echoes, then another flash, an explosion, the sound of a tree cracking on the top of the left slope. The Germans shot off small shells in the direction of the four sections. In panic the machine gunners started up their firing again, without a break.

Claude smiled. Alone, out in front of the company, quite sheltered from this blind shooting, he sized up his situation. It was good. He had not known such security for weeks; since the days he spent alone in the farm which served as headquarters for the company, when the others were digging trenches several kilometres away. He was guarding the provisions depot, and made himself chips every night, and ate the apples, pears and plums from the neighbouring orchard. War had been declared some days before, but not one gunshot had been heard, only a few bursts from aeroplanes high up in the sky, pale blue at the end of autumn. At that time Claude thought that the war would end even before it started and, as he had written to a friend, that they would see Hitler, Stalin, Daladier and the rest 'grow old and disappear without anything having been fundamentally changed'.

But now the situation was obviously different, and did not correspond with his forecasts. The regiment had entered Germany; the far end of the ravine where Claude at that moment lay in hiding *was* Germany, and shells continued to burst and light up the higher reaches of the ravine. And yet the situation was not essentially that much different; clearer, that was all. Up there they went on with their imbecilities, and here, protected from rain as from shellfire, Claude was turning things over in his mind. The only thing to do was to stand aside, to keep out of the way of their madness.

Hitler, Daladier and Stalin could grow older and get better or worse, it was all the same to Claude. The important thing was to be in Paris once again, sitting on the bank of the Seine in the sun. He did not give a damn whether the authorities would be German or French. If the real fighting started right now they would be German, of that he was sure. And bad luck for idiots like Fremigacci.

As he turned round to change his position in his rocky hiding place, Claude's right foot hurt him a lot; the fiery pain shot up as far as his knee.

As a prisoner in a camp at the other end of Germany, the days would pass, he would dream of Paris, the war would finish, and he would find himself in Paris sooner or later. He had succeeded in the most difficult task – of separating from the company with complete discretion. Now he had only to be picked up by the German patrol without being shot at. Surely that would not be too difficult, and the awful moment would not last long; he would just have to make a few signs and perhaps shout a word or two. Claude lost himself in memories of the schoolroom for a moment and constructed in German an elementary and precise phrase. Besides there was no hurry: he had the following day and night to prepare himself. By dawn he would be far away, he would be a prisoner.

He unbuckled his kit and ate half a bar of chocolate and a big piece of bread; using his drinking can he drew some water from the stream flowing under the mosses. There was no doubt he had a touch of fever, for he drank an enormous amount. Then he lay down again in his hole in the rocks. The explosions along the top of each side of the ravine made time pass quickly; he strained to guess the spot where the shells were falling, and to make out the positioning of the gunners. The machine guns had hardly stopped their chatter since morning, and with it were mingled single rifleshots. Now and then a broken branch rolled gently down the slope, like a man sliding down a tree.

It was possible to go quite a way along the bed of the stream without being hit. However, he would keep his helmet on, leaving most of his equipment where he had been hiding. For a moment sunlight lit the bottom of the ravine; dead leaves glistened, still damp from rain; and lifting his head Claude saw a hole of blue sky through the trees. How beautiful the Seine was in such weather! He was on his way up to see his young girlfriend, who was a potter and lived in the Rue de l'Échaudé; autumn sunshine lit the bed and the bowl of fruit on the table. On Claude's last leave it was already autumn in Paris.

He would never be able to tell anybody what he was doing at that moment. Certainly not her. If only the others up there, and in all the warring countries, had been less stupid; he would so much have loved to stay with them, sharing worthwhile risks, and taking the lead in good causes. Instead of cutting each other to pieces they should practise peaceful rivalry, convince the world by their example that they were nations capable of sorting themselves out, of doing away with unemployment, of making the most of their resources ... In such a state of affairs it would be possible to tell the truth. What Claude was doing now was the consequence of a just view of things; no one could reproach him for acting on his convictions. And fear? Everybody was afraid when the company set off on an attack, even the sergeant who was going to become a priest.

Or to put it bluntly, cynically, Claude saw himself stretched out on the bed with his sweetheart in the sunshine of a summer to come. Suddenly he would say: 'I deserted.' He would see how she took it.

Fear? He was not afraid when he came out from his hole in the rocks as night fell. He did not even take the precaution of following the very bottom of the ravine. There he would have had to walk over stones, taking care not to slip; and his foot hurt too much.

As the darkness grew, so the light from exploding shells became more intense, reddening and seeming closer. Each time one went off Claude threw himself forward on to his hands, then got up again and walked on. But when he heard the sound of wheels on the pebbles he lay completely flat, and did not budge for quite some time. He was at the top of the slope at the side of the ravine when he heard voices. He could not make out what they were saying; they were impatient voices, shouting orders. Then there was only the noise of the wheels. The vehicles of his company had all been left strung out at the last encampment.

Had it not been night-time, Claude might have climbed up the slope, unarmed and with his hands in the air. At any rate the terrible moment would soon be over. Claude was behind the German lines. The further he went on the better it would be for him. Surely they would not shoot at him well inside the lines. He would drag his foot; a sick, lost soldier.

At that moment, once again on his way, he stumbled into something which made him leap back. Then moving very slowly, with his face close to the ground, he looked to see what it was. A huge cable, clearly visible in the darkness, made its way down the slope and became lost in the depths of the ravine, which it must have crossed and come up the other side.

It could not have been a mine; it would have exploded. It was the cable for the German field telephone. Claude grasped it in both hands and felt its wrinkled casing.

Christiane brought in the coffee, real coffee which Claude had got by using a little flattery at the grocery shop in the Rue de l'Échaudé, where he was registered on his return to Paris. The sunlight of autumn 1945 gently lit the large room, a corner of which was stacked with flower vases and ashtrays, some of Christiane's work, brought from the pottery kiln the day before.

'I had a lot of trouble cutting the cable,' Claude went on. 'I'd never have succeeded if I hadn't had the wire cutters. And then I was scared I might electrocute myself. The hardest part was finding the section again. I'd walked for longer than I thought, I was well inside the German lines. And my foot hurt more and more. You've seen the small scar; it hasn't gone after five years.'

Christiane stroked his hair; he was lying on the bed, his arms folded.

'In fact, you could say it all hung by a thread,' he said quite dreamily.

'You didn't have to cut it,' said Christiane. 'That wasn't part of your duties.'

'Oh, my duties, I was never too clear exactly what they were. You know, one makes things up as one goes along in such cases. I might just as easily have deserted. Nobody would have suspected. I'd have been a prisoner for five years, instead of going through Dunkirk, England, North Africa.'

'You'd have died in captivity,' said Christiane. 'You're too fond of your bit of freedom to stand being held prisoner.'

'Nevertheless, I must say I regretted not having been captured, once I was back with the section. That week in the forest was the worst in the whole war for me. I could hardly move my foot, and that bastard of a Corsican sergeant refused to believe me; he kept sending me three kilometres to get the soup. It's quite simple. He'd got it into his head that I wanted to desert. If I hadn't brought back a bit of the telephone cable he'd have sent me to the commanding officer. Absent from the section one day and one night, that was serious. Funniest thing of all is that he himself was taken prisoner later on in Belgium.'

'Perhaps he wanted to give himself up too . . .'

'"Too" . . . that's a bit much,' laughed Claude. 'I never wanted to surrender.'

'Poor love,' said Christiane. 'Even if you had, it wouldn't have changed the end result of the war; the whole French army surrendered afterwards.'

'I didn't,' said Claude, 'because I went to Algeria. But I admit that I'd had enough in that blessed forest. And then my foot hurting so . . .'

'How horrible,' said Christiane. 'Something working its way up under your skin!'

'Like those insects that burrow into the flesh of cattle,' said Claude more precisely. 'You should have seen the face of the male nurse at the medical centre. He had to stun the creature with ether to make its claws let go, and pull it out slowly with tweezers.'

'Oh, keep quiet,' said Christiane, 'it makes me feel ill. I'll dream about it.'

'In the long run,' Claude went on after a pause, 'I've been lucky. I've seen a few countries, and then I've found you again, and Paris. Listen, I was always thinking about Paris on days like today, a beautiful sun, not too hot ...'

'You only have to look at the lines in your hand,' said Christiane. 'You'll always be lucky. Show me your palm again ... No, the left one, the palm of reality.'

Translated by Ken Thomson

MARGUERITE DURAS

The Boa

It happened in a large town in a French colony, around 1928.

On Sunday afternoons, the other girls of the Barbet boarding school would go out. Those girls – those girls had 'guardians' in town. They returned in the evening, gorged on cinema, on tea at 'The Pagoda', on swims in the pool, on trips in the car, on games of tennis.

No guardian for me. I stayed with Mlle Barbet all week and on Sundays.

We would go to the Botanical Gardens. It cost nothing, and it allowed *Mamoiselle Barbet* to charge my mother supplementary expenses in the name of 'Sunday outings'.

We would thus go to see the boa gulp down its Sunday chicken. During the week, the boa skipped his meal. He was given only dead meat or sickly chickens. But on Sundays his chicken was well and truly alive, because people preferred it that way.

We would also go to see the caimans. Twenty years earlier, another caiman – a great-uncle or perhaps the father of those that were there in 1928 – had severed the leg of an officer in the colonial forces. It had severed it at the height of the groin and had thereby ruined the career of this poor soldier, who had wanted to play at tickling its mouth with his leg, little realizing that when a crocodile plays, he plays in cold blood. Ever since, railings had been erected around the caiman pool and one could now observe them in perfect safety, sleeping with eyes half-closed and dreaming intensely of their past crimes.

We would also go to see the masturbating gibbons, or the black panthers from the mangrove swamps, dying parched on a cement floor, refusing to look through the iron railings at the face of men who take such sadistic delight in their suffering, and staring instead at the green mouths of Asian rivers teeming with monkeys.

If we arrived too late, we would find the boa already somnolent on a bed of chicken feathers. Even so, we would still stay a good while in front of its cage. There was nothing left to see, but we knew what had happened a moment before, and both of us would stand before the boa, lost in thought. This peace after that murder. This impeccable crime, committed in the warm snow of those feathers, which added a fascinating realness to the chicken's innocence. This stainless crime, without a trace of blood spilt, without remorse. This order, after the catastrophe, peace in the chamber of crime.

Coiled around itself, black, gleaming with a dew purer than that of the morning on a hawthorn, an admirable shape, plump in its roundness, gentle and muscular, a column of black marble which would suddenly roll with an ancient weariness and finally wrap around itself, suddenly scornful of that weighty pride, its undulating slowness quivering with coiled strength, the boa incorporated the chicken in the course of a digestion of sovereign ease, as perfect as the absorption of water by the burning sands of the desert, a form of transubstantiation accomplished in sacred tranquillity. In that magnificent inner silence, the chicken became serpent. With a pleasure that could make you dizzy, the flesh of the biped flowed into that of the reptile, within that long, uniform pipe. A shape like no other, confusing, round, with no visible grip on its exterior, yet more prehensile than any talon, hand, claw, horn or fang, and yet still naked as water and as no other in all the multitude of species is naked.

Mamoiselle Barbet was, because of her age and the very advanced state of her virginity, indifferent to the boa. Personally, it had a considerable effect on me. It was a spectacle that left me preoccupied . . . which might, had I been gifted with a livelier and better more cultivated mind, with a more scrupulous soul, with a more appealing and bigger heart, have inspired me to rediscover God the Creator and the absolute division of the world between the forces of evil and powers of good, both of them eternal, and the conflict between which is at the origin of all things; or, conversely, to rebel against the contempt in which crime is held and against the value placed on innocence.

*

When we returned to the boarding school, always too soon for my liking, a cup of tea and a banana would be waiting for us in Mamoiselle Barbet's bedroom. We would eat in silence. I would then go up to my room. It would only be after a little while that Mamoiselle Barbet would call up to me. I would not reply straightaway. She would insist:

'Come and see for a moment . . .'

I would make up my mind. She would have come to get me otherwise. I would return to Mamoiselle Barbet's bedroom. I would always find her in the same place, in front of her window, smiling, in a pink slip, her shoulders bare. I would stand before her and look at her as I was supposed to do, as it was understood I would do every Sunday after she had been good enough to take me to see the boa.

'You see,' Mlle Barbet told me in a gentle voice, 'that's fine lingerie . . .'

'I can see,' I said, 'it is indeed fine lingerie, I can see . . .'

'I bought it yesterday. I love fine lingerie,' she sighed, 'the older I get, the more I love it . . .'

She held herself quite straight for me to admire, lowering her gaze lovingly upon herself. Half-naked. She had never revealed herself like this to anyone in her life, other than me. It was too late. At seventy-five years of age, she would no longer reveal herself to anyone else other than me. She revealed herself only to me in all the house, and always on Sunday afternoons, when all the other boarders were out and after the visit to the Zoo. I would have to look at her for as long as she determined.

'How I can love it so,' she said. 'I would sooner go without food . . .'

From Mlle Barbet's body there emanated a terrible smell. There was no mistaking it. The first time she revealed herself to me I finally understood the secret of the terrible smell which floated through the house; I recognized it, a smell underlying the fragrance of carnation in which she drenched herself, a smell which drifted from the wardrobes, which mingled with the dampness of the bathrooms, which stagnated, oppressively, reeking of its twenty years, in the inner hallways of the school, and, at siesta time, flowed as if through open floodgates from Mlle Barbet's black lace blouse, as she fell asleep as usual in the living room after lunch.

'Fine lingerie is important. Learn this. I learned it too late.'

I had understood the very first time. The whole house smelled of death. Mlle Barbet's secular virginity.

'To whom would I show my lingerie if not to you? To you who understands me?'

'I understand.'

'It's too late,' she moaned.

I didn't reply. She waited for a minute but to that I could not reply.

'I wasted my life' – she waited a while and added – 'he never came . . .'

That absence devoured her, that absence of the one who had never come. The pink slip, trimmed with 'priceless' lace, covered her like a shroud, swelled her like a balloon, her middle strangled by the corset. I was the only one to whom she exposed this consumed body. The others would have told their parents. As for me, even if I had told my mother, it would have been of no importance. Mlle Barbet had accepted me into her school as a favour because my mother had been very insistent. No others in the town would have agreed to take in the daughter of a native teacher for fear of compromising their schools. There was goodness in Mlle Barbet. We were complicit, she and I. I did not say anything. She did not say that my mother would wear the same dress for two years, that she wore cotton stockings, and that she sold her jewels to cover my monthly fees. And so, as we never saw my mother, and as I never spoke of my Sunday timetable – of those free but charged Sunday outings – and as I never complained, Mlle Barbet thought highly of me.

'Thank God you are here . . .'

I would stop myself from breathing. Nonetheless there was goodness in her. And in all the town her reputation spread, perfect, as virginal as her life. I said so to myself, and told myself she was old. But it did not make any difference. I would stop myself from breathing.

'What an existence . . .' she would sigh.

To get it over with, I would tell her that was rich, that she had fine lingerie and as for the rest, maybe it was not as important as she now believed, that one could not live in regret . . . She would not reply, would sigh deeply and put back on her black lace blouse, which throughout the week served as evidence of her respectability. She moved slowly. When she buttoned up the sleeves of her blouse I knew it was over. That I would be left in peace for a week.

I would return to my bedroom. I would sit outside on the terrace. I would breathe. The succession of those two spectacles, the visit to the Zoo and the contemplation of Mlle Barbet, would inevitably trigger in me a kind of negative enthusiasm.

The street would be filled with sunshine, and the tamarinds with their giant shadows cast great sprays of green scent into the houses. Soldiers of the colonial forces would pass by. I smiled at them in the hope that one would beckon to me to come down and tell me to follow him. I would stay there a long time. Sometimes a soldier smiled to me, but none of them beckoned to me.

When evening came, I would head back into that house infected with the stench of regret. It was awful. No man had beckoned to me yet. It was awful. I was thirteen, I thought it had already taken too long for me to be yet to leave that place. Once back in my room, I would lock myself in, take off my blouse and look at myself in the mirror. My breasts were neat, white. That was the only thing in my life which I enjoyed seeing in that house. Outside the house, there was the boa, here, there were my breasts. I would cry. I would think of mummy's body, which had worked so hard, at which four children had drunk and which smelled of vanilla like every inch of mummy in her patched-up dresses. Of mummy who would tell me that she would rather die than see me have a childhood as dreadful as her own, that to find a husband one had to have studied, to be able to play the piano, know a foreign language, know how to conduct oneself in a saloon, that Mamoiselle Barbet was better placed than she was to teach me these things. I believed my mother.

I would dine opposite Mamoiselle Barbet and then quickly go up to my room to avoid the return of the other boarders. I would think of the telegram I would send the next day to mummy to tell her I love her. And yet, I never did send that telegram.

So I stayed at Mamoiselle Barbet's for two years, trying to reconcile the quarter of my mother's pay with the weekly contemplation of that woman's septuagenarian virginity, until the wonderful day when, finding herself unable to carry on meeting the monthly fees, my mother, despairing, came to get me, convinced that my interrupted education would mean she would be stuck with me for the rest of her life.

It lasted for two years. Every Sunday. For two years, once a week, it was my honour to be witness first to a violent devouring, with its dazzling stages and precise contours, and then to another devouring, this one slow, shapeless, black. All this, from thirteen to fifteen years of age. I was therefore required to be present at both, on pain of no longer receiving an adequate education, of 'bringing about my own ruin and my mother's', of not finding a husband, etc...

The boa devoured and digested the chicken, regret too devoured and digested Mamoiselle Barbet, and these two devourings which regularly succeeded each other took on a new significance in my eyes, precisely because of their unfailing succession. Had I only been exposed to the first of these as a spectacle, that of the chicken by the boa, perhaps I would have always regarded the boa with a horrified bitterness for the torments it had made me endure, through my imagination, as I put myself in the chicken's place. It is possible. Had I, likewise, seen only Mamoiselle Barbet, no doubt she would have limited herself to giving me, along with a sense of the calamities that weigh on the human race, one – just as inescapable – of an imbalance in the social order, and the multiple forms of subjection that stem from this. But no, I would see them, with only rare exceptions, one after the other, on the same day, and always in the same order. Because of this succession, the sight of Mlle Barbet would send me back to my memory of the boa, the beautiful boa which, in broad daylight, in rude health, devoured the chicken, and which, by contrast, took its place in an order dazzling with radiant simplicity and native splendour. Just as Mlle Barbet, after I had seen the boa, became the ultimate horror, black and miserly, insidious – for one did not *see* the devouring of her virginity happening, one only saw its effects, breathed in its smell – a nasty, hypocritical and timid horror and, above all else, vain. How could I have remained indifferent to the succession of these two spectacles, whose connectedness, by virtue of who knows what fate, I clung on to, gasping with despair at being unable to flee the enclosed world of Mlle Barbet, nocturnal monster, without being able to reach the world I could sense, mysteriously, thanks to the boa, that diurnal monster? I imagined it, this world, stretching out, free and hard, I foresaw it as a kind of huge botanical garden where, in the freshness of fountains and ponds, in the dense shadow of the tamarind alternating with pools of intense light, there were countless carnal exchanges going on in the form of devouring, of digesting, of coupling both orgiastic and calm – of that calmness of things beneath the sun within the light, serene and unsteady with giddy simplicity. And I would stay on my balcony, stay at the confluence of these two moral extremes, and I would smile at the soldiers of the colonial forces who were the only men there ever were around the boa's cage, because it did not cost anything either to them who did not have anything either. So I would smile, like the bird trying out its wings, without knowing, believing that this was the right way to go about reaching the green paradise of that criminal boa. This is how the boa, which also terrified me, nonetheless restored, alone, my boldness and brazenness.

It intervened in my life with the force of a regularly applied educational principle or, if you prefer, with the decisive accuracy of a tuning fork for horror, which meant that I felt no real aversion except before a certain kind of horror, which one might describe as moral: of hidden ideas, hidden vices and, also, unacknowledged illness and anything which was borne shamefully and alone, and conversely I felt no horror for murderers, for example; on the contrary, I suffered for those amongst them who were locked up in prison, not for their physical self exactly, but rather for their generous and unsung temperament, stopped in its deadly tracks. How could I fail to attribute to the boa that inclination I had to acknowledge the deadly side of temperament, the boa being in my eyes the perfect image of that? Because of the boa, I swore an invincible sympathy for all living species, the whole of which seemed to me like a symphonic necessity, so much so that the loss of one of amongst them would have been enough to mutilate the whole irredeemably. I became suspicious of people who had the temerity to pronounce on those species deemed 'horrible', on 'cold and silent' serpents, on 'hypocritical and cruel' cats, etc... Only one category of human beings seemed to me truly to belong to this idea I had formed of a species, and those were of course prostitutes. Just like murderers, prostitutes (who I imagined scattered throughout the jungle of the great capital cities, hunting their prey and consuming it with the imperiousness and shamelessness that come with fatalistic temperaments) inspired in me the same admiration, and I suffered for them too because of the ignorance in which they were kept. When my mother declared that she did not think she would find anyone to marry me, Mamoiselle Barbet immediately appeared before me, and I consoled myself with the thought that there was still the brothel, which very fortunately, if it came to that, would always be there. I pictured it as a kind of temple of deflowering where, with utter purity (I only learned of the commercial aspect of prostitution much later), young girls in my position, who were not destined for marriage, would go to reveal their bodies to strangers, to men of the same kind as they. A sort of temple of shamelessness, the brothel had to be silent, no one was to speak there, with everything being arranged so that there was no reason to utter so much as a word – a sacred anonymity. I imagined that the girls wore masks on their faces to enter there. Doubtless to acquire the anonymity of their kind, in imitation of the absolute absence of 'personality' of the boa (that model wearer of the naked, virginal mask), their kind innocently bearing alone all responsibility for the crime, the crime simply coming out of the body like the flower of a plant. The brothel, painted green, the same natural green as the one in which the boa's devouring takes place, and the same as the tall tamarinds which flooded my balcony of despair with shade, with its row of cubicles side by side where one gave oneself to men, resembled a kind of swimming pool and one went there to be washed, to be cleansed of one's virginity, to have one's solitude removed from one's body. I must speak now of a childhood memory which only corroborated this way of seeing things. When I was eight I think, my brother, who was ten, asked me one day to show him 'how' it looked. I refused. So my brother angrily declared that girls 'could die from not using it and that hiding it caused suffocation, and very serious diseases'. I did not go through with it, but I lived for a number of years with an agonizing doubt, all the more so as I confided in no one. And when Mamoiselle Barbet revealed herself to me, I saw confirmation in this of what my brother had told me. I was thus sure that Mamoiselle Barbet was only old because of this, because she had never been of use either to the children who would have suckled there, or to the man who would have revealed it. It was a gnawing of solitude that one doubtless avoided by having one's body revealed. That which had been used, used for anything – used to be looked at, for example – was protected. The moment a breast had been of use to a man, even if it was only allowing him to look at it, to examine its shape, its roundness, its bearing, the moment this breast could spark a man's desire, it was safe from any such degeneration. From this arose the great hope I placed on the brothel, the ultimate place for people to reveal themselves.

The boa confirmed this belief in no less dazzling fashion. Of course, the boa terrified me, by its devouring, just as much as the other devouring of which Mlle Barbet was the prey, but the boa could not stop itself from eating the chicken in that way. Likewise, the prostitutes could not stop themselves from revealing their bodies. Mamoiselle Barbet owed her misfortune to the fact that she had evaded this nonetheless imperious law, and that she had failed to understand, failed to-reveal-her-body. So the world, and thus my life, opened on to a double avenue, which formed a clear alternative. On one side there was the world of Mlle Barbet; on the other, the world of the imperious, the deadly world, that of the kind considered as destiny, which was the world of the future, bright and burning, singing and shouting, of difficult beauty, but the cruelty of which one had to get used to in order to reach, just as one had to get used to the spectacle of devouring boas. And I saw the world of my future life rising before me, the only possible future for a life; I saw it open up with the musicality, the purity of an uncoiling serpent, and it seemed to me that when I eventually got to know it, it would appear to me like this, in a development of majestic continuity, where my life would be gripped and gripped again, and taken to its term, in transports of terror, of rapture, without rest, without weariness.

Translated by Will McMorran

BÉATRIX BECK

The Adam Affair

God tells his creature:

'Your name is Adam.'

The aforementioned touched his chest as he repeated 'Adam' then God's chest and asked:

'Adam?'

'No. I am God.'

The other gently corrected Him:

'I am God.'

'No. There is only one God.'

The loser, beaming with the joy of understanding, exclaimed:

'Me, you, we are one, the God Adam.'

'No. It is I who made you.'

'It is I who made you.'

'You stubborn . . . before you existed, I was.'

'You were what?'

'I was, absolutely and perfectly.'

'And now that I am, you are relatively and imperfectly?'

'You're wrong, but it doesn't matter. Are you not happy to exist?'

'How could you be, without me?'

'I was premeditating you.'

'How did you put me together?'

'Couched in the clay like a corpse, I left my imprint there.'

'Like a what?'

'Nothing. Nothing.'

'What does that mean, a corpse? Explain.'

'Later.'

'Why not now?'

'It's not a word for someone your age.'

'Then why did you say it?'

'It was a slip.'

'What?'

'An anachronism.'

'What's an anachronism?'

'A forgetting of time.'

'What's time?'

'For me, time does not exist.'

'For me neither then.'

'It's different. My thoughts are not your thoughts.'

'Yet you moulded me in your image. We are twins.'

'Not identical twins.'

'You may not be identical but I am.'

'Ignoramus.'

'I don't mind not knowing what time is but I want to know what a corpse is.'

'Your curiosity is unhealthy, Adam.'

'You are hiding things from me. You don't really love me.'

'I do.'

'Well, I'm not sure I love you.'

'That's because I wanted you to be free.'

'Free?'

'Able to choose.'

'I don't want to choose. I want everything.'

'Adam, my man, I have to remove your arrogance and your curiosity from you. I want you to sleep.'

The Almighty waved his magnetizer's hands a few times and his homo erectus fell flat on his face on the flowery grass of Eden. The Almighty leaned over and, with the greatest of ease, extracted from the sleeping, dreaming man Eve, who stood up and exclaimed:

'Hi, God!'

'Oh, you know who I am – you're not like your . . . your brother. But do you know your name?'

'I'm called Goddess since you're called God.'

'You're mad and Adam is stupid. Don't make your . . . your companion suffer too much.'

'You fear for your little blue-eyed boy? Don't worry, he'll do me as much harm as I'll do him. We will be quits without quitting on each other.'

Adam was amazed at the differences between himself and his new friend.

'It's because I wasn't made in the manner of a pot like you were. I am a piece of king.'

The oaf grasped neither the insult, nor the flattery, nor the invitation. To console herself, the woman *in spe* made friends with all the animals, and notably the serpent, an unusual beast that spoke better than any other:

'Eve, my beauty, my goddaughter, my adopted daughter, I'll teach you how to take your innocent's innocence away.'

What had to happen happened. Jehovah, who had wanted man but not humanity, chased the couple from the Garden.

Adam observed with shock that his eyes were raining but Eve was stroking her belly and saying that it was a nest. Absurd talk.

Strangely, children were born, years passed. The husband asked his wife:

'You remember, when we were there?'

'I only remember that the place was called a name I have forgotten, with "terrestrial" before it. It's terrestrial here too.'

'Yes, but there's something missing – it's on the tip of my tongue.'

Adam is lying in a coffin. Eve, Cain, Abel and Seth are kneeling at its four corners. Adam raises himself up slightly and asks:

'Am I dead?'

'Yes, darling,' his widow replied with a sniffle.

Seth rushes over to his father and hugs him:

'I don't want you to be dead.'

'The main thing is that you did not see yourself die.'

'No, I didn't. We have to be sure in our hearts. Sure? Mine is indeed so sure it's as if I didn't have one any more.'

'I will massage your heart and you will live again.'

'Bring me a mirror.'

'That's it, my mirror, my mirror.'

'What are you doing running around my bed?'

'It's not a bed, it's a coffin.'

'Don't contradict your father.'

'Why am I lying in a coffin? It's macabre.'

'It's what is most appropriate for your condition, it's the done thing.'

'I didn't think I'd got to that stage yet.'

'You are further along than you thought.'

'Is it real, at least, this coffin?'

'You can see for yourself it is – it isn't fake, it doesn't have a false bottom.'

'I mean as in period.'

'Period? A coffin is always period.'

'Mummy said once that you were nobody. So your tomb will be a cenotaph?'

'What do you expect? You're dead, you're dead.'

'I *am* dead? You really used the auxiliary to be? The word death cannot be attached to the words to be. Me not dead, me not dead. There is none dead yours truly. It's good not dead. It's good *vita*.'

'Could death be a return to childhood?'

'A posthumous madness.'

'There is an incompatibility between death and me.'

'It's certainly been detrimental to your faculties.'

'It seems to me on the contrary that my wits are sharper.'

'Sharper – you can say that again.'

'The people upstairs will hear us.'

'And so?'

'As you well know we have no rights, they can throw us into the street whenever they feel like it – it's already happened to you once.'

'We're not joint owners?'

'We're dust.'

'You should make the most of your condition to say a word or two to them.'

'A word or two? What words?'

'You'll plead our case, drag a couple of guarantees out of them. It's hard to turn down someone . . . someone whose health . . . is beyond the pale.

Just don't take the lift – suppliers, servants and unaccompanied children aren't allowed.'

'I'm neither a supplier (what would I supply?), nor a servant (who could I serve?), nor an unaccompanied child (although . . .).'

'You can just take the stairs.'

'Impossible. Begging and peddling are forbidden in the building.'

'I don't beg or peddle.'

'Your situation risks being taken for begging or peddling.'

'Shall I go with you, Daddy?'

'Seth, you have no sense of propriety.'

'All the same, you could have tried to perform a miracle.'

'Oh, you've made me think I ought to buy some miracle velvet for my mourning.'

'I need to try to get out of this crib.'

'Careful, you might decompose.'

'We'll hold you up as far as the goods lift, it will be child's play. Help me, you lot.'

Adam finds himself in an ordinary living room, opposite some very affable middle-aged chap.

'I'm sorry, I went down instead of up.'

'It's perfectly fine, dear sir, perfectly fine.'

'I don't wish to be indiscreet but I've a feeling I've seen you before.'

'I've got one of those unremarkable faces typical of these parts. Besides, we must have bumped into each other. How can I be of service?'

'My family had sent me up, to the owner, and here I am down here with you. Perhaps I should put this incongruity down to my condition.'

'You couldn't have landed anywhere better than here – I'm the manager. I'm the one who takes care of everything in this building, the owner gives me carte blanche. I'm the property manager. Admit, dear sir, that goods are worth more than goodness, ho ho . . . I was joking, I'm joking, I'm joking – just killing time, my dear sir . . .'

'No offence . . .'

'Nothing offends me, dear sir, I'm very good-natured.'

'No offence, but it's the owner, in person, upstairs, whom I'd like to see.'

'He's never there.'

'I'd like to make sure all the same . . .'

'As you wish, dear sir, I won't stand in the way; I will show you my secret staircase but you're bound to hit a brick wall.'

Climbing the stairs which multiplied beneath his feet with some difficulty, in this building turning into a skyscraper, the future deceased at last reached a narrow door. He rang, knocked. In vain. Yet he thought he could clearly hear a hubbub coming from the depths of the apartment.

He took his now useless identity card from his pocket and slid it under the door having scribbled a few words: 'I was hoping to see you before my burial. My family will try to contact you. I commend my eldest to you, he's a boy with a bright future ahead of him.'

Translated by Will McMorran

BORIS VIAN

Danger from the Classics

The electronic timer on the clock buzzed twice. I jumped, and tried to tear myself from the whirlwind of images that were spinning around in my head. With some surprise, I noticed that my heart was starting to beat a little faster as well. Blushing, I quickly closed my book. It was *You and Me*, a dusty old volume written prior to the last two wars, which I had hesitated to pick up until now, because I was aware of the bold realism of the theme. It was then I noticed that the cause of my distress lay as much in the time and date as in my book. Today was Friday 27 April 1982 and, as usual, I was waiting for my intern, Florence Lorre.

The realization hit me harder than I care to admit. I consider myself to be open-minded, but the man should not be the first one smitten; we need to maintain the dignity that befits our sex at all times. Nevertheless, after the initial shock, I began thinking, and found some justification for my behaviour.

There is a preconceived idea about scientists, and about women scientists in particular, that they are severe-looking and very unattractive. Certainly, women, more so than men, have a talent for research. And in certain professions where physical appearance is part of the selection criteria, in acting for example, there is a fairly large number of women who look like goddesses. However, if you take the problem one step further, you soon notice that a pretty mathematician is not, on the whole, harder to find than an intelligent actress, even though there are more female mathematicians than actresses. In any case, when it came time to draw lots for the allocation of interns, luck was on my side. Although not a single bad thought had crossed my mind to that point, I had already recognized, quite objectively of course, that my intern had an obvious charm. And therein lies the reason for my current state of confusion.

Right on time again. She arrived as usual, at five past two.

'You look awfully smart,' I said, a little surprised at my own audacity.

She was wearing a tight-fitting pair of overalls made from shimmering pale green material, very simple, but they must have come from a factory that produced luxury lines.

'Do you like it, Bob?'

'I like it a lot.'

I am not one of those people who find colour out of place, not even when it comes to something as traditional as women's laboratory overalls, and at the risk of causing a scandal, I have to admit that even a woman wearing a skirt doesn't shock me.

'I'm pleased about that,' Florence answered mockingly.

Although I am ten years older, Florence assures me that we look the same age. For this reason, our relationship is a little different from most normal student–teacher relationships. She treats me as a friend, and that bothers me a little. Of course, I could always shave off my beard and cut my hair to look like an old scholar from the 1940s, but she insists that it would make me look effeminate and would do nothing to earn her respect.

'And how is your project coming along?' she asked.

She was referring to a rather tricky electronics problem that the Central Bureau had entrusted to me, and which I had only just resolved that very morning, much to my great satisfaction.

'It's finished,' I said.

'Bravo! Does it work?'

'I'll know tomorrow,' I said. 'Friday afternoons are set aside for your education.'

She hesitated and lowered her eyes. Nothing makes me feel more uncomfortable than a bashful woman, and she knew it.

'Bob . . . I want to ask you something.'

I was feeling very ill at ease. A woman really must avoid this sort of charming affectation around a man.

She continued, 'Explain to me what you're working on.'

It was my turn to hesitate.

'Listen, Florence . . . this work is highly confidential . . .'

She placed her hand on my arm.

'Bob ... even the cleaners in the lab know as much about all these secrets as ... er ... Antares' best spy.'

'Ah, now that would surprise me,' I said, feeling depressed.

For weeks, the radio had been bombarding us with songs from *The Grand Duchess of Antares*, the internationally acclaimed operetta by Francis Lopez. I hate all that popular music. I only like the classics, like Schoenberg, Duke Ellington or Vincent Scotto.

'Bob! Please explain it to me. I want to know what you're doing ...'

Another interruption.

'What now, Florence?' I said.

'Bob, I like you ... a lot. So you have to tell me what you're working on. I want to help.'

So there you have it. For years you read about it in novels, the description of the emotions you feel when you hear your first declaration of love. And it was finally happening to me. To me! And it was more disturbing, more delightful, than anything I had ever imagined. I looked at Florence, with her bright eyes, and red hair cut into a crew-cut that was all the rage in that year of '82. I think that there is no doubt she could have taken me in her arms then and there without a struggle on my part. And to think I used to laugh at love stories! My heart was pounding and I felt my hands shake. I had a lump in my throat.

'Florence ... You shouldn't say things like that to a man. Let's talk about something else.'

She came up to me, and before I could do anything, she threw her arms around me and gave me a kiss. I felt the ground give way beneath my feet, and I found myself sitting on a chair. At the same time, I was experiencing a state of euphoria that was as indescribable as it was unexpected. I blushed at my own depravity and noticed, with renewed astonishment, that Florence was on my knee. That's when the cat let go of my tongue.

'Florence, this isn't right. Stand up. If someone were to come in ... my reputation would be ruined. Stand up.'

'Will you show me your experiments?'

'I ... Oh! ...'

I had to give in.

'I'll explain everything to you. Everything. But stand up.'

'I always knew that you were a nice man,' she said as she stood up.

'All the same,' I said, 'you've taken advantage of the situation. Admit it.'

My voice was trembling. She patted me affectionately on the shoulder.

'Come on, Bob, dear. Don't be so old-fashioned.'

I didn't waste any time launching into the technical details.

'Do you remember the first electronic brains?' I asked.

'The ones from 1950?'

'Slightly earlier,' I corrected. 'They were calculating machines. Quite clever, actually. You remember that, very quickly, they were fitted with special tubes which allowed them to store various pieces of information that could be drawn on when needed? Memory tubes?'

'You learn that in primary school,' Florence said.

'Do you remember that this type of machine was being perfected up until around 1964, when Rossler discovered that a real human brain, properly set up in a nutrient bath, could, under certain conditions, accomplish the same tasks taking up much less space?'

'And I also know that in '68 this process was, in turn, replaced by Brenn and Renaud's super-circuit,' Florence said.

'Fine,' I answered. 'Gradually, these various devices were fitted and tested with all the different types of "effectors" that were available, the effectors themselves having been derived from the thousand and one gadgets developed by man over time, to make up the class of machines we call robots. All these machines have one thing in common. Can you tell me what it is?'

The teacher in me couldn't help himself.

'You have lovely eyes,' Florence answered. 'They're a greeny-yellow colour, with a kind of star on the iris . . .'

I stepped back.

'Florence! Are you listening to me?'

'I'm listening very carefully. The one thing all of these machines have in common is that they only act on the data provided to their internal operating systems by the users. A machine that is not given a specific problem to solve remains incapable of any initiative.'

'And why hasn't anyone tried to provide them with awareness and reason? Because it was noted that, with only a few elementary reflex functions, their behaviour was worse than that of the old scientists. Go to any old shop and buy a small electronic toy tortoise, and you'll soon see what the first electro-reflex machines were like: irritable, unpredictable ... In short, endowed with a personality. We rather quickly lost interest in these kinds of automatons, which were created solely to provide a simple illustration of certain mental processes, but were far too difficult to live with.'

'Dear old Bob,' Florence said. 'I love hearing you talk. Do you know how boring you are? I learned all that in the eleventh grade.'

'And you're insufferable,' I said seriously.

She was looking at me. I do believe she was making fun of me. I am ashamed to say it, but I would have liked her to kiss me again. I took up where I left off, very quickly, to hide my confusion.

'We're striving increasingly to introduce into these machines sustainable reflex circuits capable of interacting with a wide range of effectors. But we haven't yet tried to supply them with a broad-based education. To tell the truth, up till now there's been no point. But it so happens that the work the Central Bureau has asked me to do should allow the machine to retain a number of higher-level concepts in its memory bank. In fact, the model you see here is intended to assimilate the entire collection of knowledge contained in the sixteen volumes of the 1978 *Larousse Encyclopaedia*. Its purpose is almost purely intellectual, and it's fitted with simple effectors to allow it to move around by itself and to take hold of objects for identification and analysis, if need be.'

'And what will be done with it?'

'It's an administrative device, Florence. The Flor-Fiña ambassador, who's taking up his post in Paris next month following the Mexico City Convention, is going to use it for advice on matters of protocol. Each time there's a request for information on his part, the machine will provide the ambassador with the kind of response that someone with an extensive knowledge of French culture would give. In each instance, it will tell him the steps to follow, and explain to him the nature of the problem and how to conduct himself, whether it be on the occasion of the naming of a new polymegatron or dinner with the Emperor of Eurasia. Since French has been adopted by world decree as the most prestigious language of diplomacy, everyone wants to be able to boast that they're highly cultivated. And so this machine will be invaluable to an ambassador who doesn't have time to educate himself.'

'So!' Florence said. 'You're going to cram sixteen fat volumes of the *Larousse* into that poor little machine! You're a sadist.'

'It has to be done!' I said. 'It has to absorb everything. If we only feed it bits and pieces of information, it'll more than likely acquire a personality like one of those unresponsive old tortoises. And what will that personality be like? Impossible to know in advance. The only chance it has of being well balanced is if it knows *everything*. That's the only way it can remain objective and impartial.'

'But it can't know *everything*,' Florence said.

'If it knows something *about* everything, in equal proportions, that will be enough,' I explained. 'The *Larousse* is reasonably objective. It's a fairly good example of a piece of work written without emotion. According to my reckoning, we should end up with a machine that's polite, sensible and well-behaved.'

'That's wonderful,' Florence said.

It seemed like she was making fun of me. Obviously, some of my colleagues solve more complex problems, but nevertheless, I had drawn some good conclusions from some rather imperfect data, and I think that deserved something better than the trite, 'That's wonderful'. Women don't seem to understand just how disheartening and thankless these mundane tasks can be.

'How does it work?' she asked.

'Oh, a run-of-the-mill system,' I said, feeling a little dejected. 'A basic lectoscope. All you do is insert the book into the tube and the apparatus reads and records everything. There's nothing very fancy about it. Naturally, once the material has been assimilated, the lectoscope will be dismantled.'

'Start it up, Bob! Please!'

'I'd really like to show you how it works,' I said, 'but I don't have my volumes of the *Larousse*. They arrive tomorrow night. I can't get it to learn anything beforehand because that will upset its balance.'

I went over to the machine and plugged it in. Small red, green and blue lights flashed randomly on the control panel. A gentle humming sound was coming from the electrical supply. Despite everything, I felt rather pleased with myself.

'The book goes in there,' I said. 'You push this lever and that's all there is to it. Florence! What are you doing? Oh no . . .'

I tried to switch it off, but Florence held me back.

'I'm just trying it out, Bob. We can always delete it . . .'

'Florence! You're impossible! You can't delete it!'

She had thrown my copy of *You and Me* into the tube and had pulled the lever. I could now hear the rapid clicking of the lectoscope as it scanned the pages. In fifteen seconds it was done. The book came out, assimilated, digested and intact.

Florence was watching with interest. Suddenly she jumped. The speaker started cooing gently, almost tenderly:

I need to explain, convey, confess
That we can only feel what we can express . . .

'Bob! What's happening?'

'Oh my God,' I said, exasperated. 'It doesn't know anything else . . . It's now going to recite Géraldy non-stop.'

'But Bob, why is it talking to itself?'

'All lovers talk to themselves!'

'What if I were to ask it something?'

'Oh no!' I said. 'Not that. Leave it alone. You've already done enough damage!'

'What a grouch you are!'

The machine was making a soothing humming sound. It made a noise as if to clear its throat.

'Machine,' Florence said, 'how do you feel?'

This time it was an impassioned declaration that came from the machine.

Oh! I love you! I love you!
Do you hear? I'm crazy about you . . . Crazy! . . .

'Oh!' Florence said. 'What a cheek!'

'It was like that back then,' I said. 'Men spoke to women first and I can assure you, young Florence, that they weren't afraid to do so . . .'

'Florence!' the machine said, deep in thought. 'Her name is Florence!'

'That's not in Géraldy!' Florence protested.

'So, you haven't understood a single word I've said,' I observed somewhat annoyed. 'I haven't built a device that simply reproduces sounds. I'm telling you that inside there are lots of new reflex circuits and a complete supply of phonetics which allow it to formulate adequate responses to the sounds it accumulates … The difficult thing was to maintain its balance, and you've just ruined that by filling it with passion. It's like giving a piece of steak to a two-year-old child. This machine *is* still a child … and you've just fed it bear meat …'

'I'm old enough to take care of Florence,' the machine remarked drily.

'It can hear!' Florence said.

'Of course it can hear!'

I was becoming more and more exasperated.

'It can hear. It can see. It can speak …'

'And I can also move around!' the machine said. 'But kissing? I can see what it is, but I don't know how I'm supposed to do it,' it continued with a pensive air.

'You won't be doing anything,' I said. 'I'm going to turn you off, and tomorrow I'm going to change your tubes and we'll start all over again.'

'You, with that awful beard,' the machine said. 'You don't interest me. And you'll leave my switch alone.'

'His beard is lovely,' Florence said. 'You're very rude.'

'Maybe so,' the machine said with a lecherous laugh that made my hair stand on end, 'but in matters of love, I know a thing or two … Florence, come closer …'

For the things to you I have to say
Are things, you see, that can be said each day
With words, looks, deeds and smiles …

'Try to lighten up a little,' I said mockingly.

'I *am* able to laugh!' the machine said.

It repeated its obscene laugh.

'In any case,' I said furiously, 'you should stop reciting Géraldy parrot-fashion.'

'I'm not reciting anything parrot-fashion!' the machine said. 'And the proof is that I can call you a fool, an idiot, a blockhead, a nag, a moron, a bumpkin, a loser, a deadbeat, a twit, a nutter …'

'Okay! That's enough!' I objected.

'Anyway, if I recite Géraldy,' the machine continued, 'it's because nobody speaks the language of love any better. And besides, I like it. When *you* can talk to women the way this guy can, let me know. Until then, stay out of it. It's Florence I'm talking to.'

'Be nice,' Florence said to the machine. 'I like nice people.'

'You can tell me to be gentlemanly,' the machine pointed out, 'because I'm feeling rather masculine. Be quiet and listen.'

The things that you would say, my dear,
Are things I already know.
Come close. Draw near!
Allow me to undo your blouse.
Quickly now, let us begin.
To feel this way is not a sin.
Take off your clothes. Do not hide,
Lie down here, right by my side.
Remove your skirt, do not be shy,
The time to be as one is nigh.

'Oh, will you be quiet!' I protested, outraged.

'Bob!' Florence said. 'Is that what you've been reading? Oh dear!'

'I'm going to disconnect it,' I said. 'I can't bear to hear it speak to you that way. There are some things you read that you just don't repeat.'

The machine became silent. And then a growling sound came from deep within.

'Don't touch my switch!'

I strode up to it and, without a word of warning, the machine launched itself at me. I threw myself to the side at the last minute, but its steel housing struck my shoulder. Its wicked voice continued:

'So, you're in love with Florence, eh?'

I had taken up refuge behind the metal desk and was rubbing my shoulder.

'Run, Florence,' I said. 'Go on. Get out of here.'

'Bob! I don't want to leave you alone ... It ... He ... is going to hurt you.'

'It's okay. It's okay,' I said. 'Get out quickly.'

'She'll leave when I tell her to!' the machine said.

It made a movement towards Florence.

'Run, Florence,' I said again. 'Hurry.'

'I'm afraid, Bob,' Florence said.

In two bounds she had joined me behind the desk.

'I want to stay with you.'

'You won't come to any harm,' the machine said. 'It's the bearded one who's going to get it. Oh, so you're jealous! So you want to turn me off!'

'I don't want anything to do with you!' Florence said. 'You disgust me.'

The machine backed up slowly, preparing to launch itself. Suddenly it charged at me with the full force of its engines. Florence screamed.

'Bob! Bob! I'm scared!'

Pulling her into my arms, I got nimbly on to the desk. The machine collided full on with the desk, which sent it careering towards the wall, which it struck with irresistible force. The room shook and a lump of plaster fell from the ceiling. If we had stayed between the wall and the desk, we would have been cut in two.

'It's lucky I didn't fit more powerful effectors,' I said under my breath. 'Stay here.'

I sat Florence on the desk. She was more or less out of harm's way. I stood up.

'Bob, what are you going to do?'

'I mustn't say it out loud,' I answered.

'You don't need to,' the machine said. 'I dare you again to try to flick my switch.'

I watched it back up, and waited.

'Chicken!' I taunted.

The machine growled furiously.

'Oh yeah? We'll see.'

It charged towards the desk, which is what I had been hoping for. Just as it was about to demolish that piece of furniture to get to me, I leaped forward and landed on top of it. With my left hand, I grabbed hold of the feeder cables sticking out of the top and tried to reach the contact switch with the other. I received a violent blow to the back of the skull. The machine, using the lever of the lectoscope against me as a weapon, was trying to beat my brains out. I groaned with pain as I tried to wrench the lever back. The machine screamed. But before I could tighten my grip, it began to shake itself like an enraged bull and I shot off the top. I collapsed in a heap on the ground. I felt a sharp pain in my leg and, through blurry eyes, I saw the machine backing up, getting ready to finish me off. And then there was darkness.

When I regained consciousness, I was stretched out, eyes closed, my head resting on Florence's lap. I was experiencing a range of complex sensations. My leg was hurting, but something very soft was pressing against my lips and an extraordinary feeling swept through me. The first thing I saw was Florence's eyes two centimetres from mine. She was kissing me and I passed out a second time. This time, she slapped me and I immediately came to.

'You saved me, Florence . . .'

'Bob,' she said, 'will you marry me?'

'It wasn't my place to propose to you, Florence darling,' I answered blushing. 'But I accept with pleasure.'

Translated by Peter Hodges

DANIEL BOULANGER

The Hunters' Café

Montfavert had transformed his kitchen into a carpenter's workshop and lived in his war invalid's tricycle. He moved only around the ground floor of his house, which looked on to Jules-Taupin Walk. The first floor and the attic were his paradise. He was always thinking about them and could not get up there. When he had turned the wood to make doll's-house furniture, the proceeds from which supplemented his invalidity pension, and when he had fed the spiders that he was breeding in a sideboard with glass doors, the inside of which he lit with a neon strip light, he changed seats and set off to go round the town in a motorized wheelchair. His horn could be heard everywhere and people were glad that he never went about at night; he would have woken even the dead. This almost daily noise scarcely made him liked, although talking to him was a most enriching experience. He knew all the battles in history, and you merely had to call out to him for him to stop the din made by his machine and tell you the date of a counter-offensive in Jutland or in Cyrenaica, troop numbers and the names of the leaders. He lived the feat of arms to the point where he could be seen changing colour, and it even came about that you learned the true source of this pain, which you begged him to forgive you for having caused.

'Not at all,' he replied. 'On the contrary, it's a pleasure. You see me shaking because of Angèle. She died last night.'

'I'm so sorry.'

'She would have been two. A spider which answered whenever I called, which ran up to greet me, which danced, I'll say. Solid and supple on her star-shaped feet, she let herself be bounced like a ball.'

'You've got others!' people said to console him.

'What creature can replace another? Please!'

He was allowed to turn his engine back on and drive to the Hunters' Café, where he had his quarters for relaxation. There, without getting out of his wheelchair, he settled down at the regulars' table to play games of chance that would give way to conversations about the army, his memories, his transformations, his future, his reading of old combatants' newsletters or war magazines. Montfavert had subscriptions to various publications, not including brochures and encyclopaedias of which he had received the specimen copy and the accompanying subscription letter. Moreover, not a week went by without him giving in to a mail order, and his memory was comforted by those rows of stories of every sort which bled his finances dry. One day he arrived at the Hunters' in a state of utter confusion.

'Montfavert! You look in a real state!'

'I'm jealous,' he merely said, 'and annoyed. I've often talked to you about an old comrade: Agricole Palaneuve! We were in the same hospitals! But he's a Parisian through and through! Only Paris counts! Always Paris! Ange did not even give me a hint! As if I was buried in this hole!'

'What are you talking about?'

'Of a historic deed!'

'So, what are you complaining about?'

Montfavert took a magazine out of one of the bags of his tricycle.

'A new publication. The first edition. Very expensive, too expensive. Still, the paper is glazed. And right in the middle I come across Palaneuve! Am I still his friend? I'll let you be the judge of that.'

'We're listening.'

'It's called "The Outrage".'

The landlord brought some white wine.

'An extra-special Alsace,' he said gleefully. 'From a new supplier. You'll never drink anything else!'

'No,' interrupted Montfavert, pushing the bottle away, 'not today. A bottle of red, please.'

Everyone around the table was amazed, but the hand of the paralysed man remained authoritative. The red wine arrived, and he began:

The Outrage

When he read that a Scandinavian had cooked himself an egg over the flame dedicated to the Unknown Soldier, Agricole Palaneuve let his newspaper slide to the ground, closed his eyes as he sat in his wheelchair, and his hands went white from pain, so hard was he squeezing the armrests. It was a very long time since he had shed his last tear, over there, in the depths of his war, and if other misfortunes since then had befallen the country, no deed came close in baseness to the act of sacrilege that had just been told, in peacetime, the day before the procession to commemorate the Armistice. He picked up his telephone to call the minister who gave him his pension. He was passed from office to office by officials, but he could not get hold of the secretary-general, whom he knew sufficiently well to describe his indignation to in the name of all those who had not dared to call, but the employees, who all knew what had happened, for they spent the morning reading the newspapers, scarcely seemed to be moved. Agricole had even thought that he had made out someone sniggering at the other end of the line. 'There's nothing worth waiting for any more,' he sighed, 'nothing either in the long or the short term.' He found himself under the flow of water from a Providence relieving itself and he recalled the ants on which, in days gone by, he liked to urinate as he chanced to walk by and as the need arose. 'It's all fitting into place,' he thought, and he added: 'Since they do not want to hear me, they're going to see me!'

The caretaker of his block of flats came to take him out of his fifth-floor flat and pushed him into the lift. Agricole Palaneuve found himself in the street once more and started the little motor on his wheelchair. The busiest streets, the crossroads, did not frighten him any more, for he was aware of the danger he posed to car drivers, and in spite of his despair he always counted on inspiring pity, and thus attention. Jeers and insults never failed, however, to rain down upon him, together with advice of this sort: 'Stay with your nanny!', 'Plonk yourself in the sun and it will grow back!' Ah, he could indeed talk about human nastiness and boorishness! He retained certain expressions of spite, the most apt obscenities, in order to relate them to friends in the same condition as him, and he compared them with those that they too had heard. They even got the giggles about them. Their meetings always took place on the Champ-de-Mars and, when it rained, in the nearby cafés of the École Militaire. They were pushed beyond the back room where billiards were played into a sort of windowless pergola, where the general public scarcely went and from where they could follow the games that the players were playing or watch television programmes on the screen reserved for the staff. The waiters took their meals in there at the quiet times of the morning and the afternoon. There were sometimes four or five invalid carriages, but Agricole Palaneuve could always count on finding Jacques Mouchelin's, for he rarely left the room, lived in the area, turned his wheels only with his hands and was nicknamed Le Casanier by his friends. That day, Agricole had decided to put the problem to them, to think up a response to the blasphemous gesture of the Scandinavian and to begin by all signing a letter to the minister in order to show him that they did not intend that the outrage should go unpunished. They were comforted by the sight of a game of tennis played by disabled people in small wheelchairs. It was taking place in America and, at the end of the broadcast, the winner of the tournament seemed to throw his racket to them, bursting with joy just like players who run about on two legs. A breath of freedom passed through the pergola and the high windowless wall which enclosed it echoed their cheers.

Agricole posted the letter. Days went by without a reply, until it arrived two weeks later. In the pergola the friends listened to Palaneuve, who read it out in his fine voice. The minister allowed himself to be moved, expressed his understanding, but made it clear that it was best to forget an act of madness. Everyone could remember, he added, more unworthy acts in this sacred place, which was not, of course, a reason to use the Flame as a kitchen stove. The Scandinavian was Danish. After a heavy fine he had been sent back across the border. The letter ended with a call for vigilance 'although in this respect as in others, no being and no temple could be protected from such a filthy deed. The mentally ill are at every street corner.'

'It is not a question of a street,' said Le Casanier, 'but of the most beautiful avenue in the world.'

'Quite right,' said the others.

'They should double the number of guards!' shouted Agricole. 'Money is never wasted when it is a matter of honour.'

They could hear the click of the billiard balls in the nearby room, the muffled noise from the other rooms, so very like the din that comes out of henhouses.

'I've an idea,' said Agricole, whom the others had been looking at for quite some time. 'We're going to get you an engine and you're going to do your bit, Le Casanier.'

'I don't need one,' exclaimed the man, who moved his chair by hand.

'It's vital,' said Palaneuve. 'You would regret not having one and thus not being in with us! Even though you're a lone wolf, in a sense.'

'I'm here much more often than you!' exclaimed Le Casanier. 'It's always me who waits for you!'

'This time, all six of us will be on time, and together, and in the same row, and with others as well! Let me add that we shall all have an engine, for before and afterwards.'

'Before and after what?' asked the others.

'My friends . . .'

And he laid before them the plan that was to make the one who had done his cooking over the Unknown Soldier think, and to revive the affair that everyone was suppressing, from the minister to the last passer-by. Beneath the pergola, convolvulus-like, the peculiar silence of the plotters spread over everything and over the six invalids, and the many questions that no one dared utter, and which waited to be asked for the breath of the bravest amongst them, fluttered above them like as many pale flags. Le Casanier began:

'Surely, there aren't enough of us?'

'We're going to gather every last one of us together,' said Agricole, 'and assemble them, without explanation, for this important matter which concerns them. I will speak to them. Today is Monday. I want us all to be here in two days and we'll draw up our plan of attack.'

Although he had never been promoted above the rank of sergeant, Agricole Palaneuve spoke with complete authority, like a generalissimo, and the others accepted that he was the most resolute and the most adept of their number. Agricole took all this on board and hence scented victory with his every command. He returned home and, for once, Le Casanier went part of the way with him, substituting for the engine which he still did not have, and for which he now felt the need, a grip of steel. His steering bar in one hand, he had seized Agricole's armrest with the other and allowed himself to be towed through the arrondissement. It was with regret that he let go of Palaneuve and watched him drive off into the distance, building up to maximum speed and overtaking even the quickest pedestrians.

If we asked our fellow men what they would like to save from a total disaster, most would reply that it would be a picture or a letter, the photograph of the person most dear to them or the declaration of affection made by their most loved one. The signature might be infinitely variable in appearance, from that of a child to that of a mother, from that of a wife to that of a leader. Agricole did not make his decisions or create his dreams without having before him a note signed by General de Gaulle. He had put it under glass, framed it with a strip of horse hide, and hung it above his bedside table.

He looked at the prestigious signature and smiled: the General would approve of the event that Agricole was telling him about as he moved his lips, letting out a word now and then, as though to apologize for the farcical side of it that some might see, but he became serious again and slept deeply for all of one night, as he had previously done only on the eve of attacks, emptying himself, as it were, and getting ready a new and alert man.

It was a Friday when Agricole and his companions brought the attention of the world back to the devotion of those who had died so that others might live. He did not think that washing away the stain of an insult is to remind people of it and that holding someone like that up to public obloquy is to rank him highly. The Scandinavian was going to get roasted again, if such an image is permissible. The oblivion that is preferable is not just difficult, it is impossible.

Following the custom of this daily ceremony, the Old Soldiers from a regiment had gathered that day towards the top of the Champs-Élysées, filling the pavement before parading on the road, flags at the head of the column, towards the Étoile and the tomb of the Unknown Soldier, on whose grave they were to put flowers. A difficult problem was always posed by an increase of the ever-dense traffic at that time and in that spot, in spite of the greater number of policemen, quick-thinking and efficient, in the merry-go-round of the cars. The men, wearing their medals, berets and forage caps, were stamping their feet and exchanging news, for they had come from all over France. In spite of the cold, the traces of snow, the frost on the bare trees, everyone was in good humour for they were talking about life, about births and marriages, about the pranks of those who had left them since the last gathering at the Flame, about the simple, basic pleasure of being together, still manning the fort. The ceremony assumed a secondary importance and in small groups they thought about the reunion dinners, well supplied with wine, which would follow before they all went home. Suddenly, a hubbub could be heard coming from the roundabout, lower down, a chorus of horns which was reaching the avenue and stealthily covering all Paris in the advancing evening.

Agricole Palaneuve and the twenty or so invalids that he had gathered together had just left the lower end of the avenue that they had reached with their motors from all corners of the capital. Their engines turned off, propelling the wheels by hand, two arms' lengths separating them, and advancing in a single horizontal line, they were blocking off the half of the Champs-Élysées which rises. Before them the dense flow of cars was moving off into the distance whereas behind, unable to overtake the invalids, the vehicles were beginning to form a solid mass, to stall, to set off again with difficulty at two kilometres an hour, to roar, to sound their horns in every pitch, rhythm and fury. The din assumed the density, the strength, of a storm-tossed sea and, like the sea, the noise suddenly stopped, started again, with new, terrible, wild vigour. Now, in front of the line of wheelchairs, the avenue was almost clear. Street lamps were coming on. The Old Soldiers, at the top of the avenue, ventured out on to the road to look at the demonstration, and people out for a stroll were beginning to come down towards Palaneuve, surprised to be walking in the wrong dir-ection on the clear road, without the hint of a whistle from a policeman, without being called back into line. The lower end of the avenue was black from cars that were bumper to bumper and one suspected that the mass was increasing. Police cars arrived from adjoining streets and from the downward side of the avenue, on which cars were no longer obeying the traffic lights since their normal hurry was taking second place to the curi-osity of their drivers. Agricole, Le Casanier and the others toiled with delight, their pale faces taut to the bone. Some wondered if they would make it as far as the Flame, but they pushed on, their chests covered in medals, their forage caps square on their heads. They had reached the halfway point of their toil, halfway to triumph, their breath enveloping them in mist, when Agricole Palaneuve, feeling the muscles, but not the ardour, of his troops to be weakening, noticing also that the pedestrians, be it from goodheartedness, amusement, kindliness or as a joke, were blocking their route and their momentum, yelled out the order that his companions were waiting for:

'Engines on!'

They restarted their engines. Surprised for a moment, the chorus of horns started again even louder and followed behind them in a way that Agricole could never have hoped for. They were no longer jeering, they were a help, at least that is what he thought. What did the motive matter! All those loudmouths were the set designers in the play that he was directing. Now they were adding their sidelights and their headlights. When they came level with the Old Soldiers, the flag bearers threaded their way between them and the cars. Agricole asked his men to slow down. The police were waiting for them on the Place de l'Étoile. The only cars that were moving were threading their way along the edge. The officials amongst the guards and the Old Soldiers assumed that this unexpected demonstration had been organized without them getting wind of it and gave the wheelchairs all the assistance they needed. In the very centre of the square, a hundred feet from the Unknown Soldier, Agricole stopped his engine and his squad made a circle around him. A bank of Japanese people, amateur reporters, were clicking madly away at their cameras, running between the flags. The car horns were becoming hysterical. The city was screaming.

'Now what?' cried a brigadier.

'Advance!' shouted someone else.

The traffic police were now beginning to surround the invalids, but Agricole Palaneuve did not flinch. Solemnly, he pulled an egg from a bag on his wheelchair and dropped it on the road.

The official from the Old Soldiers went up to Le Casanier:

'What's going on?' he asked. 'What regiment are you from?'

'Go on ahead,' said Agricole. 'We'll follow you.'

The massed military band waiting under the Arc struck up 'Le Chant du départ'. Everyone was waiting for them. Horns were turned off. In the growl of the traffic, which had started to move again, a bugle sounded a cry of infinite sadness which seemed to come from another age. Le Casanier, leaning towards Palaneuve, squeezed his hand.

'We'll read about it all in the paper tomorrow,' said Agricole, 'and hard luck on those who do not believe in anything!'

From their tiny carriages they looked at the flame dedicated to the blue that the night was turning to copper. In Agricole's mind the gateway to heaven must be like this, in the shape of a lance and transparent. He gripped the armrests on his wheelchair for he could feel tears rising.

'Le Casanier,' he said as the bugle faded away, 'dismiss! Everyone goes back as we planned, everyone to the pergola! Lamps fixed to your arms! I've had the wine from Alsace chilled.'

The Hunters' Café had fallen silent. The customers who had formed a group went back to their tables, carrying their chairs.

'So,' said Montfavert, with a note of tragedy in his voice, 'couldn't Pala-neuve have got in touch?'

'Of course he could,' said a faint voice. 'A friend is primarily a man who thinks of you, but perhaps he wanted to spare you the journey?'

Montfavert tapped the armrests of his wheelchair.

'I can go from one side of France to the other in this!'

'Yes, it's a bit much. This was also an insult to you. Of course, you'll stop taking that magazine?'

'I sent the cheque for my subscription this morning,' replied Montfavert, 'as soon as the post office opened. In my view friendship is also about forgetting a whole aspect of a friend.'

Translated by Richard Coward

JACQUES STERNBERG

The Execution

The man walked slowly down the last corridor, head bare, his shirt half off, his wrists tied behind his back. His hands were relaxed, not at all tense.

He had amazed everyone with his composure. An impassive demeanour that was neither defiance nor a brave last stand. It really was the composure of a man confronting his death with indifference because he had always been indifferent, whatever the circumstances – in the face of joy as in the face of the consequences of his crime.

The rope had already been placed around his neck when the executioner turned to one of the officials and whispered a few confidential words.

The prisoner, who was an educated man, felt he was intruding. He stepped aside, politely greeted a few bystanders, and, brushing past one of the spectators, said his goodbyes and left the execution yard.

He reached the street, a little embarrassed to be wearing just a shirt in February.

So he found a job, and after a few days he could afford a suit.

He looked for another job with better pay, became a salesman, then a senior salesman, and then manager of a whole department.

A year later, he was running the business. Two years later, he had bought it, and the six other branches as well.

He married and had two children – two years went by.

He celebrated his fifth year of success with a banquet. He made a speech without faith and without feeling, and let his staff eat and drink themselves merry on the house. He went outside to take the air.

The building stood in a little garden. The garden was a blaze of green between two whitewashed walls. In one of these walls was a green door.

He pushed it open. He was smiling.
The executioner approached.
'Off we go,' he told him, 'now that you've come back.'
And, in a few quick movements, he hanged him.

Translated by Patrick McGuinness

OUSMANE SEMBÈNE

Mahmoud Fall

Mahmoud Fall, bronzed complexion, aquiline nose, quick stride – but not as quick as his hawkish eye – was descended from a line of Senegalese Muslims. Loyal to the motto of his ancestors: 'What's mine is mine; nothing's stopping you from sharing yours', Mahmoud did not work. To be more precise, he did not like to sweat. When children mockingly asked him:

'Mahmoud! Tell us why there are no cats in your country?'

'It's just that I don't know.'

It was his way of not saying that, just like him, cats like to be fed without doing anything. That is why there were none to be seen in that very hilly region of Senegal. The earth there is arid and the locals pitch their tents at dusk for the break of dawn. No animal can live at the expense of a man when he is living as a nomad. Birds of a feather, flock together, they say. Those ones, however, would flee from each other. And if, by chance, one stumbles across a cat in that place, it is a pitiful sight.

Weary of doing nothing, with empty pockets, Mahmoud Fall had embarked on a journey to the land of the Bilals to the west. For him, these ebony men were inferior, barely up to guarding a harem once they were castrated – which avoids disputes, later on, over the paternity of children.

Upon his arrival in Senegal, Mahmoud Fall changed his name; he called himself Aïdra. This name opened all doors wide open for him. He was received everywhere with the dignity due to one of his rank. Having studied the Qur'an in Mauritania – which, in Senegal, commands respect – he used all his knowledge of the Sacred Book, presided over prayers, sinking into endless genuflections. The locals were enthralled – they considered it a very great honour to have as their Iman a descendant of the noble family of Aïdra.

Mahmoud, like his kindred spirit the cat, strutted about smugly with all this praise. As nature had gifted him with a fine singing voice, he regaled those around him with it, endeavouring to modulate his syllables before swallowing them at the end of each verse. Between each of the five daily prayers he spent his time squatting on a sheepskin, the beads of his rosary rolling between his fingers.

When the time came to eat, Mahmoud insisted on being served separately. By way of thanks, he made do with spraying children and adults alike with a misty cloud of saliva they would each rub into their faces, saying, 'Amin ... Amin.' But what could Mahmoud have been making of all this, in the hidden depths of his consciousness, when he was alone with God?

Used to moving around frequently, he would go from concession to concession, received according to the tradition which demands, 'To every stranger his bowl.' At first, our man did not turn his nose up at anything, but as the days passed, he became more and more difficult. According to him, couscous was now stopping him from sleeping well; he complained of indigestion. Anxious to stay on the path which leads to paradise, his hosts made him small dishes fit to delight a palate as refined as his. And, just to be safe, he did not hesitate on occasion to go directly to the kitchen to pass on his order. It was his brotherly spirit.

Aside from the food, Mahmoud Fall accumulated some small change; he never deemed it to be enough for the trouble he went to. Evidently these Blacks held prayer in very paltry esteem. And something else – why did they insist on keeping cats like that? Every time he saw one in a house, he felt his hair bristle like the fur of an angry tomcat. He pulled faces at them and chased them off. Sometimes, he even held sermons about the uselessness of cats.

Despite these little aggravations, Mahmoud Fall felt his reputation as a preacher grow with the passing months. Everywhere the talebs, the marabouts, the tafsirs had only one phrase in their mouths: 'Souma Narr ... Souma Narr', My Moor ... My Moor. Deep down, Mahmoud took them for lunatics.

'Souma Narr! Souma Narr. What do they mean by this possessive? Where has anyone seen a Black buy a Moor? Has the world turned upside down?'

And he made more and more signs etched on paper and made to be worn, as he applied himself – more than ever – to keeping his true origins and his goal quiet. To add to his prestige, he even went as far as to declare in public that his body had been banished from Finahri Dianan . . . from hell. They swallowed it along with the rest.

Months passed, during which Mahmoud saw his hoard prosper. One morning, without saying 'Goodbye', he left, just as he had arrived one evening. The elders, in their wisdom, said, 'When a stranger has given you a sunset, don't look for him at sunrise.'

With a hunting bag on his back, and a light step, Mahmoud Fall was returning to his dear Atlas. He walked day and night, resting very little, dreaming of the use to which he would put his wealth and anxious to avoid any unpleasant encounters. To this end, he made a detour to the north. There lies the kingdom of the Tièdes, atheist fetishists, unbeknownst to Mahmoud. As he walked, he gave praise to himself: 'By the grace of Saîtané, I possess a deep understanding of the art of taking other people's property for myself.'

It was the height of the dry season. The sun's rays, veritable flame-throwers, set alight the occasional tufts of grass tormented by the wind, which tore them out, hurled them towards the riverbanks, out of sight, whistling as if it wanted to put an end to the unbearable monotony of silence. A vapour emanated from the overheated soil, drifting towards the void of the sky. Animal cadavers, scoured carcasses at every stage of decomposition, mingled with grains of sand which, beneath the gusts of wind, served as gravediggers. The birds which passed overhead uttered cries that sounded like lamentations offered to nature. A mixture of serenity and disquiet.

As far as Narr's gaze extended, he could discern no trace of a living being. Just a tree. A curious tree. Curious for its abundance of leaves. The sole survivor of this hell. A tamarind. The hour of prayer was approaching. Worn out by the long march, stifled by the heat, Mahmoud lingered quite a while in this place. Puzzled, he mulled over the prayer.

'Should I do it before or after sleeping?'

A decision needed to be made. Mahmoud finally opted to rest and stretched out under the tamarind. Abruptly – what had got into him? – he sat up on his haunches and shouted, very loudly, even though he was alone:

'Oi! . . . Oi! . . . Oi! . . . Yes, you, up there . . . Come down.'

The echo repeated his call. Three times in a row he spoke thus to an invisible interlocutor without receiving the slightest response. Then he got up, ran to the right, ran to the left . . . to the west and to the east.

Nothing there but him. And the tree. Alone, wary enough for two, his conscience commanded him to bury his treasure. He dug down a cubit deep. Went off to inspect the vicinity. Nothing. He returned, dug down another cubit, left again . . . Another race to the surrounding area. No one. He shielded his eyes with his hands, and furrowed his brow in such a manner that his eyesight, having gained in sharpness, could pierce the thick foliage of the tree. There was no one perched up there. So Mahmoud returned to his hole, and dug down further until he was in up to his trunk. Once that was done, he sat down, crossed his legs over his hiding place and counted his derhems, which jingled pleasantly in the silence. Content, and reassured, he buried it all, then lay down over it. Remembering he had yet to acquit himself of his debt to the Almighty, he called out to him:

'I owe you one . . .'

After all this merry-go-round, sleep did not delay in paying him a visit, accompanied by a sweet dream of sailing in the desert. Stretching out as far as the eye could see, an immense ocean of sand, the walls of the dunes interweaving. Vessels on this silent sea, the camels bobbed their long necks; their copper nose rings kept their guides close in this storm. Harder than steel, the grains of sand, stinging even through the layers of clothes, bit into the skin. And now the dream transformed into a sort of reality. Mahmoud Fall saw himself picked up by a very skinny, half-naked Black. The man rifled through his treasure, then calmly proceeded to shave him. Still dazed from his sleep, Mahmoud woke up, thanked Allah and yawned.

Devout worshipper that he was, he thought of the prayer. (In the absence of water, ablutions with sand are permitted.) He poured some on his hands and arms, to cleanse them of anything impure they might have touched, then on his face and head. While carrying out this ritual, he was suddenly taken aback: he had not felt any hair. He hurriedly took his head in his hands, feeling and rubbing it. His skull was bare. There were no hairs there any more. Slowly, gently – taking care to maintain his self-control – Mahmoud moved his hands down to his chin. His beard had disappeared. Bewildered, wild-eyed, Mahmoud had the feeling that something strange was happening inside him. He thought he could hear voices. It was true: he could hear voices, but they were inner voices:

'It's God who shaved you,' said the first.

'Where did you see that? God doesn't shave anyone.'

Mahmoud, listening to this dialogue, became ashen. When one voice spoke, the other laughed:

'Have faith in God, his mercy is in all things.'

'Ha, ha, ha! . . . Don't make me laugh! And when you were fleecing those poor buggers – in whose name were you doing that? Ha, ha, ha, ha, ha!'

Having tried in vain to silence these voices by shaking his head this way and that, Mahmoud stuck his palms over his ears. He didn't want to know, didn't want to hear any more. They continued nonetheless:

'Pray! You owe two prayers.'

'Look for your money. Without that you won't be respected. If you don't have any camels, you won't eat. Check on your money first. Praying comes more easily when you know a full stomach is guaranteed.

Mahmoud obeyed this last commandment. He threw himself on the ground, digging down with such fervour his movements no longer resembled those of a normal person. When backed into a corner, even a goat bites: the Mauritanian would have bitten anyone who had come between him and his casket. Hunched over, he was sweating, his tongue hanging out. A passer-by would have likened him to a pyramid crab. With his feet he swept the earth away from the hole. The collar of his boubou* was bothering him – he tore it in two and got back to work, digging faster and faster. Great indeed was Mahmoud's disappointment when he came across his hair, smooth and black. He picked it up, contemplated it a moment, disorientated, and looked down again at the empty ditch. Then he raised his eyes to the tree and took God as his witness:

'Bilahi-vahali,† it's not me . . .'

Holding this wig in one hand, stroking his shaved head in the other, he felt the tears welling up. He wept, repeating:

'Bilahi-valahi, I am not Mahmoud Fall!'

With all his strength, he called out:

'My friend, my old friend Mahmoud Fall, deliver me from my uncertainty!'

* Senegalese robe
† To swear to God/I swear to God (Arabic)

The echo seized hold of this phrase, rolled it around, hurled it across the plain like a stone on a zinc roof. The murmur died away in the distance.

'My old friend Mahmoud Fall, don't play this trick on me, I've known you for a long time . . .'

Nothing. So he extended his sense of hearing to its utmost. It went beyond the distance his eyes could cover. He concentrated all his senses on one fixed point, but his ear reported nothing. An absolute void. Zero. Mockingly, the voices returned to the fray.

'You're not praying?' asked the first.

Half-unconscious, he got up. Facing towards Mecca, his hands on his temples, he began:

'Allah Akbar! God is great.'

His gaze lingered on what had been his hiding place.

'You can pray when you've been robbed?'

'Ask God who your thief is,' the other voice said.

His arms dangling, Mahmoud did not know what to do. He remembered his dream:

'I wasn't asleep . . .' he thought.

He had seen his thief. He had even felt himself being peeled. And the Almighty had not taken his side, the Almighty had let it happen . . .

'No, I'm not praying any more,' he said very quietly to himself, thinking that Allah would not hear him.

Three times, he circled the tree in the hope of finding footprints. In vain. Up in the sky, very high, a passing bird whistled gleefully. Mahmoud hurled insults at it. Then, suddenly, he felt he was alone:

'On my Moorish life,' he murmured, 'those sons of slaves are all thieves!'

Fury overwhelmed him. Head bare, the rags of his boubou flying behind him, he started running like a madman into the desert.

It had just dawned on him that you did not have to believe in Allah to be a thief!

Translated by Will McMorran

ANNIE SAUMONT

The Finest Story in the World

Okay. Let's get things properly organized. Yes. The list. As usual.

She tears a page out from her notebook. Someone's gone off with my pencil again.

dry-cleaner's
medical bumf
parents' evening – Charlène
appointment paediatrician
water hydrangeas
paint velux
adaptor
cleaning stuff
frozen food order

She gets back from the dry-cleaner's. Crosses that off. She fills in the medical expenses claim form. Jean had flu then asthma. Jean's the one who doesn't want to go and live with his mother. She sticks the stamps on the form. Must get Pascal to sign it and send it off to his firm's insurance.

Parents' evening. Five o'clock sharp. She can drop the baby off at the playgroup.

Velux. That can wait.

There's another thing – not on the list, in her head – always being shelved, always back on the table that will have to get done one day, her wild dream of writing the finest story in the world.

Yes, everyone knows. *The Finest Story in the World* goes back nearly a century. For Kipling it was the story of the writer who tries to tell the finest story in the world but who abandons his project when the bank clerk holding the key to the story falls in love with the young salesgirl taken on by the tobacconist. And loses all interest in the story.

Woman, then, is an obstacle to writing.

But there are women who write.

She writes.

When she gets a spare minute. When everything is sparkling. When the final of the Cup Winner's Cup is live on television and she can forget that she lives with a man who needs a sympathetic listener in the evenings. After a good dinner.

She starts cooking. She starts writing. The osso bucco bubbles gently then turns to cinders. She opens all the windows, puts the charred pan in to soak. Gets out a tin of sausages with lentils, meal-in-a-minute. No way is a burnt dinner going to mean the end of the finest story in the world. She's going to get this story written. Just as soon as she's scrawled an affectionate invitation to Aunt Josiane to come for the weekend – poor Aunt Josiane, lonely and depressed.

vacuum bag
tax payment
repot geraniums
clear chest of drawers
shorten curtains

She's writing.

She's writing in her notebooks. She enters it into the Mac. She writes while the baby's asleep. She writes between bouts of anxiety – has he vomited his bottle? That little spot on his cheek that she noticed just now, could it be the first symptom of some infectious illness? Why is he so quiet? She runs to check if he's still breathing.

She's writing. She's not writing. Charlène is whining, nobody likes me. Charlène is complaining that she's fat and ugly. Don't be so silly. Look at yourself in the mirror. I got D in my end of term test. Ooh! that's rather different. Charlène resolves to give up chocolate éclairs and to go through her homework in future with her mother.

> *go through homework*
> *sort out winter clothes*
> *ironing*
> *mothball cupboards*
> *senior citizens' club visit*
> *press-studs, 50 cm velcro tape*
> *fruit vegetables*
> *subscription TV magazine*

Jean wants to have his friends round one Saturday evening. For a mega rock and rap session. She shudders. Had no idea what she was taking on when she agreed to be a stepmum. Chin up, others have been in the same boat. Listen, Jean, we'll see. Just now I have to write. And it's time for your basketball training.

Write? says Jean. Write to who? Nobody writes any more. What for, with mobiles . . .

She's not writing. She is writing. In between she decides that the kids can use the garage and make sandwiches in the kitchen on condition that . . . But what's the point in having conditions when the promises are bound to be broken, recriminations inevitable . . . Don't let Jean get on at you advises Pascal, retreating to the safety of his study. This from a man who has never been able to say no to his son.

From a man who has a study.

A room of one's own. How can she sort out a refuge for herself in a house of modest proportions in which the children all have their own room and Dad has a study?

There is no bar on writing the finest story in the world on the kitchen table. Nor on thinking about questions of syntax whilst stirring the tomato coulis with a wooden spoon.

Charlène's long hair is infested with vermin. The school nurse said to take emergency measures. Don't want my hair shaved off. The shampoo guarantees the nits will die a perfumed death. To be repeated twice more this week. Nits in the baby's hair. Bugs in the word processing system. Women and computers, Jean sniggers. You just pressed *shift* when you should've pressed *alt*. Shall I put it right for you, he suggests, good Samaritan. Okay, for the rock and rap session she will supply an enormous pizza and a whole crate of cans of coke. She will send Charlène off to her best friend's house for the night. And suggest to Pascal that it's about time they visited the grandmothers. She and Pascal and the baby will stay with one or other of them until Sunday afternoon. Heaving out through the hatchback a mountain of stuff, folding cot, high chair, pack of nappies, jars of baby food, inflatable bath, cleansing milk. Hello, stranger. Thought you'd forgotten you had parents. Armelle – (Jean again) – Armelle, is my Beachmania T-shirt ready? Still in the dirty washing basket! I've got nothing left to wear.

Baby's gums are sore. Can she imagine writing the finest story in the world with her right hand, whilst rocking a baby with teeth coming through in the crook of her left arm?

I hate to disturb you, says Pascal, I don't suppose by any chance you've seen . . .

Have I seen, haven't I seen, what can I say (the missing folder, the watch that Pascal takes off and puts down in a different place every night, the credit card that he is quite sure he put away in its case, Jean's Game Boy, Charlène's fluorescent pogs). See nothing, say nothing, hear nothing, keeping her head down, she writes. Ever since she was a kid she's dreamed of being a writer. Without ever telling her parents, they would have shrugged their shoulders, where does she get these funny ideas. Her mother would have added that girls need only

Yes: spin wool and keep house.

Peace at last. Then the telephone.

Elsa, her best friend from way back. Hello, Armelle, Gérard is having an affair.

Look, Elsa, you've thought this too many times before.

Armelle, this time I swear he is.

The tenth time at least (the twentieth even?) that Elsa has rung her in desperation, Help he's having an affair. That could be the subject of the saddest story in the world. And the most farcical.

The computer is purring. Charlène, watch the plug. Have I saved it? Pascal opens the door a crack, Armelle, would you have a second to read over my article, you're so good at spelling.

Charlène is complaining, the baby is just ridiculous, throws everything he's given on the floor. Next time, young man, I am not picking your car up. The Ferrari crashes noisily to the floor. Too bad, I warned you. The baby starts howling.

Just at that moment the health visitor rings at the door. Sorry, just a routine visit, don't take it the wrong way.

She doesn't take it the wrong way. Sighs.

While I'm here I wanted to let you know that the old lady next door is having problems remembering things. Perhaps you could, discreetly . . . Mum, you said you'd help me make some paper flowers, the teacher wants them for the school fête. You haven't got time? Don't be surprised then when I don't get to move up to secondary school next year.

Wednesday. The kids out of school in the neighbourhood are making a racket. The play area down the street is showered in bits of glass. It takes her for ever to pick them up. What is the best way to give meaning to life? Write the finest story in the world or rid the planet of broken glass?

Or take a lover. She'll pick a good one. Rich and loving and generous. She'll talk to him. When they've made love. Pascal goes to sleep after lovemaking. The lover will listen to her. She'll tell him about writing, about how demanding it is. He'll understand.

He'll take her away from this place. Somewhere where no one needs her any more. Pascal will have to cope with Jean's behaviour, Charlène's moods, his aspirations in senior management, his choice of tie, the baby's vaccinations. And the plumbing. Far away beneath a panoramic blue sky she'll open her notebooks and fill them up in future without wasting any pages on lists of domestic tasks, blissfully untroubled by thoughts of shopping baskets.

No. There would be regrets and remorse. The pain of having hurt and betrayed. There would be anguish. The sky has turned grey.

And the finest story in the world will never be written.

Translated by Elizabeth Fallaize

JACQUELINE HARPMAN

Eve

Reader's Letter

Dear Madame Harpman,

*On Mary's advice, I've just been reading the stories you've written about
her and also about Antigone and Joan. I'm not very educated – I only
learned the alphabets two or three centuries ago, and so I'm not in a position
to discuss the literary merits of your accounts, but I found in them, as Mary
had promised, much cause for amusement. She told me that she'd dictated
the text herself and that you'd been very faithful to her thinking. The liberties
you took with Antigone and Joan amused me greatly. Joan doesn't bear a
grudge – she has a good heart and understood your intentions. She's even
flattered you portrayed her as someone so little taken in by her times. I'm
not too sure what Antigone thinks: Eternity has yet to placate her bad
temper – she's wary of friendship and incommunicative. She spends much
of her time looking for Oedipus to pick a fight with him; he avoids her like
the plague – I don't think that man will ever get over his earthly destiny.*

*If I'm taking the liberty of writing to you, it's to tell you that my reading
deeply shocked me. Of course, I knew that, since the dawn of time, a lot of
nonsense has been said about me, but I didn't realize that others too had
been victims of slander. It seems clear to me now that I've been too cut off – I
didn't think we women could speak up, and I kept quiet. In truth, I was
barely thinking at all, because if one doesn't speak, how can one think?
Throughout my earthly life I was so busy with a thousand chores demanding
my attention from morning to night that I never had time to reflect; I went
to bed exhausted and if it took me a few minutes to fall asleep, they'd be*

197

taken up thinking ahead to the next day: I'd have to wake up in time to grind the grain while the fire got going because Adam could not stand his bread not being baked by the time he opened his eyes and the poor man had so much work that I did my best to please him. In one hand I'd be holding my youngest who was suckling, and with the other I'd be kneading away, and at the same time I'd have to keep an eye on my little girl as she was always getting up to mischief the moment no one was watching. Cain and Abel were always quarrelling in a corner – I'd get through the night without dreaming and the day like a beast of burden. I'd hoped to have some peace in the last years of my life, once the little ones had reached adulthood and I the menopause, and that I would stop giving birth every ten months, but there were so many tragedies that I spent all my time crying. Mary has lost a son too – she knows you never recover from that.

I was very relieved when I learned the hour of my death was approaching: at last I'd be able to stop, but Oh, my word! What a dreadful disappointment! I don't know in which dreary corner of His paradise the Lord has chosen to house us, but no one ever comes here other than family. Furious that I'd taken so long, Adam was pacing up and down waiting for me, and everything carried on as it had on Earth, except that I was baking with imaginary grain and serving him illusory bread, which he pretended to eat as he thanked God for His gifts! I didn't understand any of it. Was eternal life nothing but the infinite repetition of earthly life? I saw my sons and daughters arrive, their wives and husbands, and I finally gave in to ennui.

Out of which you've dragged me, Madame. I've left the retirement home which we'd been allocated – apparently Adam's looking for me everywhere grumbling that he's hungry and that I need to cook his lunch. Is he pretending or has he really not grasped that he's dead?

Like Mary, there's plenty for me to correct. Oh, there was no glorifying of my virginity: whatever obsession men have about claiming their mother was a virgin, in my case, it would be difficult, given I had to give birth to humanity through my immense progeniture – seventeen children, and all healthy! But I want first and foremost to tell the truth about that business with the serpent. I am outraged. I wonder why the Eternal allows so many lies to do the rounds. Mary's theory must be true: He's having fun somewhere else and has forgotten humanity.

Eden.

Let's talk about Eden!

I remember the first moment perfectly: I opened my eyes and became aware of existing, sat in the grass before an excited and nervous Adam. The Hand of God floated in the air. The first words I heard were:

'You like her, like that?'

'I would have preferred a blonde.'

'Nice start! Well, if you think I've nothing else to do . . .'

And The Hand withdrew.

I was there, stunned, looking around me and not really understanding what I was seeing. The man sat in front of me:

'Are you ready?' he asked me. 'He's ordained that we should be fertile and that we should multiply.'

'Let me catch my breath.'

'Fine, but hurry up. One can never obey the Lord's injunctions quickly enough.'

All of history was in that little phrase there and it didn't take me long to grasp my situation: His impatient injunctions always suited Adam, who, quite evidently, was the Creator's favourite – as for me, I had to be at his beck and call. He granted me a minute then shoved me back into the grass and pounced on me.

I won't play the hypocrite. I educated myself very quickly and smartly in those days – I learned surprising things. The truth is the Eternal is no dunce: as he was creating, He realized that the biology He was inventing would be very painful for women and that, while the first weeks of pregnancy go by without too much difficulty (except when there's nausea) soon the heavy tummy, the back pain, the babies carried around all day and crying all night, the cracked nipples – everything would make wives so reluctant that, were he to grant us freedom before our husbands, He would be risking a revolt. So he was prescient, in my case anyway. One has to remember that, having neither a father nor a mother, Adam and I were not bothered by an Oedipal complex, nor by the complications that come with it, and the reflexes that, in His foresight, the Lord had put in place, worked without constraints: things happened pretty quickly, and ten minutes later we were panting joyously on the lawn.

'Goodness me!' said my master. 'That was worth the trouble!'

That first day was pure bliss. We spent our time making love and eating all sorts of fruit, without worrying about the ones that were forbidden as there really was plenty of variety to satisfy us. We drifted off to sleep before night fell, and by dawn we were alert, famished and ready for more pleasure.

But He didn't foresee everything. I don't think the Eternal had thought it worthwhile to become a good psychologist; it hadn't occurred to him that one wearies of things that never change. Before us, He'd invented the animals, who seemed content with what they'd been given: when he granted us more intelligence than them, He didn't weigh up all the consequences of the situation He was creating. However pleasant the sensations we receive from our bodies may be, they end up repeating themselves, and anything which repeats itself becomes boring. No doubt He never repeats anything. There are a hundred kinds of fruit, or more, but an orange is an orange, however sweet, however juicy, and after twenty of them you look for something else, and the moment came when we'd tasted everything. We began to feel we were going round in circles.

I have to describe our moral situation to you. We'd received curiosity, a taste for exploration, a desire for discovery, and, even if it had seemed very large to us in the beginning, we realized that the garden had limits. The Eternal hadn't explicitly forbidden us from going beyond these: but the lions which, within these boundaries, came over to lie at my feet so that I'd stroke under their ears, roared and bared their teeth the moment I tried to reach the other side of the hedge. My first pregnancy still wasn't showing by the time we'd covered the whole domain in every direction and wearied of forever setting off on the same walks. In the mornings, we'd have a shower beneath the northern waterfall, in the evenings we'd dine on bananas and dates to the west to admire the beautiful sunset; in the long twilight we'd search for a patch of grass on which to sleep, then it was all just eternal repetition and our waking up became increasingly morose.

'What do you want to do today?'

'What can we do that we didn't do yesterday, and the day before, and the day before that?'

We continued to sit, yawning. Even Adam's amorous ardour was failing and he saw, nervously, apathy triumph over desire.

'What do you expect? Sure you're cute, but it's always the same!'

Still, we made a real effort to come up with variations. Grow forth and multiply, *the Eternal had said: in our ignorance, we had a mysterious sense that it had something to do with our frolics in the grass and Adam's very personal growth, but he'd reached the stage of only multiplying out of obedience. From time to time, a new fantasy would rouse him then once again we'd find ourselves consumed by monotony.*

The flesh is sad, alas!* *and I had nothing to read.*

As you must have started to suspect, the truth is there never was any serpent. I don't know who made up that story – I think it was someone who wanted to disparage human intelligence. I would have said Man and his intelligence, but the facts are the facts and I won't distort them: it's me, Woman, who, beyond exasperation, stopped before the Tree.

'Why did He forbid us from eating from this one?'

'I've no idea. He said it was the Tree of the knowledge of good and evil and that if I ate from it I would die.'

'You would die? And me?'

'He didn't say anything about you.'

That sounded like Him, always relegating me to the background.

'Good and evil? What's that about?'

'I have no idea do I, precisely because He doesn't want us to know.'

That much seemed irrefutable to me. I was annoyed.

'And that's it?'

'I don't remember. I think he also muttered something about being equal to the gods.'

'The gods? I thought He was the only one?'

'Well, I definitely haven't seen any others.'

'Maybe he was referring to Himself in the plural?'

'Listen, the Lord moves in mysterious ways, and you're too curious.'

'I don't know if you can say that to me. It amounts to a criticism of His creation, and I think He's very touchy about that.'

It was our first serious conversation and you can see it didn't last long. Adam was quite evidently more inclined to submission than me – he instinctively came down on the side of established order, which, at the time,

* A line from Mallarmé's poem 'Sea Breeze': 'The flesh is sad, alas! and I've read all the books.'

irritated me, but with hindsight I tell myself it makes sense: the Almighty made him in His image and He's the one who established order. Adam could identify with the master without any go-between: me, I was already the next generation, and so ready to cause conflict.

With every day, Adam irritated me more and Adam became more morose. Summer bloomed in all its splendour – whatever His faults, the Eternal is a great artist – the sunsets were sublime and the firmament sumptuous in the moonlight, but when I pointed the shooting stars out to the husband, he just sulked:

'Right, listen, it was the same yesterday, and it will be the same tomorrow!'

I agreed with him, but I wanted to make him feel the monotony of our existence. At the time I wouldn't have been able to explain why; today I can see I wanted interaction, conversation – in short to share my emotions with someone. So you'll understand the impulse which drove me to write to you.

In the morning, he didn't want to get up and was grumbling away. Making as if I wanted to distract him, I brought him handfuls of lovely fruit:

'Strawberries again! Kiwis again! You didn't find anything else?'

'Yes. As you can see there are lychees, a Comice pear and two mandarins.'

'I had some yesterday.'

'I know of nothing else.'

It was as if our intuition of other sorts of food was gnawing away at us without our being able to give it substance. We watched the lambs gambolling and the hares grazing on lettuce – it taught us nothing. Sometimes I'd tear off an ear of wheat and have it in my hands for a good while with a nagging sense of holding something interesting, but I never went any further and would just bite, gloomily, into my mango.

The fruit from the Tree was different, and regardless of what has been claimed, it bore no resemblance to apples, or any other ordinary fruit. We had seen that the fruit we didn't pick – and there was so much of it that, honestly, we were only eating a tiny fraction – would rot little by little on the branch or plant before falling to the ground. Those from the Tree never changed appearance, as if they were not of the same nature.

'You don't find that bizarre?'

'Stop thinking about those fruit. We can't touch them full stop. What's the point in peering at them like that?'

'I enjoy it.'

Adam frowned, a little jealous as he didn't enjoy anything any more, but I didn't manage to pique his interest.

We obviously hadn't given names to the months, because we didn't know that there were months, but the leaves were turning red and I know now it was September when the rain came.

'O Lord! Lord! We'll catch cold.'

The rain stopped and an immense grumbling filled the universe.

'I've still got to water My plants, though.'

'Lord, we're not questioning Your intentions, which can only be perfect since they're Yours, but I'm shivering and look at Eve – her hair's dripping wet and she's sneezing.'

The Eternal growled:

'Fine. Get under the Tree. It's had enough water – it's of a kind which doesn't need much; I'll see to it that the rain doesn't reach beneath its leaves. But don't forget that it's forbidden to eat from it.

As it wasn't cold, we were soon dry again. I was intrigued: everywhere else in the garden one could smell the scent of flowers, and aromatic herbs; here there was no smell at all.

'Hey!' I said to Adam, who shrugged his shoulders, 'have you noticed that this one's never flowered? What's it for?'

'Well, for sheltering from the rain!'

The fact is I'd always wondered what that damned Tree was for, until it got on my nerves. There it was, right in the middle of the garden with its fruit that didn't perish and which no one ate; from all around one could see its great thick mass of very dark green, almost black. Its leaves were particularly smooth, and when the rain had stopped and we were leaving the shelter the Lord had granted us, I glimpsed them sparkling in the moonlight. I couldn't get back to sleep. To distract myself, I watched the night birds, but I could see that none of them approached it. Had the Almighty imposed the same prohibition on them as he had on us? As they didn't speak and never seemed to understand me when I tried to say something to them, it seemed unlikely. Now that I'm a little more educated, I say to myself that

He may perhaps have inscribed it in their genetic code: but in that case, why didn't He do the same thing with us?

The more time passed, the more the Tree annoyed me. It swelled, it rose, it became gigantic – I could see nothing else in the garden. Why, if He didn't want us to touch it, had he shoved it under our noses? He could have planted it in some discreet corner so that I wouldn't have to think about it all the time! It was a provocation and I started to ask myself if He really wanted His prohibition to be respected or if He was putting our docility to the test. Were we idiots ready to follow any injunction whatever it was? Did He want to test our sense of initiative? I looked at Adam getting bored and fat, while my bad mood had ruined my appetite.

'I don't know what's wrong with you,' he told me. 'Your shoulders are getting rounder and rounder and your belly fatter and fatter. It's not very attractive.'

Because, of course, I didn't know, and nor did he, that I was pregnant. I don't think you can imagine our situation, Madame: we knew NOTH-ING, and we didn't have even the slightest suspicion that there was something to know on any given subject. I find it difficult myself to remember our state of extreme ignorance. For example, we'd got used to seeing that every night was followed by day, so that in the evening it did some-times occur to me to think of the following day: would we swim in the pond to the south or have a shower in the waterfall to the north? Would we have a siesta under a tree or in the sun on the grass? These paltry plans constituted the sum and total of our amusements. And that way, we knew that the days repeated themselves – oh boy, they repeated themselves ad nauseam – but we had no notion of the seasons, and watched the leaves turn red without suspecting it was a presage of winter. My belly was growing rounder, I had no idea what was happening, and I didn't ask myself why. I was indifferent to Adam's criticisms, and pleased if anything to see ardours which I enjoyed less than before on the wane. I wonder, if I'd already eaten the fruit by the time of the birth, what would have hap-pened and how I'd have taken care of the child. Would the Eternal have come to give me some explanation? Would He have shown me how to breastfeed? We were living from day to day – minute to minute – learning at the very most that tomorrow would succeed today, but even if we had a full stomach and sluggish desire, to say that we were asking what we were going to do with ourselves would be too precise, as we had no idea of any activity other than coming and going, under the sun, from one bush to the next, resting at the first sign of tiredness and aimlessly setting off again after.

When the next rain came, we didn't wait for permission to take shelter beneath the tree. Sitting on the ground, I looked at the fruit: none had fallen, the earth was dry and free of anything rotten. They were imperishable – whatever spoiled the other ones had no power over these. It was then and there that I gained a clear understanding of time and the word formed in my mind. At that exact moment, thunder rolled and bolts of lightning rent the sky: I think the Lord didn't like my reflections and that he didn't appreci- ate, in any shape or form, what my mind had produced.

'The Eternal isn't happy,' a frightened Adam told me.

I felt nervous, but it didn't seem to me that it was fear. I was thinking. The stems form buds, which develop into flowers, then the petals fall and the fruit is formed, which then rots and falls if we don't eat it. Perhaps you'll think, Madame, that I'm talking endlessly about these fruit and their fall, but understand that I'd nothing else to nourish my reflections. I continued: the leaves redden, they dry out and leave the branch – at that rate the trees will soon be stripped bare. It seemed to me natural to suppose that, after a while, new leaves would grow and the cycle would begin again. That is time, I told myself, we are without any doubt subject to it like the leaves – are we too going to wither and fall rotting to the ground? There is only one fruit that seems to escape time, and He doesn't want us to touch it.

'In your opinion, why does He forbid us from eating from this Tree?' I asked Adam, who seemed not to understand my question.

I insisted:

'There has to be some reason.'

'I am not sure it's lawful to question His intentions,' he replied at last with an air of superiority.

'But what could happen to us if we did forbidden things?'

'How do you expect me to know? He wouldn't be happy.'

'And He'd send us great claps of thunder?'

Adam stretched out on the ground to sleep. I wasn't sleepy. I was think- ing of the next day: it would be a beautiful day, as it was every day. We'd *eat fruit, we'd stretch out in the sun, we'd go bathe in the lukewarm water of a lake, and then the night would fall, and we'd begin the same again the following day. Exasperation suddenly overwhelmed me. So was there really nothing else to do? So my life would be this succession of identical days, and when we had multiplied, instead of two there would be ten, a hundred, I don't know how many, bumping into each other on the grass, dazed and stuffed in this sunny Eden? I saw a thousand duplicates of Adam, and my countless doubles coming and going, shallow, swollen, stupid . . . my hand reached out all by itself, took some fruit and lifted it to my mouth.*

Its skin yielded pleasantly to the bite, I was expecting some juice, some soft pulp – there was just a sort of little breeze which spread around my mouth, a discreet perfume drifted to my nostrils, and the scales fell from my eyes.

Oh, how strange and beautiful a thing it is to begin to think. One has to have lived stupid to appreciate it, which no longer happens to anyone: when I recall the delicious explosion of intelligence, I don't regret my months of imbecility. I was suddenly filled with discernment, everything made sense, the light filled my soul and I had tears in my eyes: when He created us, He gave us just enough knowledge to survive, barely more than the animals. We instinctively knew that hunger led to eating, and genital arousal to sex, we had a little language: I took stock of my ignorance. I don't know why it's called the Tree of Knowledge: I didn't learn anything when I ate the fruit, but I began to reason and I became angry. The Eternal wanted to make idiots of us? The days were getting colder, we were heading towards winter, He'd said nothing – how would we protect ourselves from the cold? Would we have to call out to Him constantly for help? 'Lord, we're shivering!' and He'd bestow a little heat? Would we have to depend on Him constantly, and then adore Him for his beneficence? Which fruit would we eat when there was nothing growing on the branches? 'Lord, we're hungry,' and He'd find us something? Grow and multiply, He'd said, without explaining how we were supposed to go about it, and I hadn't connected my fat belly to His injunction nor to our frolics in the grass which, in the beginning, I'd so enjoyed. I realized that I'd some confused idea that, from time to time, I would wake up in the morning split into two, with another Eve at my side who'd begin, her as well, to take a stroll from the north to the south, from the waterfall to the ponds. I placed my hand on my belly and felt the baby move. I'd seen the ewes lambing, and I realized I was going to do as they did. How would I protect from the cold a child who would doubtless not be enveloped in nice natural wool as lambs were, but would be as hairless as us? They suckled at their mother's udders: but as for me, what would I give my child? I could clearly see the lambs only started to graze after a certain amount of time: would the fruit that nourished us be suitable for a baby? A thousand questions over-whelmed me, Adam was snoring without a care – I couldn't stand it any longer and I picked another fruit from the Tree and placed it delicately between his parted lips. He bit into it instinctively then bolted upright with a start.

The Voice of the furious Eternal made the ground tremble.

'You disobeyed my order.'

'Lord, I didn't do anything, I was sleeping,' said my terrified husband.

'It's true. I placed it between his lips.'

'I gave you power over the woman: you are responsible for the violation.'

The rest is well known: you shall give birth in pain, you shall earn your bread with the sweat from your brow, etc., but, as you see, no serpent, no serpent at all. I dreamed up my crime all alone and I've long wondered why a serpent has been shoved into the story. Since educating myself, I've formed a hypothesis: Adam must have felt vexed at having been less curious than me, and he spread amongst our children that vicious rumour that turned me into a feeble creature incapable of resisting, when in truth no one tempted me, no one seduced me – it was my own curiosity which won out over the fear the Eternal wanted to instil in my soul.

I have sometimes regretted it, I confess, for our life has been hard: but then I'd cast my mind back to that endless wandering around the garden of Eden, from north to south and from dawn to dusk . . . a wave of nausea would rise in my throat and I'd banish all regret. I'd also banish it when we ate a lovely slice of fresh bread with a large grilled cutlet, and I've never touched fruit since, compotes aside.

But the story doesn't end there, and the rest is mentioned nowhere. You'll be surprised. Or perhaps not, as I suspect you are very difficult to surprise.

I didn't see, to the east of the garden, the cherubim with flaming swords mentioned in Genesis. It was as if invisible walls were no longer separating inside and outside, and we were completely naked in the wind. The Eternal had nonetheless left at our disposal a pile of animal pelts which we wrapped ourselves in as best we could, and then we sat down on the ground, utterly disorientated.

'We must find a way to shelter and make fire,' said Adam, who'd suddenly become active and industrious.

I won't describe to you all the difficulties that we encountered, nor how we overcame them. We were young, vigorous and resourceful – we came up with something every day and went to sleep proud of our invention. Well . . . not every night! There were times I was exhausted to the point of exasperation, and Adam, become attentive once again, tried to console me by telling me the immense honour we'd been done, and the glory of being the first men of humanity. He took such pleasure in this that I pretended to share a sentiment which, at the end of the day, didn't make me feel any less tired. Despite it all, the moment came when we'd had enough of a climate that was too harsh, and we decided to head down south, to find a more clement valley. I should also say that the children were growing older: the eldest had hit puberty and was constantly chasing after his sister, which worried me a great deal because we knew the Eternal had forbidden incest. As usual, Adam grumbled at my fretting and told me the Eternal would certainly find a way to sort things out and we just had to leave it to His Providence. Yeah . . . I preferred my own foresight, and sensed that we absolutely had to leave. I don't know if I'd have succeeded in convincing my husband, but when he found his daughter wailing half-raped by her brother, and practically had to fight with the boy to tear him away in the act, he heaved a great sigh and agreed that we had to do something.

We packed our big bags and hit the road with the children: Adam put together a cart of sorts in which I could put the pots I used for cooking, the pelts which we wore against the cold, and some provisions. I was breastfeeding my youngest and thankfully I wasn't pregnant, so I had all of my natural agility at my disposal. There we were, on the road, stopping at night to sleep, setting off again at dawn, and delighted to feel it was indeed getting warmer and warmer.

Eve

We're moving along quite briskly as we're on a slight slope having just left a forest behind us. The little ones have fallen asleep in the cart. Adam has just noticed that we're following a kind of path, like those which, up the mountain, we'd formed by dint of walking the same way, and I'm about to be surprised by this when we see some people suddenly appear.

Some people?

My eyes open wide, I rub them, and look: there are two men, there's no doubt about it, they have two legs, two arms, a head like Adam's, and there are two women – I can make out the swell of their breasts beneath the fabric.

The fabric?

I've never seen such a thing, not the pelt of an animal, even a fine one, but something else, soft and floating around their bodies. Their hair isn't loose, but held in place by little objects I will learn are called pins, they're wearing sandals – well, I don't need to describe the typical dress of a woman two thousand years before Jesus Christ.

We're gasping with astonishment. They're as surprised as we are: they've never seen people roaming around half-naked in badly stitched animal pelts; a man who, having never shaved, has a beard down to his chest; and a woman whose shoulders are covered but not her breasts, because a child is suckling while she's walking.

They speak. We are so surprised that we don't even think to ask ourselves how come we're speaking the same language.

Madame: the Eternal was taking the piss.

The first men! The first men, you must be joking! He pulled Adam out of a pile of dust, I don't dispute He plucked me from one of his ribs, and He put us somewhere that was protected from the rest of the world by one of those magic spells which is among His talents: throughout this time, humanity carried on, from Homo erectus *to* Homo sapiens, *evolving, Lucy, Neanderthal, Magdalenians and the Lascaux cave . . . I was cutting and stitching those stinking pelts, the Greeks were spinning fine woollen sheets, Egyptian civilization was dazzling in all its splendour, Adam was doing his utmost to catch a goat and ewe which were to be the start of our flock, and I was feeling queasy when he killed a lamb to feed the children while, in the cities, women were going to the butcher's.*

Oh, I didn't know these luxuries, but at any rate the tribe which took us in treated us very well. We received a tent, we were allocated some land, I learned how to make bread and to spin wool, the little ones had all the education there was to be given, the Torah and the Kashrut, we were spared the dangers of consanguinity by giving wives to our sons and husbands to our daughters, and, as no one cast doubt on our story, we even became myths. I could happily have done without that.

I don't know what the Eternal had in mind when He placed us in the situation I've described. I imagine He was already unhappy with His creatures and that He wanted to carry out some new experiment. It failed. I'd love to have a serious conversation with Him, but He shuns all company. I don't think He likes criticism, but I'm a polite woman and I'd know how to speak to Him with moderation, keeping my bitterness to myself. I'd have some advice for Him. Apparently, He feels He doesn't need any.

However, if it's true that He's trying something elsewhere, as rumour has it, He should consult His failure, to avoid repeating it.

I hope you've not found this long letter boring. According to Mary, you're not a woman who lets others bother her, and if it did annoy you'd already have tossed it away. For me, at any rate, it was a pleasure to write to you.

Yours cordially,
Eve

Translated by Will McMorran

FRANÇOISE SAGAN

The Unknown Visitor

She took the corner at full speed and pulled up sharply in front of the house. She always sounded her horn on arrival. She didn't know why, but every time she arrived home she would give David, her husband, this warning that she was back. That day, she found herself wondering how and why she had acquired the habit. After all, they had been married for ten years, they had been living for ten years in this charming cottage in Berkshire, and it hardly seemed necessary to announce herself in this way to the father of her two children, her husband and ultimate protector.

'Where can he have got to?' she said in the ensuing silence, and she got out of the car and walked with her golfer's stride towards the house, followed by the faithful Linda.

Life had not been kind to Linda Forthman. At the age of thirty-two, after an unhappy divorce, she had remained alone – often courted, but still alone – and it required all Millicent's good nature and enthusiasm to endure, for example, this entire Sunday in her company, playing golf. Though uncomplaining, Linda was infuriatingly apathetic. She looked at men (unmarried men, of course), they looked back at her, and things never seemed to go any further. To a woman like Millicent, who was full of charm and vitality, Linda Forthman's character was an enigma. From time to time, with his usual cynicism, David would offer an explanation: 'She's waiting for a chap,' he would say. 'Like every other girl, she's waiting for some chap she can get her hooks into.' Not only was it untrue, it was grossly unfair. In Millicent's view, Linda was simply waiting for someone who would love her, for all her apathy, and take her in hand.

Come to think of it, David was very contemptuous and acerbic on the subject of Linda, and indeed of the majority of their friends. She must talk to him about it. For instance, he refused to see the good side of that buffoon Jack Harris, who, even if he was as dumb as an ox, was generosity and kindness itself. David was always saying of him: 'Jack's a ladies' man . . . without the ladies', at which point he would roar with laughter at his own joke as though it were one of the inimitable witticisms of Shaw or Wilde.

She pushed open the door into the drawing room and paused, flabbergasted, on the threshold. There were overflowing ashtrays and open bottles all over the place and two dressing gowns lying in a corner in a heap: hers and David's. For one panic-stricken moment she wanted to turn round and leave, and pretend not to have seen. She cursed herself for not having telephoned beforehand, to say she was coming back earlier than expected: Sunday night instead of Monday morning. But Linda was there behind her, wide-eyed, a look of dismay on her pale face, and she would have to think up some plausible explanation for the irreparable occurrence that had evidently taken place in her house. Her house . . . ? Their house . . . ? For the past ten years, she had said 'our house' and David 'the house'. For the past ten years, she had talked about pot plants, gardenias, verandas and lawns, and for the past ten years David had said nothing in reply.

'What on earth,' said Linda, and her high-pitched voice made Millicent shudder, 'what on earth has been going on here? Has David been giving parties in your absence?'

Millicent laughed. She, at least, seemed to be taking it fairly lightly. And indeed it was perfectly possible that David, who had left for Liverpool two days before, had come back unexpectedly, spent the night there and gone out to dine at the nearby Country Club. Only there were these two dressing gowns, those two gaudy shrouds, those two banners, as it were, of adultery. She was astonished by her own astonishment. After all, David was a very attractive man. He had blue eyes, black hair and considerable wit. And yet it had never occurred to her, she had never had the slightest presentiment, let alone proof, that he was interested in any other woman. Of that much, without knowing why, she was certain. In fact she was absolutely convinced that David had never even looked at another woman.

She pulled herself together, crossed the room, picked up the two incriminating dressing gowns and threw them into the kitchen – hurriedly, but not hurriedly enough to avoid seeing the two used cups on the table and a butter-smeared plate. She shut the door hastily as though she had witnessed a rape; and, emptying the ashtrays, tidying away the bottles, chatting amiably, she set about trying to distract Linda from her initial curiosity and get her to sit down.

'Such a bore,' she said. 'Probably the maid didn't come to clean up after last weekend. Do sit down, darling. Shall I make you a cup of tea?'

Linda sat down gloomily, her hands between her knees and her bag swinging from her fingertips.

'If you don't mind,' she said, 'I'd prefer something stronger than tea. That last round of golf exhausted me . . .'

Millicent went back to the kitchen, averting her eyes from the cups, grabbed some ice cubes and a bottle of whisky and set them down in front of Linda. They sat facing one another in the drawing room furnished in bamboo and shadowed cretonne which David had brought back from somewhere or other. The room now looked – if not human – at least presentable once again, and through the french windows the elm trees could be seen swaying in the wind, that same wind which had driven them off the golf course an hour ago.

'David's in Liverpool,' said Millicent, and she realized that her voice was peremptory, as though she felt poor Linda was liable to contradict her.

'I know,' said Linda amiably, 'you told me.'

They both stared out of the window, then at their feet, then at one another.

Something was beginning to take hold in Millicent's mind. Like a wolf, or a fox, at any rate some sort of wild animal, it was gnawing at her. And the pain was getting worse. She gulped down some whisky to calm herself and caught Linda's eye again. 'Well,' she thought to herself, 'if it's what I think it is, if it's what any reasonable person might be expected to think it is, at least it isn't Linda. We've been together all weekend and she's just as appalled as I am, in fact even more so, oddly enough.' For, to her mind, the idea of David bringing a woman back to their house, whether or not the children were there, the idea of David bringing that woman here and lending her her dressing gown, still seemed absolutely unthinkable. David never looked at other women. In fact David never looked at anyone. And the word 'anyone' suddenly resounded in her head like a gong. It was true that he never looked at anyone. Not even her. David had been born hand-some and blind.

Of course it was natural enough, only seemly, really, that after ten years their physical relations should have dwindled practically to nothing. Of course it was only to be expected that after all this time nothing much should remain of the eager, hot-blooded, highly strung young man she had once known, but even so it was really rather odd that this handsome husband of hers, so blind but so attractive . . .

'Millicent,' said Linda, 'what do you make of all this?'

She gestured vaguely around the room, indicating the general disorder.

'What do you expect me to make of it?' said Millicent. 'Either Mrs Briggs, the charlady, didn't come in last Monday to clean up, or else David spent the weekend here with a call-girl.'

And she laughed. If anything she felt rather relieved. These were the two alternatives, there was no great mystery about it. There was nothing wrong with having a good laugh with a girlfriend about being deceived by one's husband and discovering it by chance because it was too windy to play golf.

'But,' said Linda (and she too was laughing), 'but what do you mean, a call-girl? David spends his entire time with you and the children and your friends. I can't see how he would have the time for girls.'

'Oh, well,' said Millicent, laughing even louder – she really did feel relieved, without knowing why – 'perhaps it's Pamela or Esther or Janie . . . Search me.'

'I don't think any of them would appeal to him,' said Linda, almost regretfully, and she made a move as if to get up, to Millicent's alarm.

'Look, Linda,' she said, 'even if we had caught them in the act, you know very well we wouldn't have made a scene. After all, we've been married for ten years, David and I. Both of us have had the odd fling . . . there's noth-ing to make a fuss about . . .'

'I know,' said Linda, 'these things don't matter very much. All the same, I must go, I want to get back to London.'

'You don't like David much, do you?'

For a second there was a look of amazement in Linda's eyes, which quickly changed to one of warmth and tenderness.

'Yes I do, I like him very much. I've known him since I was five years old, he was my brother's best friend at Eton . . .'

And, having made that pointless and uninteresting statement, she looked intently at Millicent, as though she had just said something of the utmost importance.

'Good,' said Millicent. 'In that case, I don't see why you can't forgive David for something I myself am prepared to forgive. I know the house is in a mess, but I'd rather stay here than be stuck in that awful traffic all the way back to London!'

'David is very good to you,' she said.

'Of course he is,' said Millicent unhesitatingly.

And it was true that he had been a considerate husband, courteous, protective and on occasion highly imaginative. He could also, alas, be exceedingly neurotic: but she would keep that to herself. She wasn't going to tell Linda about David lying on the sofa in London with his eyes closed for days on end, refusing to go out. She wasn't going to tell her about David's terrifying nightmares. She wasn't going to tell her about David's manic telephone conversations with some businessman whose name she couldn't even remember. She wasn't going to tell her about David's rages when one of the children failed an exam. Nor would she tell Linda how insufferable David could be about furniture or pictures, nor how forgetful David, the considerate David, sometimes was about his appointments, including those with her. Nor about the state he was sometimes in, when he came home. Least of all could she tell Linda about the marks she had seen on his back one day when she caught sight of it in the mirror . . . And the mere memory of this was enough to break down her conventional English reticence, and she asked – at least she heard herself ask – 'Do you really think it's Esther or Pamela?' Because it was true that he didn't have the time to see other women, and even women who indulge in illicit affairs demand a certain amount of time from their lovers. David's adventures, if they existed, could only be crude, frantic, hurried affairs, with prostitutes or specialists. And it was surely impossible to imagine David, proud, fastidious David, as a masochist . . .

Linda's voice seemed to come from a long way away.

'What makes you think of Pamela or Esther? They're much too demanding . . .'

'You're right,' said Millicent.

She stood up, went over to the mirror on the wall and examined herself in it. She was still beautiful – men had told her so often enough, and sometimes proved they meant it – and her husband was one of the most charming and gifted men in their circle. Why, then, did she seem to see in the mirror a sort of skeleton without flesh or nerves or blood or sinews?

'It seems a pity,' she said (she hardly knew what she was saying any longer), 'it seems a pity that David hasn't more men friends, as well as women friends. Have you noticed?'

'I've never noticed anything,' said Linda, or rather Linda's voice, since dusk had descended and all Millicent could see of her was a silhouette, a sort of mouse-like creature perched on the sofa, who knew – but what did she know? The woman's name. Why didn't she tell her? Linda was nasty enough or nice enough – how could one tell in such cases? – to murmur a name. Why then, in this July twilight, wrapped in her solitude and her pale suit, did she look as though she was scared out of her wits? One must be rational and down to earth about these things. If it was true, she would have to face up to the fact that David was having an affair with some woman, either a friend or a professional. Vulgar recriminations must be avoided at all costs, and, perhaps, later on, she might even take a light-hearted revenge with Percy or someone. One must see things in their proper perspective, like a woman of the world. She got to her feet, straightened the cushions with a regal hand, and declared:

'Listen, darling, whatever happens we'll stay here the night. I'll go and see what sort of state the rooms are in upstairs. If by any chance my husband has been having an orgy, I'll telephone Mrs Briggs, who lives down the road, and ask her to give us a hand. Does that suit you?'

'Fine,' said Linda from the shadows. 'Fine. Anything you say.'

And Millicent walked towards the staircase, giving the photograph of their sons an absent-minded smile on the way. They were to go to Eton, like David, and who else was it? Oh, yes, Linda's brother. Climbing the stairs, she was surprised to find that she needed to lean on the banisters. Something had deprived her of the use of her legs; it wasn't the golf, nor the thought of possible adultery. Anyone can envisage, indeed must envisage, the possibility of their partner's infidelity – it wasn't an excuse for creating a scene or putting on an act. Not to Millicent's way of thinking, at any rate. She went into 'their' bedroom, the bedroom of 'their' house, and noticed without the slightest embarrassment that the bed was unmade, the sheets rumpled, churned up as they had never been, it seemed to her, since her marriage to David. Then she noticed the watch on the bedside table, *her* bedside table. It was a heavy, waterproof watch, a man's watch, and she weighed it in her hand for a moment, fascinated and incredulous, until the realization that it must have been left behind by another man finally sank in. She understood everything now. Downstairs, there was Linda, worried stiff and getting more and more scared, sitting there, in the dark. Millicent went downstairs again, and with a curious, almost pitying expression in her eyes, looked at dear Linda who also knew.

'Linda, my poor pet,' she said, 'I'm afraid you were right. There's a pair of salmon-pink camiknickers in the bedroom I wouldn't be seen dead in.'

Translated by Joanna Kilmartin

MONIQUE WITTIG

The Garden

'Deformed, altered in their physique, in their gestures, in their thinking, no matter what their sex, their species, their race, creatures, enslaved by the social and political body as a whole, testify, even in the shape of their bodies, to the effects of the brutality and the violence of what we call culture.'

— Camille Larsen, *Culture or Domination*

At noon the garden is covered in a violet haze. There is no movement on the paths of rose-coloured sand. Rows of flowers of different species receive a cloud of water dispersed by big rotating sprinklers. But there is no wind to agitate them. The bodies are laid out side by side in deck chairs, immobile, naked. A voice is heard from time to time. Then silence. Numerous hours pass without anything happening. One watches the sky through the fountains' mist, one waits for a cloud to form and to disintegrate, but most of the time the sky is empty, grey, blue, white. Not even a bird passes. In the middle of the day the feeders come to nourish the bodies. They arrive from everywhere, and despite the transparency of their wings, the sky is all obscured. Their bodies are red, blue-green, very shiny, ringed in various places. The feeders fly up close, and without touching down they practise mouth-to-mouth, their beaks slide between the lips, and they vomit into the gullet thick and syrupy liquids whose composition varies every day. One closes one's eyes so as not to see the large pendulous eyes that move in all directions, but despite long habit it is still difficult to get used to them. One can, however, watch without displeasure the multiple veins of their wings that one discerns clearly despite their movement. At times some of the bodies refuse nourishment. Then the beaks are forced between the lips, and it is impossible to offer any real resistance despite their apparent fragility. When the feeders have gone, at times some of the bodies start to make long and sweet raucous howls, never-ending. Or some start to laugh and shake their heads in all directions. They are drunk, to tell the truth, and they shout, they make all kinds of noises with their throats. Others fall asleep. Time stands still. Now and then the noise of a petal falling attracts attention. Or it's the whistling of one of the numerous jets of water at the end of its run and about to stop. One hardly speaks. From the body, in this position, only the head can perceive the other parts when looking down, the cylindrical chest, the stomach, the legs both fused and divided, whose diminishing shape resembles the tail of the big blue fish that can be seen in the pools. It is said that the bodies used to live in the oceans. They were called mermaids. But the mermaids had forelimbs. The bodies have this in common with the mermaids; they swim perfectly and they sing, it is said, as the mermaids used to sing. One sings only when one is in the water, at bath time. One can do it any time when in the open air. One never does. In the water of the pools, the sound waves don't leave the surface. So one sings. This is the time of day that everyone awaits. The big apes come a bit before sunset. They walk solemnly while beating their tambourines with bare hands. Their bodies are without clothes, and on their heads they wear silver-coloured caps. One by one they carry the bodies to the pool where they let them fall with great splashes. One lets oneself go to the bottom of the pool. One comes and goes very quickly, from bottom to top, in all directions, and in passing one brushes against the enormous blue fish that move aside. Sometimes one plays with them, belly-to-belly, in a kind of battle. Most of all one sings. One sings, letting oneself drift away, head towards the sky. One makes stridencies, modulations, low and barely audible sighs. One twirls or goes upside down. When one goes back up to the surface one sees the big apes covered with hair, jumping all around the pools clapping their palms together. Or they lean down, trying to catch a body when it passes by. One always escapes them. At a given moment the big apes plunge in long-handled nets to gather the bodies one after another. They struggle violently. Many don't let themselves be taken the first time or else they manage to upset their net and they escape as fast as they can. In the end all the bodies are taken prisoner. During this capture the big apes show neither impatience nor anger. They treat the bodies very gently and rock them in their arms to calm them when they are caught. Later on they place them on tables in the relaxation rooms, and they start to massage them by covering them with benzoin oil. Their skin gleams. Sometimes one of the bodies, slipping in the hands of the masseur, falls to the floor and lets out a loud cry. The beings come to the garden when they organize parties. It's usually at nightfall after bath time, and it's only during these occasions that one has the freedom to see the night. The flowers aren't visible, but one perceives their odours much more than during the day. Girandoles and Bengal lights are lit in the paths and above the pools. Immobile in the deck chairs one always fears being struck by cinders or sparks. Coloured lanterns hung all along wires light up the rows of bodies. The beings arrive, dancing laughing very loudly shouting. They go in groups, or two by two, holding each other by the waist or by the hand. When they pass next to the mute and immobile bodies, they start to sing, O seesaw, O lilies / silver enemas, pointing at the enormous sexes stretched out on the bellies all in a row. Or else they make derisive gestures. Or they call out to one or another of the bodies inviting them to the party, challenging them to follow. For the ones so summoned, there is no other option but to bow their head to their chest or close their eyes. Sometimes the beings ask mocking questions. No one responds even when threatened with beatings. When one of the bodies in these circumstances is taken with fear and rolls in the sand of the path, one of the beings uses a whistle to call the big apes. Without waiting for them to arrive, the beings turn and leave together, laughing and making remarks. The body writhes about on the ground and rolls over, sometimes on the belly with head held high, sometimes on the back, split legs convulsively projected in the air. One of the big apes seizes the body, rocking to calm it, and wipes away the sand sticking to the recently oiled skin. At times during the feasts the milking of the bodies takes place in the garden paths instead of the relaxation rooms. The big apes place the milking machines on the sexes in the presence of the beings. On these occasions there are a lot of beings. They come and go from one machine to the next, evaluating the various bodies' productions, establishing a winner. When the winner of the milking is declared, one of the beings comes forward with a heavy garland of flowers while music, a kind of flourish of trumpets, breaks out. In the re-established silence the body receiving the garland is relieved of the milking machine and celebrated with a great pompous speech. At certain times the winner is celebrated by what the beings call the beating. The winner is then carried in triumph on to a stage and placed belly down on the knees of a being whose hands are gloved. The head hangs down on the same side as the garland. All the rest of the body is supported on its sexual bulb. The trumpets flourish as the being flings its hands in studded gloves at full speed on the body's backside. The music covers the cries except for those who are nearby. Only the satisfied bodies enjoy the beating. Everyone else systematically practises insomnia so as not to be a winner. Other than the pain caused by the blows, the face-down position on the being's knees is in itself a source of misery because of the enormous pressure exerted by the body when bellydown on the sex. Each blow applied to the buttocks is such a shock to the body that the heart stops beating. Sometimes the winner is carried away unconscious to a deck-chair to the rapturous applause of the standing beings. The parade of the bodies ends at the same time as the feast, at the moment when the lanterns are almost all out, when the smells of cooked sugars fade away. Before that the beings leaving the scene of the feast must cross back over the paths. Sometimes they pass by very quickly, yawning not talking much without stopping beside the bodies. Most often the beings come back from the feast with melting lumps of marshmallow on the end of sticks, or yams, or caramels. They take up positions in the shadows behind the deckchairs where they can't be seen, and one by one they jump out shouting to lance their hot and sticky projectiles on the faces on the torsos on the bellies on the sexes of the bodies all in a row. It's hard to not cry out when one is hit. Some beings wipe their hands right on the bodies to get rid of the rest of the food. Some nights when the full moon turns the garden white, the beings arrange races. They call them performances. The big apes bring the spheres in which the bodies are inserted before being released into the air. The pressure of the bodies on the inner walls manoeuvres the spheres. They would make excellent machines if their speed during the race were not regulated by the beings. When the beings seize the spheres, they open them by throwing them to the ground with all their might. Once cap-tured, the bodies are carried and held in the sandy path so that they can be treated according to the performance code. Rape is but one of the abuses they undergo. One hears screams, protestations, sounds of falling, whistles. Each one is carried to the pools by the big apes. Then one swims with all one's might to the bottom of the water; one screams, one struggles to escape the nets. The big apes have to work in groups to capture each of the bodies. The torches create reflections in the water. One twists in the big apes' hands in order to fall into the water of the pool. It is said that one night, one of the bodies succeeded in this way to be free and was found dead from fatigue in the morning. That one is called victorious and is celebrated by long collective murmurings the day after each feast. It is said that there are other gardens like this one and that the beings have their festivities there on the nights when they are not busy here. Some say that there are many other beings like those we know as well as other bodies and other gardens. Some rare afternoons after the feedings the regurgitations and the naps there are rebellions. One of the bodies complains, crying and yelling. Then one after the other they all make themselves heard. There are moans howls grumblings buzzes hoots curses angry incoherent speeches groans clamours. Disorder spreads in the rows of deck chairs among the shaken bodies, jumping throwing themselves down beating their heads on the ground. The disorder continues like this until bath time or until one after the other the bodies fall asleep from fatigue, even on the ground, mouths full of sand. The big apes wake them up with caresses, throaty noises, a kind of purring. The rebellions can take other forms. One or another starts to tell a story, for example, there was a time when you were not a slave, remember that. Each one in turn recovers the story of this mythical time when bodies had legs for walking when they stood upright, some even tell that they had arms like the beings. When the beings are questioned on this subject before the feasts they laugh, guffaw, pat the questioner's cheek, talk of insanity, demonstrate proof of a fundamental biological difference, crudely point out the genitals, origin, they say, of a paralysing function in itself. It is difficult for the questioner to protest when faced with the accumulation of proof. Raucous noises escape from some of the throats, stifled shrieks, grunting. The beings ignore them and move away in the midst of laughter. Rebellions are sometimes accompanied by plots to be executed during the brief moment when the beings stop near the deckchairs before going to the feasts. The plan is to spit on them or to bite if one of them comes close enough to permit it or in one great exertion to throw one's entire body against one of them like a weapon.

The day after such an attack the beings send their guardians. The guardians come with chairs and seat themselves next to a body. Their task consists of making the bodies talk. They themselves don't say anything. When the bodies refuse to talk in the course of the guardians' intervention, the feeders are called to pour the appropriate liquids into their mouths. That's what the guardians call untying the tongues. Tongues thus untied talk, and even if one plugs up one's ears the repeated recriminations are heard. There are complaints against forced feeding, forced milking, forced parading, the beatings, the performances. The guardians write on tablets. The guardians' silence has the goal of sending the speakers back to their own speech. The speakers must use their own material to organize what they are describing in a coherent manner. The description in each case, nevertheless, ends up revealing a strictly coercive system. But that is none of the guardians' business. They come back every day until the cure is complete. The cure is complete for each of the bodies when it is silent after absorbing the appropriate liquids. Some say that the guardians are also beings. Even though they have the outward appearance of it, the allure, the clothing, the limbs, one can't be sure. The face of each guardian is hidden behind a mask. The uselessness of the plots is a subject debated by the bodies during downtime in the garden. Some say that the presence of the guardians cannot be avoided except by avoiding plots altogether. Most of them say that they must try, try again. But generally the interludes with the guardians are followed by long periods of apathy during which the bodies close their eyes when the beings pass by them to go to the feasts. No one moves despite the beings' provocations in response to what they call sulkiness. What makes the afternoons particularly monotonous are the games played by the satisfied bodies. Their gatherings cut the reading sessions short. These are so-called creative games. To easily manage them the big apes regroup the satisfied bodies. They improvise in dialogues, monologues, decorous speeches but also in all kinds of poems. The themes are the quality of the food, the diversity of tastes, the garden's beauty, the sensual joys of the milking, the pleasure of receiving garlands. The violence of the beating and the performances are some of the themes that they reserve for the tragic genre. Even though the satisfied bodies are not the majority, one must listen to them. They must be read as well, unless one closes one's eyes, because their words occupy all of the reading space in which they are projected as well as emitted. Sometimes a generalized buzzing that little by little covers up the sound of their voices interrupts the satisfied bodies' exercises. Here and there a body suffocated by shame throws itself to the ground, crawling to hide under its deckchair. When the commotion becomes uncontrollable and all of the bodies in their excitement have thrown themselves to the ground, the big apes interrupt the so-called creative games and project holograms of the alphabet into the reading space. Calm is re-established instantaneously. One goes on then without transition to some grand story about a being or to a philosophical dissertation. The big apes take care of the bodies that have hurt themselves in jumping from their deckchairs and reinstall each one of them in their initial place. It is often debated after the reading sessions why the beings teach the bodies to read their books. The most accepted response is that in order for the servitude of the bodies to be pleasant for the beings and not just profitable, it has to be guessed at and even rationally understood by the bodies. That's why so much time is devoted to reading in the garden. Some argue that the beings thus run a risk because those who understand can change the situation and that the beings endanger themselves with the readings that they allow. They are given the answer that the beings' books never call into question the bodies' existence such as it is and that at the root of their systems and serving as their foundation is what the bodies call servitude. The beings call it something else. Some of the bodies even claim to be able to use the beings' concepts in order to disrupt their system as a whole. Either by the beings or by the bodies themselves, they are sent back to their deckchairs from which they cannot budge. Some being can say, get up and walk, and think itself mischievous. To add to the despondency about reading there are those who go around repeating that truth is blinding. There is no exaggeration to the preceding formula if it is true that the print in the books, by their holographic form, burns the retinas of the eyes in the end. At least the bodies don't run the fatal risk of confusing, as do the beings, the words composed of solid and bulky letters in their books with the real things to which they refer. As to whether it is reason enough to go on living, many are those who respond in the negative. Those are the ones who organize suicide campaigns instead of useless plots. The suicides can be by indigestion at feeding time or by suffocation in the waters of the pools at bath time. They are prepared for over a long time, like the plots, to be collective demonstrations. The results of the waves of suicides are not clear. In practice the bodies are immediately replaced. Most say that the exchange, inasmuch as it is carried out against the satisfied bodies, is of no benefit. They say that they have to cease behaving like that if one does not want to ensure definitive elimination. Some of them say that inasmuch as one can never leave the garden for lack of legs the only thing to do is to let oneself be drugged by the food. They say that in so doing the state that they attain other than being pleasant contributes to insomnia and guarantees that they will not be the winners of the milking. Despite the unending debates on the impossibility of getting out of the garden there are those who do not give up on finding a way to escape. They get the big apes to let them gather together for consultations. Their rallying sign is a saying from one of the beings' tales whose meaning they have twisted. Whoever wants to join them sings this saying until one of the big apes carries them over to the group of allies. Even if every initiative seems unsuitable to the concrete situation, even when the temptation is to enjoy the garden without doing anything, it's hard to remain outside the plans that they are constructing. One of them, for example, claims to have discovered that the food stored in the fleshy part of the cheeks, once putrefied, is a noxious poison to the beings. The tactics then consist in biting one of the beings until the flesh is opened and projecting a stream of the decomposed liquids into the open wound. The speaker claims that the being thus bitten was executed in several minutes and died in the midst of convulsions in the sand of the path. This one says that if this event went unnoticed it was because one of the big apes immediately concealed the cadaver from view. Right after that most of them become restless. Hope without precedent runs through the rows of bodies. The discussions are accomplished in pairs, in threes, in groups of several. Large groups are avoided. The beings seem to not see a cause and effect relation between the bite carried out by the body and the being's death. They have apparently been content to seize the biter. Some stricken with fear say that for right now it is necessary to postpone any action for fear of reprisals and because the beings are doubtlessly performing tests on the body that they have confiscated. Others say that the longer they wait, the more they risk being discovered. They say that they must act quickly while there is still time. Some of them say that the beings have no way to identify the bodies' weapons. Everyone says, what to do? The restlessness grows. More and more bodies in their excitement fall from the deckchairs. Gradually each one realizes that quick action is necessary and that they betray themselves by all of the commotion. Not to mention that the satisfied bodies are on the lookout and that it will be more and more difficult to hide the facts from them. Some say that as soon as they know their new strength the satisfied bodies will rally all of the allied bodies. Some of them protest this reasoning, saying that the satisfied bodies have been brainwashed for ever by the beings' guardians. The last plan to date is the one that was adopted unanimously. It has the advantage of responding to the objection of those who say that even if all the beings are killed the bodies will still be equally powerless. They say, do you intend to take the beings' legs or what? There are still the spheres and the big apes. The plan is simple and consists of a signal given to rush the most beings possible. It can be done during performances at the moment when the beings open the spheres to appropriate the bodies. It will take biting, spitting, and throwing oneself back into the sphere all in one movement. If one has been ejected, immediately getting the help of a big ape to be put back in. And then it will take leaving the garden as quickly as possible. Some say that to kill a larger number of beings, all of them maybe, it will take going into action during a big milking ceremony, one of those that are followed by a pompous speech, when the beings are all assembled in the same place. To that it was objected that it would be better to divide up their forces and that in attacking the beings individually during the performances their confusion would be increased. It was also objected that on these special occasions at the time of the pompous speeches the spheres are nowhere in sight and that the big apes will not have time to produce them at the site of combat. Some among the bodies don't share the general enthusiasm. They stay silently slumped in their deckchairs. Sometimes they say, to what good anyway, we will all be killed in the end. Or still they say, what will the bodies find at the gates of the gardens; they say that the bodies' ignorance about the things of the world outside is absolute, that the beings have carefully removed all possibility for concrete knowledge for the bodies, including in their books. They say that the bodies without the feeders and the big apes cannot survive. Nevertheless, one waits for the next performances. One spends the long nap times after the feedings preparing the poison; one distils it; it goes from the fleshy part of the cheeks to the mouths where it is ruminated for a long time and rehashed until it becomes a concentration of the original liquid. It is preserved in this form in the cheeks that have developed interior pockets from uninterrupted suction. It is there that the desired putrefaction or fermentation takes place. This action is systematically carried out by all of the bodies, including those that are slumping in their deckchairs. Each one contributes a concentration so intense that the restlessness is calmed. From now on silence reigns in the garden paths. The creative games of the satisfied bodies are not interrupted. The reading sessions go on, too, with eyes shut, all of one's attention fixed on the putrefaction in progress. The time to act may be tomorrow. And if it takes dying, hold on to this sovereign happiness, vile creature to whom nothing on this earth belongs, except to die. Is it not written that in risking death you will cease to be a slave?

Translated by Lorie Sauble-Otto

GEORGES PEREC

The Winter Journey

In the last week of August 1939, as the talk of war invaded Paris, a young literature teacher, Vincent Degraël, was invited to spend a few days at the place outside Le Havre belonging to the parents of one of his colleagues, Denis Borrade. The day before his departure, while exploring his hosts' shelves in search of one of those books one has always promised oneself one will read, but that one will generally only have time to leaf inattentively through beside the fire before going to make up a fourth at bridge, Degraël lit upon a slim volume entitled *The Winter Journey*, whose author, Hugo Vernier, was quite unknown to him but whose opening pages made so strong an impression on him that he barely found time to make his excuses to his friend and his parents before going up to his room to read it.

The Winter Journey was a sort of narrative written in the first person, and set in a semi-imaginary country whose heavy skies, gloomy forests, mild hills and canals transected by greenish locks evoked with an insidious insistence the landscapes of Flanders and the Ardennes. The book was divided into two parts. The first, shorter part retraced in sybilline terms a journey which had all the appearances of an initiation, whose every stage seemed certainly to have been marked by a failure, and at the end of which the anonymous hero, a man whom everything gave one to suppose was young, arrived beside a lake that was submerged in a thick mist; there, a ferryman was waiting for him, who took him to a steep-sided, small island in the middle of which there rose a tall, gloomy building; hardly had the young man set foot on the narrow pontoon that afforded the only access to the island when a strange-looking couple appeared: an old man and an old woman, both clad in long black capes, who seemed to rise up out of the fog and who came and placed themselves on either side of him, took him by the elbows and pressed themselves as tightly as they could against his sides; welded together almost, they scaled a rock-strewn path, entered the house, climbed a wooden staircase and came to a chamber. There, as inexplicably as they had appeared, the old people vanished, leaving the young man alone in the middle of the room. It was perfunctorily furnished: a bed covered with a flowery cretonne, a table, a chair. A fire was blazing in the fireplace. On the table a meal had been laid: bean soup, a shoulder of beef. Through the tall window of the room, the young man watched the full moon emerging from the clouds; then he sat down at the table and began to eat. This solitary supper brought the first part to an end.

The second part alone formed nearly four-fifths of the book and it quickly appeared that the brief narrative preceding it was merely an anecdotal pretext. It was a long confession of an exacerbated lyricism, mixed in with poems, with enigmatic maxims, with blasphemous incantations. Hardly had he begun reading it before Vincent Degraël felt a sense of unease that he found it impossible to define exactly, but which only grew more pronounced as he turned the pages of the volume with an increasingly shaky hand; it was as if the phrases he had in front of him had become suddenly familiar, were starting irresistibly to remind him of *something*, as if on to each one that he read there had been imposed, or rather superimposed, the at once precise yet blurred memory of a phrase almost identical to it that he had perhaps already read somewhere else; as if these words, more tender than a caress or more treacherous than a poison, words that were alternately limpid and hermetic, obscene and cordial, dazzling, labyrinthine, endlessly swinging like the frantic needle of a compass between a hallucinated violence and a fabulous serenity, formed the outline of a vague configuration in which could be found, jumbled together, Germain Nouveau and Tristan Corbière, Rimbaud and Verhaeren, Charles Cros and Léon Bloy.

These were the very authors with whom Vincent Degraël was concerned – for several years he had been working on a thesis on 'the evolution of French poetry from the Parnassians to the Symbolists' – and his first thought was that he might well have chanced to read this book as part of his researches, then, more likely, that he was the victim of an illusory *déjà vu* in which, as when the simple taste of a sip of tea suddenly carries you back thirty years to England, a mere trifle had succeeded, a sound, a smell, a gesture – perhaps the moment's hesitation he had noticed before taking the book from the shelf where it had been arranged between Verhaeren and Viélé-Griffin, or else the eager way in which he had perused the opening pages – for the false memory of a previous reading to super-impose itself and so to disturb his present reading as to render it impossible. Soon, however, doubt was no longer possible and Degraël had to yield to the evidence. Perhaps his memory was playing tricks on him, perhaps it was only by chance that Vernier seemed to have borrowed his 'solitary jackal haunting stone sepulchres' from Catulle Mendès, perhaps it should be put down to a fortuitous convergence, to a parading of influence, a deliberate homage, unconscious copying, wilful pastiche, a liking for quota-tion, a fortunate coincidence, perhaps expressions such as 'the flight of time', 'winter fogs', 'dim horizon', 'deep caves', 'vaporous fountains', 'uncertain light of the wild undergrowth' should be seen as belonging by right to all poets so that it was just as normal to meet with them in a paragraph by Hugo Vernier as in the stanzas of Jean Moréas, but it was quite impossible not to recognize, word for word, or almost, reading at random, in one place a fragment from Rimbaud ('I readily could see a mosque in place of a factory, a drum school built by angels') or Mallarmé ('the lucid winter, the season of serene art'), in another Lautréamont ('I gazed in a mirror at that mouth bruised by my own volition'), Gustave Kahn ('Let the song expire ... my heart weeps / A bistre crawls around the brightness. The solemn / silence has risen slowly, it frightens / The familiar sounds of the shadowy staff') or, only slightly modified, Verlaine ('in the interminable tedium of the plain, the snow gleamed like sand. The sky was the colour of copper. The train slid without a murmur ...'), etc.

It was four o'clock in the morning when Degraël finished reading *The Winter Journey*. He had pinpointed some thirty borrowings. There were certainly others. Hugo Vernier's book seemed to be nothing more than a prodigious compilation from the poets of the end of the nineteenth century, a disproportionate cento, a mosaic almost every piece of which was the work of someone else. But at the same time as he was struggling to imagine this unknown author who had wanted to extract the very substance of his own text from the books of others, when he was attempt-ing to picture this admirable and senseless project to himself in its entirety, Degraël felt a wild suspicion arise in him: he had just remembered that in taking the book from the shelf he had automatically made a note of the date, impelled by that reflex of the young researcher who never consults a work without remarking the bibliographical details. Perhaps he had made a mistake, but he certainly thought he had read 1864. He checked it, his heart pounding. He had read it correctly. That would mean Vernier had 'quoted' a line of Mallarmé two years in advance, had plagiarized Verlaine ten years before his 'Forgotten Ariettas', had written some Gustave Kahn nearly a quarter of a century before Kahn did! It would mean that Lautréamont, Germain Nouveau, Rimbaud, Corbière and quite a few others were merely the copyists of an unrecognized poet of genius who, in a single work, had been able to bring together the very substance off which three or four generations would be feeding after him!

Unless, obviously, the printer's date that appeared on the book were wrong. But Degraël refused to entertain that hypothesis: his discovery was too beautiful, too obvious, too necessary not to be true, and he was already imagining the vertiginous consequences it would provoke: the prodigious scandal that the public revelation of this 'premonitory anthology' would occasion, the extent of the fallout, the enormous doubt that would be cast on all that the critics and literary historians had been imperturbably teaching for years and years. Such was his impatience that, abandoning sleep once and for all, he dashed down to the library to try and find out a little more about this Vernier and his work.

He found nothing. The few dictionaries and directories to be found in the Borrades' library knew nothing of the existence of Hugo Vernier. Neither Denis nor his parents were able to tell him anything further; the book had been bought at an auction, ten years before, in Honfleur; they had looked through it without paying it much attention.

All through the day, with Denis's help, Degraël proceeded to make a systematic examination of the book, going to look up its splintered shards in dozens of anthologies and collections. They found almost three hundred and fifty, shared among almost thirty authors; the most celebrated along with the most obscure poets of the *fin de siècle*, and sometimes even a few prose writers (Léon Bloy, Ernest Hello) seemed to have used *The Winter Journey* as a bible from which they had extracted the best of themselves: Banville, Richepin, Huysmans, Charles Cros, Léon Valade rubbed shoulders with Mallarmé and Verlaine and others now fallen into oblivion whose names were Charles de Pomairols, Hippolyte Vaillant, Maurice Rollinat (the godson of George Sand), Laprade, Albert Mérat, Charles Morice or Antony Valabrègue.

Degraël made a careful note of the list of authors and the source of their borrowings and returned to Paris, fully determined to continue his researches the very next day in the Bibliothèque Nationale. But events did not allow him to. In Paris his call-up papers were waiting for him. Joining his unit in Compiègne, he found himself, without really having had the time to understand why, in Saint-Jean-de-Luz, passed over into Spain and from there to England, and only came back to France in 1945. Throughout the war he had carried his notebook with him and had miraculously succeeded in not losing it. His researches had obviously not progressed much, but he had made one, for him capital, discovery all the same. In the British Museum he had been able to consult the *Catalogue général de la librairie française* and the *Bibliographie de la France* and had been able to confirm his tremendous hypothesis: *The Winter Journey*, by Vernier (Hugo), had indeed been published in 1864, at Valenciennes, by Hervé Frères, Publishers and Booksellers, had been registered legally like all books published in France, and had been deposited in the Bibliothèque Nationale, where it had been given the shelfmark Z87912.

Appointed to a teaching post in Beauvais, Vincent Degraël henceforth devoted all his free time to *The Winter Journey*.

Going thoroughly into the private journals and correspondence of most of the poets of the end of the nineteenth century quickly convinced him that, in his day, Hugo Vernier had known the celebrity he deserved: notes such as 'received a letter from Hugo today', or 'wrote Hugo a long letter', 'read V.H. all night', or even Valentin Havercamp's celebrated 'Hugo, Hugo alone' definitely did not refer to 'Victor' Hugo, but to this doomed poet whose brief oeuvre had apparently inflamed all those who had held it in their hands. Glaring contradictions which criticism and literary history had never been able to explain thus found their one logical solution: it was obviously with Hugo Vernier in mind and what they owed to his *Winter Journey* that Rimbaud had written 'I is another' and Lautréamont 'Poetry should be made by all and not by one'.

But the more he established the preponderant place that Hugo Vernier was going to have to occupy in the literary history of late nineteenth-century France, the less was he in a position to furnish tangible proof, for he was never able again to lay his hands on a copy of *The Winter Journey*. The one that he had consulted had been destroyed – along with the villa – during the bombing of Le Havre; the copy deposited in the Bibliothèque Nationale wasn't there when he asked for it and it was only after long enquiries that he was able to learn that, in 1926, the book had been sent to a binder who had never received it. All the researches that he caused to be undertaken by dozens, by hundreds of librarians, archivists and booksellers proved fruitless, and Degraël soon persuaded himself that the edition of five hundred copies had been deliberately destroyed by the very people who had been so directly inspired by it.

Of Hugo Vernier's life, Vincent Degraël learned nothing, or next to nothing. An unlooked-for brief mention, unearthed in an obscure *Biographie des hommes remarquables de la France du Nord et de la Belgique* (Verviers, 1882), informed him that he had been born in Vimy (Pas-de-Calais) on 3 September 1836. But the records of the Vimy registry office had been burned in 1916, along with duplicate copies lodged in the prefecture in Arras. No death certificate seemed ever to have been made out.

For close on thirty years, Vincent Degraël strove in vain to assemble proof of the existence of this poet and of his work. When he died, in the psychiatric hospital in Verrières, a few of his former pupils undertook to sort the vast pile of documents and manuscripts he had left behind. Among them figured a thick register bound in black cloth whose label bore, carefully and ornamentally inscribed, *The Winter Journey*. The first eight pages retraced the history of his fruitless researches; the other 392 pages were blank.

Translated by John Sturrock

ASSIA DJEBAR

There Is No Exile

That particular morning, I'd finished the housework a little earlier, by nine o'clock. Mother had put on her veil, taken her basket; in the opening of the door, she repeated as she had been repeating every day for three years: 'Not until we had been chased out of our own country did I find myself forced to go out to market like a man.'

'Our men have other things to do,' I answered, as I'd been answering every day for three years.

'May God protect us!'

I saw Mother to the staircase, then watched her go down heavily because of her legs: 'May God protect us,' I said again to myself as I went back in.

The cries began around ten o'clock, more or less. They were coming from the apartment next door and soon changed into shrieks. All three of us, my two sisters – Aïcha, Anissa and I – recognized it by the way in which the women received it: it was death.

Aïcha, the eldest, ran to the door, opened it in order to hear more clearly: 'May misfortune stay away from us,' she mumbled. 'Death has paid the Smaïn family a visit.'

At that moment, Mother came in. She put the basket on the floor, stopped where she stood, her face distraught, and began to beat her chest spasmodically with her hands. She was uttering little stifled cries, as when she was about to get sick.

Anissa, although she was the youngest of us, never lost her calm. She ran to close the door, lifted Mother's veil, took her by the shoulders and made her sit down on a mattress.

'Now don't get yourself in that state on account of someone else's misfortune,' she said. 'Don't forget you have a bad heart. May God shelter and keep us always.'

While she repeated the phrase several more times, she went to get some water and sprinkled it on Mother, who now, stretched out full length on the mattress, was moaning. Then Anissa washed her entire face, took a bottle of cologne from the wardrobe, opened it, and put it under her nostrils.

'No!' Mother said. 'Bring me some lemon.'

And she started to moan again.

Anissa continued to bustle about. I was just watching her. I've always been slow to react. I'd begun to listen to the sobs outside that hadn't ceased, would surely not cease before nightfall. There were five or six women in the Smaïn family, and they were all lamenting in chorus, each one settling, for ever it seemed, into the muddled outbreak of their grief. Later, of course, they'd have to prepare the meal, busy themselves with the poor, wash the body . . . There are so many things to do, the day of a burial.

For now, the voices of the hired mourners, all alike without any one of them distinguishable from the other if only by a more anguished tone, were making one long, gasping chant, and I knew that it would hang over the entire day like a fog in winter.

'Who actually died over there?' I asked Mother, who had almost quieted down.

'Their young son,' she said, inhaling the lemon deeply. 'A car drove over him in front of the door. I was coming home when my eyes saw him twisting one last time, like a worm. The ambulance took him to the hospital, but he was already dead.'

Then she began to sigh again.

'Those poor people,' she was saying. 'They saw him go out jumping with life and now they're going to bring him back in a bloodstained sheet.'

She raised herself halfway, repeated: 'jumping with life'. Then she fell back down on the mattress and said nothing other than the ritual formulas to keep misfortune away. But the low voice she always used to address God had a touch of hardness, vehemence.

'This day has an evil smell,' I said, still standing in front of Mother, motionlessly. 'I've sensed it since this morning, but I didn't know then that it was the smell of death.'

'You have to add: May God protect us!' Mother said sharply. Then she raised her eyes to me. We were alone in the room, Anissa and Aïcha had gone back to the kitchen.

'What's the matter with you?' she said. 'You look pale. Are you feeling sick, too?'

'May God protect us!' I said and left the room.

At noon, Omar was the first one home. The weeping continued. I'd attended to the meal while listening to the threnody and its modulations. I was growing used to them. I thought Omar would start asking questions. But no. He must have heard about it in the street.

He pulled Aïcha into a room. Then I heard them whispering. When some important event occurred, Omar spoke first to Aïcha in this way, because she was the eldest and the most serious one. Previously, Father used to do the same thing, but outside, with Omar, for he was the only son.

So there was something new; and it had nothing to do with death visiting the Smaïn family. I wasn't curious at all. Today is the day of death, all the rest becomes immaterial.

'Isn't that so?' I said to Anissa, who jumped.

'What's the matter now?'

'Nothing,' I said without belabouring the point, for I was familiar with her always disconcerted answers whenever I'd start thinking out loud. Even this morning . . .

But why this sudden, blatant desire to stare at myself in a mirror, to confront my own image at some length, and to say, while letting my hair fall down my back so that Anissa would gaze upon it: 'Look. At twenty-five, after having been married, after having lost my two children one after the other, having been divorced, after this exile and after this war, here I am busy admiring myself, smiling at myself like a young girl, like you . . .'

'Like me!' Anissa said, and she shrugged her shoulders.

Father came home a little late because it was Friday and he'd gone to say the prayer of *dhor* at the mosque. He immediately asked why they were in mourning.

'Death has visited the Smaïns,' I said, running towards him to kiss his hand. 'It has taken their young son away.'

'Those poor people,' he said after a silence.

I helped him get settled in his usual place, on the same mattress. Then, as I put his meal in front of him and made sure he didn't have to wait for anything, I forgot about the neighbours for a while. I liked to serve Father; it was, I think, the only household task I enjoyed. Especially now. Since our departure, Father had aged a great deal. He gave too much thought to those who weren't with us, even though he never spoke of them, unless a letter arrived from Algeria and he asked Omar to read it.

In the middle of the meal I heard Mother murmur: 'They can't possibly feel like eating today.'

'The body is still at the hospital,' someone said.

Father said nothing. He rarely spoke during meals.

'I'm not really hungry,' I said, getting up, to excuse myself.

The sobs outside seemed more muffled, but I could still distinguish their sing-song. Their gentle sing-song. This is the moment, I said to myself, when grief becomes familiar, and pleasurable, and nostalgic. This is the moment when you weep almost voluptuously, for this gift of tears is a gift without end. This was the moment when the bodies of my children would turn cold fast, so fast, and when I knew it . . .

At the end of the meal, Aïcha came into the kitchen, where I was by myself. First she went to close the windows that looked out over the neighbouring terraces, through which the weeping reached me. But I could still hear it. And, oddly, it was that which made me so tranquil today, a little gloomy.

'There are some women coming this afternoon to see you and to propose marriage,' she began. 'Father says the candidate is suitable in every way.'

Without answering, I turned my back to her and went to the window.

'Now what's your problem?' she said a little sharply.

'I need some air,' I said and opened the window all the way, so that the song could come in. It had already been a while since the breathing of death had become, for me, 'the song'.

Aïcha remained a moment without answering. 'When Father goes out, you'll attend to yourself a little,' she said at last. 'These women know very well that we're refugees like so many others, and that they're not going to find you dressed like a queen. But you should look your best, nevertheless.'

'They've stopped weeping,' I remarked. 'Or perhaps they're already tired,' I said, thinking of that strange fatigue that grasps us at the depth of our sorrow.

'Why don't you keep your mind on the women who're coming?' Aïcha replied in a slightly louder voice.

Father had left. Omar too, when Hafsa arrived. Like us, she was Algerian and we'd known her there, a young girl of twenty with an education. She was a teacher but had been working only since her mother and she had been exiled, as had so many others. 'An honourable woman doesn't work outside her home,' her mother used to say. She still said it, but with a sigh of helplessness. One had to live, and there was no man in their household now.

Hafsa found Mother and Anissa in the process of preparing pastries, as if these were a must for refugees like us. But her sense of protocol was instinctive in Mother; an inheritance from her past life that she could not readily abandon.

'These women you're waiting for,' I asked, 'who are they?'

'Refugees like us!' Aïcha exclaimed. 'You don't really think we'd give you away in marriage to strangers?' Then with heart and soul: 'Remember,' she said, 'the day we return to our own country, we shall all go back home, all of us, without exception.'

'The day that we return,' Hafsa, standing in the middle of the room, suddenly cried out, her eyes wide with dreams. 'The day that we return to our country!' she repeated. 'How I'd like to go back there on foot, the better to feel the Algerian soil under my feet, the better to see all our women, one after the other, all the widows, and all the orphans, and finally all the men, exhausted, sad perhaps, but free – free! And then I'll take a bit of soil in my hands, oh, just a tiny handful of soil, and I'll say to them: "See, my brothers, see these drops of blood in these grains of soil in this hand, that's how much Algeria has bled throughout her body, all over her vast body, that's how much Algeria has paid for our freedom and for this, our return, with her own soil. But her martyrdom now speaks in terms of grace. So you see, my brothers . . ."

'The day that we return,' Mother repeated softly in the silence that followed . . . 'If God wills it.'

It was then that the cries began again through the open window. Like an orchestra that brusquely starts a piece of music. Then, in a different tone, Hafsa reminded us: 'I'm here for the lesson.'

Aïcha pulled her into the next room.

During their meeting, I didn't know what to do. The windows of the kitchen and of the other two rooms looked out over the terraces. I went from one to the other, opening them, closing them, opening them again. All of this without hurrying, as if I weren't listening to the song.

Anissa caught me in my rounds.

'You can tell they're not Algerian,' she said. 'They're not even accustomed to being in mourning.'

'At home, in the mountains,' Mother answered, 'the dead have nobody to weep over them before they grow cold.'

'Weeping serves no purpose,' Anissa was stoic, 'whether you die in your bed or on the bare ground for your country.'

'What do you know about it?' I suddenly said to her. 'You're too young to know.'

'Soon they're going to bury him,' Mother whispered.

Then she raised her head and looked at me. I had once again closed the window behind me. I couldn't hear anything any more.

'They're going to bury him this very day,' Mother said again a little louder. 'That's our custom.'

'They shouldn't,' I said. 'It's a hateful custom to deliver a body to the earth when beauty still shines on it. Really quite hateful ... It seems to me they're burying him while he's still shivering, still ...' (but I couldn't control my voice any longer).

'Stop thinking about your children!' Mother said. 'The earth that was thrown on them is a blanket of gold. My poor daughter, stop thinking about your children!' Mother said again.

'I'm not thinking about anything,' I said. 'No, really. I don't want to think about anything. About anything at all.'

It was already four o'clock in the afternoon when they came in. From the kitchen where I was hiding, I heard them exclaim, once the normal phrases of courtesy had been uttered: 'What is that weeping?'

'May misfortune stay far away from us! May God protect us!'

'It gives me goose bumps,' the third one was saying. 'I've almost forgotten death and tears, these days. I've forgotten them, even though our hearts are always heavy.'

'That is the will of God,' the second one would respond.

In a placid voice, Mother explained the reason for the mourning next door as she invited them into the only room we had been able to furnish decently. Anissa, close by me, was already making the first comments on the way the women looked. She was questioning Aïcha, who had been with Mother to welcome them. I had opened the window again and watched them exchange their first impressions.

'What are you thinking?' Anissa said, her eye still on me.

'Nothing,' I said feebly; then, after a pause: 'I was thinking of the different faces of fate. I was thinking of God's will. Behind that wall, there is a dead person and women going mad with grief. Here, in our house, other women are talking of marriage ... I was thinking of that difference.'

'Just stop "thinking",' Aïcha cut in sharply. Then to Hafsa, who was coming in: 'You ought to be teaching *her,* not me. She spends all her time thinking. You'd almost believe she's read as many books as you have.'

'And why not?' Hafsa asked.

'I don't need to learn French,' I answered. 'What purpose would it serve? Father has taught us all our language. "That's all you need," he always says.'

'It's useful to know languages other than your own,' Hafsa said slowly. 'It's like knowing other people, other countries.'

I didn't answer. Perhaps she was right. Perhaps you ought to learn and not waste your time letting your mind wander, like mine, through the deserted corridors of the past. Perhaps I should take lessons and study French, or anything else. But I, I never felt the need to jostle my body or my mind ... Aïcha was different. Like a man: hard and hardworking. She was thirty. She hadn't seen her husband in three years, who was still incarcerated in Barberousse prison, where he had been since the first days of the war. Yet, she was getting an education and didn't settle for household work. Now, after just a few months of Hafsa's lessons, Omar no longer read her husband's infrequent letters, the few that might reach her. She managed to decipher them by herself. Sometimes I caught myself being envious of her.

'Hafsa,' she said, 'it's time for my sister to go in and greet these ladies. Please go with her.'

But Hafsa didn't want to. Aïcha insisted, and I was watching them play their little game of politeness.

'Does anyone know if they've come for the body yet?' I asked.

'What? Didn't you hear the chanters just now?' Anissa said.

'So that's why the weeping stopped for a moment,' I said. 'It's strange, as soon as some parts of the Koranic verses are chanted, the women imme-diately stop weeping. And yet, that's the most painful moment, I know it all too well myself. As long as the body is there in front of you, it seems the child isn't quite dead yet, can't be dead, you see? . . . Then comes the moment when the men get up, and that is to take him, wrapped in a sheet, on their shoulders. That's how he leaves, quickly, as on the day that he came . . . For me, may God forgive me, they can chant Koranic verses all they want, the house is still empty after they've gone, completely empty . . .'

Hafsa was listening, her head leaning towards the window. With a shiver, she turned towards me. She seemed younger even than Anissa, then.

'My God,' she said, emotion in her voice, 'I've just turned twenty and yet I've never encountered death. Never in my whole life!'

'Haven't you lost anyone in your family in this war?' Anissa asked.

'Oh yes,' she said, 'but the news always comes by mail. And death by mail, you see, I can't believe it. A first cousin of mine died under the guil-lotine as one of the first in Barberousse. Well, I've never shed a tear over him because I cannot believe that he's dead. And yet he was like a brother to me, I swear. But I just can't believe he's dead, you understand?' she said in a voice already wrapped in tears.

'Those who've died for the Cause aren't really dead,' Anissa answered with a touch of pride.

'So, let's think of the present. Let's think about today,' Aïcha said in a dry voice. 'The rest is in God's hand.'

There were three of them: an old woman who had to be the suitor's mother and who hastily put on her glasses as soon as I arrived; two other women, seated side by side, resembled each other. Hafsa, who'd come in behind me, sat down next to me. I lowered my eyes.

241

I knew my part, it was one I'd played before; stay mute like this, eyes lowered, and patiently let myself be examined until the very end: it was simple. Everything is simple, beforehand, for a girl who's being married off.

Mother was talking. I was barely listening. I knew the themes to be developed all too well: Mother was talking about our sad state as refugees; then they'd be exchanging opinions on when the end might be announced: '. . . another Ramadan to be spent away from home . . . perhaps this was the last one . . . perhaps, if God wills it! Of course, we were saying the same thing last year, and the year before that . . . Let's not complain too much . . . In any event, victory is certain, all our men say the same thing. And we, we know the day of our return will come . . . We should be thinking of those who stayed behind . . . We should be thinking of those who are suffering . . . The Algerian people are a people whom God loves . . . And our fighters are made of steel . . .' Then they'd come back to the tale of the flight, to the different means by which each one had left her soil where the fires were burning . . . Then they'd evoke the sadness of exile, the heart yearning for its country . . . And the fear of dying far from the land of one's birth . . . Then . . . 'But may God be praised and may he grant our prayers!'

This time it lasted a bit longer; an hour perhaps, or more. Until the time came to serve coffee. By then, I was hardly listening at all. I too was thinking in my own way of this exile, of these sombre days.

I was thinking how everything had changed, how on the day of my first engagement we had been in the long, bright living room of our house in the hills of Algiers; how we'd been prosperous then, we had prosperity and peace; how Father used to laugh, how he used to give thanks to God for the abundance of his home . . . And I, I wasn't as I was today, my soul grey, gloomy and with this idea of death beating faintly inside me since the morning . . . Yes, I was thinking how everything had changed and that, still, in some way everything remained the same. They were still concerned with marrying me off. And why exactly? I suddenly wondered. And why exactly? I repeated to myself, feeling something like fury inside me, or its echo. Just so I could have worries that never change whether it's peace or wartime, so I could wake up in the middle of the night and question myself on what it is that sleeps in the depths of the heart of the man sharing my bed . . . Just so I could give birth and weep, for life never comes unaccompanied to a woman, death is always right behind, furtive, quick, and smiling at the mothers . . . Yes, why indeed? I said to myself.

Coffee had now been served. Mother was inviting them to drink.

'We won't take even one sip,' the old woman began, 'before you've given us your word about your daughter.'

'Yes,' the other one said, 'my brother impressed upon us that we weren't to come back without your promising to give her to him as his wife.'

I was listening to Mother avoid answering, have herself be begged hypocritically, and then again invite them to drink. Aïcha joined in with her. The women were repeating their request . . . It was all as it should be.

The game went on a few minutes longer. Mother invoked the father's authority: 'I, of course, would give her to you . . . I know you are people of means . . . But there is her father.'

'Her father has already said yes to my brother,' one of the two women who resembled each other replied. 'The question remains only to be discussed between us.'

'Yes,' said the second one, 'it's up to us now. Let's settle the question.'

I raised my head; it was then, I think, that I met Hafsa's gaze. There was, deep in her eyes, a strange light, surely of interest or of irony, I don't know, but you could feel Hafsa as an outsider, attentive and curious at the same time, but an outsider. I met that look.

'I don't want to marry,' I said. 'I don't want to marry,' I repeated, barely shouting.

There was much commotion in the room: Mother got up with a deep sigh; Aïcha was blushing, I saw. And the two women who turned to me, with the same slow movement of shock: 'And why not?' one of them asked.

'My son,' the old woman exclaimed with some arrogance, 'my son is a man of science. In a few days he is leaving for the Orient.'

'Of course,' Mother said with touching haste. 'We know he's a scholar. We know him to have a righteous heart . . . Of course . . .'

'It's not because of your son,' I said. 'But I don't want to get married. I see the future before my eyes, it's totally black. I don't know how to explain it, surely it must come from God . . . But I see the future totally black before my eyes!' I said again, sobbing, as Aïcha led me out of the room in silence.

*

Later, but why even tell the rest, except that I was consumed with shame and I didn't understand. Only Hafsa stayed close to me after the women had left.

'You're engaged,' she said sadly. 'Your mother said she'd give you away. Will you accept?' and she stared at me with imploring eyes.

'What difference does it make?' I said and really thought inside myself: What difference does it make? 'I don't know what came over me before. But they were all talking about the present and its changes and its misfortunes. And I was saying to myself: of what possible use is it to be suffering like this, far away from home, if I have to continue here as before in Algiers, to stay home and sit and pretend . . . Perhaps when life changes, everything should change with it, absolutely everything. I was thinking of all that,' I said, 'but I don't even know if that's bad or good . . . You, you're smart, and you know these things, perhaps you'll understand . . .'

'I do understand,' she said, hesitating as if she were going to start talking and then preferred to remain silent.

'Open the window,' I said. 'It's almost dark.'

She went to open it and then came back to my bed where I'd been lying down to cry, without reason, crying for shame and fatigue all at the same time. In the silence that followed, I was feeling distant, pondering the night that little by little engulfed the room. The sounds from the kitchen, where my sisters were, seemed to be coming from somewhere else.

Then Hafsa began to speak: 'Your father,' she said, 'once spoke of exile, of our present exile, and he said – oh, I remember it well, for nobody speaks like your father – he said: "There is no exile for any man loved by God. There is no exile for the one who is on God's path. There are only trials."'

She went on a while, but I've forgotten the rest, except that she repeated *we* very often with a note of passion. She said that word with a peculiar vehemence, so much so that I began to wonder towards the end whether that word really meant the two of us alone, or rather other women, all the women of our country.

To tell the truth, even if I'd known, what could I have answered? Hafsa was too knowledgeable for me. And that's what I would have liked to have told her when she stopped talking, perhaps in the expectation that I would speak.

But it was another voice that answered, a woman's voice that rose, through the open window, rose straight as an arrow towards the sky, that rounded itself out, spread out in its flight, a flight ample as a bird's after the storm, then came falling back down in sudden torrents.

'The other women have grown silent,' I said. 'The only one left to weep now is the mother . . . Such is life,' I added a moment later. 'There are those who forget or who simply sleep. And then there are those who keep bumping into the walls of the past. May God take pity on them!'

'Those are the true exiles,' said Hafsa.

Translated by Marjolijn de Jager

MARYSE CONDÉ

Family Portrait

If someone had asked my parents what they thought about the Second World War, they would have no doubt replied it was the darkest period they had ever known. Not because France was cut in two or because of the camps in Drancy or Auschwitz, or the extermination of six million Jews and all those crimes against humanity that are still being paid for, but because for seven long years they were deprived of what meant the most to them: their trips to France. Since my father was a former civil servant and my mother was still working as a teacher, they were regularly entitled to a paid vacation from their home in Guadeloupe to the *métropole* with their children. For them France was in no way the seat of colonial power. It was truly the Mother Country and Paris, the City of Light that lit up their lives. My mother would cram our heads with descriptions of the marvels of the Carreau du Temple and the Saint-Pierre market, throwing in as a bonus the Sainte-Chapelle and Versailles. My father preferred the Louvre and the Cigale dance hall, where as a bachelor he had gone to get his juices flowing. So we were only halfway through 1946 before they set sail again in sheer delight on the steam-ship that was to carry them to Le Havre, the first stop on their way back to their country of adoption.

I was the very youngest. One of the family's mythical stories was the circumstances of my birth. My father was still going strong at sixty-three. My mother had just celebrated her forty-third birthday. When she missed her period she thought it was the first sign of menopause and rushed over to her gynaecologist, Dr Mélas, who had delivered her seven times. After examining her, he burst out laughing.

'I was so ashamed,' my mother would tell her friends, 'that during the first few months I walked around like an unmarried mother and tried to cover myself up.'

However much she showered me with kisses, saying that her little 'late-comer' had become her walking stick in her old age, I had the same feeling every time I heard this story: I had not been desired.

Today, I can imagine the somewhat unusual sight we must have made, sitting in the sidewalk cafés of the Latin Quarter in a gloomy postwar Paris: my father, a former Don Juan, still looking good for his age, my mother decked out with lavish Creole jewellery, their eight children, my sisters, eyes lowered, rigged out like shrines, my teenage brothers, one of them already in his first year at medical school, and me, a spoiled, precocious little brat. Their trays balanced on their hips, the *garçons de café* would hover around us admiringly like honey bees. Setting down the *diabolos menthe*, they never failed to come out with: 'You speak excellent French, you know!'

My parents bore the compliment without turning a hair or smiling, merely a nod of the head. Once the *garçon* had gone, they turned to us as witnesses: 'Yet, we're as much French as they are,' my father sighed.

'Even more so,' my mother continued vehemently, adding by way of explanation, 'We're more educated. We have better manners. We read more. Some of them have never left Paris, whereas we have visited Mont Saint-Michel, the Riviera, and the Basque coast.'

There was something pathetic in this conversation which, though I was very young, upset me. They were complaining of a serious injustice. For no reason, the roles were reversed. The white-aproned, black-vested *garçons* scrambling for tips considered themselves superior to their generous customers. They were endowed with this French identity which was denied my parents, refused them despite their good appearances. As for me, I could not understand why such people, so proud and pleased with themselves, part of the Establishment back home, were competing with some *garçon de café* who was serving them.

One day I decided to get things straight. Whenever I was in a quandary I would turn to my brother Alexandre, who had renamed himself Sandrino 'to sound more American'. At the top of his class, his pockets stuffed with love letters from his girlfriends, Sandrino was the sunshine of my life. He was a protective, loving brother. But I would have liked to have been more than just his little sister – forgotten as soon as a bit of skirt flashed past or a soccer match began. Could he explain my parents' behaviour? Why were they so envious of people who, in their very own words, couldn't hold a candle to them?

We lived in a ground-floor apartment on a quiet street in the seventh arrondissement. It wasn't like in La Pointe, in Guadeloupe, where we were kept locked up at home. In Paris our parents allowed us to go out as much as we liked and even play with other children. At the time I was amazed by their attitude. Later I understood that in France our parents had no reason to fear we would speak Creole or take a liking to the *gwoka* drums like the ragamuffins in La Pointe. I can remember it was the day we were playing tag with the blond-haired children on the second floor and sharing their tea of dried fruit in a Paris still plagued with food shortages. Darkness began to transform the sky into a starry sieve. We were getting ready to go home before one of my sisters put her head out the window and cried: 'Children! Papa and Maman say it's time to come in!'

Before giving me an answer, Sandrino leaned back against a carriage entrance. A dark shadow fell over his jovial face, still bearing the chubby cheeks of childhood. His voice turned serious. 'Don't worry your head about it,' he blurted out. 'Papa and Maman are a pair of alienated individuals.'

Alienated? What did that mean? I didn't dare ask. It wasn't the first time I'd heard Sandrino poke fun at my parents. My mother had pinned a photo she'd cut out of *Ebony* over her bed. An African-American family with eight children like ours stood for all to admire. All doctors, lawyers engineers, and architects. In short, the pride of their parents. This photo sent Sandrino into fits of mockery, convinced he would become a famous writer and little knowing that he would die before life had barely laid hands on him. He never showed me the first pages of his novel, but he would recite his poems that left me puzzled, which, according to him, was what poetry should do. I spent the following night tossing and turning in my bed at the risk of waking my sister, Thérèse, who slept in the top bunk bed over my head. I worshipped my father and mother, I reasoned to myself. It was true I was none too pleased with their greying hair and wrinkles. I would have preferred them to be younger. For my mother to be mistaken for my older sister like my best friend Yvelise's mother when she took her to catechism. It was true I was in agony when my father peppered his conversation with Latin phrases which, I discovered later, could be found in the *Petit Larousse Illustré*. *Verba volent. Scripta manent. Carpe diem. Pater familias. Deus ex machina.* I especially suffered from the stockings two tones too light for her dark skin that my mother wore in the heat. But I knew the fondness at the bottom of their hearts and I knew they were endeavouring to prepare us for what they believed to be a wonderful life.

At the same time I had too much faith in my brother to doubt his judgement. From his expression and tone of voice I sensed that the mysterious word *alienated* designated a type of shameful ailment like gonorrhea, perhaps even fatal, like the typhoid fever last year that carried off so many folk in La Pointe. At midnight, after piecing all the clues together, I came up with a vague theory. An alienated person is someone who is trying to be what he can't be because he does not like what he is. At two in the morning, just as I was dropping off, I swore in a confused sort of way never to become alienated.

As a result, I woke up a completely changed little girl. From a model child, I became a child who answered back and argued. Since I did not quite know what I was aiming for, I merely contested everything my parents suggested: An evening at the opera to listen to the trumpets in *Aïda* or the bells in *Lakmé*; a visit to the Orangerie to admire Monet's *Nymphéas*; or quite simply a dress, a pair of shoes, or ribbons for my hair. My mother, whose virtue was not patience, did not skimp on the number of cuffs she dealt out. Twenty times a day she would exclaim: 'Good Lord! What has got into the child?'

A picture taken at the end of that particular visit to France shows us in the Luxembourg Gardens. My brothers and sisters all in a row. My father, sporting a moustache, dressed in an overcoat with a fur collar. My mother smiling with all her pearly-white teeth, her almond-shaped eyes squinting under her shiny, rabbit-skin fedora. Standing between her legs, skinny me, disfigured by that sulky, exasperated expression I was to cultivate until the end of my adolescence, until the hand of fate, that always comes down too hard on ungrateful children, made me an orphan at the early age of twenty.

Ever since, I have had plenty of time to understand the word *alienated* and especially to wonder whether Sandrino was right. Were my parents alienated? To be sure, they took no pride in their African ancestry. They knew nothing about it. That's a fact! During their visits to France my father never set foot in the Rue des Écoles, where the journal *Présence Africaine* was the brainchild of Alioune Diop. Like my mother, he was convinced that only Western culture was worthy of existence and was ever grateful to France for allowing them to obtain it. At the same time, neither one of them felt the slightest inferiority complex because of their colour. They believed they were the most brilliant and the most intelligent people alive, positive proof of the progress achieved by the Black Race.

Was that the meaning of 'alienated'?

Translated by Richard Philcox

LEÏLA SEBBAR

Women of Algiers, Women of Shame

Three women. Look for them. Yes, the museum's huge, enormous. Run everywhere, go right, left, upstairs, downstairs, you'll find them. Don't stop every time you see a woman, you won't take a step without seeing a body, standing, sitting, lying down, exposed for anyone to see, with white skin, smooth and soft, yes, they're beautiful, yes, bright eyes with the devil hiding behind them and hair, floating, golden, in ringlets, no headscarf, no veil, I'm telling you, they're naked and there's one of them, horror and damnation, you'll go straight to hell if you look up at her and her black bush, open to everyone, you hear me, don't stop, run away and don't turn round, get right away, far away, and don't look, don't look whatever you do, you'll be burned up like when you view an eclipse with the naked eye, run, the gaping flesh of that bush will swallow you up, it's greedy, insatiable, you'll never escape that bush, black as coal and a mass of curls, it's swallowed men after men, powerful men, more experienced in war than you, men who had swords and shields, men with Kalashnikovs, invincible men. Let the infidels disappear one after another into that cavern, let them fall into the dark hole, body and soul. Don't stay there in front of the monster, you won't be spared, and don't allow yourself to stray like weak men, their lust will destroy them, they will die and you will survive.

Here's the ground plan of the Museum and Art Gallery. Study it carefully. Be patient, all of you, you know that patience is a divine virtue, the last of Allah's virtues before the hundredth that must not be revealed to anyone. You'll know where to run, and where not to run. Just imagine you're blind until God grants you sight because you've deserved it, because you have a mission to carry out. God did not allow artistic creation to exist before the Book and the word of the Book. You know all this. That the forbidden work of art must be destroyed. But there, in that labyrinth of a gallery, where you must stop is at these three women, in an oriental room. They're your target, the Women of Algiers.

An infidel insisted on painting them. He went to an Islamic country, accompanying soldiers fresh from the conquest of another Islamic country, may they be cursed, how far will they go, these sun-worshippers who call themselves Christians. God is not on their side. They claim we have the same God, the only God. The All-Merciful, the Kind, don't believe them. Their words drip venom, every word is a snake.

This foreigner walked through the streets, sketchbook in hand, he drew pictures, morning, noon and night, I think he can never sleep, does he even eat? There is nobody to forbid this phantom, who goes here and there, spying . . . A spy? Women, children, old men . . . What does he see in our veiled women? He does not know that women cannot go about with their hair loose, they can't go alone, as they do in the reserved quarters. He does not understand that those women are women destined for Sheitan, for Hell, for torments beyond the grave. Perhaps he went inside those houses to sketch them naked on sofas, singing and dancing before the godless bedchamber. They say that foreigners, contaminated by these sorceresses, have never seen their native land again, they died in torment and were thrown to the jackals behind the hills north of the city. That will be this infidel's fate.

He was the one who painted this picture. The three women are seated, silks, muslins, Ottoman fabrics. In the cool of the siesta, they're chatting indolently, waiting for men from palaces and barracks, officers and courtiers, if the men don't have gold coins, they are thrown out. The woman standing, the negress, the men don't want her, she's a slave. Don't attack her. Leave her alone. If she escapes, don't chase her, the slave is not a whore.

Pay special attention to the Koranic lettering near the negress. Don't let it survive there for the impious. The painter does not understand what he has written. A sacred verse in the bedroom of a brothel. If he were alive today . . . Others will pay for him, I tell, you, but when? That I don't know, but their blasphemous drawings condemn them to violent death. They don't know that. Some day soon will be the day of judgement for every one of them.

Go directly to those Women of Algiers. You have the ground plan. Don't make a mistake.

The painter lived days and nights peacefully in his house, a studio with a garden in the centre of the city, the city of light they call it, the most beautiful of cities, I've never been there, the city of debauchery, it was not bombed during wartime when it might have disappeared, and with it the cursed museum and those Women of Algiers, who are still living. He had women come to his house, friends, neighbours, whores perhaps? He dressed them up. Those eastern clothes, he picked them out from trunks full of precious fabrics that you can't find today, because the most famous weaving workshops have disappeared. His models posed according to his wishes and he drew and painted until nightfall. The models dropped off to sleep, exhausted. He would drink a last cup of coffee in the garden, he said he liked the smell of box, like in Grenada, the box hedges of the Alhambra, where he had never been but where he would like to go for the beauty of Islamic art, the beauty of the mosques, the mosaics, the arabesques, the cupolas and the minarets. And Istanbul too, which he never had time to visit. He's old now. Istanbul will be for another life.

These Women of Algiers, he loves them. He talks about his women. He doesn't say 'my harem', he says 'my women', his beloved women, until eternity.

But the eternity of Art does not exist. God alone protects Art, the Art he permits. The only kind on earth.

Don't wait for the museum to close. Just go there. Don't forget your hoodies and your Kalashes. Don't be afraid of the crowds. Those men and women who are looking at the pictures on the walls, I don't know what they are seeing. God has not permitted the reproduction of the living in dead images. These idolaters ought not be living either, but don't kill them. Think only of the mission you're carrying out. Don't fire the Kalashes. Take out your knives. Slash the canvas to shreds, so that no one will be able to make out an eye, a finger, a jewel, a flower, not even a colour.

We'll burn to ashes those accursed women, that will be their hell, nothing will remain, nothing, not even the ashes, drowned in the river that flows through the city.

On you go!
   You are the heroes of a new world.

Translated by Siân Reynolds

PATRICK MODIANO

The Hat

At the age of eighteen, my mother embarked on a movie career in her native city of Antwerp. Until then, she had worked for the gas company and taken some elocution courses, but when a studio was built on the Pyckestraat, at the initiative of a certain Jan Vanderheyden, she walked in the door and was hired.

Before long, a team had formed around Vanderheyden, who always used the same actors and the same crew. He oversaw both production and direction, and he shot his films in record time. The Pyckestraat studio was such a hive of activity that journalists called it '*de Antwerpsche Hollywood*', the Hollywood of Antwerp.

My mother was the very young lead actress in four Vanderheyden pictures. He made the first two, *This Man Is an Angel* and *Janssens v. Peeters*, over the course of 1939. The next two, *Janssens and Peeters Reconciled* and *Good Luck, Monique*, date from 1941. Three of the films are popular comedies, set in Antwerp, and made Vanderheyden – as one critic put it at the time – the 'Pagnol of the Schelde'. The fourth, *Good Luck, Monique*, is a musical.

By then, the Vanderheyden production company had been placed under German control, and my mother was sent for several weeks to Berlin, where she took a small part in Willi Forst's *Bel Ami*.

In the year 1939, my mother also signed a contract with Antwerp's Empire Theatre. She was a showgirl. From June through December, they staged an adaptation of *No, No, Nanette*, and my mother appeared in that. Then, starting in January 1940, she was part of a 'current events' revue entitled *Tomorrow Will Be Better*. She was at the centre of the final tableau. As the other showgirls danced with 'Chamberlain' umbrellas, my mother could be seen rising up in a basket, her head wreathed in golden rays. Up, up she went, and the rain stopped, the umbrellas came down. She was the image of the rising sun whose light banished all the shadows of the coming year. From up in her basket, maman waved to the audience, and the orchestra played a medley. The curtain fell. Every time, as a joke, the crew would leave her there in her basket, way up high, in the dark.

She lived on the second floor of a little house near the Quai Van Dyck. One of her windows looked out over the Schelde and the riverside promenade, with the big café at the end. There was the Empire Theatre, with the dressing room where she did her make-up every evening. There was the custom house. There were the streets along the waterfront, the port and the docks. I see her cross the avenue as a streetcar rattles by, its yellow light fizzling out in the fog. Now it is night. The steamers sound their horns.

The wardrobe man at the Empire had grown fond of my mother and offered to serve as her manager. He was a jowly man, with large horn-rimmed glasses and very slow of speech. But by night, at a cabaret in the Greek quarter, frequented by sailors, he sang in a musical number as Madame Butterfly. According to him, the films of Vanderheyden, charming and numerous though they were, could not make an actress's career. My dear, you must think bigger. And as it happened, he knew a couple of important producers who were about to shoot a film but were still looking for a girl to play the second lead. He took my mother to meet them.

These producers turned out to be a man named Felix Openfeld and his father, known to everyone as Openfeld Senior. A Berlin gem dealer, this Openfeld Senior had retreated to Antwerp when Hitler seized power in Germany and Jewish businesses first came under threat. The son, once head producer at the German movie studio Terra Film, had found work in the United States.

They liked my mother. They didn't even give her a screen test, they simply asked her to read a scene from the script, right then and there. The movie had an English title, *Swimmers and Detectives*, and had been written to spec for the young Dutch Olympic swimming champion Willy den Ouden, who wanted to go into film. From what my mother told me, the rather lame detective subplot served as a pretext for various dives and aquatic ballets. My mother was to play the role of Willy den Ouden's best friend.

I have the contract my mother signed that day. Two sheets of great thick sky-blue paper, watermarked, with the Openfeld Films letterhead at the top. The *O* of Openfeld is very large, with an elegant loop executed in calligraphic thicks and thins. Inside the *O* stands a miniature Brandenburg Gate, finely engraved. It is there, I suppose, to recall the origins of the two producers, in Berlin.

It is agreed that my future mother shall receive a fixed sum of seventy-five thousand Belgian francs, payable in instalments at the commencement of each week of shooting. And it is understood by both parties that this fee shall not be subject to any augmentation or diminution until the contract should expire or, in due course, be extended. It is further stipulated that time spent in make up and wardrobe shall be considered work preparation, not work as such.

At the bottom of the page, my mother's careful signature. Then the dashed-off signature of Felix Openfeld. And the third signature, in an even choppier spidery hand, under which someone has typed: Mr Openfeld Senior.

The contract is dated April 21, 1940.

They invited my mother to dine with them that evening. The wardrobe man was also in attendance, and the screenwriter, Henri Putmann, whose nationality was unclear: Belgian? English? German? Willy den Ouden was supposed to come meet my mother but at the last minute was detained. It was very cheerful. The two Openfelds – Felix especially – possessed that courtesy, at once rigid and playful, so typical of Berlin. Felix Openfeld had high hopes for the picture. An American studio had already expressed interest. Hadn't he always said they should launch a series of detective comedies with a 'sporting angle'? At some point during the dinner they took a photo, which I have, here on my desk. The man with the dark, slicked-back hair is Felix Openfeld. The two fat men, slightly behind him: Putmann and the wardrobe man. The old man with the weaselish face but magnificent round eyes – that's Openfeld Senior. And the girl who looks like Vivien Leigh is my mother.

In the opening sequence of the film, she was to appear all by herself. She would tidy her bedroom, singing to herself, and answer the phone. Felix Openfeld, who was directing, had decided to take the scenes in chronological order.

The first day of shooting was set for Friday, May 10, 1940, at Sonor Studios in Brussels. My mother would arrive at ten thirty a.m. Since she lived in Antwerp, she would take a very early train.

The day before, she received an advance on her fee, which she used to buy a leather overnight bag, a pretty one, and some Elizabeth Arden products. She went home at the end of the afternoon, worked a bit more on her part, had her dinner, and went to bed.

Around four in the morning, she woke to what she thought was thunder. But this noise was even louder – a long, muffled roar. There were ambulances on the Quai Van Dyck, people were leaning out of their windows. Sirens howled across the city. The woman from the next apartment explained, trembling, that the German air force was bombing the port. The noise stopped, and my mother went back to sleep. At seven her alarm went off. She hurried downstairs to wait for the streetcar, in the little square, overnight bag in hand. The streetcar didn't come. Groups of people walked past, speaking in lowered voices.

Finally she found a taxi, and all the way to the station the driver kept repeating, as if saying the responses at Mass, 'We're fucked ... we're fucked ... we're fucked.'

The station was packed, and it was all my mother could do to fight her way to the platform for the train to Brussels. People gathered around the conductor, asking him questions: No, the train wasn't leaving. He was waiting for instructions. And the same sentence was on everyone's lips: 'The Germans have crossed the border ... The Germans have crossed the border.'

On the radio, on the six-thirty news, they had announced that the Wehrmacht had just invaded Belgium, Holland and Luxembourg.

My mother felt someone touch her arm. She turned – it was Openfeld Senior, in a black felt hat. He was unshaven, his weaselish face had shrunken by half, and his eyes were enormous. Two immense blue eyes, in the middle of a tiny head, the sort of head collected by the Jivaro people. He led her out of the station.

'We have to meet Felix at the studio – in Brussels – a taxi – quick – a taxi.'

He swallowed half his words.

The taxi drivers refused to take them such a long way, for fear of the bombings. Openfeld Senior managed to convince one with a hundred-franc note. In the taxi, Openfeld Senior said to my mother,

'We'll split the fare.'

My mother explained that all she had was twenty francs.

'That's all right. We'll sort it out at the studio.'

He said very little in the car. Now and then he consulted an address book and rummaged feverishly through the pockets of his overcoat and jacket.

'Don't you have another suitcase?' he said to my mother, nodding towards the leather bag on her knees.

'A suitcase?'

'I beg your pardon – that's right . . . you're staying here . . .'

He muttered something inaudible. He turned back to my mother:

'I could never have thought that they would fail to respect Belgian neutrality.'

He stressed each syllable, Bel-gian neu-tral-i-ty. Until that day, obviously, he had clung to those two words like a vague hope, and he must have said them over and over to himself, not believing in them, but with abundant goodwill. Now they were swept aside, along with everything else. *Belgian neutrality.*

The taxi brought them into Brussels and down Avenue de Tervueren, where several buildings had burned to the ground. Teams of firemen were sifting through the rubble. The driver asked what had happened – a bombing around eight o'clock.

In the courtyard of Sonor Studios, they found a truck and a large convertible crammed with luggage. When Openfeld Senior and my mother appeared on soundstage B, Felix Openfeld was giving instructions to various crew members, who were packing up the cameras and projectors.

'We're off to America,' Felix Openfeld said in a confident voice.

She sat on a stool. Openfeld Senior held out a cigarette case.

'Won't you come with us? We'll see if we can shoot the film over there.'

'You won't have any trouble at the borders,' Felix Openfeld said. 'You have a passport.'

Their plan was to get to Lisbon as fast as they could, through Spain. Felix Openfeld had obtained papers from the Portuguese consul, a great friend of his, he said.

'By tomorrow the Germans will be in Paris, and in two weeks they'll be in London,' declared Openfeld Senior, and shook his head.

They loaded the equipment on to the truck. There were three of them, the two Openfelds and Grunebaum, a former Tobis cameraman who, although he was Jewish, could have passed for Wilhelm II. My mother knew him because, the week before, he had had her do a lighting test for the close-ups. Grunebaum climbed behind the wheel of the truck.

'Marc, you follow me,' said Felix Openfeld.

He hopped into the convertible. My mother and Openfeld Senior squeezed into the front seat, beside him. The back seat was encumbered with several suitcases and a trunk.

The crew wished them bon voyage. Now Felix Openfeld was driving rather fast. The truck followed behind.

'We'll see if we can shoot the film in America,' Openfeld Senior said again.

My mother didn't answer. She was feeling somewhat bewildered by this turn of events.

At Place de Brouckère, Felix Openfeld parked the car in front of the Hôtel Métropole. The truck stopped, too.

'Wait here – I'll be right back.'

He went running into the hotel. A few minutes later he emerged with two bottles of mineral water and a large sack.

'Sandwiches for the road.'

They were about to drive off when, all at once, my mother leapt from the car.

'I . . . I have to . . . stay here,' she said.

The two men looked at her, half smiling. They didn't say a word to change her mind. She, they must have thought, had nothing to lose. And really, why should she go? Her parents were waiting for her in Antwerp. The truck left first. The two Openfelds gave her a wave goodbye. My mother waved, too. Felix Openfeld pulled out of the parking space with a jerk of the wheel – or was there a gust of wind? Openfeld Senior lost his felt hat, which went rolling down the sidewalk. But what was a hat. They hadn't a second to lose.

My mother picked up the hat and began walking, without quite knowing where.

In front of the credit union stood an endless line of men and women, wanting to withdraw their money. She walked down the Avenue Nord to the station. There she found the same chaos, the same stunned crowd, that she'd seen at the station in Antwerp. A porter told her that a train would be leaving for Antwerp around three that afternoon, although they might not get in until late that night.

In the cafeteria, she sank down in a corner seat. People went in and out, men were already in uniform. She overheard someone say that a general mobilization had been called at nine. From a radio at the back of the room came news bulletins. In Antwerp, the port had been bombed a second time. French troops had just crossed the border. The Germans had already taken Rotterdam. Squatting next to her, a woman was tying a little boy's shoes. Some travellers were shouting for coffee, others were pushing and shoving, others dragged suitcases, out of breath.

She would have to wait until three o'clock. She felt a slight headache coming on. Suddenly she realized that she'd lost her overnight bag, with the Elizabeth Arden products and the script. Maybe she'd left them at Sonor Studios, or in the car. What she held in her hand, but had not noticed until just then, was Openfeld Senior's black felt, curly-brimmed hat.

Translated by Lorin Stein

BOUALEM SANSAL

The Voice

Not all awakenings are alike. Even a perfectly ordered routine can come undone. Nor is it ordained that the supernatural and the fantastic must come into our lives like an irruption or in some unexpected form. Often, always, without departing from the banal path, things come at us one after the other, little by little, and find us in their way, yawning with quiet boredom. They settle in, and straightaway the undermining begins. You curse the unpleasantness, occasionally time is short, people rush around, underlings get their fingers caught in the works, the machine gives a lurch, mail gets lost, power goes out, you don't know whether you're coming or going, and now and again there are real threats in the air; things stall. Such upheavals are ridiculous if you think about them philosophically. Routine has its own tricks, its hidden flaws and wondrous inner workings, it can get back on track, it always does, and gravity can recover its good old power of oppression. You can shake yourself into action and off you go again, hunched over inside your shell. So the days go on, slowly in the morning, not too fast in the evening, never doubting their good old tireless hum-drum round. From one knowing glance to another, life poses for a snap, nothing moves save for the people taken for a ride by that glance. Yet there are catastrophic awakenings. Ancient groans worn out by the steady hum of the days explode in infernal dungeons and belch into our mouths like volcanic lava. The collapse occurs when everything seems fine, when tomorrow looks like being the perfect replica of the day before. But good God, what do we know of the soul's cries, of the fractures of our being, of the silent miseries that poison our legs? Where the mind never ventures for want of light and walkways and a safety harness tight enough to cope with death rattles, the smell of putrefaction and viscous couplings, in those depths there arise colossal ruptures, infinite dramas, final ends; and of the last hopes you cling to by reflex, only vague debris remains at the bottom of the cliff. 'The ruins of the world struck him but did not move him' is another fine and majestically antique way of saying that man, be he a fair one or a coward, always lives too near to the end. You die of astonishment, of revulsion, more than of being broken. Shock opens on to an extraordinary universe, a terrifying drift into the absurd and the extreme.

In that respect the story of Si Flène is exemplary. Reading it will surely make you feel sick, we are innocent, we dream of love and our hands of caresses, our tragedies come from lack, all we know are the agonies of expectation. That's the name we'll give him, Si Flène, meaning Mr Somebody or better still Mr Boss. He heads a government department that people have never heard of, somewhere to the side of the main machinery of state, an extension that was bolted on some time ago, of no obvious use, probably a secondary one, like a box of old tools in a large, beautiful, automatic factory that's been put down in a cautiously forgetful way between a wall and a post or under a flight of stairs. Why, nobody knows, the years stumble on, accumulating dust behind them, routine dims the awareness we have of things, and as we know eyesight declines faster than age. Members call it the airlock, and in truth it is a kind of decompression chamber between two power zones with contradictory aims, a little like the revenue service that sucks up taxpayers' money with great difficulty and the budget department that spends it without constraint.

A kind of Grand Inspector or rather, as its Members understand it, a Judge that must not be distracted.

In the course of time the department draped itself with various signs and seals, some official, others shared under cover, revealing the regime's internal struggles, and that is maybe why its Members, irremovable in the service of continuity, gave it the name of airlock. On entering or leaving you have to prove you're one of them, and up to no good.

Si Flène is a cultivated man with experience of humans and systems. He has a brilliant revolutionary past. He stood beside the great bowsprits of History who fell for the cause but live on in the pantheon of pantheons, the hearts of the heirs of November. Nobody's left to authenticate his acts of valour, that's how decisive they were. He is respected, adored, feared, insulted and cursed like all men of power. Though he is without use, he is indispensible; though unknown, his name is on everyone's lips. He is much sought after. High officials visit him on set dates, on the eve of commemorations, and occasionally, a little hurriedly, almost by magic, when the town's muffled drums announce the new moon and the coming of a new era. Other folk, trembling little monkeys, wait their turn as they gauge the length of the queue in the hope that Allah will still be around on the Day of Judgement. In times of trouble people go to him, they know he throws nothing away, forgets nobody, can deal with anything. Support, favour, service, a hand and all expressions suggestive of eternal gratitude, such are the words his callers use. Their favourite pastime is to be in need, despite the fact that they all have innumerable fortunes behind them, weightier by far than the country can dream of. To listen the way he does is a veritable exploit. He has his own entirely hieratic way of drinking tea, with his glass suspended in mid-air right in front of his eyes, almost eclipsing them. His eyes give nothing away, his façade is insurmountable, and an imperial moustache stands like an armed guard over his mouth. Nonetheless, his silence promises what his pouting lips make conditional, it puts the supplicant at ease and incites him to say more and above all to conceal nothing. The greatest need among friends is to hide nothing from one another. Callers smile at the secretary on their way out, she has the memory of an elephant. She is as old as the Department and from one point of view even more locked. In influential circles people talk of her influence as something formidable, that's how important she is.

Is he happy? he wonders, giving the same slightly transcendent answer that serves as a full stop at the end of unnecessary words: the State has no feelings. His men, the Members, experienced to the point of sickness, see him as the pro, the irremovable, always himself, superior to others. They admire him and their admiration allows them to see miracles of no common order. Nothing impresses him, they tell each other as they feverishly leaf through the newspaper. Massacres, screams, scandals, accusations, verbiage, floods – all slide off the armour of the grandmaster of the order of the Faithful Ones. The Members have given him all kinds of names appropriate to his many qualities: duck, eagle, spider, steel glove, trustman ... His friends, who are also his enemies, credit him with everything they lack: money, power, good health, and they are jealous of the miraculous longevity which allows him to enjoy life without haste or excess of appetite. Ah impunity, it's a real plus, but you can't have it all. His bosses – o, there are not so many of them – let's call them his peers, swear by him. His Department is doubled by others that may be newer or older; but as the moles in each of them know the others like the backs of their hands, that does not constitute a fundamental threat to collegial bonhomie. Outside cases of jealousy, their wives mix, eagerly share hairdressers and caterers and the same private jet; their boys and girls phone each other often, like crazy, and as soon as they are old enough, cousins of both genders tango together, not fearing to let themselves go wild. This world of women and children too happy to bother with homework is marginal, it knows nothing, apart from the mysteries of fashion and the misery of domesticity.

Despite twenty-four-hour workdays Si Flène gives the best of himself to his family. He pays particular attention to its comfort and insists on deciding where it will travel, within and beyond the Kingdom. The improvised appearance of their comings and goings is just that, an appearance. The boys' jousting, the girls' screaming with wide-eyed rage, the old wives' snapping, the servants' bustling, the gardeners' yawns of relief all contribute to the deception. And the fine ladies' eyes express the exact opposite of their thoughts. And so off the tribe goes without the dogs even guessing what's going on.

Times have changed. Behind the dusty decorum and the great Friday prayers, deep splits arose, blind-eyed missteps, mortal discords, and seismic tremors undermined minds great and small, infatuated without distinction, and unbelievable bankruptcies appeared in the sky; and naturally war came and had its word to say. Leaks sprang in all quarters of the ship. The storm, far from abating, fed on collective panic. No morality exists to hold back the maelstrom in any way. The machine is broken, deep down, the beast wallows in its excrement, rot sweeps everything away in disorder. Good folk who have all the world's wisdom in them and love their children stop even hoping for peace. Believing in it once more seems to them the greatest sin of all. What they want to reach is the end of the disaster. Is it a death wish? Or do they want to be certain that Evil can no longer do any harm? To cast eternal shame on those responsible? Or, woe betide us, is it because when you get to such a state of despair you cherish your own decline and no longer love your offspring?

Great men have their own worries. The most pressing is to deal with emergencies. That's when there are no plans, no magically interlocking guidelines, no debates on strategy taken to the point where imagination hits the brick wall of impossibility, no time for anything. Improvise, recover, run on, head off, reverse the situation, regain the initiative, attack, harass, step aside to get your breath back, put your head in your hands in order to think, count the ammo, wait for night or for the light to come out as if nothing had happened. Trust nothing, especially not yourself, the perfect crime does not exist, fatigue is a trap, vertigo, the edge of the cliff is never very far. Send out decoys. Change your address. Change your codes. Change your route. Those are the stakes and that is the law of this world.

For some time now Si Flène has been exhibiting signs of superhuman fatigue. Members are biting the dust more often than their allotted turns. Nobody knows where the blows are coming from, nor do they know whom they are striking. Things vanish, whole buildings, whole villages, whole chunks of the state, and the void sucks up everything else. Everything gets done on the wing. People change their clan, their language, their religion, their country. Pseudonyms have become legion, insignia have got muddled up, media coups erupt one after the other, the Web has been hacked and sites corrupted. Thanks to sloppiness stoked by the internal enemy, foreign powers are keeping a close watch, reducing wriggle room, putting spotlights into murky corners, secret places, the dark side of history and ancient plots where, in the last analysis, traitors, heroes and straw men shared the same roles, publishing names, numbers, charts, scouring memories and bottom drawers, unearthing files, key documents, fostering doubt and suspense, and thereby creating those shifts of perspective that put the pathetic glimmer of ignorance in the eye of the beholder. What is said is as nothing next to what is not said. It would be a huge and strange revelation if one day we were to learn that the truth is what we knew all along but could never say. The main part is still to come but there's no time to hear it all and you can't do anything about that.

Si Flène was watching television, staring at the leading anchor, in fact, and cursing between clenched teeth. 'That careerist is just a dwarf we plucked from the desert . . . Why ever does he want to foul his own nest? Who gave him his job? His coach? His entourage? His plane? His glittering guard, his diamond crown, his false prophet's crook, his ecstatic fans, his magic mirror? ... Does he know all we know about him?' An artist who knows he's admired twenty-four hours a day eggs it up to the left, to the right, in your face, to make a show of his magical dexterity. Only when he's lost to TV (for he is surely, truly, mortal) will we find out whether he was dog or pork.

Si Flène had his head in his hands, it had been happening quite often for a while. He would be prostrate like that for a whole period of time, making his elbows go numb as he rocked back and forth like a Taliban regurgitating his prayers in a fever. Fatigue has got nothing to do with it, he knew it intuitively, nor was it the ever-growing threat of danger, because that was the routine. Something was telling him that a boundary had been crossed and that neither God nor the Devil had wanted that to happen. He was struggling with ... 'Good God what is this pain that's eating me up? ... Well, I'm not going to let that finish me off,' he thought as he shook himself so as to get back on top of things.

The mysterious secretary came in, tottering. That's a surprise, my secretary has feelings, he thought with a sigh: you just can't trust anybody.

'Si Flène, yesterday late, I got a phone call that was peculiar ... I mean, it was different from the calls I usually get.'

'I'm listening.'

'The caller masked his voice, but I think I've heard it before. Definitely one of your friends ... I mean, an acquaintance who is playing a trick on you.'

'Indeed.'

'Um ... Not sure how to say this ... He asked after you and then told me, you'll pardon the expression, to say these precise words to you: "The cut-throat of Tablat sends greetings to the old swindler." Then he said: "I'll call again when that's sunk in."'

'Is that all?'

'That is all.'

'Tape the calls from now on. Thank you. Ah, wait ... mmm ... ask ... yes, ask Krimo from the tech section to pinpoint where the call came from ... and to report to me – only to me.'

'That's food for thought. As if there were not enough of it already. A prank? ... A signal? ... A new actor? ... A deep throat about to spill?

Why one and not the other? Who is the cut-throat of Tablat? . . . Someone's trying to trip me up, knock me off balance, that's it, trying to make me act and show my hand . . . Someone's trying to manipulate me, damn it, control me, lead me step by step towards . . . Good grief, are there any compass points left? I have to refresh my bearings, change methods, adjust the pressure . . . invent more traps, set decoys in every field . . . find a shooting solution, as submariners say . . . Meanwhile, I'll say nothing . . . keep right on . . . seal the airlock. And yes, I must keep an eye on the secretary too, she is old and loyal but what does that mean, you can be old and loyal and all and still be in cahoots.

'What's all this silence, damn it? Nobody running down the corridors, no slamming doors, you can't hear the hum of the city . . . no sirens, either, nor the rumbling of the Machine in the basement . . . but it's a fine piece of engineering all the same . . . No, it's tension, I've lost touch . . . that's right, yes, my head is screaming, my ears are bleeding, my heart is suffocating . . . my knees . . . o yes, yes, my knees are knocking like drums, my fleas are dancing and my owls are clapping . . . but . . . what am I saying? I'm going mad, it's crazy . . . I can feel something soaring in my soul . . . as if it was trying to escape . . . or to get in, unsuccessfully . . . What if it were a sick person? . . . yes, a SICK person. I am the one who is ill, I'm incubating something.'

The calls keep on coming. Always at the same time, at the end of the day, when Si Flène leaves the office for his mysterious evening meetings. Nobody in the airlock knows what they are, co-workers talk about them confidentially, partly to imagine the unthinkable, partly to practise theory. The mysterious Tuesday encounters are known and they suspect the Thursday appointment to be no less murky, but it's part of the job, nothing more. Clan chiefs keep away from their troops to co-operate, to map out the terrain, to get into step, to set up new agreements, to share out jobs, to settle the crucial issue of kickbacks, and to smoke the pipe of peace. The Monday appointment used to be of an official or even festive kind but it no longer is. Si Flène goes along intending solely to put an end to it. 'This mess has really got up my nose, I'm going to cast those guys down,' he'd been heard to say behind two bullet-proof doors. But his other contacts can only be guessed at. Maybe not the Friday outing, it's everyone's day of relief, people go to the stadium and then get so plastered they can't find their way home. A man is a man or else he's not Muslim. And later on you indulge in a vanload of starving whores. Si Flène is a man, a real one, and his chicks are healthy, they're worth their weight in gold.

The series of calls made the picture clearer but didn't reveal what it was all about. Si Flène listened to the recordings over and over with fascinated ears and his body in a state of complete suspension. The secretary brought them in every morning first thing, on the tray, between the coffee and the croissant and under the newspapers. It is a serious gesture when a celebrant presents a long-lost relic to a magus ... or the testicles of a boss of the Bronx who's finally ousted. Despite knowing everything about her and the bees in her bonnet, he sometimes wondered where this perfect good woman slept: surely not in a bed, he reckoned, smiling behind his fine boxer's moustache. The cut-throat of Tablat had a nickname, Debbah, meaning the butcher. A primitive trick, it didn't ring any bells. Common among the guerrillas ... they're all called Debbah, the knife is their flag, blood is their religion, and for a rosary they have a miserable string that dreams of swallowing the whole planet without holding back ... The voice was fake but familiar ... the more he listened to it, the less he could pin it down. Si Flène had been drawn into the game, a sordid, supernatural tension that was at the same time pregnant with a tremendous revelation: the news of an end of the world the size of the world itself. In any case, he wanted to smash everything, starting with himself, and the dog next door, and to cut the throat of every cut-throat on earth.

Translated by David Bellos

DIDIER DAENINCKX

Youth, Suburb of Life

If childhood is the centre of life, youth is the first of its outer suburbs. A way of escaping as much as a way of being counted. And as in urban geography, a simple trip round the ring road is enough to confirm that no suburb is like any other. Take Paris: from the Porte de la Chapelle to the Portes of Passy, Montreuil and Saint-Cloud, the gateways are permanently open. It might look as if the city is no longer closed. Yet these frontiers – far more solid than the ancient dotted lines on maps of Europe – dictate people's movements. Some areas are more favourable to prolonged adolescence, others plunge you straight into adulthood. Peter Pan is still a contemporary of Oliver Twist. Between one métro terminus and another, the time of youth is not equal for everybody.

I am only dimly aware of the youth that goes to swanky soirées, or of their stereophonic counterbalance, the youth of the gang-rape. What I see around me, in the unvarnished world of reality, isn't a middle way between those two. Many of the young people I meet have in their eyes that veil of dreams, the fragmented clouds that bring the fantastic into the everyday.

For the last two years, Francis has spent half his life leaning up against the restaurant window, inside in winter, on the terrace in summer. At first, he used to talk to the five other delivery guys, but since then, he's got in the habit of simply listening to his music. He gets a tap on the shoulder to tell him it's ready, he puts the pizzas in the box fixed to the carrier of his bike, takes the street map and puts his helmet on over his headphones. He works Saturdays and Sundays and odd times on three other days of the week, he rides the wrong way up one-way streets, he goes on to the pavements, taking no notice of the yells of pedestrians. For now, the future is confined to the sight of his front wheel. At twenty-two, the one thing he really cares about is saving up enough to get away from his parents' place, find a flat and live with Laurent, who's a salesman at Virgin and provides him with plenty of CDs borrowed on trust.

Nasser doesn't know that the neighbourhood he lives in is one of those that French government policy has labelled 'Sensitive Urban Zones', where unemployment has hit 25 per cent of the population when the national figure had fallen below 10 per cent. Nobody explained to him when there was still time that there might be some connection between these stats and his own life. He's crazy about computers and sport. His life changed for good when he went into a night club, on holiday, and a bouncer aimed a gun at him. The bullet nicked his ear, just a burning sensation then above all a deafening pounding inside his head that's never left him. Some time back, a mock métro station went up on the main square opposite Auber-villiers town hall, part of a campaign to get an extension of the Porte de La Chapelle métro line to the city centre. A brilliant pastiche of the old Guimard design, straight out of a film set. It stayed up for a month, then they took it down. I bumped into Nasser. He took me on one side to show me the empty space.

'Funny things happen here too. They've stolen the town hall métro station.'

Last time I heard news of him, he had smashed a shop window. He was picked up by the cops and in his delirium one name kept coming up: Richard Durn, the madman of the Nanterre massacre.

Stéphanie has always been fascinated by the mysteries of the human body. Her most treasured Christmas present was a surgeon's kit that turned up under the tree when she was ten. Eye glued to the microscope, she would observe a drop of blood with the same passion as an astro-physicist discovering a new planet. With the support of her entire family, she worked her butt off to pass the bac and get into medical school. After two years, she had to give up, so now she's working for peanuts in a care home. She's full of resentment, she knows that one day she'll go back to her medical studies, she'll prove they were right to give her that chance in the first place. And she'll manage it. All she needs is ten times more determination than other kids in other suburbs, the children of top civil servants, who represent 13 per cent of all lycée pupils, but walk off with 47 per cent of the passes in the competitive Bac C stream. The children of manual workers, who represent 40 per cent of the age group, have to be satisfied with 8 per cent of those coveted Bac C passes.

Lisa has always wanted to look like the girls in the glossy magazines. And yes, you have to admit she had a pretty good start: long legs, slim figure, cupid's-bow mouth and deep, deep eyes. She added a tattoo on her shoulder, a diamond in one nostril and a breast enlargement. The world of nightlife had always fascinated her. I was afraid for her when she got too close to its quicksands. As a receptionist, waitress and barmaid, she rubbed shoulders often enough with showbiz types to believe briefly that if they called you 'tu', it meant there'd be an opening for you. She auditioned for the cast of the reality show *Loft Story 2*, but didn't get in. With two hundred other hopefuls like her, she works part-time in a call centre with headphones and a mic, talking to mobile phone customers. She's slimming, in hopes of getting into *Loft Story 3*.

A civil war in Africa cast Abdul's family on to the Spanish coast and then to the outskirts of Paris. What he had seen back home had turned him into a wild beast. In school, no one understood that the only relations anyone had had with him were of unspeakable violence, that his own verbal and physical aggression was simply a way of fending it off. If anyone took any notice of him, it was to note that he was going downhill even faster. Until the day a hand landed on his shoulder, one of the educators who should have chucked him out of the centre, after a hundredth stupid fuck-up, but who, instead of talking to him about France, talked to him about 'his own' country, 'his own' history, the African continent, its storytellers, its poets, Amadou Hampâté Bâ, Wole Solinka. Abdul ended up reading them and recognizing himself. Nowadays, he writes funny stories, African stories about the Seine-Saint-Denis neighbourhood, in which the traditional figures of his childhood and their beliefs people the life of these outer suburbs. He's starting to give readings in schools and in exchange he receives hundreds of innocent smiles, something missing for a good while from his life.

Or I could mention Bouba, from Burkina Faso, who has no ID papers, and for whom I'm acting as republican sponsor. Bouba who, after moonlighting for a while, is now teaching traditional carving on wood or gourds to kids in the Landy neighbourhood. Or Coralie, who's progressing from one internship to another, learning to be a journalist. Or Renaud, who at twenty-three has just got his first *non-temporary* job – and still can't believe it. And I could mention Aurélie, who's friends with all the above, and is writing a thesis about the north-west Paris suburbs and their image in the cinema, while also helping kids who have gone off the rails to get back on track.

I look at them all and tell myself that one dream could fulfil all their dreams. And that dream consists of a single word: equality.

Translated by Siân Reynolds

GILLES ORTLIEB

Portrait of Saxl

Melancolia è una ninfa gentile . . . And he had said that in an almost absent-minded tone, but serenely, as he had on another day declared himself to be looking at the 'destiny of the rain', as one might caress the flanks of a sleeping dog. And had he not once replied to me, when I advised him to participate as little as possible in the life of the agency, because it seemed to have become so painful to him, to act dead in his office: 'But I don't need to act, I am already dead . . .'

Sometimes, I find myself comparing him to a matt surface, with an infinite capacity for impregnation, that reflects only a tiny part of what it absorbs. A bottomless well, never filled by the widest possible and most contradictory reading matter, the substance of his Sundays that hang like fathomless, unsilvered mirrors: from a string of crime novels to the writings of Lie Tseu, via some learned work on the motifs in Oriental carpets, or the obscure Life of some minor Viennese Master.

Calling him one evening at home:
    'Am I disturbing you? Were you having supper?'
    'Having supper – me? I "sup", as you put it, very rarely. No, I eat standing up, like a horse . . .'

Behind his smooth, glabrous face, mostly in repose, what eddies and whirlpools must there be, worsening at times into some kind of private, everyday carnage? What he once called, and in a way I found, though I never told him so, somewhat mannered (but perhaps he was not thinking of himself so much as of the four walls of his office) 'my little metamorphic theatre', meaning undoubtedly, 'changes for the worse'. And yet, assuredly, on other days, what peace.

'Oh no, I have nothing against happy people. It's simply that after two hours, and often less, I get bored.'

'And unhappy people?'

'That depends. If they are intelligent . . .'

'What about people who are both happy and intelligent, do you never meet them?'

'Not often . . .'

Saxl, who appreciates more than anything 'the meek, the dreamers, the failures, the unfulfilled', once told me he realized that his life had started going wrong here the day he came to believe that 'every cloud has a silver lining'. When I meet him in the lift this morning, he tells me he had to take a few days off to look after his next-door neighbour, an octogenarian Romanian who had been suffering from a terminal illness, and who had finally died last Sunday.

'All that gave a little meaning to my existence, which it badly needed. The rest of the time, I am still engaged in examining my conscience. It goes on, and on . . . I cannot say that I come out of it enhanced, but then I can't really spend my time making excuses for my existence . . . Or can I?

'For someone like me, so little in control of my life, and for whom much of existence is ungraspable, punctuality is all I have left. When I first got here, my concierge claimed he could set his watch by my departure every morning: 8.20 was when I crossed the hall and exited the building. It took me around twenty minutes to walk to the Agency. At around 8.35 I would pass an old people's home. It was much bigger than a house, more like a small town complete with private chapel, bursary, gardens and a surrounding fence. The building was huge, with several wings – a veritable gerontopolis. Sometimes, in winter, the vision was quite nightmarish, with all these little old people teetering cautiously through the fog, grasping their sticks or leaning on their zimmers, or else in pairs, arm in arm, for fear of falling. They made me think of those little votary candles in churches, at the mercy of the slightest breeze of any strength. One of the façades of the building bordered the street I had to take, and in one of the windows on the third floor was a little old lady who would watch me go past. She had got into the habit of making a little signal to me with her hand, to which I would always reply. She was seated at a table strangely lighted by a globe, and most probably having her breakfast. One day, I arrived ten minutes late. There she was, at her accustomed place, and she wagged her finger, almost as though she were scolding me ... Our little exchange continued in this way for nearly a year. And then, last year, shortly before I moved to the blood-boltered house, I noticed one morning that she was not at her usual place. Nor the next day, nor the days following. Then they changed the curtains, and the room was rearranged. You can guess what had happened. But I used to miss her when I walked past every morning.'

For a long time, he would wonder whether the first words of Purcell's *O Solitude* were *my sweetest joy* or *my sweetest choice*. 'Not that it makes much difference ...' With that rather metallic laugh of his, which took a little getting used to. There was also his fascination for certain expressions he came across in his reading: 'caught red-handed', 'a red-letter day', 'the bread of tears', 'ashes in the mouth', 'the seven-year itch' (which in his case he insisted was rather the 'five- or six-year itch').

A colleague who was also a friend once boarded her cat with him for the November long weekend holiday, and while on the phone to me he would have to leave off and scold the animal for sharpening its claws on the furniture in the next room. I could hear, down the receiver, foreign expletives and exclamations. Then he came back on the line:

'Yes, I speak to him in English. It's the language one should use with animals. I use it on my mother, too ...'

On one of the very rare occasions, many months ago now, when we met outside of the Agency, we happened to pass in front of a cinema, and Saxl suddenly got vociferously indignant at the terminal stupidity of the by-lines on the posters that try to sum up the content of B-movies: *He's his worst enemy, but he doesn't know it yet. He'll have one long night to find out ...* Or this: *You can escape your past, but not your destiny ...* Or this: *She had lost her memory: he should never have helped her get it back* . . . And when I registered my astonishment at seeing him get so angry at something really so trivial, he riposted, and I still can't decide quite how seriously he meant it: 'There are false angers. But you need them too. Like false emotions . . . To distinguish them from real ones.'

'The spasm of the prole, the prole of spasms,' he joked once, speaking of masturbation. One of his very rare confessions concerning his emotional life, and from which I deduced his abstinence: 'Beware the coming together of bodies because that is what you will miss most when it is withdrawn. And why should it be withdrawn? Because. From which I glean my vision, a little sulphurous, impoverished and mistrustful, of reality. Perhaps it is the one I know best . . .'

And again: 'Everything that exceeded me, and I mean the whole of me, having been progressively whittled away by time, habit and necessity, the feeling of relief and depth can only come to me now through little abyssal interior moments. Which have, I admit, the advantage of being without substance. For I know from experience that when the volume of what I think and do not say exceeds, and by a long way, the volume of what I say without always thinking it, then my inner equilibrium is seriously threat-ened, compromised, and it becomes as friable as the backbone of a tinned sardine . . .'

When he visited the flat for rent in Bellevue, the residential quarter of the town coveted by many colleagues because of its proximity to the Agency, a large carpet had been laid over the parquet floor of the living room. This couldn't fail to intrigue him, especially as the room was otherwise quite empty of furniture. Out of curiosity he lifted it up, and found a large cir-cular and brownish stain, which the owner assured him was a spillage of varnish. Some weeks after he had moved in, his neighbour across the corridor rang at his door:

'– I just wanted to make sure that everything was okay. Surely you know what happened here? The last tenant was murdered. By his wife, who stabbed him with a knife. Out of jealousy. He just had the strength to drag himself to the telephone, leaving a trail of blood and a big pool on the parquet. You can't have failed to notice it . . . In the event it was the wife who phoned the police herself, so they would come and take her away. That's why the flat remained empty for so long. Everyone in the neighbourhood knew about it. Except for you, apparently . . .'

Half-jokingly, in his usual vein: 'Oh no, one mustn't suppose that we are all out of the same mould: there are those who fix their paper clip top left of the sheaf, or else top right; or else at one third along the top, aligned with the margin . . .' And he also came out with this observation, which I have never forgotten: 'Where is the point, the lever, the oyster-knife with which to force open the muscle and tear apart the tendons that control the closing of the valves? I know very well what wearies and will one day destroy us here, if it hasn't already done so: the fact of being stretched on the rack, every day, between a state of resignation ("One has to earn one's living") and of being privately in revolt at the inanity of the job. Without ever being able to choose, once and for all, one side or the other. Somewhere between revolt and submission is the worst solution of all. It is the one I seem to have opted for. And I'm sure I'm not alone in that . . .'

Saxl, who has witnessed more than one metamorphosis by money, by a material comfort all the more enveloping in that it has come late, tells me about a new colleague who recently joined his section: 'Oh, I've seen quite a few like him, with their beards and velvet jackets, their degrees in sociology and unfinished theses, their beat-up cars and their agonizing love affairs, finishing or finished. You should see them, a few months later, close-shaven and wearing a tie, already caught up in their careers, set upon promotion to the next grade and impatient because it seems to them delayed – and leaving in the evening, accompanied by a colleague or a secretary, at the wheel of a four-wheel drive done out in gunmetal grey . . .'

Monday morning. He told me he had spent his weekend looking after his cleaning lady, who was the victim of a long and tortuous depression, by plying her with packet soups. And then:

'When I get in early to the office: a cavelike gloom in the early morning lit barely by a veiled, almost miserly sort of light . . . Then I turn on the lamp, and finding my files exactly where I had left them when I went home on Friday is somehow appeasing. In short, it is the guarantee of a quiet day that nothing can disturb which one has not oneself, so to speak, already prepared and willed. Nonetheless it sobers me rather to think that one morning in the office is enough to shelve the chaos of the weekend, and reduce it to the rank of a threat that is too imprecise to be real, to a vague form that is already being diluted. What should one believe?'

Yielding to the affectionate and insistent requests of a group of younger colleagues recently arrived in his department, Saxl finally agreed to go with them yesterday evening to the circus, whose tent, pitched on a central reservation and covered in multicoloured bulbs, has been visible from the Agency for about a week. I got a brief *résumé* this morning, when by chance we met in the queue for the canteen, longer than usual as is often the case when it is raining outside): '. . . You should have seen the tamer in his groom's get-up with golden buttons, in the midst of some rather moth-eaten tigers and two or three black panthers, one with swinging udders that he had more or less to carry on his back to get moving. He wouldn't stop hopping about on the track like a waterfly, and stinging the beasts with his whip, to get them to roar, or to pretend to roar, when all they wanted was to get back to their quarters. Several times I was on the point of getting up and leaving, but once again my courage failed me . . .'

'I should take up a sport. I've thought about fencing. What do you think? I'm attracted to the idea of being masked, protected, and, at the same time, on the offensive.'

Saxl inherited an ancient chess set from his grandfather, with pieces in high polished woods, that he deploys only rarely on the board so that the odour (of greased leather, tobacco and even, he has persuaded himself, 'of Prussian battlefield') does not completely fade and disappear entirely. In the same vein he once confessed that he had avoided any prolonged *tête-à-tête* with X, because he had trouble putting up with the slightly bitter and muted, but nevertheless tenacious, body odour. 'It's not my fault that I have a very developed, overdeveloped, sense of smell: a half hour after-wards, I can still tell you, unerringly, which of my colleagues has taken the lift before me . . .' A hypersensitivity that sometimes makes him feel a drop of rain falling on the back of his hand like a hammer blow, and a gust of cool wind like an arctic draught.

And then there are his migraines: a cloudy veil that prevents him from reading or listening to music, and even from speaking (he explains as much to me in a voice that is, effectively, slowed and muffled, as though stuck permanently in a minor key); and it makes him 'fearful of the light'. But he hastens to add, thereby cutting short any sympathetic noises: 'But they are companionable. I'm not sure that I want to be cured, and never have them again . . .'

One lunchtime in the canteen, in the medley of voices above the clatter of trays, finally giving way to uninterrupted conversation, I sense he is distracted, preoccupied, somewhere else. That evening, I called him at home:

'It'll pass – it's nothing . . . Just like a minor toothache.'

I understood the reason a few weeks later, when he told me that he had had an affair with his neighbour on the floor above his, a Swiss German married to someone from here. Now he feels bad for having practised upon her, to perfection, every classic strategy, refusing to see her unless it be understood, vaguely and tacitly, that this would be one of the last times, the absolutely last time being of course deferrable *ad infinitum*; or displacing, by means of a kind of visual and olfactory fetishism, all the burdens of an attachment he didn't dare assume, and all the torment issuing from decisions he could not take, on to the slightest traces of perfume that he would recognize in the lift, or the red silhouette of her car, which he would look out for in front of the house, or parked in a nearby street. Nearly a year had passed like this, marked by as many break-ups as reconciliations, by as many mornings-after crushed by guilt as they had been preceded by fraught anticipations. The day of that lunch in the canteen was the day of the final separation, with the couple leaving definitively for a town in Switzerland.

'Well, at least they've gone now, and it is better that way . . .'

And I sensed, from his intonation, that his sole and scarcely convincing consolation derived from the fact that the depression of being on his own again was, in spite of all, still less than what he would have felt at times, if the affair had been prolonged interminably. The habit of sadness, when it is not merely self-pity: one of the worst, in his opinion, one can fall into. But he doesn't recall ever having cried since he was twenty. 'Since I have dry eyes,' he added, 'I mean eyes without tears, it makes things harder . . .'

'No, I do not feel better . . . I have the feeling that everything is going more to pieces by the day. This morning, for instance, when I was getting up, I looked at my watch, and in the little square that shows the date, I seemed to see a tiny prison window, with its two bars: the eleventh of the month . . . And my nights are no better: the feeling of a huge tree trunk resting across my chest, whose weight finally wakes me up. After which, rather satisfied by the accuracy of the image, I go to sleep again, a little calmer . . .'

He was struck, this morning, by the prematurely wrinkled hands of a young colleague sitting opposite him during the weekly department meeting. So out of harmony, it seemed to him, with the rest of her body, with her face. 'As if she had put on a pair of wrinkling gloves . . .'

'The very thin interstice between which I try, not without effort or contorsion, to slide. To shake off this species of forsaken monad I seem to have become. This is what I seek and at bottom it's the only thing that interests me . . . But I sense that these fissures are becoming narrower, and rarer.'

'I too must speak, from time to time . . .' is how he sort of excused himself, the day after I had tried in vain to phone him the evening before, when his phone was busy for a long time. Those times when he hasn't left the receiver off the hook or unplugggd the phone to guarantee himself a bit of peace, and when he is not persecuted by one or other of his asthma attacks ('I don't know whether it's the asthma that depresses me, or my depression that gives me asthma, in any case I don't answer to avoid hearing myself wheezing in the ear-piece . . .'), he is in fact much more open and relaxed than when we meet in the corridors of the Agency, where he appears to be constantly on the alert, as though apprehensive of some spirit that haunts the place, which he has learned to distrust.

*

Something else he claims to have noticed, that started half a year ago: nearly every one of his thoughts that comes to him is immediately followed by another, which annuls the first, anaesthetizes it, sucking all cohesion and even all meaning out of it. Which is how he explains – though without trying to excuse it – his lack of energy and the inertial drag he acknowledges to be considerable. 'I spend hours at my table, unable to read, unable to write, just turning over dead ideas. And if my pen falls from my hands, I can remain a quarter of an hour staring at it on the ground, and cannot summon the force within me to get it, the courage to pick it up. This must be why all my travel plans have come to naught over the last few years: what is the point of going to the other end of the world if it is only find myself at the end, alone before the Great Nothing? Better to stay at home, on my kitchen balcony, and watch the birds carrying on in the tree opposite, on the other side of the street . . .' Other times he speaks of the number and the insignificance of the ideas that can visit him in a single day, and how their minimal existence evaporates instantly and how he cannot even describe a single one of them to me. 'An inchoate mass of private spasms, of regurgitations similar to those in blocked drains, accompanied always by a sense of absence that sometimes leaves me dazed and gasping . . .'

Hypothesis: it may be that the permanent sense of discordancy he feels – his prolonged effort to live a life frustrated, and in deferral – can be explained by his persistent attempt to take refuge in a previous existence which everything now conspires to deny him, and which he vigorously refuses to consider lost or redefined by those around him. The only identity, which is ideal and barely sketched out, the one he should like to have claimed, has been abolished in the interim: 'Saxl the pianist'. Pianist or nothing. Nothing, then. (And I suspect him of wondering whether, combined with his fear of change, that this nothing will never end.)

Another long telephone conversation. He has just returned from England where he had to go and see to some family duties, 'sell some acres of forest' belonging to him, and to try and 'sever my links with the country'. He recounted the scandal that has riven his family, during his stay there, when one of his aunts found out that her son was carrying on with the girl from the local chemist's, considerably older than him. A violent family row succeeded merely in driving the young man, out of rage and impotence, to jump out of the first-floor window, thereby breaking his leg. To put a stop to gossip and avoid a scandal, they asked Saxl to call a doctor, claiming the boy had fallen from his horse. This he refused to do, naturally enough, especially as no physician would have been taken in. 'Now do you understand why I can't live there?'

A dinner party with colleagues. This had become, according to him, inevitable, after he had refused so many times. So he had to undergo the full visit of the house and then of the garden, with its rows of gooseberry bushes and newly planted trees, admire the bookcase in teak or rosewood ('some precious wood anyway'), 'marvellously fitted, to the nearest centimetre' under the ceiling, then the apéritif, served from a low glass table, very 'design' also, with some car magazines on it, because the host was about to buy a new car (its colour – metallic off-white tinged with champagne – had already been determined by catalogue and sample chart); but also on the table, carelessly opened and laid down, as though the doorbell had interrupted the mistress of the house in the middle of her reading, was a volume of *Exemplary Tales* by Cervantes, who conferred upon this wealthy and almost perfect couple a finishing touch of cultivation and distinction. 'Then we went through to the dining room, but not before Maria-Magdalena – her name is Maria-Magdalena – had discreetly touched a button on the hi-fi system, which ensured that suitable background music accompanied us throughout the entire length of the meal. And so we dined in the slanting, golden light that came from the garden in which, thanks to a wide bay window, we had the impression of being seated. I shall spare you the details of the conversation, that slipped from subject to subject with as much goodwill as, I felt, lack of conviction. Then came the dessert, wild berries from the woods with a scoop of vanilla drizzled with vodka, that I tactlessly compared – as I was made to feel, more gently than I deserved – to a magazine recipe 'suggestion'. But so often, when I'm with other people, I feel I have to lug around my soul, whatever that may be, like a basin full to the brim, and carry it in both hands across seriously uneven ground. Then came the fateful phrase: "Shall we go through to the living-room? ..." So we returned to the settee where, for want of anything better, our gaze falling once more upon the coffee table, we started talking about cars again (the old Fiat, in which they first arrived, and then there was another, and then the one after that). Around midnight, unable to bear it any longer, I felt that the moment had perhaps come, having in any case endlessly consulted it furtively, to look at my watch and make a show of surprise at the lateness of the hour, as if to congratulate ourselves that the evening seemed to have flown so amiably and rapidly. Then I got up with a decisive movement, as if no less an effort would allow me to tear myself from such a warm and friendly atmosphere ... I spoke the usual words of thanks, left, and that was that.

'I think I shall be left in peace for a while now, and they won't be that keen to invite me back again ...'

'Sometimes, at the end of the afternoon, when work lets up a bit, I look at the office walls around me, as the last of the sun starts to disappear like a fragment of ember laid on the hills, nibbled at by their ashen contours. And it lasts, and lasts, like an agony ... It's usually at that moment I feel so strongly that I've been doing the wrong thing all these years. And I cannot discount the possibility, it is in fact a certainty, that I shall follow this road, the wrong road, to the bitter end. Then I wait on a little, the time it takes to gather my things, bid good evening to my neighbour if he has not already left, and go home as if nothing were wrong. Sometimes, at around seven o'clock, I pass the cleaning ladies on the square outside, as they alight from the bus, ready to start work in a tight-knit little band. They are all middle-aged, a bit heavy, and chatter loudly. Despite their laughter and their jokes, I don't know why, but I always find the scene of an almost infinite melancholy ...'

A few days ago he discovered, while on the subject, that in Dürer's famous etching what he had taken to be 'map' of Melancholy fixed on the wall – just as there is one devoted to 'Tenderness' – represented in reality a bat with its wings spread. (He also told me, on the same occasion, that he had noticed something that 'looked almost human' in the shadows on the polyhedron in the background.)

*

This morning, when I recognized Saxl's unmistakable silhouette, going to the archives at exactly the same moment as another colleague emerged from his office, I could not help but admire the slight turning of his body and rapid movement of his hips to avoid meeting the other face to face; a preventive action that did not escape the other, who continued on his way stiff and frozen, like a brand new pack of cards. Which revealed to me, yet again, the wholesale, violent antipathy that can arise between two beings who are equally unhappy, but – as one says of wood – not of the same grain.

'Do you want my opinion? We are too sensitive about what people think, too sensitive in general. We live here as though on a windswept, over-exposed plateau, where things grow, but rather twisted and deformed. And where people are in clearer relief, and more distinct. Their characters, too. A meagre consolation ... For showing one's suffering in this place is to incur more suffering. If this were not so our days here might be lighter, or at least less full of misplaced heaviness. I try hard to resist, but in a way that is so interiorized it comes to resemble a form of absolute submission. In the end, staying in this job is like being in a hospital bed with a long-term illness: he wants for nothing, he is looked after, there are visiting hours. And he doesn't know how to get comfortable because of his bed-sores ...' And then this, after which he let a meditative silence take hold, which prompted me not to tarry any longer in his office: 'I am always amazed at the ease, the brutality, and the very selective scruples with which others conduct their lives. I have, myself, the impression that I am simply waiting to become a bit deaf, a bit dumb, a bit dead. But not blind, Oh no, not blind ...'

Under the bus shelter, one evening. Motionless, pensive and still angry, even if he would have preferred not to show this, after the meeting with his superior that afternoon, who wanted to transfer him for a few months to the foreign contracts department.

'In the end I told him that he could send me to the cow byre or the pigsty, it was all the same to me. That the snout of stupidity pushes in round here at every door. And that water in this place wears away the stone faster than the reverse. He looked at me with a little smile, and said nothing. I shall go. And the worst of it is that I *really* do not care. I came out of there all bruised, or blemished, or whatever the word is for fallen fruit?'

Our growing apart will have been mutual, gradual and by consent. The phone calls became rarer, and then stopped altogether after several months. By an excess of tact, really, both parties dreading nothing so much as to intrude when their presence, even to the slightest degree, might not be wholly welcome. And the feeling of solidarity cannot, I think, have been sufficiently strong, otherwise it would surely have survived Saxl's transfer to his new section, at the other end of the building. These days we bump into each other much more rarely, which in no way diminishes our genuine pleasure when it does happen. Apart, possibly, from a very slight trace of regret which, again out of tact, both parties would find incongruous were it to take the form of a reproach.

Second Monday of September. We arrived together this morning, from our separate directions, in front of the tall revolving door of the Agency. Saxl was dressed in a light linen jacket and a pair of camomile cords that emphasized the suntan on his hands. The short ride in the lift, up to our respective floors, left him only the time to tell me that he had just returned from Spain, where he had spent two weeks in a rather luxurious hotel, swimming and diving. His gaze still seemed to be full of submarine shadows and vibrant reflections.

'Let's try and meet up soon?'

'We always say that . . .'

'I'll call you.'

I know he will not call. And it is probably better that way. I am not offended. We have remained, after our fashion, friends.

Translated by Stephen Romer

HERVÉ GUIBERT

A Man's Secrets

When it came to trepanning, the specialist said: I could never touch this brain, it would be a crime, I would feel like I was attacking a work of art, or hacking at perfection, or burning a masterpiece, or flooding a landscape that needed to stay dry, or throwing a grenade into an exquisitely structured termite mound, scratching a polished diamond, ruining beauty, sterilizing fertility, tying off the canals of all creation, every cut of the blade would be an assault upon intelligence, thrusting iron into this divine mass would be an auto-da-fé for this genius; only a barbarian, an illiterate, an enemy would commit such a crime! The enemy existed. Sarcastically, examining the three lesions spreading across the scanner's images, he says: how could such brilliance be left to rot? We have to open this. This intelligence had pierced him, personally, not by name, but by condemning all the deceit in his system, in several books. The man of the mind had castigated the man of law: the doctor, the judge; the philosopher had ultimately accused his ancient predecessors of abuse of thoughts; in their texts, he tried to find the exact moment when the thread was lost, imperceptibly but insidiously, when the right words, drawn from the right thoughts, slipped ever so slightly, were recovered maladroitly, and turned into wrong words, oppressive words. The surgeon took pride in assailing such a fortress, especially considering how he called his prestige groundless; a man's head, he said to his assistants, is nothing more than a bit of flab, of cured meat. But when the orb was opened, he was astonished by the powerful beauty that matter exuded; his disdain was as mute as his tongue, and his stylet fell from his hands; all he could do, now that he had been converted, was contemplate. The brain was no longer a simple, tender walnut with manifold, indecipherable convolutions, but a luminescent, teeming terrain as yet uncongealed by anaesthesia, and every fiefdom was busy working, gathering, connecting, charting, drifting, damming, rerouting, refining; three strongholds had collapsed, that was easy to see, but all around the moat kept golden thoughts and laughter flowing. The most noticeable veins carried along all sorts of nasty old ruined things, prison turrets, torture vices; but the whips seemed to gleam royally like sceptres, and the gags were woven like finery. Exposed discourses glittered on the surface, opened up to derision; their reek of arrogance was absolved by their aroma. Digging just a little revealed corridors full of savings, reserves, secrets, childhood memories, and unpublished theories. The childhood memories were buried deepest of all, in order not to clash against idiotic interpretations or poorly woven veils that were meant to be enlightening but which instead shrouded the work. Two or three images were buried in his vessels' depths like vile dioramas. The first one showed the young philosopher led by his father, himself a surgeon, through a Poitiers hospital room where a man's leg had been amputated, that's how the boy's manliness gets shaped. The second revealed a typical backyard the little philosopher was walking past, which was aquiver with the recent news: right there, on a straw mattress, in this sort of garage, was where the woman all the papers were calling the Poitiers Prisoner had lived for dozens of years. The third retold the beginning of a story, wax figures coming to life through the machinery hidden beneath their clothes: in high school, the little philosopher, who had been the top of his class, was threatened by the sudden and seemingly inexplicable invasion of an arrogant band of little Parisians who were sure to be more talented than the rest. The ousted philosopher-child came to hate them, insult them, hurl all sorts of curses upon them: the refugee Jewish children in the area did disappear by being deported to the camps. These secrets would have sunk in the Atlantis ever so slowly, ever so sumptuously chiselled, suddenly shattered by lighting, had a vow of friendship not raised the vague and uncertain possibility of their being passed on . . .

Each of these strongholds were threatened, one by one: the cache of proper names emptied. Then it was personal memories that were very nearly ruined: he fought to keep the scourge from winning out. Even the existence of his books vanished: what had he written? had he even written? Sometimes he wasn't sure at all. The books there, in his hands, could have borne witness. But the books weren't himself, he had once written that and he remembered it still: that the book wasn't the man, that between the book and the man was the labour that had dissociated the two, and sometimes drove them apart like two enemies. But was that actually what he had written? He hesitated to return to the text itself, he was afraid to find himself locked out as an idiot. So he wrote and rewrote his name on a piece of paper, and underneath he drew rows of squares, circles and triangles, a ritual he had taught himself to verify his mental integrity. When people came into his room, he hid the paper.

He had to finish his books, this book he had written and rewritten, destroyed, renounced, destroyed once more, imagined once more, created once more, shortened and stretched out for ten years, this infinite book, of doubt, rebirth, modest grandiosity. He was inclined to destroy it for ever, to offer his enemies their stupid victory, so they could go around clamouring that he was no longer able to write a book, that his mind had been dead for ages, that his silence was just proof of his failure. He burned or destroyed all the drafts, all the evidence of his work, all he left on his table were two manuscripts, side by side, he instructed a friend that this abolition was to continue. He had three abscesses in his brain but he went to the library every day to check his notes.

His death was stolen from he who wished to be master of his own death, and even the truth of his death was stolen from he who wished to be master of the truth. Above all the name of the plague was not to be spoken, it was to be disguised in the death records, false reports were given to the media. Although he wasn't dead yet, the family he had always been ostracized from took in his body. The doctors spoke abjectly of blood relatives. His friends could no longer see him, unless they broke and entered: he saw a few of them, unrecognizable behind their plastic-bag-covered hair, masked faces, swaddled feet, torsos covered in jackets, gloved hands reeking of alcohol he had been forbidden to drink himself.

All the strongholds had collapsed, except for the one protecting love: it left an unchangeable smile on his lips when exhaustion closed his eyes. If he only kept a single image, it would be the one of their last walk in the

Alhambra gardens, or just his face. Love kept on thrusting its tongue in his mouth despite the plague. And as for his death it was he who negotiated with his family: he exchanged his name on the death announcement for being able to choose his death shroud. For his carcass he chose a cloth in which they had made love, which came from his mother's trousseau. The intertwined initials in the embroidery could bear other messages.

As the body was collected in the morgue's rear courtyard, masses of flowers lay all around the coffin: in wreaths, in rows, from editors, from the institute where he had taught, from foreign universities. On the coffin itself stood a small pyramid of roses among which a band of mauve taffeta revealed and concealed the letters of three names. The bier travelled the whole day, from the capital to the rural village, from the hospital to the church and from the church to the cemetery, it passed from hand to hand, but the pyramid of roses, which the florist had not stapled or taped to the wood, was never knocked off the structure. Several hands tried to move it. Either those hands were immediately caught in a moment's hesitation after which they reconsidered, or other hands reached out to stop them. An occult, imperious order bound the pyramid of roses with its three names to the coffin. When the coffin was gently set in the pit, the mother was asked what should be done with this spray of flowers, and she gestured, she who was not crying, to leave them on the coffin. Nobody got rid of the letter that someone had left when the body was collected, or worried about whether it contained love or hurt, the cut flowers buried it. A tall young man with bare shoulders, in a leather jacket, sunglasses, stood in the distance, accompanied by an old crooked man who seemed to be his father, or servant, or driver; from the capital to the village, from the morgue to the church, from the church to the cemetery they had travelled in an elegant sports car. I had never seen this young man and when he threw flowers into the ditch after me with his sunglasses still on, I suddenly recognized him and I went up to him, I said: Are you Martin? He said: Hello, Hervé. I said: He always wanted us to meet, and now we have. We kissed each other and perhaps we kissed him at the same time over the grave.

Translated by Jeffrey Zuckerman

ANANDA DEVI

The Melancholy Ambassador

He cried at night without holding back. He had to. He was sad.

He also cried in the daytime, but in secret, in the toilet, or else when his staff were nodding off in the empty hours between noon and two. Because of this, his tear glands had become hyperactive, and sometimes he cried when he was watching a reality show on TV where contestants had forgotten they were humans.

He dreamed of fjords and volcanic rock. Of an ashen sky where light sometimes pierced the clouds like a knife and blinded eyes accustomed to darkness. The air was so white it broke your heart. But he greeted each new day with alacrity, for he knew how precious the paltry sunshine was and that those so short days had to be lived with the intensity of a warrior. Each day was thus both a gift and a struggle.

He was dreaming of the country he had lost.

But what did he really know, what did the ambassador with his frost-dazzled eyes know of real struggle? What he saw here, in this other world, was the dust of humanity, and not actual people. It spoke of the colour of the earth, not of history. Dust and soil that he took in through his nostrils and expelled through his pores, percolating subtle poison at each breath. It had made him believe that he was dissolving into the sulphuric gases and diesel fumes that the toxic air dissipated through his pure flesh.

He had cried from the very first days. He cried every night, in the arms of his equally downcast but more pragmatic wife, who took solace from knowing that they would have staff to clean for them, to cook for them, to drive them around and even to keep the lawn in perfect shape. She whispered that being ambassador in New Delhi was a career move, that it would be a stepping stone to New York, Berlin or London. In two years' time, she told him, or three at the most, we'll be at the Metropolitan for Wagner's *Ring*; just be patient. He promised he would. But just three months later she was the one who packed her bags and left India, and her husband, for good.

And so it was that for the last ten years he had been dying and weeping, or the other way round. Each tear robbed him of a few milliseconds of life. At least that meant he would not have to live on this accursed land for all eternity, he thought. He reckoned he had been forgotten by everyone and especially by his land of fjords and rocks, of a land as smooth as this one was hairy, of a land where people did not smell of sweat and rancid oil but of frost and wood ash.

The proud but anxious appearance of this lonely man aroused my curiosity when I first encountered him at a literary festival in India. Perhaps I recognized in him the same feeling of displacement that I had suffered since getting here and that made me feel dizzy, like a ringing in the ear that won't go away. Excess and shortage. The magical and the iniquitous. Generosity and infamy. Wherever you looked, opposites clashed. There was no middle term.

The first evening of the festival, held in the gardens of a palace that had become a luxury hotel, consisted of one of those notoriously extravagant parties that Indians throw. Everything about it dripped with money and power, it was all excess and overabundance, a showy display in which writers, I have to say, were rather drab beings lost among the aggressively gregarious butterflies of Indian high society. The attractiveness of such extravagance was short-lived and the party soon became mildly disagreeable. On each side of the walkway leading to the marquee stood turbaned waiters holding heavy brass torches aloft, as straight-backed as soldiers of the old Anglo-Indian army. 'Will they have to stay there the whole night long?' I asked. There was no answer. I drew my coat around my shoulders. I was chilled by this country, by its customs and its perversions.

The dinner was quite as lavish as the party. Dozens of nomad women with foggy eyes and pock-marked faces reddened by the heat of the stoves laboured behind a long row of tandoors. Their angular hands worked in strict coordination, flipping naans directly over the burners, sprinkling them with melted butter, and stacking them on plates. Dishes, served in grand style, tickled guests' palates with exquisite flavours, especially the desserts with their fragrance of saffron, honey and grated pistachio.

Towards the end of the meal, someone directed my attention to a tall, thin and curiously fleeting figure of a man gliding one more time along the buffet display table at a time when everyone else had finished eating. 'He's the ambassador of X,' I was told. 'He comes to every conference, every festival, every dinner.' To me he looked dignified and at the same time evanescent. My informant added: 'I suppose the poor man doesn't have anything else to do.' Indeed, I could not myself imagine what purpose an embassy in India could have for a Nordic land such as his.

He wasn't a writer, and he had no role in the circles of power that surrounded us. He was just there. Tall, white-haired, pale-skinned. Melancholy. Infinitely.

He'd forgotten who it was who'd thought that the country's economic salvation lay in trade agreements with the giants of Asia. It might have made sense if the country had had anything to export, but its whole economy was based on an elaborately impenetrable banking system whose recent eruptions had been accompanied as if in a tragic opera by the volcanoes looming over it. That's why the ambassador's dispatch to these parts had been accompanied by trumpet blasts and electoral promises of economic revival. But once he got here, he hit a brick wall masked by wordy shows of friendship.

It was inevitable that the slow pace of Indian bureaucracy would collide with the efficiency of his own land. Correspondence composed of baroque formulae piled up on his desk, and in time began to smell of damp and to disappear under a galaxy of cobwebs; there were just as many instructions from his own ministry, ever more strident in tone. Misunderstandings piled up as well, pulling the rug from under the plans. However, despite his requests, which turned into pleas, he was not allowed to return to his own land or to move on to another posting. As he well knew, that was the consequence of failure.

However, nobody was aware of how quickly he was fading away. He'd noticed it himself in the first week – a few ounces off when he stood on the scales. He put it down to the stress of travel and especially to his reception by officials with impressive moustaches and ill-fitting suits who had greeted him without a smile whilst shamelessly harassing their sub-ordinates. An exquisitely courteous man, he had felt the humiliation of 'inferiors' as an almost physical affront. And there were inferiors all over the place in this country, where hierarchy mattered above all else. Each person took comfort in the fact that there was always somebody else on a lower rung. So each time he behaved with consideration towards one of them, he created palpable embarrassment, and made more enemies than friends by acting respectfully towards people who didn't deserve it in their own eyes.

He was disturbed to the root of his being. Everything he believed in had been harmed. Was he still a man if he gave way to a woman? If he shook a servant's hand, was he offending the very person he thought he was respecting? He no longer knew.

So then he wept.

Do you understand the nature of his melancholy? I mean, when it is all the harsher for being senseless, when it is an incoming tide slowly eroding the ground of your inner being? You are an ambassador in one of the world's largest countries. You are treated like a king. You have more staff than you know what to do with. You don't need to lift a finger to have your smallest need met. And yet.

Who is there to whom you can say you are miserable? Your wife, of course. But she understood only too well and packed her bags because she could do so before the place swallowed her whole.

Who else?

The ten million people around you? Pick one, at random. He'll take a look at you, a well-dressed man in a chauffeur-driven luxury car with an uncomfortably oversize house, and his eyes will say it all: only a wealthy idiot such as you are could have the gall to wail about being lonely.

So he held it all back.

And he lost weight. He'd cut an imposing figure when he arrived in New Delhi, but as the months and years went by he slimmed down to the point of gauntness, with a neck as scraggy as a scavenging chicken's and wrists too narrow for hands grown blotchy with age. The suits he'd brought with him, handmade in Savile Row (for he was a bit of a dandy), got looser and looser until one day, dressing in the huge closet he had for that task, he was stunned to see his trousers slip off his hips and down to the ground, revealing jutting pelvic bones and flabby skin that was so pale as to be grey. His belt ran out of notches. To cap it all, even his shoes were now too big for him. He had to put shame aside and get himself a complete new set of clothes made by the best tailor he could find in town. A few months later he had lost more weight and had to go back to have new clothes made again by the same tailor, who took down his measurements with a tiny pencil stub that he licked. He compared them to the measurements he'd noted the last time in the same school exercise book, and pursed his lips.

'Too thin, then. You reducing too much,' the tailor says in approximate English. Frowning, he adds, 'Are you sick?'

The ambassador shakes his head, He smiles faintly, pats his belly and says: 'I can't manage local food very well.'

The tailor recommends him to go and see an Ayurvedic practitioner who performs miracles. The ambassador pays scant attention: he knows that no form of medical treatment can cure sadness – at any rate, not a sadness of that kind, as hard and cold as a gravestone.

On the first day of the festival, I bumped into him several times. He was always alone, standing a head higher than the milling crowd, and paler than the few other white skins that could be seen here and there – as pale as the winter that follows in his wake with its haze of *ennui*. The other attendees, by contrast, dash between lectures and round tables like a word-starved horde, which, for the writers who were there, made up for past literary events where they'd spoken to empty seats. Here, they've got an audience of thousands. Here, people hurry, swarm, stand and camp out on chairs as if they'd decided to spend the day and the whole night there if necessary, so as not to miss any treasures that might spill from literary lips. As for the ambassador, he stands on the fringe of the crowd. He listens in to a bit of a reading, to a fragment of a debate. Sometimes a smile hovers on his lips, but never when a writer makes a joke. Perhaps it was because a sentence or a clause or a tone of voice summoned up a sketchy, fleeting memory of a familiar image? Then he goes to lunch in the writers' canteen, stands in line to have his badge scanned, and then ponders over the various options on the buffet table for so long you might think he were about to make the most important decision in his life. He eats on his own. He does not look at anybody. He puts the paper napkin on his lap and eats and drinks like a well-behaved child. He wipes his mouth with the corner of the napkin. Because he ate his chapatti with his fingers, he sprinkles water over his hands. My heart breaks to see him like that, with his blue eyes all foggy from the void inside.

He had engaged in only two official actions since he'd been in post – apart from visa issues raised by tourists, which were dealt with by his secretary via the embassy's website. (There was in fact one occasion when a strange man looking for work in his country came to see him, but as he was sure the person would never adapt to the climate, the ambassador cleverly redirected him to the US embassy with the assurance that there were jobs to be found in Alaska. He never saw the man again.)

One of the notable cases he had to deal with concerned a couple that had been arrested on their return from Katmandu with their backpacks stuffed with cannabis. In fact they would not have been caught if one of their ruck-sacks hadn't been stolen on the station platform when they arrived in Delhi. Their plan was to get to the border and cross over on foot. They shouted out loud and a policeman had the presence of mind to grab the thief and tackle him to the ground. Other policemen came running, and they beat the unfor-tunate thief so hard that the rucksack burst open and packages wrapped in sealed transparent plastic fell out of the torn lining. The cops collected up packages that weighed several kilos, and discovered that they contained can-nabis of a particularly pure kind. The tourist couple abandoned the rucksack and tried to flee, but the police, suspecting foul play, came after them. They were spared the customary beating only because they were white.

Alerted by the Foreign Ministry, the ambassador went to the prison where they were being held. The two detainees, who were hardly more than eighteen years old, were already in a pitiful state. Confined to stinking, filthy cells infested by roaches, among criminals whose gaze came from the other side of hope and reason, they thought they would moulder away for years and die from the slow torture of being forgotten. They went on their knees in pools of piss to beg for repatriation. 'We plead guilty,' they said, 'and we accept the penalty that the courts of our own country will impose on us. But for heaven's sake, allow us to serve our time at home!'

The ambassador was disgusted by the sight of the place they were in, but he felt no pity. They could only blame themselves for having come to this country of their own free will and then breaking its laws. However, slightly stimulated by the thought that he had a job to do at last, he told them to be patient, and proceeded at his own slow pace to get the matter dealt with.

Throughout the case, he woke each day with a degree of eagerness. At last he had a purpose. He had acquired some importance. He shaved and did his hair with care, resuming the habits of the dandy that he'd put away in the trunk of his melancholy, and reckoned he looked better than usual, that his complexion was pinker, less wan, and his eyes a sharper tint of blue. As he got dressed he was surprised that he had to pull in his paunch to buckle the belt. But he'd not had a paunch for years! He had a little trouble buttoning his shirt. His jacket felt a little tight on the shoulders.

He spent the day calling members of the government of his own country, conducting discussions with the Foreign Ministry, taking advice from eminent lawyers. The greatest surprise and the apogee of it all was a call from the Prime Minister! He stood up straight and gave clear and well-ordered answers. The Prime Minister congratulated him on his efficiency and entrusted him with the task of making sure that the couple would be repatriated with the least possible fuss in the media. When the ambassador suggested that the Indian authorities were likely to be hesitant about an extradition, given that there was no bilateral treaty on the matter, the Prime Minister's response took his breath away: 'I have full confidence in you, my dear friend. If anyone can do it, you can!'

He was so overcome that he burst a button on his shirt.

It turned out that the Indian authorities were not at all unwilling to allow extradition. As they were only too aware of the media's taste for stories of drug smugglers imprisoned in atrocious conditions, they would be glad to be rid of this unwelcome burden as quickly as possible. The blond weaklings would obviously not survive more than six months. They'd end up with their throats cut by their cellmates or else hanging from their own bed sheets. And that would put the authorities themselves in a bind for human rights violations. After all, India wasn't China. The world's largest democracy had to answer for its crimes, even if it was occasionally nostalgic for the time of dictators.

And so officials from the Indian Foreign Ministry made it clear to the ambassador that they were prepared to negotiate the extradition of the two citizens. He was surprised and initially pleased, but then irritated that the case had been solved so quickly. His newfound fitness convinced him that he needed to feel useful in order to survive. And what could be more useful than saving two young people from a life in jail, or even from the death sentence? He therefore applied the rules of purposeful deferral that he had learned from those self-same Indian officials. He claimed that letters had been mislaid, he didn't answer calls from the ministry, he told his own government that the local authorities were dragging their feet. He made one press statement after the other, implying first that there would be a positive resolution to the case, then that it would not work out well. The officials were mystified, as they thought it had all been sorted out some time ago.

Weeks turned into months. The youngsters were losing weight whilst the ambassador was filling out. He whistled as he dressed in the morning and was overjoyed to return to the suits he had brought with him. Their cut had never seemed so becoming, the line of his silk jacket had never seemed more elegant. He chose a pocket handkerchief to match his tie, and lost himself in contemplation of the hues that went so well with the rest of his attire. He could hardly keep his delight to himself.

One day they found the young woman drowning in her own blood. She had cut her wrists with a piece of iron she'd prised from the frame of her bed. The ambassador got an emergency call from the hospital. Seeing such a frail creature under drab and crumpled bed sheets hovering between life and death like a damaged butterfly, he realized that he could not keep the masquerade going any longer. He passed on the messages he'd put in limbo and before the week was out the two defendants were taken back to their country to be hounded by journalists with an insatiable hunger for morbid stories and to be housed in a neat and tidy prison cell with a television set and DVD reader, which was in their eyes utter paradise.

The ambassador went back to his residence trying to hold on the feeling of a job well done. He kept it up until the next evening. The day after, he started to shrink again.

His second case concerned a man who suffered a massive heart attack while crossing the desert on camelback. He was a wealthy businessman who sought extreme experiences in the most unwelcoming places on the planet. He'd put a lot of work into planning this trip with local nomads and had it all laid out in the smallest detail on spreadsheets and on cutting-edge communication devices. He was so confident in himself and in his efficiency that it never occurred to him that he might die on the trip. In his view, death came only from bad planning. But it came for him all the same.

The nomads accompanying him saw him fall off his camel just as he was urging them to go faster. They thought it was a rich man's joke, but when they found that they could not make him move, they panicked. It has to be said that they were a people on the brink, as their territory had been so diminished that all they had left for their wanderings was an area bounded on all sides by aggressively expanding settlements. Demand for their cattle had dropped in the face of frozen produce from New Zealand. Their handicrafts had been sidelined by identical objects made in China. They survived thanks to tourists who were fascinated by their strangeness, their pale eyes and skin etched by wind and sun, and also because tourist hotels hired them to sing, dance, cook traditional dishes and display themselves like circus dogs. Their eyes had the hue of the horizon, for travelling was written in their genes.

When the businessman thought he saw rising on the horizon the fortress-city of Jaisalmer (he was wrong, it was only a mirage), he grew excited and gestured wildly to the nomads to make them hurry up, even to have a camel race, he went as red as a scalded lobster and fell off his mount. He'd stopped breathing even before his large plump body hit the ground. The nomads shook him about, poured water into his mouth and over his face, but they had to admit in the end that the tourist was well and truly deceased. They fled, for they knew that they would face unending police harassment if they declared the death officially. They reckoned that sun, sand, wind and vultures would not take long to dispose of the awkward corpse, by which time they would have vanished without trace.

The man's wife was worried not to have had news and as she couldn't reach him on his cellphone she called the embassy. The ambassador, woken from the blank torpor that had overcome him since the departure of the two drug dealers, sprang back into action, took the necessary steps and, acting like a detective, eventually found out where the man was.

They found him a guide who knew the desert as well as the nomads. The fee was huge but his government had given him carte blanche. The missing man was sufficiently important to spend whatever it took. So he ventured into the desert in a clapped-out jeep, considerably fearful of getting lost and never coming back. But when he sat down in the jeep and buckled his safety belt, he saw he had a small belly poking out of his middle. The paunch of satisfaction.

This second case arose shortly before the festival where I met the ambassador. However, he was thin and pale once again, and I noticed that he took several servings from the lavish buffets at our disposal but ate without enthusiasm and apparently without relish.

One day before the end of the festival, I found myself sitting at the same lunch table. With exquisite manners he stopped eating and stood up for me as I sat down. I smiled at him as engagingly as possible and introduced myself. He seemed distracted and as if consumed by hidden anxiety. There was an awkward pause.

But then, maybe because he guessed from my look that I was sympathetic without saying so, he drank a mouthful of the Indian wine that was served at meals in large quantities and launched into the story I have told you. When he got to his departure in the jeep, he stopped.

'So what happened next?' I asked. 'Did you find the body?'

He nodded.

'I thought I would die from the unbearable desert heat. I drank water all the time, but shortly after setting off – please forgive me mentioning this unpalatable detail at table – I suffered a dreadful attack of diarrhoea. My guide had to stop every ten minutes so I could relieve my bowels. I was writhing in pain. He wanted us to go back, but I knew I had to fulfil my mission. I was convinced that if I carried it off, my government would allow me to go back home. If I failed, I would die in the coming days. There was no doubt about it.'

His eyes went vague and his blue irises went so pale as to be almost white, as if they were the reflection of the emptiness that the ambassador never ceased to contemplate. I saw his skin was flabby, like a gourd stripped of flesh.

'But after two days in the fearsomely coloured desert, where golden rocks mingled with bloody sediments, in the bellowing noise of the winds that arose and then stopped with brutal suddenness, I grasped a truth that had escaped me up to then: that this country detested me . . . no, abhorred me, begrudged me with persistent hatred as if I was a virus it had to be rid of.'

It took them two days and two nights to reach a place where nomads met, at a point where several tracks crossed. Nobody was there, but their tracks remained. And what they also found not far off was what remained of a corpse after the sun, the wind and the vultures had done their work – a piece of torn and carbonized flesh, consumed by all the pitiless forces of the place. And as he looked at these unspeakable scraps, these inhuman remnants, the ambassador was convinced he was looking at himself as he really was in face of the voracious carnage of this land.

By a curious transposition of the kind that arises in a fever dream or when you spend too long in the sun in the open desert, he told me, he became quite certain that what he had found were his own mortal remains. He didn't tell his guide. But that blue shirt rent by talons, and that torn hat, and the cross caught on a rock, all these traces of life and struggle and refusal, each as futile as the other, he felt quite sure – that was him.

After police and forensics had taken what they needed, gathered up the pieces of the corpse and packed them in sealed containers that would be returned to the man's homeland once the inquiry was over, the ambassador went back to his residence. He sat on the balcony and downed several whiskies to the sound of birds chattering furiously at sunset. He didn't see the cleaner who took his grimy clothes to the wash or the butler who made sure to refill his crystal glass when it was empty.

From then on this grey and insubstantial man spun out his idle and useless time by checking his weight every evening. He worked out that he had quite exactly two hundred and eleven days left before he would vanish entirely to be reunited with his remains scattered in the desert sand.

He was not recalled to his home country. He resumed his regular life and tried to pack it with futile activities like literary festivals, which filled his schedule, but not his soul, or his paunch.

Translated by David Bellos

CHRISTIAN GARCIN

The Goldfish

At night, before going to bed, I spend a minute or two watching the gold-fish in his bowl, slipping through the plastic seaweed my son insisted on buying for him. It's an odd fish, not because it's black with a huge tail and big bulbous eyes, because in those respects it resembles pretty much all the fish one finds in fishbowls in Chinese restaurants, but because it swims backwards and sometimes on its back. I had no idea it was possible for fish to swim on their backs. I've often seen dolphins on TV doing that sort of thing, and plenty of other weird things besides, like standing upright on the water's surface balancing on their tails, but as far as I know, dolphins are not fish. Be that as it may, mine, or rather my son's, swims on its back and swims backwards. It's a very unusual fish.

To tell the truth, I've never been very fond of fish. Nor have I had much experience of them. Except in the days when I worked at the fish market, but of course back then the fish were dead. It was tough work: I started at 11 p.m., and it was non-stop, or pretty much, until 6 a.m. There was just one break, around 4 a.m., when I had the chance to have a coffee and a croissant. Except that with the smell that permeated my fingers, dipping my croissant into my coffee or even bringing the croissant up to my mouth, or even holding the coffee cup to my lips was unpleasant. During the night, there were a few stretches with not much going on. I made the most of them by heading out for a smoke on the dock, still with that smell in my nostrils each time I brought my hand up to my mouth. The cigarette breaks were pleasant enough. Mainly because in those days I wasn't unloading the lorries from the trawlers, I wasn't lugging armfuls of floppy fish around the place, nor was I hosing them down or packing them in layers of ice in boxes, ready to be sold on the other side. But also because, in the dead of night, there was something melancholy and mysterious that I liked very much in the slow lapping of the dark water, and in the silence of the sea filling the horizon. If there was a break around sunrise, it was even better: the dawn colours were sometimes spectacular, the day's noises beginning to edge out the cold of the night, and the great seabirds arriving noisily and waiting beside me for offcuts or entrails, or sometimes whole fish I'd throw them without telling the boss. I went home dirty and stinking, and the smell of fish never left my nostrils even once I had showered – scoured myself, I should say – even when I slept and even when I woke hours later. It wasn't pleasant. But not too unpleasant either.

That said, living fish are a species I have no knowledge of. The one I have at home, apart from the fact that it swims in that peculiar way, is a mystery to me. Let me reiterate, I am no expert in fish, but I had no idea these creatures, the little ones who live in fishbowls, could live beyond two or three years. My son bought this one almost five years ago. It's probably an old man, or an old woman – how does one tell? And I'll tell you this: it's in fine fettle. It swims backwards and forwards, on its front and on its back, with equal ease. Sometimes I wonder if it has been exposed to radiation, if it's a mutant.

It was my son who looked after it. It wasn't an onerous job: just changing the water every week or so, adding some antibacterial drops and feeding it once a day and no more. He took the job very seriously. He was still small, and the goldfish-bowl looked enormous in his arms as he carried it from the table to the sink. But I've been looking after it myself for two years now. My son no longer lives here: he lives with his mother and some sort of company director who earns a lot and doesn't want a goldfish in his house. On the other hand, he has a garden, and in this garden he has a labrador. Labradors are very fashionable apparently. I'll admit that it's probably more fun than a goldfish – even an ancient acrobatic one. Let's just say there are probably more opportunities for emotional bonding.

When my son comes to mine, every other Saturday afternoon and Sunday night, in other words two nights and three full days per month, he doesn't really bother with the fish. Most of the time he barely notices it. I get that – we have other things to be getting on with. The other day, however, he wanted me to buy a plastic plant to put in the bowl. He chose it himself, paying special attention to the size, because he didn't want it taking up too much space in the bowl. Back at the house, he put it in, lodged between two stones we brought back from a walk. Then he watched the goldfish. I watched him, glad of his renewed interest in this peculiar old creature who swims so strangely. He stayed there a minute or two, leaning over the bowl, his hands on his knees, watching the fish, who couldn't have cared less about the plastic plant. I was behind him, and I was happy. I felt I was seeing myself in the movements I make every night before going to bed, and I felt the invisible, unbreakable, thread binding us together, my son and me.

Translated by Patrick McGuinness

CHARLES DANTZIG

Looking Inwards on the Autobahn

12 May

The office was a large room with suede on three walls and brushed steel panels on the fourth, pierced by two tall windows giving on to beech foliage. The outdated, mid-seventies interior decoration told me its owner was maybe tight-fisted but undoubtedly distinguished. There were no paintings or bookshelves, there was nothing to distract the attention required by the *top doctor*. The desk, a long, broad, thick mahogany bureau with gilded sphinx talons standing on a beige carpet, was similarly bare, displaying only the broad hands of Dr Querlédec. One of which slowly rose to support the doctor's heavy jawbone as he gave me an intense look. All right, all right, I thought, but is he piling up all these details out of professorial punctiliousness, or as a way of not saying something?

'Professor, is it fatal?'

The relief the question gave him released sincerities for my own instruction. Truth. Strength of character. Frankness always preferable to hypocrisy. Liver cancer, metastases, eight to twelve months with treatment, if not, four to six.

At one o'clock, at the restaurant, Warren T. Atsuhito was telling me about the Phuket conference. Panel discussion, swimming pool, panel discussion, full-body massage *und so weiter*, plenary session, banquet with guest of honour ... Good God, had I really donated my experience to circles that made such heinous use of their leisure time?

Go. Leave the business, leave home. Go in order to find myself. What a family! Blessed be the malady that forced me to admit I had married a garden rose and fathered a sloth! What's more, doing without them would look good to posterity: dear old Henri, *he chose to spare them the sight of his frailty.*

Montfort l'Amaury? Monfort is only three-quarters of an hour from Nicole, I mean, from Saint-Cloud. Nicole would smother with discretion and suffocate out of pity. Or somewhere abroad, like Sri Lanka, where the conference was held two years ago? I would need a good hospital nearby, and you're more easily identified when abroad than at home, see for example the Lacaze boy who was found in Italy only five days after being kidnapped. What a pity the USSR is no more! What a great black-comedy lark that could have been! 'French industrialist defects to the East.' And I could have taunted all the insincere mourners in my family and my circle from a hidey-hole known to the entire world. Look at me, all my many sniffling underlings! . . . I've been given a palatial residence on the Black Sea . . . I'd be taking the lid off the company's tax havens and hit men on state television! . . . In the car in the lane to the right a young woman with a thoughtful look is biting off a nail skin. In the car in front of hers a man is talking to himself as he beats time on the steering wheel with his index finger. In the car on my left a pretty girl scowls as the man in the passenger seat raises his knees to the glove box, crosses his arms and falls into thought. Traffic jams . . . Driving . . . Meditation all round . . .

Stocked up on cigarettes twelve days later. 'Four to six months' probably means two or two and a half before going into hospital, two and a half months times two and a half packets a day makes . . . I reached the requisite number after five calls at cigarette shops. As I write this (I am writing on my lap) I can see the boxes I have left on the parcel shelf, in the mirror. The remaining details of my futile life were settled in nine days, including a mini-crisis at the board described in veiled terms in the minutes. I took twenty thousand euros in cash from my various stashes, providing me with a per diem of two hundred and twenty-eight euros and twenty-two centimes. At the following consultation, Querlédec respected my decision not to have chemotherapy. Old school, Querlédec, straight up and down guy, doesn't announce the disease to lay down a burden that it is his duty to share and then go and play golf, he respects the moral choices others make. On Sunday the 15th, because Nicole was at her mother's and Ludovic was asleep – that ne'er-do-well only comes home at weekends to get his laundry done – I packed my stuff and put it in the car. On the 16th, at the time when usually I set off for the office, I drove out to the ring road.

13 May

Where can you be alone? In a crowd. How can you be nowhere? If you don't stop moving. Where had I seen people meditating? In cars. What place is most conducive to introspection? The motorway.

On such roads which are abstractions of roads I would progress towards knowledge. As they are plain and always the same, skirting towns and flattening the landscapes they cross, they teach people that what's important is purification.

14 May

I've been gone thirty days. On the first day as I drove away from home I thought of my two-and-a-half months, maybe three, three months, a hundred days. The one hundred days, Napoleon. Napoleon, the landing. Landing, Fréjus. Motorway A4.

The faster you run, the sooner you find. At a hundred and twenty I overtook the lorries, swept past trailers, keeping an eye out for speed radars. By nine thirty in the evening I was in Nice.

I had to slow down.

I gave a false name and paid cash for two nights at the Negresco. For two whole days I went for walks, swam in water that was still cold, on my own, in the Baie des Anges, the Bay of Angels, alone, getting closer to the angels. What a pleasure. What a mistake. Drive and think! On my way. Hang on, it's time for the . . . 'Here is the news on Thursday, 16 April. The businessman Henri Defrétier has disappeared from his home in Paris.' Was it the lead story? A reporter standing in front of that 'home in Paris' (Saint-Cloud, actually) and shouting out every fourth word, usually adjectives, explained that for the last two days 'all branches of the *French* police' had been looking for 'Henri Defrétier, an *influential* leader of the *aeronautical* industry' and that right now, right behind him, two inspectors were talking with 'his *wife* Nicole Defrétier'. Back to the studio, where a journalist recited my CV in a low voice, as if a high pitch were reserved for reporters, excitement, things happening. Cutting-edge electronic components business. In the sights of several multinational groups. I was the owner of the famous racehorse Helvetica de Garamond (I'd sold it two years ago). I listened to myself saying in a clip from one of the few interviews I ever did that nobody in this country was interested in entrepreneurs, that I was keen on reading and chess. Chess was a lie, and reading barely true, how can you have the time to read when you're on the telephone or in meetings all day long and play golf at weekends, but a successful man has to have *passions*, and noble ones at that. (By the way, I do like history a lot. I've read everything about Churchill.) The anchor man said that nobody had yet claimed the kidnapping; in Iraq . . . I stop the car on the hard shoulder, get out, cross my hands behind me. Lit up in the growing dusk, the citadel of Carcassonne looked like a cartoon mosque. Cigarette between index and middle finger, arm stretched out in front of me. Through the eye I've not closed I can see smoke rising from the gabled roof. Hey? Is that how you think about fate? Why, you've done five hundred kilometres without noticing? I got back on the move. The following news headlines said that suicide 'was not ruled out' because I had recently learned I had cancer. 'Why hide it,' the newscaster added, 'by calling it "a long and painful disease"?'

With my hands loosely draped over the top of the wheel, my mind wandered to the harsh way we sacked the deputy director for recommending a merger with the Germans when I saw in the distance a dome of pink light hanging over the flatland.

TOULOUSE,

said the blue sign that rushed over the top of the windscreen. I parked in a service area, sat in the passenger seat and lowered the seatback.

15 May

I woke up with aches and pains. So much the better: comfort is an easy way out. From the suitcase with a 'First Class. Priority Handling' tag still attached to its handle I took out my toilet bag and went over to the yellow concrete toilet block thinking about my idiot son who, on getting back to his flat (his mother paid the rent) must be pouring himself a glass of Oxyboldine and . . . Ugh! Cold water! I'll let my beard grow. That'll make for a new Henri. More detached, more pure.

Drive slowly. Think. All right, OK, see if the radio . . . All the stations run funny stories, jokes and songs in the morning hours. Getting near Agen, electronic sound: 'and here is the news. In Iraq, the president . . . The UN . . . The American president . . . The secretary-general . . . Saddam Hussein . . . The Spanish prime minister . . . The Azores . . . Marseille vs Monaco . . .' My name came up only at the end in a list of short announcements, and only to say there was nothing new to report. You can't imagine how little the Middle East matters to me!

For ten days, from Agen to Bordeaux, Bordeaux to Poitiers, Poitiers to Orléans, Orléans to Tours, I followed a radio serial like so many others, *Garonne* or *The Flames of Love* (usefulness of having a wife who strives to improve her education). By 25 April there'd been no mention of Henri Defrétier for several days.

16 May

Say how I spend my days. In the morning I wash at the tap in the concrete toilet blocks, then I jog for ten minutes and do some push-ups in the rest area where you find four to eight large tables made of the same rough-hewn wood as the stall doors in the toilets, and an equal number of spindly trees, very exposed to the wind, as if to dissuade you from lingering: on the road! I eat at service area cafeterias. Petrol pumps like Easter Island statues under a metal awning on which the brand name is lit up at night as if it were a tabernacle. Beyond it, a glass-walled hut. Floor tiles, white lighting, vacuum-packed food displayed in refrigerated cases, hot drinks from machines with bulging middles, and some CDs of tasteless music on a carousel. You come across gloomy truckers, bawling families, a bleary-eyed sales rep (he'd had such a lively, persuasive look in those eyes earlier on), and pasty-faced check-out assistants (harsh lighting, ill-fitting orange uniform). Those examples of humanity won't make me sorry to leave it behind. It turns out I'd overestimated the importance of habits. A man does not have very deep roots. I've put up quite easily with the less 'civilized' state I'm now in. It even gives me satisfaction. And if what I miss the most is not Nicole but a shower, then I understood, on the eighth day of showerlessness, that showering is an act of self-comfort. Comfort is a vice of the soul.

Motorway restaurants looking like pyramids. You go in through glass doors covered in stickers advertising subsidized meal tickets. Musty, penetrating smell (stale grease + honeysuckle air freshener). Stack of imitation-wood plastic trays. Zinc hoppers with stainless steel cutlery. Pyrex glasses on plastic stands. Manufactured bread in imitation-wicker ceramic bread baskets. Long glass shield protecting a display of hors d'oeuvres made with manufactured mayonnaise. I slide my tray along steel runners. A lass with faded coloured hair fixed with a pink plastic peg and wearing a nylon jerkin retracts her head from a dumb waiter, turns towards me and hands me the sausage with a hose-pipe skin that I'd picked out on the illustrated panel, with a blob of putty-like mashed potatoes for ballast. A piece of cottony cheese, a biscuit enhanced by electronic-green sprinkles. I sit at a table, leaning back on a plywood trellis draped with a cloth creeper, and as I chew I read one of the books I've brought with me. Personal development books, not history. It's no longer about their past but about my future. The meaning to give to the small amount of life left to me so as to put the meaning of my death in the correct direction. I never thought I would read that kind of book. This challenge will help me make up for the vanity of the first fifty years of my life. And who knows whether I am facing the challenge for precisely that reason? To abstract myself. To think. Windy service areas, bleary box buildings, reconstituted foods – it is all put on to stop us forgetting the non-human essence of motorways, and that is all to the good.

17 May

Road sign semiotics. Blue only on the signboards that hang over the lanes: they give distant destinations, ideals. White is for the nearside boards, giving exit numbers and mileage to nearby destinations: materialist hope. Large upper-case letters for foreign countries, italic lower case for small towns. The distant and the nameless are capital. I noticed subtle differences in the lettering used by operating companies running different stretches of motorway: italics at Angers aren't the same as the italics of Lyon. Does that mean that regional accents leak into script? Realist corruption? Thankfully, on the median strip there are very small rectangular panels with numbers I haven't been able to fathom – numbers that are mysterious, abstract and, for that reason, admirable.

Right before the tollbooth, as a wide signboard has just told me to

SLOW DOWN

and another one declares

TOLL 1.5 KM

a final sign emerges before the battery of booths topped with illuminated crosses (open or closed) telling us what we owe according to our vehicle. A white bicorn levitating over two coins owes x euros; idem pursued by a square over a single coin, x'; a rectangle significantly longer than it is high suspended over one coin to the right and two to the left owes x''. I hand my money over to an employee with a rotating torso, a semi-divine collector of dues who reigns over us from the booth. Signage contributes to the advance towards abstraction. Am I granting its inventors more subtlety than they deserve? They just did it like that, one way is as good as another, no thought involved. Most people only have thoughts when looking on their graves.

18 May

What about the tourist signage, white on ditch brown? Yesterday on my nth crossing from the Atlantic to the Mediterranean I read outside Villefranche-de-Laurageais:

TOULOUSAIN BELL GABLE

I looked around and saw it on the hill, a gable-end flanked by two towers in fired brick. OK, I thought. What's that? Johnny Hallyday? Eddy Mitchell? . . . Later

PÉZENAS
(MOLIÈRE)

Ah, that's Jean Ferrat. These quiz shows are absurd.

MONTAGNE SAINTE-VICTOIRE

And this morning, after leaving and returning to Menton (Schengen or not, I don't want to risk getting stopped by the border police), I forced myself to stare at the wide abstract carpet of the motorway as if trying to keep a taste in my mouth and came upon:

GORBIO VILLAGE
LA TURBIE TROPHY OF THE ALPS
ÈZE MEDIEVAL VILLAGE
ROQUEBRUNE MEDIEVAL CASTLE

Sometimes there is just the name, other times there's a shape to fill it out. Before the word CHARTRES there's a cartoon cathedral, in front of LA BEAUCE three heads of wheat, in front of LA SOLOGNE three birds in flight. Might the motorway be seeking a pardon for having a pure soul? Or to plunge us back into materiality? I avoid places, but you should know they are there?

Chartres and its cathedral . . . Hunting in Sologne . . . Beauce and its wheat. . .: these signs are postcards. Clichés. False images. Phew. The motorway is the purest of the pure. It inscribes grooves of disincarnation across the land and, thus freed from vulgarity, we are able to think.

It is pleasant to realize I was right.

19 May

To think, to think! Up to now all I have produced are (in restaurant language) shaved ideas. Shaved ideas on a bed of cancer. I have to accept thinking about the enemy that lives inside me and that means there are two of us, which is to say, very different from the rest of humanity in good health, consisting of unitary bodies which proceed without a care. Must stop distracting myself by wondering what could happen in the business, etcetera. No more etceteras. I've stopped childish telephone calls to hear the voice of someone from before and then hanging up. You are weak, Defrétier.

20 May

I was travelling northwards across Anjou by night and the headlamps lit up

YOU ARE 150 KM FROM PARIS NOTRE-DAME

Notre-Dame. Quai Saint-Michel. The *bouquinistes'* display cases, all shut up at this time of the night. Just before the Institut, the frame of white houses around the statue of a great man. A jam. Use a flipper to dive down the slip road on to the riverside expressway.

YOU ARE 50 KM FROM PARIS NOTRE-DAME

Up and down, camelback style, from the riverside expressway to the *quais*, from the *quais* to the riverside expressway. The Eiffel Tower on club feet. Pont de Garigliano. Porte de Saint-Cloud. Home.

SLOW DOWN

Darling where were you we were so worried Marie-Agnès was so kind

313

would you like it's silly Ludovic dropped in this evening but he's gone out clubbing tomorrow we could

At the moment I was about to veer on to the link to Porte d'Orleans I suddenly swerved and the car rolled in the direction of Porte d'Italie. I kept my eyes straight ahead on the ring road so as not to be tempted by Paris on my left-hand side, so near, so warm, palpitating like a pigeon, so dangerous. Motorway east. I left it at Troyes. I overcame temptation.

23 May

Noon. A roar comes up at the back of my neck, slips past my cheekbone, wraps itself round my head. I sit up with a start: a truck the size of a black mountain is overtaking, and I correct the steering with a sharp tug at the wheel. Do analgesics contain tranquillizer?

12.15. In a rest area at the summit of a hill where cicadas screech, I throw a bag of dirty laundry into an openwork refuse bin from where a black plastic bag flaps in anger as it tries to escape.

00.37. Crossed the border. While waiting in line, I zapped radio stations: nothing about Defrétier on any of them. Watched people in cars. A fat man in a little Fiat furiously grasping the wheel. A woman leaning over backwards to slap the kids. A playboy in a red Ferrari emitting the threatening noise of a female rocker. Two silent women dolled up to the nines smoking cigarettes and looking out of their respective side windows, which they'd lowered. A family singing together (parents' arms waving like windscreen wipers). A boy with his neck straining towards the mirror and bursting a pimple in the corner of his lip. All in all, the masses with their small joys and small worries, knowing nothing of the grandeur of suffering. A policeman waves me on. Italian radio crackles over the French station and then smothers it entirely. *Ti amo. Amore mio. Ricordati, amore. Voglio l'amore.* Sentimental spaghetti. Beneath a blazing sun, I follow the dark dotted lines through the tunnels. Sun, a tunnel swallows me, then another sun, another tunnel, and now I'm suddenly borne through the air by a very high and very long viaduct. The greatness of Rome lives on. As does the mediocrity of man.

What if French motorways were the inheritance of Versailles? The fact that there aren't any here reminded me that ours are decorated with flowers and bushes. Better that they were not. Beautification is deception. Anyway, motorway landscapes are not as uniform as all that. When you go through Provence, there's an air of Provence about it. When you go through Brittany, there's an air of Brittany. You have not done enough purification, you tarmac tongues. In spite of myself I'd remained in reality, the reality I had spent my whole life trying to overcome, as a manufacturer of airplane fixings, so beautiful and so alike, but imperfect, because despite the efforts of machines and engineers, they still had variations at the scale of one thousand millionths of a centimetre. By way of punishment my body opened a gap of one thousand millionth of a centimetre, that's how the killer cells creep in.

24 May

I've driven into Genoa by mistake. So many different noises after the peaceful hum of the motorway. So many men standing. Walking. Tired out and confused by the one-way system and forever coming back to the 'centro città' that I wanted to leave, I took refuge in an inn where I spent the night, near the bay. I lay fully dressed on the smelly pink velvet counterpane and read the toll ticket issued by Autouroutes du sud de la France that I had claimed to have lost. ('You'll have to pay for the longest portion. – I know, can't be helped, I'm in a hurry.') The reverse crutch symbolizes the stretch from Barcelona to Lyon on the vertical and the route from Toulouse on the horizontal. Those names, those numbers. Le Boulou 272. Perpignan-sud 255. Perpignan-nord 241. Leucate 219. Sigean 208. Narbonne. Béziers. Agde. Forks for motorway restaurants, mushrooms for filling stations. The motorway is right. It will help me become more perfect. Through the window the black arch of the road bridge that gives the Bay of Genoa its funeral diadem cried out to me: Come back!

25 May

Slept badly. Bowels in a twist. Triple dose of medicine.

26 May

On the area servizio near Florence I am almost jolly as I whistle my way from the toilets back to my car that I left with its windows open. The car radio has been stolen. Thunder rolls, lightning flashes over the grey landscape. Another twinge. So you were jolly, were you? Singing like a cicada?

27 May

The motorway remains the same whatever the country. The ribbon of abstraction unrolls over a whole continent. Purity, to thee do I run!

28 May

Complete improvement. I panicked for nothing. Could Querlédec not have been wrong?

29–30 May

Nausea. Vomiting. Stomach cramps. Medicines. Three hours on the hard shoulder trying not to make a movement. The cause of cancer is that we agree to lead lives that are beneath us. The cause of cancer is sin. And our soul takes revenge on our body, on our lazybones of a body that always draws us on to facility, pleasure, comfort. Bodies collaborate with the enemy.

31 May

Better. Keeping up the high dose of medications as a precaution. When I was fifteen I asked Father L: is death expiation for original sin? 'Come, come, my lad, don't be so black.' I'm telling you, God punishes men for the futility of His ministers; and I who turned away from Him because of that know now that I have to return to Him. Malraux said: 'The twenty-first century will be religious or it will not be', and he was right. On all sides, in every country, we see writers, intellectuals, singers and politicians speak about their beliefs without embarrassment and tell us they must be applied to society. Now there's depth at last!

1 June

Four-hour wait at the Brenner crossing. Retched for an hour – 1.15 a.m. Note story Malraux against religion.

2 June

State of drowsiness. I look at myself in the rear-view mirror. Horizontal slice of a pending corpse. Ragged beard, cheeks like collapsed pumpkins, irises outshining pupils, could be Rasputin, who was a monk.

3 June

[*Illegible.*]

7 June

Drove for several days through valleys dotted with church towers shaped like the ace of spades and not sure of being on the motorway any more. Spent a whole day in death throes in a ditch. Amazed to have pain in the lungs that hurt. Sensation of the organs themselves inside me. Or is it pain that brings back memories of anatomical drawings? Better today. The medications really do me good. I'm in a service station fifty kilometres from Vienna. Burial of ex-empress Zita on television: the priest heading the procession knocks on the door, a voice from inside responds with 'Who is there?' Empress Zita. No answer, another knock, who is there. Zita the sinner, come in. Family members take off their masks, gaunt faces appear beneath top hats, skirts sweep open to reveal sugar-white tibias wrapped in fishnet stockings, cabaret music. That's Death!

8 June

Double dose. [*Illegible.*] Flowers and wreaths. Which I will have gone through.

9 June

For the first time since I was fifteen, I am praying. I beseech God to spare me these tortures. To finish me off. To let me live. As he chooses, as long as they stop. I do not want to die. Munich. Going back.

10 June

No reduction. I curse my body. Hard shoulder. [*Illegible.*]

11 June

Fribourg. What a ridiculous bout of panic! You can cure yourself by will-power alone. Solzhenitsyn managed. He beat cancer same way he beat communism. Cancer is a kind of communism. Healthy minds reject it. Illumination is stronger than thought. What I took to be an enemy is at bottom a friend. Washed up in a service station toilet. Shaved. Tucked into dinner in a green pyramid.

12 June

Vomiting. Retractable metaphysics. Lacaze suggesting one day to hold a meditation seminar so as to motivate managers. Trashed the plan as Buddha nonsense. Wrong. All Searching is. Conviction Alone [*illegible*] treasure. Violent retching avoided crash. Brakes.

16 June

Two days [*illegible*]. Sicksock? mistake slit road Basel way home. Border. france. CAVERN. Zita. Benzidoamycin. Benzitamycin. Benzido benzita. Faith. Benzita! Benzita! Opioom of the queenycins! Cries, cries, eternal and sublime Cries, strumpet tsarinanines, Postures! Postures! purity.

19 June

Near Meaux. I will soon be home. I've lost weight, I'm dirty, I'm better and I know it.

I put the key in the lock. I'd had the key all the time. I knew it without realizing.

Me, me, me, me!

Sharp pain in the bend of my arm. Strange joy. It feels like trumpets are sounding in the sky, that the clouds are clearing, that cascades of putti tumble over themselves through the gaps and that a tall, massive, rectangular white-coated man with a small, grey-haired cube-shaped head, as like as dammit to my jar of Jazz by Saint-Laurent, one of the many corruptions I gave up on my march to purity, appears, and with broad open hands calls me to him up on high.

Translated by David Bellos

MARIE NDIAYE

Revelation

This woman and her son had walked the long road from their house to the bus stop, and because for two months it had rained without respite, not even one morning or a few hours in the night without rainfall, the road was now only a muddy trail between the ploughed fields.

Now and then the son observed that you couldn't tell the road from the fields any more, and the woman patiently pointed out that the fields were dark brown, almost black, apart from the glistening, stagnant puddles in the corners, while the waterlogged road was still a dull grey.

He nodded, as if thoroughly pleased with this answer. They walked on in silence for a few moments, then the son said again, as if making a startling discovery, '. . . can't tell the road from the fields, do you see,' and within herself the woman was once again painfully surprised that he could repeat the most trivial thoughts with the same untarnished fascination, but she answered him gently, patient, detached, no longer listening to herself. And he nodded gravely, his brow clenched in concentration, and the woman's words seemed to her absurd and even enigmatic in their utter banality, and suddenly she wanted to laugh out loud at the both of them, at their senile prattle, but she did no such thing, she didn't even smile, knowing the son was now beyond all understanding or perception of irony. That thought left her morose until her son said again: '. . . isn't it funny, you can't tell the . . .' turning towards her in search of an explanation, then her irritation and torment banished all sadness for a time, and the woman carefully put on a voice and expression adapted to what she thought she knew of the thing in him that was broken, the thing that had broken.

He's unbearable, she sometimes thought. And also: he seems not so much insane as stupid, appallingly stupid.

She was angry with herself for that. This son was not cruel. His capacity for meanness had waned even as the mother's aggressive rancour grew. She realized that her despair and her rage were fuelled by nothing other than the progressive disappearance of those emotions in the son.

No, this son wasn't cruel, alas. And they would both take the bus to Rouen, since the rain had at long last stopped falling, but that evening the woman would come home to Corneville alone.

She'd take the bus back in the other direction, and the son wouldn't be with her, and maybe he knew that and maybe he didn't, it was too late now to find out. He might then abruptly refuse to get on to the bus, and the woman pictured him standing still by the roadside, calmly shaking his head and repeating, calm and incredulous: What an idea, mama, what an idea.

They were reaching the end of the road, and now they were nearing the sign that marked the stop, on the grassy strip between the fields and the highway. The sign was leaning and rusted. On it she could read the name *Corneville*. Could her son still do the same? She wanted to spit out at him, in her hard voice: So what do you think? You think you're going to come home with me tonight? You think you'll be coming home someday?

The sky suddenly cleared, and at the same instant the bus braked in front of them – appearing, the woman thought, in a flood of sunlight that nothing could have foretold. So long ago had all radiance disappeared from the atmosphere that the woman's eyes stung. She squinted, scowled. Close at her side, the son raised his head and smiled broadly. 'Mama,' he murmured, 'oh, mama, isn't it peculiar!' And, as always when he opened his mouth, she found herself irritated beyond all reason. She had to restrain herself from snapping back at him: You think there's anything on this earth as peculiar as you? Instead, she pushed him indelicately towards the bus door, which had just opened with a sort of deep, weary sigh.

This son never showed any unhappiness at being treated little better than the dog of the house, and the woman was not unaware that she often took advantage of that, raising her voice to him, shoving him aside need-lessly, but pained to see him so unaffected by these small humiliations, by his own lack of dignity, and then trying in vain, knowing perfectly well it was pointless, to rouse him to even the most fleeting fit of anger.

Nevertheless, she whispered when she asked the driver for one round-trip ticket and one one-way.

Yes, she wanted him to resist, she thought bitterly, but not about this.

The son was starting towards the narrow aisle between the two rows of seats when the driver caught sight of him. He stopped looking at the woman and stared at the son's face, then at his back, his pale little eyes suddenly filling with wonder and, she observed, mystified, with unconcealed, cordial admiration. And when the son sat down towards the middle of the bus, on the aisle so he could stretch out his long legs, the driver went on gazing at him in the rear-view mirror with a wise smile on his lips.

The driver was not a young man.

Clutching her money, the woman waited for the thought of handing over the tickets to occur to him. He shook his head, as if trying to wake himself. Finally he turned towards her, his gaze still veiled by an airy, distracted pleasure.

As time went by and the bus rolled down the road through the fields in this sudden abundance of light, the woman noticed the other passengers often turning around towards the son, or eyeing him furtively, she saw their benevolence and delight, and she realized that the son, this endlessly troublesome son, noticed none of it. She felt her own face grow pink with guilt and incomprehension. She hid it by looking out of the window. She told herself she was in this bus as if in the heart of a country so utterly foreign that every gesture of those around her was beyond her understanding. Every face was nevertheless of a type she knew well: wizened old ladies in beige raincoats, a farmer in glasses with smoked lenses, teenagers on their way home from school, a woman who resembled her in every way.

But why were they all staring at her son?

And why did the simple act of turning their gaze towards that son's beatific, distant face seem to illuminate them with such happiness?

She couldn't understand. None of them realized: there was no way to live with a son such as hers, and yet she thought this so utterly self-evident that people would do anything to avoid laying eyes on him.

The heat and the rumble of the bus left her drowsy. As long as the journey went on, there were no decisions of any kind to be made. She could scarcely bring herself to imagine the moment when she'd have to get off the bus and turn her thoughts to her son, and begin silently plotting.

Was this son, she suddenly thought, some animal she was going to sell at the market in Rouen? Was she ridding herself of him for personal gain?

No, no – she smiled wearily – it was simply intolerable, infuriating, to have him beside you, under your roof, breathing the same air as you, this son with his mysterious manias, his stifling, monotonous thoughts.

When the bus stopped at Saint-Wandrille, the woman half rose from her seat to glance at the broad rear-view mirror. She saw exactly what she was expecting – the two pale slits of the driver's eyes fixed on her son, on the reflection of his face over the seatbacks, the son's handsome, calm face, she thought to herself in amazement, and she wondered, incredulous, sardonic, if the driver and all the others openly staring at the son's face realized that that face was so beautiful and so calm only because it had no awareness of the loving attention it inspired, and so beautiful and so calm that the time had now come to put it away, never again to be seen in the streets of Corneville, and, at home, never again to burden the atmosphere with its oppressive, unending presence.

This woman thought that she couldn't bear the beauty of that son's face one moment longer – and that, in the old days, when he was still right, his face was never as handsome. No one would have turned to look at the son back when there was no need to keep from him where he was being taken. His face then had no reason to be as beautiful as it was now, since it expressed only ordinary thoughts. Nevertheless, thought the woman, rebelling, no one had the right to demand that she feel grateful or pleased at this change, no one could ask her to admire that face herself, however handsome and calm it may be.

She whispered in his ear: 'I'll be coming back to Corneville without you.'

'I know,' he said.

He smiled at her, amiable, reassuring. He went so far as to pat her arm, and then she couldn't help confiding that she wished the bus would never stop, which the son, he told her, understood perfectly. Those other sons of hers wouldn't have understood at all, it occurred to her, and she missed this one already. She'd be coming home alone, thank God: how she would miss him!

Translated by Jordan Stump

VIRGINIE DESPENTES

Hairs on Me

Him – I knew we'd fight the moment I saw him.

One of those nice surprises, the 'proverbial moment' when you're least expecting it.

I didn't try to dodge it. Wasn't even worth the effort of making that effort, that's how full on it hit me.

As soon as it started, with that first insistent look, I could feel the scale of my fear, and it was massive . . . it hadn't done that to me in ages.

We held out for a good half an hour, discussing this and that, and then we pulled back the sheets. It was so blatant, what we both wanted, and we weren't remotely embarrassed.

The first few days . . . a state of grace. Fruit never tasted before, fervent sweats, backs turned, flashes of sunlight glued to white skin, his neck my hands his back my belly limbs all sticking to each other, pumping away.

Flawless, pleasure, intertwined, trying to break our backs with all that howling, summoning old powers. Each time he stuck his shaft against my opening and then pushed a little, pulling away and coming back, his fucking head looking for work, it was breathtaking, the heavy artillery of sensations, as if he was caressing me beneath my skin. That prick, hard as a hammer, a miracle each time, too much power, I wanted it in my belly all the time, convulsions, it opened doors deep within, unexpected stirrings of the soul.

Often, I'd hold him in my arms, tight against me, like an old mother, lying on her side.

I'd spent so many years, of prudence and renunciation. And as for him, imposing himself suddenly ... He arrived at just the right time.

His minor miracle of a body, which made me a little dizzy when I looked at him with eyes wide open as we grasped each other and bent this way and that the better to gorge on each other. So many vulnerabilities flirting with so many strengths, and he let himself be watched, bc admired and loved, practically adored. A young man still a friend to women, yet to be properly separated from them.

All that power proud to rise up, we wrestled with each other, we really were living the high life, come here so I can give you what's coming to you, hit you with all I have in the depths of poems, spread me nice and wide with your tool, it feels, truly, like you're taking what is, deep down, the most precious part of me and it was always there just for you.

. . .

But I was being careful, all the same, at the start. I thought being careful would be enough ... I made it a test of my vigilance, and also my inventiveness. I was lying to myself. I'd been avoiding this for years, because I knew perfectly well it was strictly forbidden for me. But I liked him so much I lulled prudence to sleep.

The first few times with him, I'd wake up first, spontaneously. I'd go and check myself over briefly, in the bathroom. Running my fingers everywhere to see if anything was showing, then taking my pulse, examining myself in the mirror. Everything would be fine, I'd get back into bed next to him. Often, I'd fall back to sleep.

And, as the days passed, there were times when I stayed asleep next to him, letting the sun rise without worrying about it. I checked myself when I remembered to, by feel, under the covers.

Really, what was I thinking ...

*

One fine morning – him, with his hard-on pressed against my back, and me not properly aware of what was happening, pulling him over to climb on to me.

He was kissing my mouth; he planted a single kiss on my chin, 'Huh . . . a bit prickly, today', as if was no big deal.

Panic-extrication of breasts, the world retreated all at once, taking all my blood with it. I thought quicker than words, as I leapt from the bed, 'Shit, shit, shit – I've forgotten a fucking massive thing I have to do, today, leave me alone, come on, no I don't have time . . .'

And I shifted – I was out the door in two minutes.

Terrified – in the metro. I checked myself over, casually, tried to figure out exactly what stage I was at. But when there were hairs growing on your chin, the acceleration had already taken hold. Heartbeats, the sound of blood growing conspicuously louder – something I should already have clocked.

It had been years since I'd wound up like that, outside, as 'that' was starting . . . The warning signs were numerous and discernible enough. Unless one was intensely concentrated on something else, with a strong emotion to top it off. Like his cute little arse, and watching it bounce, feeling it getting busy, beavering away.

I had my mind on other things, I hadn't dwelled on it . . . on my nails splitting, my voice growing hoarse, my appetite all over the place, my mouth always a little dry . . . And then, when I didn't have a lover, the best warning sign of all would be that sudden craving for sex, like a force separate from me and wanting to devour others. So, when everything manifested itself, usually, I'd go down and stock up on fags and food, I'd make three or four phone calls to say I'd be away and I'd lock myself in. Curtains drawn, video cassettes piled up, recorded for moments like these, flopped in front of the telly.

It had started in puberty; it had happened gradually at first, without any alarm bells even for a second. Almost completely in subtle hints, sensitive mood changes, transformations in the range of the probable. For a long time, I attributed it to the mysteries of 'my cycle'. I don't know exactly what I understood by 'my cycle', but it seemed a good answer to me. I'd already noticed a light down covering my temples, and then there were tantrums, a pain-in-the-arse personality, hips getting heavier for several days, and my hair, like it was growing by the handful every day. Nothing particularly earth-shattering.

Until a day in July, when it really announced itself. I must have been old enough for it by then. Lucky for me, it was right at the end of my adolescence, and everyone was on acid. It was filed under 'collective hallucination'; it even became an old favourite in the gang I was hanging around with. 'The night Jeanne turned into a sort of wolf . . . I swear, and the worst is, we all saw it at the same time. We were in fits – we were bricking it, but we were still all in hysterics . . . She was pacing around the room like one of the damned, with her hairy head and long yellow teeth and these little piercing, menacing eyes. She kept repeating over and over, 'So it's payback time', and pulling the most unbelievable faces . . . That must have been how it started, faces so weird we took her for a monster. Can you imagine that? And we all saw her like that . . . Unbelievable or what? Acid – it's mad, man . . .'

At dawn, that hour when there's almost no one around – it's either too early or too late – I weaved my way home, head hunched between my shoulders. It was a bright and beautiful day, I tried to avoid any looks, and got back to mine sharpish. I still hoped, not thinking straight, that it would pass after I'd come down, that it was something to do with the tabs.

I waited. Smoked myself stupid, collapsed, slept.

The first time I saw myself completely transformed, the initial shock was that I liked how I looked. Bizarrely, there was something powerful, strangely seductive, there. I was a kind of massive beast, with a gleam in my eye, a human one.

But straight away, almost at the same time, I imagined somebody seeing me that way and it was shattering.

At first, I would have said I looked like a man, because of the very pale fur that covered me down to my navel, but, looking more closely, I was more like a monkey. One of those women from planet monkey, but with a less pleasant mug. There was something stubborn, determined, a cunning brutality, in my expression.

I didn't dwell on the fascinating aspect of it all for very long. I was just disgusted. To be me in a body like that. Ashamed that this unknown thing was happening to me, strongly suspecting that I'd had something to do with it, but not knowing what exactly. So ashamed I wanted to be swallowed up and disappear.

My first explanation – it was something to do with Chernobyl, innit.

My thighs had doubled in size, shoulders, wrists, jaw likewise. I got dressed, including gloves, the loosest clothing possible, but there was no forgetting myself. And I just couldn't go out at all. I honestly thought I'd die of it. Considered possible deaths that wouldn't leave a trace of my body. So no one would suspect, ever, so no one would see what I'd become. What I was, in fact.

There was also anger, gripping me. Fury, in terrible surges, the bitterness I felt towards all the others for not being like this, for knowing exactly what to do so that it didn't happen to them, but just, inevitably, to me.

Suddenly, from one day to the next, without any obvious reason, my mood had changed. I got up, examined my limbs, feeling them through the layers of clothes. Everything had gone back to plausible proportions. The hairs all over me had massively whitened and were falling by the handful like those of an old pooch.

I returned to my mirror. I shaved off what was left. The weirdest thing about it, as I faced myself in the mirror, razor in hand, doing 'that', was in the end not that I looked like a guy, but that actually no I didn't. I was a very young girl shaving – like a funny joke.

Everything went completely back to normal, chapter closed, a night that lasted barely four days. I got back to my old life, intact, the mates I'd left at dawn worrying about what I'd done afterwards, grinning at the mad time we'd had, hoping I hadn't had a bad trip. I felt unsettled for another week, and then forgot about the whole episode.

Except that, obviously, it happened again. At irregular intervals, around once a season – it's never let go of me since. I'd feel my body swinging into action, preparing itself to start all that again, so I'd closet myself away at my place, unshowable, abject, and bursting with shame until it festered.

Shut inside, double-locked, heart pounding whenever the telephone rings, because in the end even my voice changes and goes all gravelly and creepy.

I'd be haunted by terrible thoughts, demanding blood, revenge, it howled from every part of me, it took complete hold of everything. Morbid scenes – I'd spontaneously concentrate on what people's deaths would be like. It was an exercise. Concentrate, on how to cut a throat, feeling the blade beneath my fingers and someone's body, struggling, then growing calmer, then letting go. Having done it. For brief moments, my imagination would be so vivid it was like memories. There was a hunger to sate, which was way too strong for me. It came into being centuries before mine and stretched out infinitely further into the future than me. It accounted for what I was, but also thousands of other souls.

These efforts of concentration were all interconnected, the universe became more precise, we were on a mission, there were other beings with me, which I couldn't make out, we were on a mission, it was to do with a bloodbath. Warriors. All trained to know what had to be done. Out of absolute necessity. Frenetically but patiently, something fell into place inside me which would try to come out and wouldn't give a damn about tearing me apart all the way up one day just to see the light.

There was nothing remotely enjoyable about them, these few days which hit me, from time to time. Obviously I've never said a word about it. Extreme repulsion, total and fearful solitude. It passed. And me, each time, I'd make out it was nothing.

I observed myself despite it all, from every angle, hoping to find an explanation, something to avoid in order to avoid 'that' from happening again; I studied the different moons, my diet, my highs, my pills, the weather . . .

It took me whenever it wanted and all I could do was limit the damage, rush home to hide myself away and triple-lock myself in.

*

It transformed me, including the rest of the time, it infiltrated everything. Anxious and peevish. I had it in for everyone. For being able to know, for not being like this, for being a privileged fuck and why did I know these things and why was it me all alone carrying this weight of shame. Always something to reproach myself for, to blame myself for, always having to think about it, never exposing myself to danger.

I had to avoid even thinking about it, deep down, I didn't name this 'thing' and didn't formulate anything relating to it.

I made do with wringing my hands and moping around, trying to hide under the pillows every time it happened.

It became so messed-up that I shied away from all the boys. The first few years, when it was safe, I had brief nights of passion. Flashes of fireworks, here and there, good things, often. But nothing which could last, not even till dawn. I didn't trust myself enough, had no desire to wake up in a boy's bed transformed into an orangutan. That thought was unpleasant enough to turn me off full stop.

Until this guy, this one here . . . I wanted him, so much . . . that I convinced myself that I knew myself well enough to imagine a future with him, to be careful, and to figure out a way to disappear for a few days from time to time . . . I even made up a job for myself – I had to travel abroad sometimes. I thought I'd anticipated every eventuality, until that fateful morning he pointed to my chin, smiling like an idiot, must have thought I had a bit of an issue with facial hair, the kind of thing you go to a beautician for. I'd have loved to have seen that beautician's face if I'd shown up at hers all transformed.

With him . . . stretched over me, glued to me, our scents mingling, utter bliss reigning over me, I charged on, head down, all prudence forgotten.

I legged it like a lunatic, no way I could make him believe I had a plane to catch . . . I ran down the stairs then likewise through the streets. Such a long time, years, without this happening to me. Having to be in the street with hairs growing everywhere and my body packing up and leaving. Having to get to mine as quickly as possible. I just looked straight down, not to see if people were watching me. No chance of putting up a front when you've come down with a case of monkey-face. How to hide as much of it as possible . . . sticking it between my hands, playing the poor heartbroken girl. My shoulders ached, I was so tensed up. Get home, fast as. Shut the door on the outside world to – finally – fall apart in peace and above all without anyone to witness it.

I'd have liked to telephone him, to call to tell him some bullshit, but I'd already changed too much, my voice more and more guttural. I worried about him – what would he think, or imagine? Gutted to have this come between us. Gutted to be away from him. Torn apart forced apart by this thing. Over the years, I'd almost got used to it, it was my own routine, my dirty secret kept on a leash. But that night was more awful than the others. I didn't want it any more. I didn't want to be her. Chosen for God knows what.

And then, he started to call me, until I unplugged the phone; he came and knocked on the door to my building, I had to turn off all the lights and wait for him to leave, to make it look like I wasn't home. He even called up from the street, below my window, like a nutcase.

I began to hate him, as brutally as I did myself. For insisting, without suspecting, for not knowing, for being an arsehole.

I started to concentrate on those foul tales of slaughter. I crossed paths with the first of the others, other women, like me, transforming here or there. We recognized each other. One evening, in a bar, I saw a girl, a curvy brunette with big green eyes. Something, a sort of sixth sense, told me. And when I stared at her to make sure, she returned my gaze, smiling discreetly. And she brushed against me as she left, saying yes with her eyes. From that day on, I learned how to recognize them better. I even chatted with one of them, at a party. She was an old hand, she told me.

Some became mares, others wonderful mermaids, still others became sows. We were rehearsing, all at the same time, a sacrilegious choreography, and everything burned in our wake. A horde of furies, perfectly synchronized.

I was relieved when I realized that others too were hiding themselves away, like me, and having to face up to the same thing. And relieved, though worried at the same time, when I began to understand that the moment would come one day to get out there as we were. And that no one would have time to laugh.

But as soon as it had passed, I met up again with my young lover, desperate for him to forgive me; I didn't want to think about it any more, and just pretended that nothing had happened.

And the guy seriously began to ruin both our appetites, all the time bringing things back up, wanting to know what I was up to. Something, next to nothing – four days here or there – would slip from his grasp, and it would be way too much for him.

It was less fun between us now, a lot less light-hearted than before. But the sex, it goes without saying, kept us from biting the bullet.

Until the fateful day when I was shut away reading my cards on the bed. I'd noticed that the transformation heightened my ability to read cards. I was just passing the time. I knew that he'd head over to mine, like he did every time, having completely lost it. In a much more discreet way, his own metamorphosis was just as radical as mine. He turned into a barking idiot, a full-blown pain in the arse.

Until the fucking day he got hold of my keys.

When I heard the key turn in the lock, I wasn't even dressed. I was hoping it was from next door – you could hear everything that went on in there, but then . . . noises in the corridor, it was coming from my place after all.

I burrowed under the big duvet and moaned like some horrendous animal – I was terrified, incapable of holding it in. I pushed him back with both hands, curled up into a ball at the foot of the bed. Seeing me was impossible . . . impossible, and yet it was bound to happen.

The film *Elephant Man* came into my head at the same time . . . It was a bit out of kilter because I was there howling and struggling like a frightened animal. But a little part of my brain had started thinking about the Elephant Man, the poor sod.

It was mayhem before he managed to calm me down, reassuring me and saying I should let him see me. I was drenched in tears. I was angry enough to kill him at the same time as I wanted to die – it was all a bit mixed up.

And he saw me. He seemed overwhelmed, but not in the way I expected. He wasn't repulsed. He acted as if it was nothing. His eyes wandered over my swollen body ready for battle, over my skin covered in animal hair, my narrowed eyes, my jutting jaw . . . He discovered all this, and acted as if it was nothing.

It was then that I understood. He thought he had me. 'But you're beautiful, there's nothing wrong with you, you're beautiful like all the other times . . .' he said as he stroked my hair.

And he made love to me without any revulsion – even, *au contraire*, with a little more vigour than usual. I let him scheme away without letting on that I'd twigged.

The truth was, he'd been assigned. That was why he'd shown up. It had seemed like a sweet love story, innocent, something that would stop me from stumbling and lead me into the light. But that, that was just bullshit . . . That's why this guy was here.

All that fucking dirty work, that sordid, strong body, all that pent-up power . . . And him, kissing my misshapen belly. He'd come to give the beast a baby. I don't know if he even realized. He'd come to hump the beast, to get it pregnant, so it could multiply. That's why he was so insistent, every time I got away from him. What he was looking for, really, perhaps even in all innocence, was to get hold of the beast, to get it pregnant, so it could multiply.

That's what led them to this anyhow. They were all carrying baby beasts. They were clearing the decks for their little ones. Let no one even think about causing shit, or taking a moment to judge, or try to judge, the privileges they'd claim.

And him, I loved him worse than loving a child, I loved him like the centre of the world a body that would forgive mine and would never abandon it.

I liked that, at the climax, that last time we did it . . . he was going at it at full pelt but was very very attentive to me – and me, I even spoke up, I said how I wanted it and when to slow down and at the end it had me in pieces, shaken, a sensory overload that I'd never known, an absolute peak. The moment he came, it splattered me inside and utterly dazzled me from within.

*

Next, I smashed him in with a hammer; I'd got up, just after … he was still resting. I went to get the tool and I whacked him. The first blow made my head spin, a barrier to break through, and after that, again and again, I was furious with him, for being part of the plan instead of wanting to save me from it. For saddling the monster with a brat.

I knew I had serious trouble ahead. But it was all I could do to stop myself from letting it go any further, to stop myself becoming a beast, to not take part in the carnage.

After that, it was seriously mental. They all piled in, judging me for this and that, but what did they know that gave them the right to spout off. That story about the acid we'd popped, as kids, came up again. It saved my skin to be fair. Rumour had it that I'd got stuck in a bad trip. That's right, that's what the morons told themselves. It must be that … I'd lost my grip after one tab too many. Me, I wouldn't want to do them any harm, but they'll see, in a little while, where – and how deep – they can shove my infamous case of acid indigestion.

Translated by Will McMorran

Acknowledgements

We are grateful to the following for permission to reproduce copyright material:

'The Man Who Walked Through Walls' by Marcel Aymé.
   Translated by Sophie Lewis in *Beautiful Image*, Pushkin Press, 2008, pp.9–23. Reproduced by permission of the publisher.
'The Adam Affair' by Béatrix Beck.
   From *Guidée par le songe*, copyright © Éditions Grasset & Fasquelle, 1998. Translated by Will McMorran, with permission of Éditions Grasset & Fasquelle.
'Sarzan' by Birago Diop.
   Translated by Dorothy S. Blair in *Tales of Amadou Koumba*, Oxford University Press, 1966. Originally published in *Les Contes d'Amadou Koumba*, Présence Africaine, 1960, copyright © Présence Africaine Editions. Reproduced with permission of Présence Africaine.
'The Madness of the Day' by Maurice Blanchot.
   Translated by Lydia Davis in *The Madness of the Day*, Station Hill Press, 2000, pp.5–18, copyright © 1981. Reproduced by permission of the publisher.
'The Hunters' Café' by Daniel Boulanger.
   Translated by Richard Coward in *French Short Stories: Nouvelles Françaises*, Penguin, 1999, pp.106–123. Originally published as 'Le café des chasseurs' from *Les jeux du tour de ville*, Gallimard, 1983. Reproduced by permission of Éditions Gallimard.
'A Nail, A Rose' by Madeleine Bourdouxhe.
   Translated by Faith Evans in *A Nail, A Rose*, Pushkin Press, 2019, pp.27–42. Reproduced by permission of the publisher.
'What I Saw' by Emmanuel Bove.
   Translated by Alyson Waters in *Henri Dychemin and his Shadows*, NYRB. First published in English by *New York Review Books*,

Acknowledgements

translation copyright © Alyson Waters, 2015. Reproduced by permission of the publisher.

'Cinderella, the Humble and Haughty Child' by Claude Cahun. Translated by Gretchen Schultz and Lewis Seifert in *Fairy Tales for the Disillusioned*, Princeton University Press, 2016, pp.243–246. Permission conveyed through Copyright Clearance Center.

'Bois sec bois vert' by Charles-Albert Cingria. From *Bois sec bois vert*, Gallimard, 1948, pp.91–106. Translated by Patrick McGuinness, with permission by Éditions Gallimard.

'Green Sealing Wax' by Sidonie-Gabrielle Colette. Translated by Antonia White in *The Collected Stories of Colette*, Vintage, first published in Great Britain by Secker & Warburg, 1984, copyright © Estate of Colette, 1920. First published in Le Képi, copyright 1943 by Fayard. Reprinted by permission of The Random House Group Limited.

'Family Portrait' by Maryse Condé. Translated by Richard Philcox in *Tales from the Heart*, Soho Press, pp.3–18, copyright © Maryse Condé, 2016. Reproduced with permission of Soho Press, Inc. All rights reserved.

'Jeunesse, banlieu de la vie' by Didier Daeninckx. From *L'espoir en contrebande*, Le Cherche Midi, pp.85–90, copyright © Le Cherche Midi, 2012. Translated by Sian Reynolds, with permission of Le Cherche Midi.

'Tentative d'introspection sur l'autoroute' by Charles Dantzig. From *Le Courage n°5 / Orphée retourne toi: Revue annuelle dirigée*, Grasset, 2019, pp.143–163. Translated by David Bellos, with permission of the author.

'Des poils sur moi' by Virginie Despentes. From *Mordre au travers*, J'ai lu, 1999, pp.111–123, copyright © Éditions J'ai lu, Paris, 1999, 2020. Translated by Will McMorran, with permission of Éditions Flammarion.

'L'ambassadeur triste' by Ananda Devi. From *L'ambassadeur triste*, Gallimard, 2015, pp.9–25. Translated by David Bellos, with permission of Éditions Gallimard.

'There Is No Exile' by Assia Djebar. Translated by Marjolijn de Jager in *Women of Algiers in Their Apartment*, University of Virginia Press, 1999, pp.61–73, copyright © the Rector and

Acknowledgements

Visitors of the University of Virginia, 1999. Reproduced with permission of the University of Virginia Press.

'Le boa' by Marguerite Duras.

From *Des journées entières dans les arbres*, Gallimard, 1954. Translated by Will McMorran, with permission of Éditions Gallimard.

'The Monologue' by Simone de Beauvoir.

Translated by Patrick O'Brien. Monologue in *The Woman Destroyed*, translation copyright © Collins Publishers, 1969 and G. P. Putnam's Sons. Originally published as 'Monologue' from *La Femme Rompue*, Gallimard, 1967. Reproduced by permission of HarperCollins Publishers Ltd; Pantheon Books, an imprint of the Knopf Doubleday Publishing Group, a division of Penguin Random House LLC; and Éditions Gallimard. All rights reserved.

'The Goldfish' by Christian Garcin.

From *La neige gelée ne permet que de tout petits pas*, Verdier 2005. Translated by Patrick McGuinness, with kind permission of the publisher and author.

'A Man's Secrets' by Hervé Guibert.

Translated by Jeffrey Zuckerman in *Written in Invisible Ink*, MIT Press, 2020, pp.251–256. Reproduced by permission of Semiotexte.

'Eve' by Jacqueline Harpman.

From *Eve et autres nouvelles*, Espace Nord, 2005, pp.9–30. Translated by Will McMorran, with permission of Espace Nord.

'The Hat' by Patrick Modiano.

Translated by Mark Polizzotti in *Family Record*, Yale University Press, 2019, pp.27–34. Reproduced with permission of the Licensor through PLSclear.

'Révélation' by Marie Ndiaye.

Translated by Jordan Stump in *All My Friends*, Two Lines Press, 2013. Originally published as *Tous mes amis*, Minuit, 2004, copyright © Les Éditions de Minuit. Reproduced by kind permission of Les Éditions de Minuit, Marie NDiaye and Jordan Stump.

'Sunday' by Irène Nemirovsky.

Translated by Bridget Patterson in *Dimanche and Other Stories*, Persephone Books 2010, pp.1–23, translation copyright © Persephone Books, 2010. Reproduced by permission of Persephone Books; and Vintage

Books, an imprint of the Knopf Doubleday Publishing Group, a division of Penguin *La Nuit de Moyeuvre*. Translated by Stephen Romer with kind permission of the author.

'The Sow' by Thomas Owen.

From *La truie et autres histoires secrètes*, Espace Nord, 2016, pp.7–16. Translated by Will McMorran by permission of Archives & Musée de la Littérature.

'The Winter Voyage' by Georges Perec.

Translated by John Sturrock in *Species of Spaces and Other Pieces*, Penguin Classics, 2008, pp.279–285, copyright © Georges Perec 2008. Reproduced by permission of Penguin Books Limited.

'The Mysterious Correspondent' by Marcel Proust.

Translated by Charlotte Mandell, Oneworld Classics, 2021, pp.41–55. Reproduced with permission of the Licensor through PLSclear.

'Conte à Votre Façon: A Tale for Your Shaping' by Raymond Queneau.

Translated by Harry Gilonis in *Eonta*, Vol. 2 (1), 1993/94. Reproduced by permission of Harry Gilonis (with thanks to Steven Holt).

'The Unknown Visitor' by Françoise Sagan.

Translated by Joanna Kilmartin in *The Gigolo*, Penguin Classics, copyright © Françoise Sagan, 2018. Originally published as 'Le Gigolo' in *Des yeux de soie*. Reproduced by permission of Penguin Books Limited and Éditions Stock.

'La voix' by Boualem Sansal.

From *Le Monde*, 2001. Translated by David Bellos, with permission of Le Monde.

'The greatest story in the world' by Annie Saumont.

Translated by Elizabeth Fallaize in *Oxford Book of French Short Stories*, Oxford University Press, 2011, pp.339–343. Reproduced with permission of the Licensor through PLSclear.

'Femmes d'Algiers, filles de joie' by Leïla Sebbar.

From *L'Orient est rouge*, Elyzad, 2017, copyright © Éditions Elyzad, 2017. Translated by Sian Reynolds, with permission of Éditions Elyzad.

'Mahmoud Fall' by Ousmane Sembène.

From *Voltaïque*, Présence Africaine, 1962, pp.148–163, copyright © Présence Africaine Editions, 1962. Translated by Will McMorran, with permission of Présence Africaine.

'L'exècution' by Jacques Sternberg.

From *Contes glacés*, MIJADE, 2009, pp.270–271. Translated by Patrick McGuinness, with permission from MIJADE.

'Danger of the Classics' by Boris Vian.

Translated by Peter Hodges in *If I say If: The Poems and Short Stories of Boris Vian*, edited by Alistair Rolls, Professor John West-Sooby and Professor Jean Fornasiero, University of Adelaide Press, 2014, pp.213–224. Reproduced by permission of the translator, editors and La cohérie des ayants droit de Boris Vian.

'The Woman of the Wolf' by Renée Vivien.

Translated by Karla Jay and Yvonne M. Klein in *The Woman of the Wolf and Other Stories*, Gallic Editions, 2020, pp.17–26. Reproduced by permission of Gallic Books; and North American rights by permission of the translators.

'The Garden' by Monique Wittig.

Translated by Lorie Sauble-Otto in *GLQ*, Vol. 13 (4), pp.553–561, translation copyright © Duke University Press, 2007. Reproduced with permission of the copyright holder, and the Publisher. www.dukepress.edu. All rights reserved.

'The Man Who Loved the Nereids' by Marguerite Yourcenar.

Translated by Alberto Manguel in *Oriental Tales*, Farrar Strauss Giroux, 1985, pp.73–83, translation copyright © Alberto Manguel, 1985. Originally published as '*L'homme qui a aimé les Néréides*' from *Nouvelles orientales*, Gallimard, 1938. Reproduced by permission of Farrar, Straus and Giroux; and Éditions Gallimard. All rights reserved.

In some instances, we have been unable to trace the owners of copyright material, and we would appreciate any information that would enable us to do so.

Author Biographies

COLETTE (SIDONIE-GABRIELLE COLETTE) (1873–1954) was a writer, journalist and actress, and one of the leading literary figures of her generation. Her first four books, the autobiographical *Claudine* novels, were published under the name of her first husband, Henry Gauthier-Villars, known as 'Willy'. Among her best-known works are *The Tendrils of the Vine* (1908), *Chéri* (1920) and *The Ripening Seed* (1923). She was the first woman in France to receive a state funeral.

RENÉE VIVIEN (PAULINE MARY TARN) (1877–1909) was an Anglo-American writer who wrote in French. After an early childhood in England, she moved to Paris where she cut an unconventional figure in *Belle époque* society. Nicknamed 'Sappho 1900', Vivien wrote poetry that was Symbolist in inspiration, while her stories, including the volume *The Woman of the Wolf* (1904), take a subversive approach to mythology and fairy tale. The prestigious poetry prize the 'Prix Renée Vivien' was inaugurated in her honour in 1935 and funded by two of her former lovers, Natalie Clifford Barney and Hélène van Zuylen. After a long period of neglect, her work has recently begun to find its audience.

CHARLES-ALBERT CINGRIA (1883–1954) was a Swiss novelist, journalist and short story writer. In 1915, after several years of travelling around the world, he moved to Montparnasse, where he threw himself into the bohemian lifestyle of the Parisian avant-garde until war forced his return to Switzerland. A largely self-taught polymath who abandoned his education, he wrote novels, stories, studies of music and linguistics, books about travel and hiking, and his 1935 study of Petrarch won the Prix Rambert. The story in this anthology is from *Dry Wood, Green Wood*, which appeared from Gallimard in 1948.

GUILLAUME APOLLINAIRE (GUILLAUME ALBERT VLADIMIR ALEXANDRE APOLLINAIRE DE KOSTROWITZKY) (1880–1918) was one of the greatest French poets of the twentieth century. The son of a minor Polish aristocrat mother and an unknown father, he was born in Rome and moved to Paris in 1900. He became a French citizen in 1916 and joined the French army, where he was wounded in action. He died in 1918 of Spanish flu. As well as poetry of extraordinary originality, he wrote stories, art criticism, erotic fiction and novels. It was Apollinaire who coined the word '*surréalisme*'. In the preface to his play *The Breasts of Tiresias* (1916) he wrote: 'When man wanted to imitate walking, he invented the wheel, which does not resemble a leg. He thus invented surrealism without knowing it.'

JEAN DE LA VILLE DE MIRMONT (1886–1914) was a novelist and poet, whose work includes a melancholy novel, *The Sundays of Jean Dézert* (1914), and a collection of romantic-symbolist poems, *Chimerical Horizons*, which was posthumously published in 1920. He died in battle at Verneuil in November 1914. His short stories appeared in 1923.

CLAUDE CAHUN (LUCY RENÉE MATHILDE SCHWOB) (1894–1954) was a writer, photographer and performer associated with the surrealist movement. The niece of Marcel Schwob (who appears in Volume One), she was educated in England and studied at the Sorbonne. With her partner Suzanne Malherbe (known as Marcel Moore), she hosted literary salons frequented by the surrealists. In 1937, she and Moore moved to Jersey. Under the German occupation, they were both active in the resistance and were arrested and sentenced to death in 1944. The liberation of the island in 1945 meant the sentence was never carried out.

EMMANUEL BOVE (EMMANUEL BOBOVNIKOFF) (1898–1945) was a French writer and journalist of Russian-Jewish and Luxembourgian parentage. Born in Paris and educated partly in England, one of his early stories came to the attention of Colette, who helped him publish his successful first novel, *My Friends* (1924). Refusing to publish during the Occupation, he went into exile in Algiers, where he wrote three of his major novels, unpublished until 1945, the year of his death: *The Trap*, *Night Departure* and *Case Dismissed*.

MARCEL AYMÉ (1902–1967) was a novelist, essayist, playwright and scriptwriter, and the translator of Tennessee Williams and Arthur Miller. His classic tale, 'The Man Who Walked Through Walls' is the title story of his 1943 collection, which merges the '*fantastique*' with the surreal, in which ordinary people are possessed of extraordinary (and ambiguous) gifts. His novels include *The Street Without a Name* (1930) and *The Green Mare* (1933), and the WWII trilogy: *Travelingue* (1941), *The Detour* (1946) and *Uranus* (1948). The latter explores wartime Paris, from the arrival of the Germans to the post-war '*épuration*' and the purging of collaborators. Aymé's own stance in the war was opaque, and the shadow of collaboration clung to him until his death.

RAYMOND QUENEAU (1903–1976) was a poet, novelist, dramatist and editor, and one of the founders of OuLiPo, '*Ouvroir de littérature poten-tielle*', or 'Workshop of potential literature'. Expelled from the surrealist group in 1930, his first substantial work, *Encyclopaedia of Inexact Sciences*, was refused by Gallimard (where he later became an editor and board member). His work is humorous, inventive and ingeniously subversive, and displays a creative fascination with rules and structures (grammatical, mathematical, logical). His books include *Exercises in Style* (1947) and *Zazie in the Metro* (1959), which achieved huge popular success. The classic song '*Si tu t'imagines*', sung by Juliette Gréco in 1947, is a poem from Queneau's 1948 collection *The Fatal Instant*.

MARGUERITE YOURCENAR (MARGUERITE ANTOINETTE JEANNE MARIE GHISLAINE CLEENEWERCK DE CRAYENCOUR (1903–1987) was a novelist and essayist of French and Belgian parentage. Born in Brussels, she moved to the United States in 1939 and became a US citizen in 1947. The first woman to be elected to the Académie française (in 1980), her works include *Coup de grâce* (1939) and the masterpiece *The Memoirs of Hadrian* (1951), as well as *The Abyss* (1968). The story in this anthology is taken from her collection *Oriental Tales* (1938).

IRÈNE NEMIROVSKY (1903–1942) was a French novelist and short story writer born in Kyiv, Ukraine. Her family moved to Paris, where she was educated at the Sorbonne. Denied French citizenship in 1938, she was arrested as a Jew in July 1942 under France's Vichy racial laws and deported to Auschwitz, where she died. Though several of her works were published during her lifetime (*The Ball* (1930), *The Wine of Solitude* (1935), and *The Prey* (1938)), it was the discovery and publication in 2004 of *Suite Française*, the first two of a series of novels about the German Occupation, that brought her work to international attention.

BIRAGO DIOP (1906–1989) was a Senegalese poet, prose writer, veterinarian and diplomat, educated at the French *lycée* in Saint-Louis, Senegal. A leading figure in the 'Négritude' movement of black francophone intellectuals, he recorded and adapted traditional Wolof folktales. His *Tales of Amadou Koumba*, from which the present story is taken, appeared in 1947 and were first translated into English in 1966. He is the author of a collection of poems, *Lures and Glimmers* (1960), and several books of memoirs of public life.

MADELEINE BOURDOUXHE (1906–1996) was a Belgian novelist and short story writer. After an early association with the Belgian surrealists in Brussels, Bourdouxhe lived intermittently in Paris, where she was championed by Jean Paulhan (who published her first novel, *Gilles's Wife* in 1937) and Simone de Beauvoir. After decades of inattention, her work was republished by Actes Sud in France and Labor in Belgium. It has recently been translated into English to critical acclaim.

MAURICE BLANCHOT (1907–2003) was a thinker, novelist and literary critic. The influence of his work on French thought is comparable in its importance to that of Roland Barthes and Jacques Derrida. Though principally known for his literary criticism, notably *The Space of Literature* (1955), *The Book to Come* (1959) and *The Infinite Conversation* (1969), he is the author of several haunting and original works of fiction: *Thomas the Obscure* (1941), *Death Sentence* (1948) and *The Most High* (1949).

SIMONE DE BEAUVOIR (1908–1986) was one of the leading writers and thinkers of her generation. With her partner Jean-Paul Sartre and the philosopher Maurice Merleau-Ponty, she founded the journal *Les Temps Modernes* in 1945 (it closed in 2019). In 1949 she published *The Second Sex*, a foundational work in feminist thought, and in 1954 her novel *The Mandarins* won the Prix Goncourt. Among her other works are *Memoirs of a Dutiful Daughter* (1958), *A Very Easy Death* (1964) and the recently rediscovered *The Inseparables*. The story in this anthology is taken from her collection of stories, *The Woman Destroyed* (1967).

THOMAS OWEN (GERALD BERTOT, ALSO KNOWN AS STÉPHANE REY) (1910–2002) was a Belgian writer and lawyer. As Thomas Owen, he specialised in dark detective fiction and in the modern *'fantastique'*, in which he wrote hundreds of short stories and several novellas. As Stéphane Rey, he was an art critic and journalist. His first major success came in 1941 with his detective novel *Tonight, Eight O'clock*. This was followed by *Initiation into Fear* in 1942. 'The Sow' was first published in 1972 in a collection of thirteen of Owen's short stories.

HENRI THOMAS (1912–1993) was a poet, novelist, critic, translator and broadcaster who lived in Paris and in London, where he worked for the BBC. He began publishing poetry in the late 1930s and his first novel, *The Coal Bucket* appeared in 1940. A prolific but underappreciated writer, he is the author of more than twenty novels, several collections of short stories and poems, and thousands of pages of published notebooks.

MARGUERITE DURAS (MARGUERITE DONNADIEU) (1914–1996) was a novelist, essayist, playwright, screenwriter and filmmaker. Born in Saigon, she moved to Paris in 1933 and trained as a lawyer. She published her first novel, the autobiographical *The Impudent Ones*, in 1943, which she later disowned. Her major works include *Moderato Cantabile* (1958), for which she won the Prix Goncourt, *The Rapture of Lol V. Stein* (1964) and *The Lover* (1984), for which she won a second Goncourt. She also wrote the script for Alain Resnais's film *Hiroshima mon amour* (1959).

BÉATRIX BECK (1914–2008) was a Swiss-born Belgian novelist and short story writer who became a French citizen in 1955. She published her first novel, *Barny*, in 1948 and worked as André Gide's secretary until his death in 1951. In 1952 her novel, *Léon Morin, Priest*, won the Prix Goncourt. In 1966 she took up a teaching post at the University of California, Berkeley, and, later, universities in Québec and Ontario. In 1997, she was awarded the Grand prix de littérature de l'Académie française for her life's work.

BORIS VIAN (1920–1959) was a poet, novelist, lyricist and music critic, as well as a jazz trumpeter, actor and scriptwriter. Under the pseudonym of Vernon Sullivan, he wrote *I Spit on Your Graves* (1946), claiming to have translated it from English. A violent and erotic anti-racist novel set in the American South, it was banned and Vian was prosecuted for obscenity. In 1947 he wrote a follow-up, *The Dead All Have the Same Skin*, and two more 'Vernon Sullivan' novels followed. Though Vian used dozens of pseudonyms, his most important works were published under his own name, notably *The Froth of Days* (1947), *Autumn in Peking* (1947) and *Heartsnatcher* (1953). He died aged 39 during the film showing of *I Spit on Your Graves*.

DANIEL BOULANGER (1922-2014) was a poet, novelist, playwright, actor and scriptwriter. Author of twenty-nine novels, twenty-seven collections of poetry and fifteen volumes of short stories, he won both the Académie française short story prize and the Goncourt prize for short stories, as well as the Prix Max Jacob for his poetry. Also an actor, he played small roles in various French 'Nouvelle vague' films, including François Truffaut's *Shoot the Piano Player* (1960).

JACQUES STERNBERG (1923–2006) was a Belgian writer, children's author, scriptwriter and sailor. Born in Antwerp to a Jewish family, his father died in Majdanek. The author of more than 1,500 short stories, he specialized in science fiction and the *'fantastique'*. He collaborated with the film director Alan Resnais, scripting the film *Je t'aime, je t'aime* (1968) and working with Resnais, Jean-Luc Godard, Agnès Varda and others on *Loin du Vietnam* (1967). The story in this anthology is from his collection *Icy Tales* (1974).

OUSMANE SEMBÈNE (1923–2007) was a Senegalese writer and film-maker. In 1944, he was drafted into the Senegalese *Tirailleurs* and later served with the Free French Forces. His first novel, *The Black Docker*, appeared in 1956, followed in 1957 by *O Country, My Beautiful People*. His best-known novels are *God's Bits of Wood* (1960) and *Xala* (1973), the film of which Sembène directed in 1975. Sembène began making films in 1963 and in 1966 his film *The Black Girl* won the prestigious Prix Jean Vigo.

ANNIE SAUMONT (1927–2017) was a writer and translator (notably of V. S. Naipaul, Nadine Gordimer and John Fowles), and the author of several novels and more than thirty collections of short stories. She won the Goncourt short story prize in 1981 and the Académie française short story prize in 2004.

JACQUELINE HARPMAN (1929–2012) was a Belgian writer and psycho-analyst. Her Jewish family, several of whom died in the Holocaust, lived in Casablanca during the war, where Jacqueline was educated at the French *lycée*. Her major works include *Brief Arcadia* (1959), *The Beach at Ostend* (1991) and *Orlanda* (1996) which won the Prix Médicis. Her work has begun to find an audience in the English-speaking world with the recent translation of her novel, *I Who Have Never Known Men* (first published in 1995). Throughout her writing life, she maintained a career as a psychoanalyst and her *Writing and Psychoanalysis* appeared in 2011.

FRANÇOISE SAGAN (FRANÇOISE QUOIREZ) (1935–2004) became a literary star at the age of seventeen with the publication, in 1954, of *Bonjour Tristesse*. She chose the pseudonym 'Sagan' after a Parisian socialite and minor character in Proust's *In Search of Lost Time* when her parents refused to see the family name on the cover of her book. *Bonjour Tristesse* won the prestigious Prix des Critiques and a celebrity career was launched. Though none of her subsequent novels were as successful, her work remained in the public eye, as did her eventful private life. In Jérôme Garcin's *Dictionary of French Writers in Their Own Words* she wrote her own obituary: 'Made her début in 1954 with a slim novel, *Bonjour Tristesse*, that caused worldwide scandal. Her death, after a life and an *oeuvre* in equal parts happy and botched, was a scandal only for her'.

MONIQUE WITTIG (1935–2003) was a writer and feminist thinker, and one of the founders of the French Women's Liberation Movement. Her first novel, *The Opoponax*, appeared in 1964 and her second, *Les Guérillères*, in 1969, about a war between the sexes in which women are victorious. An influential theorist of sexuality and gender, her book of essays *The Straight Mind* appeared in 1992 and is a foundational text in queer studies. She moved to the USA in 1976 and was visiting professor in a number of universities, including California, Berkeley, Vassar College and Tucson, Arizona.

GEORGES PEREC (GEORGE PERETZ) (1936–1982) was a novelist, essayist and filmmaker, and a member of the OuLiPo group that included Queneau, Umberto Eco and Italo Calvino. His father died fighting in WWII and his mother was murdered in the Holocaust, and his work is haunted by the absent and the unstated. His best-known works are *Things: A Story of the Sixties* (1965), *A Man Asleep* (1967), *A Void* (1969), *W, or the Memory of Childhood* (1975) and *Life: A User's Manual* (1978), which won the Prix Médicis.

ASSIA DJEBAR (FATIMA-ZOHRA IMALAYEN) (1936–2015) was an Algerian writer and filmmaker, and the first Maghrebian woman to be elected to the Académie française. She was born in Cherchell and educated in France at the École normale supérieure de jeunes filles in Sèvres. She taught at the university of Rabat between 1959 and 1962, before moving to the University of Algiers, where she taught until 1980. Her first novel, *The Thirst*, appeared in 1957, followed a year later by *The Impatient Ones*. *Children of the New World* (1962) and *The Naïve Larks* (1967) describe the lives of Algerian women in the war of independence. The author of a substantial body of fiction and autobiographical writing about colonial legacies and women's lives, Djebar was spoken of as future Nobel laureate. The story in this anthology is from the collection, *Women of Algiers in Their Apartment* (1980).

MARYSE CONDÉ (b. 1937) is a novelist, playwright and academic, born in Pointe-à-Pitre, Guadeloupe. Educated in Guadeloupe and Paris, where she attended the Sorbonne, she taught in universities in Ghana and Senegal, before moving to the US where she was professor at the universities of Berkeley, Maryland and Columbia. Her books include *Segu* (1984) and *The Children of Segu* (1985), *Tree of Life* (for which she won the Prix de l'Académie française) and *Crossing the Mangrove* (1989). In 2018 she won the New Academy Prize for Literature.

LEÏLA SEBBAR (b. 1941) was born in Aflou, Algeria, the daughter of an Algerian father and a French mother. Novelist, essayist and academic, her work focuses on the relationship between France and its former colonies. Her first novel, *Fatima, or the Algerian Women in the Square*, appeared in 1981, followed by *Scheherazade* in 1982, the first in a trilogy of novels about a teenage Algerian runaway in Paris. The author of more than a dozen novels and collections of short stories, Sebbar is also a travel writer and critic. With Nancy Huston, she wrote *Parisian Letters: Autopsies of Exile* (1986). The story in this anthology comes from the volume *Seven Girls* (2003).

PATRICK MODIANO (b. 1945) is the author of more than forty novels, starting with *La place de l'étoile* in 1967, which was an immediate success, won the Prix Roger Nimier and enabled him to dedicate himself to full-time writing. The next two books, *The Night Watch* and *Ring Roads*, make up the 'Occupation Trilogy'. In 1972, he won the Académie française Grand Prix du roman, and in 1978 the Prix Goncourt. His work focuses on memory and repetition, on hauntings and reiterations, and is often set in and around wartime Paris. In 1973 he wrote the screenplay to Louis Malle's wartime drama *Lacombe, Lucien*. He won the Nobel Prize for Literature in 2014.

BOUALEM SANSAL (b. 1949) was born in Théniet El Had, Algeria. Variously a teacher, company director and civil servant, he was dismissed from his job in the Algerian civil service for his political views. A novelist and essayist, his first novel, *The Barbarians' Oath* appeared in 1999 and won the French first novel prize (the Prix du premier roman).

Several of his essays and works of fiction have been banned in his home country. He won the Arabic novel prize for *Rue Darwin* in 2011, a novel about an Algerian family during the war of independence.

DIDIER DAENINCKX (b. 1949) is a novelist, essayist and crime writer, and a leftist political activist. He published his first novel, *Murder in the First Round*, in 1982, followed by *Murders in Memoriam* in 1984, which explores the links between French atrocities in Algeria and wartime collaboration. Among his many novels are the 1996 *Nazis in the Metro* (a play on Queneau's *Zazie dans le metro*), *The Jailer and His Double* (1986) and *The Fateful Postman* (1990). He has won numerous prizes for his crime fiction and won the 2012 Prix Goncourt for short stories for the volume *Contraband Hope*.

GILLES ORTLIEB (b. 1953) was born in Ksar es-Souk, Morocco and educated in Paris. The author of several collections of poems, including *Place au cirque* (2002) and *Meuse Métal, etc.* (2005), he has also published two volumes of short stories (*Soldats et autres récits* (2014) and *La nuit de Moyeuvre* (2022)), as well as a series of notebooks (*Sous le crible, Le train des jours, Vraquier,* 2008, 2010 and 2013) that blend the poetic and the documentary in unique ways. He is also the author of book length essays on writers such as Baudelaire, Ângelo de Lima and Arthur Adamov, and is a translator, notably of Cavafy, Seferis and contemporary Greek authors.

HERVÉ GUIBERT (1955–1991) was a writer, journalist and photographer, best-known for his autofictional novel, *To the Friend Who Did Note Save My Life* (1990), in which he revealed his HIV positive diagnosis. Part of a trilogy that includes *The Compassion Protocol* and *The Man in the Red Hat*, it won the Prix Colette and brought Guibert national recognition. His final work, *Paradise*, appeared in 1992, and is a moving account of the lives he might have led. The short story in this anthology is taken from his collection *Virgin Mauve* (1988) and is about the French philosopher Michel Foucault, a friend of Guibert.

ANANDA DEVI (b. 1957) was born in Grand Port, Mauritius and studied at the School of Oriental and African Studies in London. Poet, novelist

and short story writer, she won the Prix des cinq continents de la Fran-
cophonie in 2006 for her novel *Eve Out of Her Ruins* and the Prix
Louis-Guilloux for *The Green Sari* in 2009. Her most recent novel, *The
Laugh of the Goddesses*, won the Prix Fémina des lycéens in 2021.

CHRISTIAN GARCIN (b. 1959) is a novelist, poet, critic and travel writer,
as well as a translator, notably of Edgar Allan Poe and Herman Melville.
He has won the Prix Roland de Jouvenel for his fiction and the Prix
Roger-Caillois for his study of Jorge Luis Borges, and has published
over a dozen collections of short stories.

CHARLES DANTZIG (b. 1961) is a poet, novelist, critic and editor. Among
his best-known works are the hugely successful *Egotistical Dictionary
of French Literature* (2005), which won the Académie française essay
prize and the Prix Décembre, and *Why Read* (2010). His most recent
novel is *History of Love and Hate* (2015).

MARIE NDIAYE (b. 1967) was born of French and Senegalese parents.
One of France's leading contemporary novelists, she is also a playwright
and children's author. Her works include *Rosie Carpe* (2001), which won
the Prix Fémina, and the Goncourt-winning *Three Strong Women* (2009).

VIRGINIE DESPENTES (b. 1969) is a novelist and filmmaker. Her novel
Baise-moi appeared in 1994 and was adapted by Despentes and Coralie
Trinh Thi into a film of the same name in 2000. In 1998 her novel
Beautiful Things won the Prix de Flore and in 2010 *Apocalypse Baby* won
the Prix Renaudot. She was shortlisted for the International Booker
Prize in 2018 for *Vernon Subutex 1*.